KAR

Where Home Is

Outskirts Press, Inc.
Denver, Colorado

Outskirts Press, Inc.
http://www.outskirtspress.com

ISBN: 978-1-4327-3419-0

PRINTED IN THE UNITED STATES OF AMERICA

Jane Addams
1860—1935

Alice Hamilton
1869—1970

Ida B. Wells-Barnett
1862—1931

and

Mary Cassatt
1844—1926

Remarkable Women All

PROLOGUE

I recall down to the smallest detail the moment I decided to become a doctor. I could tell you the color of the dress my mother wore and which supper dishes remained on the table. The moment formed me in an unexpected and irrevocable way.

My younger brother, Gus, not quite four, lay flushed and feverish, and my parents were worried enough about him to send Uncle Billy to town to fetch the doctor. Years before they had lost one child to scarlet fever and must have feared losing another. Times were different then, distances seemed greater and transportation slower, and the doctor's arrival had been anxiously anticipated for what seemed a very long time. I remember my mother's repeated trips through the kitchen to the front window and her quiet but intense "Thank God" when we heard the knock on the door.

"Come in," she called, moving to stand in the doorway of the little bedroom where Gus lay. Tuned to the inflection in Mother's voice, I heard the hope and relief in her tone and felt comforted. As the doctor pushed open the front door and took a step into the kitchen, however, I saw my mother lift her head like a wild creature sensing danger. Even I, just six years old and well sheltered from the world's vices, knew something wasn't right. The doctor stumbled as he entered, then swayed unsteadily in the open doorway as if uncertain what to do next. His words of greeting sounded slurred and too slow, and he smelled strongly of some odor I didn't recognize but which my mother must have.

Without a word Mother took several purposeful steps toward the doctor as he paused at the threshold, grabbed hold of his shoulders, and turned him back to face the open doorway through which he had just entered. My father came onto the porch at the same time and my mother stood facing him, the doctor trapped between my parents.

In a voice empty of expression Mother said, "Dr. Frank isn't well, John. He needs to leave." Then, underestimating the reach of young ears, she added in a low, much more passionate voice, "You are a disgrace to your profession, Doctor! How many lives have you endangered by your excess?" I had never heard that cold and contemptuous tone of rebuke in my mother's voice before and could only stand spellbound as my father grabbed the doctor firmly by one arm and propelled him immediately outside, closing the door behind them.

"What was wrong with him, Mama?" I asked warily, made uneasy by her voice and demeanor. She turned to look at me slowly, as if she had forgotten I was there, then smiled reassurance at my expression.

"It's all right, Katherine." Instead of answering my question directly she added, "Being a physician is a noble calling. It's a great honor and responsibility to care for the weak and heal the sick, and a doctor must always conduct himself with dignity and compassion. Dr. Frank wasn't able to do that just now, so your papa will send him home until he can."

Then Gus called, "Mama!" peevishly, repeated the summons a second time with greater urgency and demand, and she hurried into his room. After she left, I stood immobile in thought, digesting all she had just said.

My older brother, John Thomas, who had somehow slid into the room along with the doctor, commented with disgust at my ignorance, "Dr. Frank was drunk. I wouldn't be surprised if Father wasn't dunking his head in the horse trough right now." He and my older sister, Becca, shared a glance before they both hurried outside, hoping, I'm sure, to see such an entertaining spectacle, but I continued to stand spellbound and thoughtful.

That incident happened a long time ago—Dr. Frank gone for many, many years and my siblings, including Gus, all grown up—but I still vividly recall how transfixed I was by my mother's comments and how gripped by the romance of the expressions she used. I rolled the syllables around in my mind and whispered them into the empty kitchen: *noble, honor, dignity, compassion.* How thrilling the words sounded to me! Exactly at that moment I knew I had no other future but to be a doctor, to care for the weak and heal the sick, to answer a noble calling.

That singular experience sent me to Kansas Medical School, motivated me through years of training there, brought me unexpectedly, delightedly to Chicago, and changed me forever. Whenever I have time for introspection, admittedly rare in my busy schedule, I can trace the line of my life from Dr. Frank's arrival in our small, cluttered Wyoming kitchen to the moment I met Douglas Gallagher—like Dr. Frank another man who would unwittingly and irreversibly affect the course of my future.

My mother often said with assurance that everything in

our lives happened for a reason. I'm of a different generation, however. I've lived through a war that engulfed the world, have seen too much pain inflicted on the vulnerable, have witnessed too much needless death and searing grief to hold her certainty that good can spring from bad. I regret that deficiency in my character and through the years have often wished I had my mother's faith and warmth and genuine goodness of heart that shone from her, that drew people to her and made her so easy to love. I am made of sterner, more skeptical stuff.

Still, my own life seems to bear out her belief in a divine plan that uses the worst of our experiences to mold us into better, stronger human beings because I know without a single doubt that I would not, could not be the person I am today if many years ago my little brother had not been terribly ill and Dr. Frank had not staggered into our kitchen. Neither would I be the woman I am today if Douglas Gallagher had not stepped into my life, so at least in two instances my mother's firmly held confidence in God's good intentions has proved true. And I think twice in a lifetime should be enough for anyone.

PART ONE

1910

CHAPTER 1

I boarded the train at Lawrence, Kansas, on a cold, dark night in early January and almost immediately caught my reflection in the glass as I maneuvered the train's aisle toward my seat. A stranger looked back at me from the window: a self-possessed young woman, sensibly dressed in a dark traveling suit, thick hair plaited and wound against the back of a too-thin neck. She looked all grown up, that woman in the glass, calm and controlled, pleasant and professional.

"Good evening, Dr. Davis," I murmured to myself, then caught my own eye and smiled a little at my foolishness. That reflection is how other people will view me from now on, I thought, caught unawares by a sudden feeling of panic: a full-grown woman, sober, mature, knowledgeable, and decisive. They will expect me to know what to do and how to act because they will see, not a country girl from the western plains and not a struggling student, but a doctor. A doctor. For a moment the thought, still new and exciting, caught at the base of my throat and made me breathless. A dream ended. A dream begun.

I found my seat and settled myself into the inadequate cushions, then watched my reflection fade as the train gained speed and rushed into the black night. I would have many long hours to remind myself that I was indeed a physician, educated at a fine school and graduated with honors, now on my way to a prize internship in the great metropolis of Chicago. That such an extraordinary award had dropped into my lap still took some getting used to. As the train rumbled east through the night, I knew I should try to sleep but instead spent the hours reexamining how I came to be Chicago bound. At my feet sat a large valise that held all my worldly goods and on the empty seat next to me rested my doctor's bag of instruments, a graduation gift from my parents, the bag's still-shiny leather tangible proof that the woman I had seen in the window glass was indeed *Doctor* Katherine Davis.

In some respects, my past years at Kansas Medical School seemed more blurred than the passing scenery I glimpsed through the train windows. Sixteen-hour days that started at four in the morning, complicated lectures, course exercises, hard study, clinical and laboratory lessons, and eventually work with patients at the local hospital had consumed my life. Nine women began the course of study with my class but only three of us finished, yet I did not fault those who quit. The work itself was grueling and made even more arduous by the disapproval we women faced every day. Many of our male classmates and a majority of the faculty did not attempt to hide their displeasure at our presence.

Not that disapproval, overt or subtle, ever held any importance to me. As any member of my family could attest, once I set my mind to a course of action, it was almost impossible to deter me. Besides, I so loved everything I did that for most of my years there I was completely oblivious to male censure. Their disapprobation did not keep me from being at the top of my class in anatomy or possessing a steady hand and stomach with my first cadaver. I welcomed quizzes, loved research and challenging questions, and remained focused on learning all I could, determined to be the kind of doctor my mother had described: one who, with dignity and compassion, healed the sick and cared for the weak.

I always thought I would go home to Wyoming to practice and had begun to make plans to do just that when a rare and unexpected opportunity opened up for me in Chicago, a city of wonder for someone who had never been farther east than Lawrence, Kansas. Because sleep eluded me, I considered the good fortune that had brought me to Dr. Emil Pasca's attention, although Mother would have said good fortune had nothing to do with it. In her positive way, she would have said it was the natural result of certain choices I made. How often did she tell my sister and brothers and me that there were consequences to the choices we made in life, that we should think them through carefully and be prepared to live with the results? Mother gave little credit to serendipity or luck. Informed decision, she called it. Personal choice.

As usual she was right because if I hadn't decided to forego the school's annual spring cotillion and spend the time in the research library, I might not have run across a rare article written nearly fifteen years earlier by a French medical student commenting on the effectiveness of something called *penicillium* in reducing infection in cattle. If I hadn't been intrigued by the article, I wouldn't have questioned Dr. Pasca, guest lecturer in bacteriology, about it, and if I hadn't asked the question, I'm sure he would never have noticed me.

But I did ask the question and he did notice me, raised thick gray eyebrows over the tops of his glasses to examine me as if he'd never seen me before, answered my question, and then asked me to stay after the lecture. We talked more on the subject of *penicillium* then, or rather he talked and I scribbled, fascinated by what he knew and wondering if I would ever have that breadth of knowledge and experience. After our first meeting, we had daily exchanges for the entire twenty weeks he remained at the school.

When it came time for the doctor to leave and for me to graduate, he asked me to come to his office. Our last meeting and one final opportunity for the personal lectures I had come to treasure, I thought regretfully, but when I got there I didn't need my notebook. In his usual methodical fashion Dr. Pasca poured each of us a cup of tea, then leaned back to examine me much as if I'd been a specimen under a microscope.

"You have a very good mind, Miss Davis, and I think a good heart as well. What will you do after you graduate?" It was the first personal reference he had ever made to me and I was surprised at the question.

"I plan to go home."

"And where is home?"

"Wyoming. Laramie, Wyoming."

He gave a little shrug as if the name were new to him. "What will you do there?"

"I thought I'd apply for work at the county's hospital for the poor and then eventually start my own practice. All I've ever wanted to be is a family doctor and as Laramie grows, it will need more physicians."

"Do you think you could put off those plans for a year?"

"I have some flexibility," I responded cautiously.

"Good. Good." He paused as if giving his words a last

mental inspection before he continued, "I have an opportunity that I think would suit you, Miss Davis. Have you heard of Miss Jane Addams?"

"Of course. I've read *Democracy and Social Ethics* and *Newer Ideals of Peace,* and I've followed the progress of the social settlement in Chicago, where she works with immigrants."

"Jane Addams is a remarkable woman of vision and great character. I've known her for twenty years, since the beginning of Hull-House in fact. When I first met you I saw something of Jane in you, and I don't believe I was mistaken, although I would be hard pressed to define exactly what it is the two of you have in common. Have you ever been to Chicago?"

"I've never been farther east than Lawrence," I admitted. "Why?"

"Every year Miss Addams trusts me to select one young doctor to spend a year at Hull-House and intern there under my tutelage. It's an especially rich opportunity. Hull-House sponsors a neighborhood dispensary, a day nursery for infants, and childcare classes for new mothers, all of which need a doctor's services. I've also recently been informed that Dr. Alice Hamilton, the noted epidemiologist, will return to Hull-House, this time to undertake a bacteriological study of infectious diseases and she has requested assistance with her study. The year promises to be full and challenging for the right candidate."

As Dr. Pasca spoke I watched him carefully, not daring to hope that he considered me that 'right candidate.' Why should he? Although I had finished in the top ten percent of my class overall, I had not been the best student in any one area. Surely the graduating class of Kansas Medical School presented more qualified and deserving candidates than I.

As if he had read my mind, the doctor explained with a

smile, "Miss Addams is very particular about who works with 'her people,' as she calls them. She does not require just a good mind. She demands the best heart, too. I see both in you and wonder if you would be interested in spending a year in Chicago. There's hardly any pay—room and board and the smallest of stipends is all. The work is demanding, the hours long, the people needy, the neighborhood rough, but that said, I don't believe there's a better environment for a young family doctor than such a setting. What do you say?"

I hesitated for only a moment and that just to catch my breath at the tantalizing prospect he had just offered me.

"I'm honored that you would consider me for the position, Dr. Pasca, and I can't think of anyplace I'd rather spend the next year than Chicago in exactly the environment you've described. My only question is When do I start?"

"I'll wire Miss Addams and tell her you've accepted," he answered, smiling at my enthusiasm, "and I know she'll want you as soon as you can get there. I'll arrange a ticket to Chicago immediately following graduation." He paused to add, "Unless you must return to Wyoming first."

"Oh, no. No. My family did expect me home for Christmas, but I'm sure they'll understand why I must change my plans. I can always go home later."

Dr. Pasca gave me a look that made me feel fleetingly very young and naïve before he leaned forward.

"Be careful about taking home for granted, Miss Davis," was all he said as I grasped his outstretched hand with both of mine.

"Thank you, Dr. Pasca," I told him fervently, ignoring his comment. "You won't have cause to regret your recommendation."

"I don't doubt that for a minute. I only hope you don't

regret your acceptance. The tenements of Chicago are a far cry from the wide open spaces of Kansas and Wyoming."

"My mother says people are people wherever you go, all alike under the skin, so I think I'll be all right."

"Yes," he agreed, "I think you'll be all right, too."

In support of my casual words to Dr. Pasca, my parents and siblings did not say or write a word of disappointment at my unexpected absence from home but sounded resolutely congratulatory and pleased about the unexpected opportunity I'd been offered. Only my brother's wife, Hope, wrote any regret, and she coupled that with a sincere congratulation for being selected to such an assignment.

Always a quiet woman, Hope was not given to excess in speech so I was touched when she wrote that she was disappointed I would not be coming home for another whole year. Of the entire family, my sister-in-law was my most faithful correspondent during the years I was away, so much so that I sometimes felt closer to her than to my own sister or mother. Certainly I was more like Hope in temperament, neither of us as spontaneous or as animated as Mother and Becca, both of us hanging a little to the outside at family gatherings. All my life I had felt like the changeling in the family, adopted in and certainly loved but somehow different. Hope intuitively understood my feelings.

The last hours of the trip to Chicago I spent dozing intermittently and when not sleeping to the rhythm of the train took time to consider my family. I regretted missing the most recent Christmas because I truly enjoyed my niece and nephew and hadn't yet had a chance to meet the latest addition to the family, baby Thomas, born last summer to my brother and Hope.

In some respects I wished I could spend more time with all of them, adults and children, but I also realized that my departure for medical school years earlier had begun a gradual separation from my family, a distancing in more than miles. Only to myself could I admit that one reason I was so pleased to be going to Chicago was that it postponed my return to Wyoming. I had had a happy childhood there and loved my family but felt real doubts about whether I could go back home and be happy. I no longer knew where I belonged and questioned whether I could slip into the old relationships again. The years away at school had shown me different worlds, had given me different dreams, and I didn't think I could be content with the rural confines in which I'd been raised. I needed a place fitted to me, a place of my own.

If someone asked where home was, I invariably answered Wyoming, but I no longer believed that wholeheartedly. I had even interrupted my studies to volunteer an extra year at the Lawrence hospital in order to gain time to deliberate about my future. The unexpected invitation to Hull-House couldn't have come at a better time, and I had high hopes that the new year would finally answer my private questions about what home would look like for me and where it would be.

I first glimpsed Chicago on a cold, gloomy, gray morning, the sky spitting an uncomfortable combination of snow and sleet and the sun nowhere to be seen. Dr. Pasca waited on the platform for me and hurried me off to a waiting motorcar, the first one I'd ever ridden in despite their increasing presence, even in Lawrence, Kansas. Another man drove, allowing Dr. Pasca and me to sit in the back, but the noisy ride made conversation difficult. I tried to catch glimpses of the city I'd heard so much about and hoped there was more to it than what I saw: large, close, brick tenement houses, dirty streets, everything cramped and dark. For a moment I wondered if I had made a mistake. I had been raised in open spaces with the exhilarating freedom to ride for miles—on horseback, not in an automobile—without the sight of another human. I was accustomed to mountains out the back door and a broad expanse of uninterrupted sky. This gray Chicago seemed literally a different world to me.

We pulled up in front of a sprawling complex of brick buildings and Dr. Pasca came around to help me out of the automobile. Even with the vehicle quiet, the city's noise still surrounded us: the constant undercurrent of people's voices, distant horns, the clang of bells, and the disconcerting blare of factory whistles. I wondered if I would ever become accustomed to the activity or the din. Once we walked through the courtyard and into the stately house that sat slightly concealed in the shadows of the more prominent buildings, however, Chicago's hubbub completely and miraculously disappeared.

Hull-House proper was the most beautiful place I'd ever seen, more elegant than even the Ivinsons' lavish Laramie mansion, which from childhood on I had deemed the embodiment of luxurious residential living. But Hull-House was more gracious and more welcoming than that hometown residence had ever been. The reception area gave the impression that no furnishing was included simply for show, that someone had selected everything carefully, even lovingly, to ensure that people felt at home and elegantly comfortable: beautiful carpets, fine paintings on the walls, a welcoming blaze in the fireplace, and warm wooden furniture upholstered in rich brocades. The interior was hardly what I expected considering Miss Addams's clientele and the surrounding neighborhood. Who would have imagined that such an oasis could exist in the middle of so drab a part of the city? My expression must have reflected my surprise because Dr. Pasca, who had been watching me surreptitiously from the moment we stepped through the front door, smiled.

"The look on your face tells me this is not what you anticipated."

"It's so gracious and beautiful! I'm not sure what I expected exactly, but I know it wasn't this warm elegance."

A pretty, dark-haired woman of about forty, who had been standing next to the fireplace, came forward to greet Dr. Pasca with both hands extended.

"Emil, we haven't seen you in such a while! How was Kansas?"

"Interesting but not enough city for me. The trip was worthwhile, though, because I have brought a treasure back with me." He turned to me. "Mary, this is Katherine Davis—Dr. Katherine Davis I should say. Katherine, this is Mary Rozet Smith, whose dedication to the mission of Hull-House is surpassed only by her dedication to Miss Addams."

I shook the woman's hand, conscious of her unhidden scrutiny as she met my look with an unsmiling one of her own. Then, as if I had passed some test that only she understood, Miss Smith smiled and spoke.

"We're so happy you're here, Dr. Davis. Dr. Comstock had to leave a full month early and we've been without a resident physician the whole month of December. We can't count Dr. Hamilton because she's already begun work on the disease report Miss Addams commissioned. When she's not out tracking down germs, she's sequestered in her study and laboratory. I know if Emil recommends you, we will be very ably served. He's never failed to bring us any but the most qualified and compassionate doctors."

Before I could respond, the door behind her opened and another woman entered the room. Dr. Pasca's eyes brightened and he stepped forward to give the newcomer a friendly and enthusiastic embrace.

"My dear," he greeted, "how good to see you!" The woman stepped away from him, smiling.

"And you, Emil. You know how much we miss you when you're not here." Then she saw me and came forward. "You must be Dr. Davis. How very generous of you to give us a year of your life. I'm Jane Addams."

The woman before me was slight in build and short, about fifty years old, with luminous blue eyes and soft, graying hair that was twisted into a bun at the back of her head. I knew Miss Addams to be about fifty years old and my first thought as she approached was that she looked older than her years, too thin, perhaps ill, and certainly more worn and tired than I had expected. But for all her apparent fragility, she radiated a sincere and heartfelt welcome as if she had been waiting just for me and now that I had arrived her cup simply overflowed.

For a sudden, very clear moment I saw my mother in her, in the rich smile, in the welcoming look and the warm tone of voice that made us instantly friends. In fact, Jane Addams reminded me so much of Mother that at first I was speechless, caught up in a brief but surprisingly intense pang of homesickness, but the feeling passed and I took her hand.

"What an honor to meet you, Miss Addams! I'm the one who should thank you for giving me the opportunity to be part of this worthwhile venture." I think my response pleased her, although her remarkable eyes might have held that same warm expression if I'd recited the train schedule.

"You'll see soon enough how really worthwhile it is," she responded. "Mary, will you show Dr. Davis where her room is? We gave you a small first floor apartment, Dr. Davis, where you'll be close to the nursery and to the dispensary's alley door. We often have visitors arrive unexpectedly at the dispensary in need of medical services, and you'll be able to get to them quickly from your room without having to go outside. You're invited to take your meals in our dining room or we can send a tray over to you if you find yourself too busy to take a break. That's happened often enough with your predecessors for us to expect it now. You and I will spend some time together at supper this evening and talk more then. I know after such a long trip you may want to rest for a while in your room. We can arrange a luncheon tray there for you if you'd like."

As Mary Smith and I left the room, I heard Dr. Pasca ask, "How are you feeling since your surgery, Jane? I'd guess you haven't been following doctor's orders to rest as much as you should."

The door closed on her answer but Miss Smith had heard the exchange, too, and volunteered, "Miss Addams had an attack of appendicitis last year and gave us all a scare. The surgery was successful, but Dr. Pasca's right. She hasn't slowed down one little bit since then. If anything, her schedule has become more hectic. With no resident doctor, she felt the need to be present at the nursery every day in December and at the dispensary almost that often. The schedule was too much for her so I'm glad you're here, Dr. Davis. Maybe between the two of us, we can convince her that more rest will hasten her recuperation."

"Shall I give her doctor's orders?" I asked, smiling. Mary Smith smiled in return but shook her head a little as she did so.

"You'll learn that does no good at all. Miss Addams is so concerned about others that she pays little attention to her own well being."

We walked outside, crossed a larger area, and entered an old brick building, somewhat the worse for wear on the outside but once again displaying a well-planned and comfortable interior. The two simple and unaffected rooms on the first floor to which Miss Smith led me contained all I needed: a bed and bureau in one, a loveseat, chair, writing table, and desk in the connecting, larger room. The luxury of indoor plumbing that included a commode and bathtub was available in a room down the hall.

Mary Smith explained simply, “We aren’t ostentatious and perhaps you’re used to something finer, but I hope you’ll be comfortable and happy here. I know we’re happy to have you. For all the interns Dr. Pasca has brought us, he has never sung anyone’s praises as enthusiastically as he did yours.” I felt myself flush with pleasure, embarrassed by her words.

“That’s very kind of him. I intend to make him proud of me and only hope I can live up to everything he’s said. And these rooms are fine, Miss Smith. I come from a family with simple tastes, and my own room at home wasn’t nearly this grand.”

“Dr. Pasca said you were from out west somewhere.” She made the statement more of a question.

“Wyoming. My parents run a cattle ranch near Laramie, and my brother raises cattle and sheep on the neighboring range.”

“I’ve seen pictures of Yellowstone Park. It looks like beautiful country.”

“We live in the southeast corner of the state so the park is some distance from us, but it’s all beautiful country. The snowy peaks of mountains are always in sight wherever you are, it’s the biggest sky you can imagine, and the countryside is so open you can see without interruption for miles.” She looked at me kindly.

“I hope you won’t feel too homesick here, Dr. Davis. Sometimes we can’t see the sky at all because of the smoke from the factories, and everyone is crowded on top of one another. The packinghouses stink and the river is so thick with refuse you can practically walk on top of the water, but our people are grateful and the work is worthwhile. I predict that when you look back, this will be a year you will never forget." As it turned out, Mary Smith was more accurate in her prediction than she—or I—could ever have imagined.

That evening I dined with Miss Addams in "The Octagon," as her second-floor study was called, and the two of us talked well into the night. Even now, despite the intervening years, I remember what an absolutely mesmerizing woman she was, how convinced of the value of her work, how impassioned on behalf of the immigrants crowding the neighborhoods, how firm in her vision of democracy and of what life could be like for the people new to that idea, how sure of her own purpose. She had a way of inspiring mutual dreams that I have never experienced from anyone since. I will always treasure that evening when I was given a rare glimpse into the heart and mind of a woman whose like I believe the world will never see again. Miss Addams must have found whatever she was looking for in me that evening because from that first night she never questioned my judgment or expertise or was ever anything but supportive and encouraging all the time I was there.

It didn't take long to fall into the rhythm of Hull-House, the name a misnomer of sorts because it was not so much a house as a complex of several buildings on several blocks. My main residence and place of work were on the north end of Gilpin Place, but on adjoining blocks there were also a gymnasium, a large theater, the Hull-House Music School, buildings for the boys' and girls' clubs, kindergarten classrooms, a boardinghouse and apartments, handicraft centers, and a labor museum to name only some of the structures, halls, and displays. There were endless activities for all ages and no one was ever turned away, whether from reading groups or music lessons or astronomy classes. The place seemed to draw energy from the stream of committed teachers and volunteers who constantly came and went and from the excited neighborhood children and young people, whose worlds were enlarged by the rich buffet of knowledge and activities spread out before them. Hundreds of people passed through the doors daily; Hull-House always felt as busy as a train station.

At the end of my first week I turned to Miss Flaherty, the day nurse who worked with me in the dispensary, and asked, "Is it always like this? I had no idea."

Whatever was in my tone, whether admiration or amazement or panic, made her laugh. Miss Flaherty was a decade older than I with carrot-orange hair and a round, freckled face.

"Oh, no. Usually it's busier. We slowed down a bit for Christmas and we had a spell of bad weather that kept a lot of people home but now that we're into the new year, we'll see things get back to their old pace."

She and I had just returned from a cramped, dark apartment where a young mother had given birth to her first child. The girl couldn't have been older than sixteen, thin and worn already at that age, her husband older and more worn than she, but the baby was a healthy boy with a good set of lungs so we were all feeling satisfied. It wasn't the first birth I'd participated in but the first one I'd handled on my own, and I felt exhilarated and happy at its success. Now a man with a bandaged foot waited for me and behind him a mother with a fussy baby in her arms. I still had all the children in the day nursery to see, a child was en route from the kindergarten with stomach cramps, and I was expected to make my first visit to the baby class that afternoon to supervise the instruction on washing newborns. Every day of that week had been filled to overflowing and today was no different. It was exhausting and invigorating and I couldn't recall ever being happier in all my life.

"Busier!" I exclaimed, making her laugh again. "I don't see how that can be unless Miss Addams has found a way to add hours to the day."

"Well, I believe Jane Addams can do anything so I suppose she could do that if she chose, but no, right now we have to settle for the standard twenty-four and do the best we can with them."

Which is what we did. I removed a huge splinter from the man's foot and assured the mother that her baby was fussy because his first teeth had begun to poke through. The kindergartner diagnosed her own stomach pains by admitting she had eaten her own as well as several of her classmates' mid-morning treats and the class on newborns went off without a hitch.

I especially enjoyed making rounds in the nursery to check each child and confer with the caregivers. The nursery itself was almost like a museum with beautiful paintings on all the walls, everything pretty and sparkling clean.

"We're glad you're here, Dr. Davis," said Mrs. Teague, the woman in charge of the nursery. She looked the part of a grandmother, stout with gray hair, pink cheeks, and a constant cheerfulness. "We thoroughly appreciated Dr. Comstock, but I believe there's nothing quite like a woman's touch with babies. Do you have any of your own?"

"No. I'm unmarried, but I have two nephews and a niece I'm very fond of."

"Well, you've got a mother's touch, and there's time enough to have a family of your own."

"I'm not sure that's in my future, Mrs. Teague. I think Miss Addams and Miss Smith are proof that women can accomplish a great deal of good in the world even without a husband." Mrs. Teague made a clucking sound and gave me a knowing look.

"There's not a person here who'd dispute that, Doctor, but I've been around a while and I don't predict that for you. We'll see."

"Yes," I said brusquely, deciding the conversation had grown too familiar, "we will," and moved to the next child.

As I lay in bed that night, I tried to picture myself with a husband of my own, but the image wouldn't come. I couldn't imagine what kind of man would welcome a doctor as a wife, who would handle the unexpected interruptions that came with the vocation and be willing to share his wife with a profession that demanded so much of her time and energy. My limited experience had shown me that—except for the men in my own family—they were not a sex willing to accept anything other than complete allegiance and attention from their wives. Too helpless to survive on their own, I thought with some disdain as I drifted off to sleep, needing a woman to keep them fed and dressed and presentable for society. Such a partner would never do for me.

After the first six weeks it was as if I had always lived and worked at Hull-House. I learned the routines, recognized faces, and enjoyed the myriad activities of the place. I finally met Dr. Alice Hamilton, a renowned scientist and physician, a woman of great intellect and untiring energy. Keeping up with her both physically and mentally took all my strength and concentration. She always spoke of disease as a personal enemy, said the names *typhoid* and *diphtheria* and *poliomyelitis* in a challenging tone with a curl of her lip, staring them down, their sworn enemy and determined to triumph.

"I have several theories, Dr. Davis, about the spread of disease and I am currently disposed to cast much of the blame on flies."

"Pasteur said, 'Look for the germ,'" I responded seriously, "so I believe you could be right about flies spreading illness. I've watched them land with their nasty little feet in something unhealthy and then generously try to share it with humans by depositing it on food. I've had my private suspicions for some time."

Dr. Hamilton seemed to eye me with more respect but only responded briskly, "Suspicions won't convince the Health Department, Doctor, so if I send you off to trap flies in a bottle, bear with me and don't look at me as if I've lost control of my faculties. The only thing I promise you is that I won't knowingly send you on any fool's errands." Then she gave me an undignified wink and added, "But unknowingly is another matter altogether." Her droll tone made me laugh, as did the picture of me wandering up and down the streets of Chicago swooping at flies with a tiny net like some lost butterfly fancier who'd taken a wrong turn at St. Louis and was desperately searching for an elusive flower garden in the middle of tenement houses.

CHAPTER 2

The second Monday in February Miss Addams stopped me as I left the dining room. She looked better than she had when I'd first arrived, not so tired and she had put on some healthy pounds.

"Do I pass inspection?" Miss Addams asked, smiling, and I realized I must have been examining her more noticeably than I'd intended.

"Not entirely but you do look more rested than when I first met you and your face has begun to fill out, which means your appetite must be improving. Those are all good signs that you're feeling better." With a smile, I added, "There's no charge for my professional opinion, either."

She took my arm, saying, "Come by the fireplace, Katherine, I have a favor to ask." Once there she sat down close to the flames and held out both her hands to the fire. I sat, too, curious about the favor.

"A great deal of my time is spent doing things I really do not want to do," Miss Addams said finally. "If I had my wishes, I'd stay here and spend time with my friends and with all the children who come here every day. I'd write, learn more about nutritional theories because I don't think we're doing them justice in our kitchen, and devote myself simply and contentedly to the running of the House. Unfortunately, I have little time to spend on the things I love most because I must constantly be concerned about financing, pleasing donors, and keeping the public informed. I lead an unwilling social life that consumes too much of my time with speeches and dinners and parties." She paused, then added, "Which is where I could use your help." Miss Addams looked over at me and said with unmistakable sincerity, "Dr. Comstock was a wonderful doctor and we miss him. He was splendid with patients, an untiring worker who never complained, but he would be the first to admit that he wasn't good in social settings. He had no tolerance for the fripperies of life and even less for the type of people who often make up our financial base. I am not condemning anyone and I have many dear and generous friends among the privileged and wealthy classes of the city, but Dr. Comstock simply had no time for any of them. He saw such people as elitist, and I believe he was truly repelled by social occasions and celebrations. He was a passionate socialist, zealous in his support of labor unions and intolerant of anyone who had what he considered to be too much money. How he thought we would exist without our wealthy patrons I have no idea."

She sighed and was silent for a moment before continuing, "This is a long explanation for a relatively simple request, Dr. Davis, but I wanted you to understand why I never asked Dr. Comstock to do what I am going to ask of you. It has nothing to do with your gender. Chicago society's annual Sweethearts Ball will be held this weekend and I wondered whether you would accompany me. I consider it my duty to attend every year, but I find less and less enjoyment in it. I know you would be a much better ambassador for us in such a setting than Dr. Comstock ever was, and I would appreciate your supporting company more than I could say."

Whatever I had expected the favor to be, a party invitation certainly wasn't it.

"Miss Addams, I would be honored to go with you but frankly, I have nothing suitable to wear to such an occasion and not enough money to go out and buy something. My white doctor's smock is as dressed up as I get, and I can't imagine that you would want me to go dressed in that, even with a stethoscope hanging around my neck for ornament." She stood up and I did too, hoping I hadn't offended her.

"I believe we can find something suitable for you to wear, Katherine, but I draw the line at wearing medical instruments for jewelry. If you can tolerate a night among the rich, I can dress you for the occasion." Then she added quietly, "Thank you. I've forced Mary to go on earlier occasions, but she's grown even more wearied than I of the obligation. Frankly, I think I must still be tired out from the surgery last year because I don't recall ever contemplating a social evening with less anticipation. I know your ready smile and warm disposition will make up for my lack of enthusiasm."

Later I thought to myself that no one had ever said I had a warm disposition before. In fact, I would have said I had just the opposite temperament, accused on more than one occasion of being cool and unfeminine. How else to explain that I handled my first autopsy with a steady hand and stomach, while two men in the class fainted and another two were busy vomiting in the hallway? Decidedly unfeminine, I was told at the time, and I had believed it. I always considered myself to be much like my father, who was a good man but formal in his habits, a man of deep feeling and strong affection but not given to public exhibition of his emotions. It was my mother who wore her sentiments on her sleeve and expressed her feelings easily and passionately, and I knew I was nothing like her. Whatever Jane Addams had seen in me was contrary to what I had always seen in myself, and I was surprised and intrigued by her observation.

The week of the Sweethearts Ball was the same week Petra came to us. The bell that connected to the dispensary's outside bell rang in my room as I was getting ready for bed one night. I pulled my dress back on and threw a coat over it before heading down the hall to see who was waiting for me. I'd already had several nights interrupted by sick children and adult injuries, many of those from fights, so it was nothing new to hear the bell ring after dark.

The night nurse who slept on site was Mrs. Tabachnik, and I heard her footsteps in the hallway behind me as I opened the alley door. In the doorway huddled a girl shivering from the cold night air, a small satchel on the ground next to her, her covered head bent against the wind, and one arm desperately holding the other arm immobile against her chest. I couldn't see her face but she seemed so small and young, just a child, that my first thought was to wonder where her parents were, surprised that she was out by herself at this late hour. I stepped outside, put an arm around the child's shoulders, and drew her back inside as Mrs. Tabachnik closed the door behind us.

"I'm Dr. Davis," I said gently. "Have you hurt your arm?"

The girl lifted her face when I spoke, showing large, violet-colored eyes and a heart-shaped face. Not as young as I'd thought, maybe sixteen, but petite and delicate. It wasn't her eyes or pretty face that caught my attention, however. It was the ugly purple-red bruise that started at the corner of her left eye and spread like a piece of raw meat across her cheek, over to her nose, and down to her mouth. The whole side of her face was swollen and discolored. Clearly someone had struck her, and for just a moment the sight of that substantial bruise on her fragile face made me angry and outraged. I knew I couldn't afford that kind of emotional reaction, though, and took a quick, deep breath so I could speak calmly.

"Mrs. Tabachnik, I'll need a cold compress for the bruise." The girl stood dumbly as if she were so exhausted in body and spirit that she couldn't move one more step. I knelt down in front of her, repeated my name, and said, "You needn't be afraid. Just come with me. No one will hurt you here. Is your arm injured?"

She nodded, but when she tried to stretch out her arm for me to see, she gave a gasp of pain at the attempt and quickly cradled it back against her chest.

"It's all right," I told her. "We'll fix it. You're safe here." I steered her gently into the examination room and had her sit in a chair as I took the cold compress from the nurse and placed it against the girl's face.

"Can you hold this with your good hand while I look at your arm? I won't hurt you." My hasty examination confirmed that her arm was broken. As Mrs. Tabachnik moved away to get things ready so I could set the bone, I handed a little vial of laudanum to the girl, explaining, "Your arm is broken and I'll need to set it. That procedure could hurt quite a bit, I'm afraid, so you should take this. Then you won't feel the pain from the procedure."

She looked at me soberly, her one eye almost swollen shut, and then, as if making a deliberate decision to trust me, did as I asked. Later, when we were done and the girl lay sleeping in one of the infirmary beds, I sat down next to her.

"I can stay up with her, Doctor," Mrs. Tabachnick volunteered. "I don't mind."

But something in the girl's face, in the way she'd purposefully decided to trust me, had touched me, and I wasn't ready to turn her over to someone else just yet.

"Thank you, Mrs. Tabachnick, but I'm wide awake now and I believe I'll just sit here a while. I'll come and get you if I need you." When it was just the two of us in the room, I spoke softly to the still figure on the bed. "Poor child. Were you very frightened? You've come to the right place. There's no one who will hurt you here, I promise." I took her good hand in mine and sat by her bed most of the night, dozing on and off until Mrs. Tabachnik came in dressed to go home.

"Dr. Davis, you never rang me! Have you sat here all night?"

I stood and stretched, feeling remarkably rested for a night spent in a chair, and answered, "Yes. Time got away from me."

"How's our patient then?"

I put a hand against the girl's forehead, lightly brushing the swollen side of her face.

"There's no fever and her breathing is nice and even. She'll make a full recovery, I think, with not even a scar to show."

"That's good. A working girl, I'd say, who ran into a man who wanted to play too rough."

"She's awfully young, Mrs. Tabachnik."

"We've had them younger than that, Doctor, if you don't mind my speaking of it. These girls bring in money any way they can to keep the family from starving, and there's always a man willing to take advantage of their situation. The Levy on the south side is famous for its red light district."

"Infamous, maybe," I commented grimly.

"Well, yes, infamous might be a better choice of words, but you understand what I'm saying. I'm on my way out, Doctor. Do you need anything before I go?"

I shook my head. "When Miss Flaherty comes in, I'll catch an hour or so of sleep. Thank you, Nurse. I appreciated your help last night."

After she left, the patient briefly awoke, stirred restlessly, and whimpered a name I couldn't catch.

I said quietly, "It's all right. I'm Dr. Davis and you're safe here. You should try to go back to sleep." My voice seemed to calm her and she did exactly that.

I turned the girl's care over to Miss Flaherty when she arrived and went to my room to try to catch a brief nap, but my attempts were useless. Disease or illness never brought me up short or made me question my choice of profession, but I would never grow accustomed to the damage one human could inflict on another. My instructors had routinely stressed the need for objectivity in patient care, but that was one lesson I didn't seem able to master. How could one remain objective with the mental picture of someone taking a brutal hand to the sweet, heart-shaped face of that girl-child? I thought I could live to be a hundred and still not be able to rid myself of the burning revulsion and anger I felt at the sight of injuries inflicted on the weak by the strong, by the bullies and thugs with whom, in my opinion, the planet was over populated. I knew a quick sympathy for Dr. Comstock and his socialist tendencies. If I wasn't careful, I'd be carrying a banner and leading a street march myself. I understood how my predecessor could easily and quickly come to despise the trappings of privilege when he was exposed to the degradations of poverty and violence on such a regular basis.

Some time after lunch I stopped by the dispensary to confer with Miss Flaherty.

"Your patient's awake, Doctor, and sitting up, but she won't say a word to me. She asked for you and when I said you weren't available, she pressed her lips together and curled up like a child under the covers. Maybe she'll talk to you."

The girl lay curled up on her side like a baby, covers pulled up to her chin and one hand still cradling the wrapped and splinted arm. When I put a hand to her throat to measure her heartbeat she awoke suddenly and pulled away from me with a fearful look on her face.

"It's all right," I assured her quickly. "I'm Dr. Davis. There's nothing to be frightened of here." I saw her come back from whatever terrible place she'd been and orient herself to her surroundings before she raised her sweet face to me.

"Dr. Davis," she repeated softly, then gave me a lopsided smile, the bruised corner of her mouth stiff and immobile. She sat up, pushing her body back against the pillow with one arm and said in a formal tone, as if we were sitting down to tea together, "How do you do? I'm sorry if I've been any trouble for you." I sat down on the chair next to her bed.

"No trouble at all. How are you feeling?"

"My arm throbs a little and I can tell my eye is swollen so I must have quite a bruise on my face, but nothing hurts exactly. I'm sure I'll be fine."

"I'm sure you'll be fine, too. You know I'm Dr. Davis, but I don't know your name."

"I'm Petra."

I repeated her name and added, "How pretty! I don't think I've ever heard that name before. Do you have a last name to go with it?"

"Stravinsky."

"Miss Petra Stravinsky, then," I said pleasantly. "Are you up to telling me how you came to our doorstep? Your parents must be frantic with worry and we should try to reach them. They'll want to have you home with them as soon as possible." At my words a spasm crossed her face—whether of fear or panic or revulsion, it was hard to tell.

"I didn't know where else to go," she responded simply. Petra had a pretty, lyrical voice that was light and slightly accented with a Russian or eastern European inflection. I still wasn't very good at identifying all the dialects and languages of the inhabitants of the surrounding neighborhoods. "Someone told me how nice it was here. I was going to come before because I'd heard there were classes and a piano and music lessons, but I wasn't allowed to come."

"Not allowed by whom?"

"My father. He said I couldn't come."

"He probably didn't understand what Hull-House offered."

"We have no money to pay for it, he said, and he did not want me to leave home. My mother is gone and who would take care of my brothers, he said."

"He'll be worried about you then, Petra, and your brothers, too. We should let them know you're here. In fact, I don't see any reason you couldn't go home now. Perhaps I could go with you and explain to your father what we do at Hull-House. I'm sure he'd allow you to attend some of the classes then."

"My father isn't worried about me," Petra replied without noticeable emotion, "and I don't want to go home."

"Why is that?"

"I just don't." She spoke the three words quite firmly,

as if the idea was not to be considered let alone discussed, and I thought with surprise that the girl had more steel in her than I'd originally given her credit for.

"Petra," I said, rising, "I have a class to supervise now, but we really must tell your father you're here. I'll come back later in the afternoon, and we'll talk about it again." She looked at me reproachfully out of that small bruised face.

"You don't understand."

"No, I don't," I agreed, "but sometimes I'm a little slow about understanding things, or so my older brother has told me often enough. When I come back, perhaps you'll take the time to explain what it is I don't understand."

But when I later returned to the infirmary, Petra's bed was empty, the sheets stripped from it and the blankets tumbled on the floor.

"Nurse, where did Miss Stravinsky go?"

I couldn't keep the disapproval and worry out of my voice and Miss Flaherty heard it, drawing herself up straight to say, "She said she had to go home, Doctor. She said her mother would be worried about her. I checked and she wasn't feverish. It was only a broken arm after all, and I saw no reason to keep her here and worry her parents for another night."

"How long ago did she leave?"

"Fifteen minutes or so."

I turned, saying over my shoulder, "I'm going out to look for her. She told me she doesn't have a mother so I'm not convinced she's going home at all, and I don't like the idea of her wandering about the streets on such a night."

I realized the chances of finding Petra Stravinsky were slim if not impossible, one of a multitude of lost girls, a black-haired needle in a haystack the size of Chicago, but I felt an inexplicable urgency to bring her back to the warm shelter of Hull-House. Something in her tone had told me there was more to her story, and I wished I would have stayed longer at her bedside, long enough to find out what exactly had happened to her.

A touch of late afternoon light still illumined the sky and the glow of the streetlamps was still faint when I stepped outside, pulling on heavy gloves and wrapping a scarf around my neck as I went. She wouldn't have gone north and continued down the alley, I thought. That way was too dark and dangerous. More likely she would head toward movement and light and people, southeast toward Halsted Street where she could find a streetcar. Each pedestrian only shrugged indifferently when I asked after a small, black-haired girl with a bruised face, and despite the flurry of prayers I sent heavenward, I had almost decided to give up the search when I saw Petra sitting on a bench waiting for the next trolley. The worn satchel was at her feet, her head was uncovered, and she sat hunched against the cold, cradling her injured arm in a familiar pose. Without apology I squeezed myself next to her, forcing the others on the seat to move down and nearly shoving one portly man, who sputtered at my rudeness, off the opposite end of the bench.

"Miss Stravinsky," I said, "I was sorry to find that you left without giving me a chance to talk with you again or say good-bye."

She remained quiet and studiously ignored me, looking down the street, clearly willing the streetcar to appear so she could escape the insistent woman, who sat next to her.

"Have you decided to go home, after all?" Still she said nothing and I kept talking. "Do you know what I think, Miss Stravinsky? I think you're running away from something and from someone, maybe from the person who hurt you. I don't think you have any place to go at all, and it doesn't make sense to me that you should be out in this cold night when we have a warm bed for you at Hull-House. Won't you trust me? I promise I won't tell anyone where you are or try to send you back to any place you would rather not go. Just come back with me. Please."

Without looking at me she asked, "Why are you being kind to me? You don't know me."

"I'm a doctor. In the doctors' rule book it says we have to be kind to people. It's our job." She gave a little snort of contempt at my feeble humor and turned to face me.

"Do you promise?" I understood what she asked.

"Yes, unless you've done something illegal, murdered someone or robbed a bank or kidnapped a baby, for example. I'd have to let the authorities know if you've done something really horrible. Have you?"

"Of course, I haven't," she answered, her accent, unmistakably Russian, made more noticeable by the scorn in her voice. "I wouldn't hurt or rob anyone, and I'd never steal a child unless—." She faltered, suddenly sounding like a child herself.

"Unless what?"

"Unless it was in danger. Unless someone was going to hurt it. Then I'd take it away without a second thought."

"I believe I'd do the same," I responded agreeably, then stood and extended a hand. "Will you come home with me now, please?"

Petra gave me a sober look out of those extraordinary violet eyes, gauging my sincerity and her own vulnerability. Finally she put her ungloved hand into mine, her injured arm unsupported and pressed against her chest as I reached for her bag with my other hand.

"Yes, I will," she answered, "but remember you promised." She sounded even more like a child, too fearful and hesitant, a child who had been abused somehow and was afraid it would happen again.

"I know. I won't forget. Come along now. We'll miss supper if we wait any longer." I could hear the streetcar in the distance and wondered if she would change her mind and at the last minute bolt onto the car and away, but she didn't. Instead, she clung to my hand and walked beside me all the way back to our residence. After dinner I asked Mary Smith if there was space for Petra in the boarding-house.

She replied, "Of course," without question or hesitation, trusting my judgment that this young woman needed shelter and protection for a while.

When I showed Petra the room where she would be staying, tears pooled in her eyes, two escaping and running in perfectly straight and parallel lines down both her cheeks.

"I'm sorry." She rubbed the tears away with her fists as I had seen my little niece Lily Kate do often enough. "I don't mean to cry."

"Fiddle tears," I said, smiling. At her questioning look I added, "When I was a little girl, my mother always called sudden tears that you didn't expect fiddle tears. I'm not sure how she came up with the name, but that's what we call them in our family to this day."

"Fiddle tears," Petra repeated with a fleeting smile at such nonsense. Then she added hesitantly, "I don't have any money to pay for all this."

"I suspect you don't," I agreed, "but we can use help in the nursery and the kindergarten, and when your arm's healed, in the kitchen as well, so if you're willing to work for your room and board I think we can reach an agreement. Are you?"

"Yes." She spoke a little breathlessly as if she couldn't believe her good fortune and wanted to answer quickly in case I changed my mind. "I'm a good worker."

"Petra, you understand that sooner or later you'll need to tell me the truth. You can trust me, but I need to feel the same about you." I held up a hand as she started to speak. "No, not now. You're tired and so am I. Meet me at the dispensary in the morning. If you can't find your way, just ask anyone you meet and they'll direct you. You can accompany me on my rounds in the nursery and meet Mrs. Teague, who I'm sure can put you to work. If she runs out of things for you to do, she can send you over to the kindergarten, where there are two dozen five-year-olds in need of amusement and instruction. Can you read?"

"Of course, I can." I heard indignation in her tone and considered the small display of temper a good sign that she was regaining strength and confidence.

"Good. The girls' club meets tomorrow afternoon. You might enjoy participating in that. I believe they're reading something by Nathaniel Hawthorne. Are you acquainted with him?" When she shook her head I added, "That's all right. I expect you will be by the end of the hour. Is there anything else you need? There are other women and children staying here so you only have to ask them if I've forgotten to tell you anything important. I'll see you in the morning then."

I started down the hall but stopped as Petra quietly called my name behind me. She stood in the doorway of her room, oblivious to the other people in the hallway, a small figure with a halo of coal-black hair. When I turned around, she spoke with dignity beyond her years.

"Thank you, Dr. Davis. I don't know why you've been so kind to me, but thank you." Then she stepped back into her room and closed the door behind her.

CHAPTER 3

Petra waited for me at the door of the infirmary the next morning, the bruise on her face more startling in the daylight, showing vivid against her pale skin.

"I saw myself in a mirror," she said. "I think I'll scare the children the way I look." I opened the door and she followed me into the room.

"Oh, I don't think so. You just need to show that pretty smile and they'll be fine. Did you have breakfast?" She nodded and I started to say more when Nurse Flaherty came to the door.

"I think you should come, Doctor. There's a woman with a child in the waiting room and I'm not easy about it."

I knew from the nurse's face that the matter was serious and forgetting Petra entirely, threw on my white coat and hurried out to the little patient held in his mother's arms. The woman was frantic—hysterical even—and she raised her voice as I approached, holding out her little burden toward me as if offering a gift. She spoke rapidly and loudly in a language I didn't understand.

Behind me Petra addressed the woman calmly in what must have been the same language, listened to the woman's response, and explained, "She says she gave the baby something to quiet his crying and now he won't wake up."

I took the wisp of a child into my arms. A skeletal infant, who had been crying from hunger, I thought, and feared from the sunken cheeks, dry skin, and minimal breathing that whatever I attempted would be too little and too late. The baby would soon be gone and there was nothing I could do for him.

But in defiance of that knowledge I directed, "Get me tea and broth from the kitchen, Nurse. Right away. Petra, ask the woman what she gave the child."

"She says she doesn't know what it was. Her husband brought it home and told her it would quiet the baby so they could all sleep through the night for once. He said it was whiskey, harmless he said, but she says it didn't smell like whiskey. After her husband left this morning to look for work, she looked in on the baby and he was like this." Petra talked at the same time as the woman, translating quickly and without emotion.

I carried the child into the back room and laid his feather-light body on the examination table. His breathing was now so slow that after each inhale I thought he would not catch another. Flaherty brought in hot tea and a cup of warm broth and as she held the child, I tried to get something warm and strengthening between his lips, speaking to him all the while, murmuring endearments as my mother had done whenever any of her children had been ill, always assuring us that we were loved and that she would never leave us. After a time I lifted the child and began to walk with him, holding him close against my chest for warmth.

"What's his name?" I asked, pacing.

"She says it's Leonid. Leo she calls him."

"Hello, little Leo," I said, looking down at the colorless, too thin face. "I'm Dr. Davis. Your mama wants you to live and so do I. There's a world waiting for you and we don't want you to miss it." The child stirred a little, took a trembling baby breath, relaxed again in my arms, and for a moment I thought with a sharp pang of grief and anger that he was gone. But then little Leo took another breath, briefly flailed one bony arm as if to acknowledge my introduction, and I allowed myself to hope that he might live after all.

For the rest of the morning Flaherty and I fed the child warm liquids and walked him in our arms, talking to him all the while as the mother sat stolidly on a bench along the wall and Petra stood by her side, still and watching.

Finally I said, "Nurse, fix Leo up a little crib here so we can keep an eye on him. Petra, tell the mother Leo must stay here all day and all night tonight. Tell her she can stay here, too, if she wishes, or she can leave and come back later in the day. If little Leo is still with us tomorrow morning, I will need to speak to the mother about his care. I'll need you to help me talk to her."

Later, having spent the afternoon with a few less serious patients and returned from the well-attended baby-care classes, I went to check on Leo. Miss Flaherty held a finger to her lips and brought me to the doorway so I could watch Petra holding the child awkwardly in her arms, his slight figure supported by her wrapped arm and her good arm surrounding his little body as if for protection. As she walked with him, she sang to him in a low but clear and beautiful voice.

"She's been doing that all afternoon," Flaherty whispered. "As pretty a voice as I've ever heard, and it seems to calm the child more than anything I can do." When I walked in, Petra looked up and her bruised face broke into a glowing smile.

"I think he'll live, Dr. Davis, but he's such a little thing we need to keep him safe until he's stronger."

"Yes, we do," I agreed, relieved to find a solid pulse and see Leo's chest rise and fall in regular breaths. "What did his mother say?"

"She said she'd be back tonight. She has other children and no one to watch them, she said. I told her Leo must stay here a long time, and I told her to bring her other children here for a warm meal. Was that all right?"

"Yes, that was exactly right."

Petra smiled again and leaned down over the baby, echoing the words I had used to her, "See little Leo, I told you no one will hurt you here."

The child's mother came to the dispensary after supper that night and she, Petra, and I sat down together in a small room.

"Tell her Leo needs to stay with us a while and get fattened up. Tell her she must come to our baby classes so we can help her take good care of her children. Tell her—"

"I know," interrupted Petra and she began to speak quickly and vehemently to the mother. When the woman tried to speak, Petra held up an imperious hand to her, brooking no interruption, and continued her monologue. I had no idea what Petra said, but her words made a dramatic impression on the mother, who turned to me, grabbed my hand, and raised it to her lips. I pulled my hand away quickly.

"No, no, Mrs. Lubchik, please." I stood up, uselessly smoothing down my skirts to hide my embarrassment. "Does she understand everything about Leo, Petra?"

"Yes. I made sure. She can't stay the night, but she would like to see the baby before she goes home."

"Of course. Will you take her and then show her out

when she's ready to leave? Tell her she can come in the morning whenever she wants but certainly by ten o'clock for the baby class. Are you willing to sit in the class with her and help her understand what's being taught?" At Petra's nod, I smiled and laid a hand on the girl's head on my way out. "See, we have plenty for you to do here, even with a broken arm. You've more than earned your keep today."

From that day, Petra became invaluable to me and to all of us at Hull-House. There was nothing she wouldn't attempt, no job too humble, no request too small. As the bruise on her face faded, her features became more recognizable. With that perfect face, stunning eyes, and cloud of soft black hair, Petra was beautiful but evasive, too, so that in the days that followed I never found the time or energy to sit with her and hear her story, and she never showed a willingness to volunteer it.

Whether busy in the kitchen, nursery, or infirmary, Petra brought a kind of joy with her. Her splendid voice, her smile, her warm nature all had the gift of making people happy. I planned to mention Petra to Mr. Sweeney, who volunteered music lessons three afternoons a week at the Music School, and ask him to hear her because even my amateur's ear could tell she was talented and would be a willing pupil, but I never made the time to follow through on my good intention. Petra would eventually handle that task for me, however, in the firm and concentrated manner I had detected in her.

As I dressed for the Sweethearts Ball I would attend with Miss Addams, the girl knocked on my door. When I opened it, her eyes, both nearly back to their regular size and color, widened.

"Dr. Davis, you look beautiful." I turned and looked at myself objectively in the mirror.

"That's very kind of you, Petra, but I'm afraid not exactly true. My sister, Becca, inherited all the beauty in my family, but I think I'm presentable enough that I won't embarrass Miss Addams." I was dressed in borrowed finery: a gown of patterned deep green silk, deeply cut at the neckline but saved from immodesty by an insert of ivory lace, and ivory gloves that met the fitted sleeves just below the elbow. I had never before worn such a beautiful garment and felt decidedly out of my element, nearly regretting that I had agreed to the evening. The only familiar thing I wore was a slender gold bracelet that had been Grandmother Caldecott's and that, although small and out of fashion, held great sentimental value for me.

"Was there something you needed, Petra?" She stood staring at me as if she'd never seen me before, and I had to repeat the question.

"I wanted to ask you something," she stammered, "but I didn't realize you were going out. I can talk to you tomorrow."

"If it's important, we can talk now. I still have a few minutes before I'm to meet Miss Addams at the front door, although I'll probably need all that time to do something with my hair." Petra came in and pushed me along to the stool in front of my small dressing table.

"Sit," she commanded. "I can help you." She had become quite deft with her unwieldy, still-wrapped arm and without my quite knowing how, she managed to wrap my hair at the back of my neck in an attractive configuration, pulling a few loose curls around my face before she stepped back to observe me objectively.

"It's not the current style, but it's becoming on you with that long neck of yours. Now you're perfect." The words said in a practical tone made me laugh.

"A very far cry from perfect, I'm afraid, but"—I turned

to view myself in the full mirror—"with this borrowed dress from Miss Smith and with what you've managed to accomplish with my hair, I may make it through the night without incident. Thank you, Petra. You're a talented young woman."

She flushed when I said that but answered staunchly, "You *are* beautiful, Dr. Davis, no matter what you say. You look quite—" she paused to find the right word, "grand. You look like a grand lady." Then she handed me my cape. "You'd better go or you'll keep Miss Addams waiting."

"Could we talk tomorrow, Petra? It's Sunday, and I'll be with Dr. Hamilton all afternoon. Come and find me when you're ready." She nodded, but I had the feeling that this evening I had missed an opportunity to talk to her that I might not find again for quite a while.

The Sweethearts Ball was Chicago's first social occasion following the Christmas holidays, and I think everyone, wearied of the cold wind off the lake and the piles of dirty snow, came eager and prepared for a good time. The gala was held on two levels of the main court of The Rookery on LaSalle Street, a breathtaking building, recently redone, Miss Addams informed me, by the architect Frank Lloyd Wright. I stood motionless and staring when I first entered The Rookery, a country mouse unused to such splendor, astonished at the beauty of the white marble columns and inlaid gold leaf, the huge domed skylight, and the cantilevered staircase that led to the mezzanine. Miss Addams smiled at my expression and patted my arm to stir me from my small-town stupor.

"It is impressive," she agreed, steering me past several groups of people who tried to catch her attention. "There's Emil and Josephine." Dr. Pasca came forward with a woman on his arm.

"Jane, I wondered if you'd be up to the evening. You

look wonderful, much improved since I last saw you, and Dr. Davis, I didn't recognize you at first. You look lovely. May I introduce you to my wife? Josephine, this is Dr. Katherine Davis, the young physician I brought back with me from Kansas." I thought Dr. Pasca's wife a cool beauty, fair hair threaded through with gray and appraising blue eyes, nothing like the woman I would have chosen for him, nothing kind or generous about her.

"Hello, Jane. I'm glad to see you up and about." She turned her attention to me. "Dr. Davis," Mrs. Pasca said with a slight nod and a slighter smile. "I'm pleased to finally meet you after hearing Emil sing your praises these last weeks. How are you adjusting to Chicago after your years on the Kansas plains?"

"I haven't had much time to think about it," I admitted. "From my first day here I've been so busy that I sometimes forget what state I'm in. I haven't been able to appreciate the city at all, but after seeing this building, I know I must be missing some beautiful sights."

Later I found out that Mrs. Pasca came from an old Chicago family that had been instrumental in the renewal of The Rookery, which explained why my response pleased her. At my words, her eyes warmed and she smiled more charitably.

"You must get out and see some of Chicago in your year here, Dr. Davis. Warmer weather will make it easier for you and more pleasant. Emil, you mustn't let your protégé work herself to skin and bones. She'll be no good to Jane or to you if that happens."

Miss Addams responded pleasantly, with just the slightest edge to her voice, "We wouldn't think of turning our Dr. Davis into skin and bones, Josephine. We are too appreciative of her donating a year of her life to us." Then she turned to me to say, "Come, Katherine, I see the mayor over in the corner, and it never does to keep him waiting." Walking away, she murmured, "Josephine is kinder than she sounded just now, Katherine, but she's very protective of Emil and sometimes that colors her tone. I don't think she expected the young lady doctor from Kansas to look so stunning and cosmopolitan. You threw her off balance for a moment."

"That's kind of you to say," I said, "but you know I'm in borrowed finery and would feel much more comfortable in my doctor's smock."

Miss Addams didn't have time to respond because just then the mayor came forward to greet her, and after that the night was a whirlwind of faces, names, music, and conversation so that the astonishment I had felt at being called cosmopolitan was forgotten.

Much later, when I would eventually return to my rooms and lie in bed reliving the evening, I would remember Miss Addams's comment and laugh out loud, picturing my older brother's reactionary snort of disdain if he ever heard it. John Thomas had seen me tossed from a horse and slathered with mud after pulling a steer out of a sinkhole. He'd outdistanced me more than once in cow pie competitions.

"Cosmopolitan?" John Thomas would hoot. "You? That's rich, Katherine, and you know it!"

I did know it, of course, which explained why I spent that evening always conscious that I was an ambassador for Hull-House and its founder, careful to say the right thing, to listen attentively and compliment sincerely. I never allowed myself to forget that the funds that supported us—supported *me*—came from many of the people in that very room. I wouldn't take the chance of alienating any of them with my behavior or attitude, but it was soon obvious that I had an easy task. Not once did anyone ever have anything but the most generous and heartfelt comments to make about Miss Addams. All I had to do was smile and agree. I thought she must be the most admired woman in the city and was proud to be affiliated with her and her mission.

Mid-evening I made my way to the refreshment table for something to drink and, stepping back too quickly, jostled the arm of the man standing beside me. The punch in his cup splashed onto his dark jacket, dripped down his trousers, and finally formed a little puddle on the floor.

"I'm so sorry," I said, embarrassed. "I wasn't watching where I was going. Please forgive me." I reached forward with my handkerchief to brush the liquid off his lapel, but he was already doing that, head bent, dabbing with his own linen at the spot on his jacket.

"My fault entirely," he responded, but his tone wasn't as gracious as his words. "Don't give it a second thought. It's very crowded here." Then he looked up and his slightly aggrieved expression disappeared entirely when he met my eyes. "Really, don't give it a second thought, Miss—"

"Davis," I supplied, lightly brushing his jacket with my own handkerchief. "Katherine Davis. And it's too late, I've already given it more than a second thought, actually a third and just now a fourth. I'd like to blame the man who was standing next to me but I'm afraid doing so would be cowardly, impolite, and untrue."

The man smiled at that and looked at me, really looked, as if he'd never seen anything like me before. I thought the look too flattering to be rude, but it was borderline.

He stood about my height, clean-shaven with black hair and glittering dark eyes, eyes darker than brown, almost as black as his impeccably tailored coat. He wore a pristine white shirt with a high starched collar and absolutely flawless tie and tails. On the hand brushing his lapel a large diamond ring caught the lights and glittered almost as much as his eyes; and a small stick pin with more brilliant diamonds scrolled into the shape of a graceful letter G adorned his tie with elegant good taste. I thought him the most dazzling man I had ever seen, polished, handsome, and sophisticated, as unlike the medical students I had spent the last few years with as the sun is unlike a candle.

He took me gently by the elbow and propelled me to the side of the large room, competently dodging both dancers and talkers.

"Miss Davis, I don't believe I've had the pleasure. I'm Douglas Gallagher. I can't think how I could have missed meeting you but I must have. I don't know any Davises and I'm absolutely certain I didn't meet any this evening."

"I'm certain you didn't, too, at least not from my branch of the family. We're not Chicagoans. I'm here as Miss Jane Addams's companion this evening and a sort of ambassador for Hull-House. If I go around spilling drinks on people, however, I'm likely to be relieved of my assignment."

The orchestra started up a new tune and Douglas Gallagher asked me to dance. I accepted the invitation but did not handle myself nearly as well as he. His dancing was as polished as his appearance, smooth and confident steps, a good leader with nothing hesitant or fumbling in his manner so that for the first time in my life I truly felt as if I were floating on the dance floor. I could recall other dances from earlier times ending with sore toes and even a bruised shin, but that would never happen with a man of his impeccable style.

When he asked me for a second dance, I had to shake my head regretfully.

"Thank you, but I'm here to circulate among the crowd and I wouldn't be comfortable with a second dance. I hope

I didn't do too much damage to your jacket, Mr. Gallagher." When I extended my hand, he startled me by lifting it lightly to his lips.

"More damage to my heart than to my jacket, Miss Davis," he replied lightly, with just the right amount of casual charm to make the remark inoffensive.

Before I could reply, Dr. Pasca came up behind me and said quietly, "I think Jane's ready to leave, Katherine. She's looking more exhausted than I'm comfortable with."

I disengaged my hand from Douglas Gallagher's without a second thought, smiled a good night to him, and followed Dr. Pasca across the floor. He had been right to be concerned, I thought, because Miss Addams appeared pale and fatigued.

She looked at me apologetically as I approached and spoke in a low voice. "I'm sorry to spoil your evening, Katherine."

"Nonsense. The evening is not about me. I'm here at your bidding, and I agree that the night has gone on long enough." Dr. Pasca brought our wraps and bundled us outside into a waiting motorcar.

"Good night, ladies." He patted Miss Addams's hand with an intimate gesture of longstanding friendship. "You've overdone it, Jane. I'm commissioning Dr. Davis to make sure you rest tomorrow and as both your friend and physician, I recommend a vacation for you." She leaned back against the seat with a sigh and a small smile.

"Mary has been pestering me about the same thing, Emil, so I might do just that, but you mustn't think it's because I'm some swooning female who can't travel anywhere without smelling salts. You know I'm plucky and can generally sleep at the drop of a hat."

"I know that very well, Jane. I know of no woman less likely to swoon than you."

"I am tired," Miss Addams admitted to me quietly as the vehicle carried us back to Hull-House, "but it's just the long night, too much handshaking and polite conversation. I still feel better than I've felt in some time." We sat in silence for a while, then she continued, "Everyone who met you this evening was charmed, Katherine. Thank you. It was such a relief not to worry that you were back in the kitchens fomenting a strike among the cooks or that you were going to sneer at someone's showy jewelry. Not," she hastened to add, "that Dr. Comstock wasn't a wonderful doctor or that I think there's anything wrong with unions or even strikes when necessary. We have four women's unions that meet at Hull-House, after all, but there is a time and place for everything, and tonight was not the occasion for organizing workers."

"No," I responded thoughtfully, "I agree it wasn't, but I saw enough showy jewelry lying on ample bosoms to curl Dr. Comstock's lip several times over." I remembered how the light had caught the stones in Douglas Gallagher's ring.

Miss Addams chuckled. "Sometimes more gems than taste, I'm afraid, but there were a number of generous people present this evening, and I have two extravagant checks in my pocket as we speak, so it was all worth it." After a pause she said, "How mercenary I can be sometimes! I hope I don't shock you."

"No. After six weeks at Hull-House, I understand perfectly. You should think of it as giving others the rare opportunity to participate in something great and not give those checks a second thought. From my perspective, you're doing the favor by accepting the donation." At her quiet, I supposed that Miss Addams had fallen lightly asleep and hadn't heard me, but after a while she spoke from the darkness.

"I do like you, Dr. Davis," laughter inflecting her words

as if with a shared joke, "We think alike."

Still dressed in my finery, I stopped by to greet Mrs. Tabachnik before I went to bed.

"Is everything quiet?" I asked.

Only one elderly man, whose deep hacking cough periodically brought up blood, lay in the infirmary. His cough was not just the effect of dry, cold air, I thought somberly, and there was little we could do for him except give him a warm bed in which to sleep, in which to die.

"Mr. Pilzner is sleeping as quietly as he can, God bless him. I don't think he looks good, Doctor."

"No," I agreed. "We should send him on to the hospital tomorrow. They're better prepared than we are to handle his illness. How long has he been here now?"

"Two days."

"Well, two days with no improvement is making me uneasy. Tomorrow I'll ask Dr. Pasca how we can be sure Mr. Pilzner isn't just dumped into a hospital hallway somewhere but gets the care he needs." I looked around the room of beds and let my glance linger at the little cot in the corner. "I miss our Leo."

"Has he been coming to the day nursery?"

"Yes, and his mother's coming to the classes, too, so perhaps he'll grow to a ripe old age, after all."

"Like Mr. Pilzner?" she asked with a grimace.

Her comment saddened me as I thought of the deadly effects of poverty and pictured Leo growing old on the cold streets, dying slowly among strangers in a strange room like Mr. Pilzner.

"I hope not, Mrs. Tabachnik. I hope not like Mr. Pilzner at all." I went over to the old man, who lay on his back with the blanket pulled up to his stubbled chin and placed my hand on his forehead. My touch startled him, perhaps felt cold, because he opened his eyes to stare at me.

"It's an angel," he muttered after a moment, his voice slurred and breathy. "God's sent me an angel with honey-colored hair."

"God sent you a doctor, Mr. Pilzner. Do you remember me? I'm Dr. Davis."

He hesitated for a moment then answered, "I do remember you, but you look different."

"I'm just dressed up now. How do you feel?"

"Awful tired." His eyes were bleary, the skin of his cheeks sagging and mottled red, his lips cracked. He looked exhausted beyond words.

"Then I shouldn't be talking to you. I'll come back in the morning. You go back to sleep."

On my way out Mrs. Tabachnik commented, "You're looking very fine tonight, Doctor. I hope you had a nice evening."

"I was on good behavior and careful to say only what was unremarkable. It was a nice evening but boring. It needed one of my brothers present to poke a hole in all that self-importance."

"Now you're sounding like Dr. Comstock."

"I'll take that as a compliment, Nurse. Good night."

Lying in bed, close to sleep but not quite there, I thought of home and how my parents would have reacted to that room full of the rich and powerful and important. I tried to imagine the two of them there, tried to picture how they would have looked, but the image wouldn't come. My parents were the least pretentious people I knew, more at home on horseback than at a ball, especially my mother, who wore men's trousers and rode astride without a bit of feminine self-consciousness.

Out of nowhere, I recalled one time when Mother stood frazzled and fatigued over the stove and then suddenly surprised us all by grabbing my unsuspecting father and spinning him around the small kitchen in an impromptu waltz that made him grin and all us children giggle. When the dance was over, he kissed her so passionately that she finally murmured, "John, the children," which caused my siblings and me to giggle again. Such a public display was rare for my austere father, and we were all mesmerized at the sight. Not a piece of showy jewelry anywhere in those early years, I thought as I fell asleep, but we had been rich in our own way, even then.

Very early that same morning Nurse Tabachnick roused me from sleep. "It's Mr. Pilzner," she said. "He's worse," but the old man was gone by the time I got to him, the blanket pushed halfway off the bed, his head thrown back against the pillow, and his mouth partly open as if he'd been trying to say something or perhaps had been gasping for breath.

I sat next to him until they came for the body, the least I could do since I could not give him life. Mrs. Tabachnik and I both knew the routine. We would pay for the burial and the accompanying graveside service and someone from Hull-House would attend as a gesture of respect. I wanted to go for Mr. Pilzner and hoped he had entered the presence of real angels. The poor old man certainly hadn't experienced much heaven during his time on earth.

I usually attended the chaplain-led Sunday services at the boarding house. That morning I rose under protest, tired from the late night, interrupted sleep, and the early morning death, but once I was there, I was glad I had made the effort. How else to explain the great mysteries of life and death except through the providence of God? How else to try to make sense of it all?

Sunday afternoons were usually my own to do with as I chose. That day I knew I had letters to write, and I was behind by several days in my personal journal entries, too, but

Dr. Hamilton had asked me to spend some time with her in the afternoon and I was hardly going to refuse. Her fame as a scientist and toxicologist was such that she had recently been appointed to the state's Occupational Disease Commission, an honor for anyone but especially for a woman. Working with Dr. Hamilton was an opportunity I would never have again, and I wanted to learn everything I could from her.

So different from Miss Addams, Alice Hamilton was a sharp-tongued and impatient woman, and it seemed the two women could have nothing in common. But when she related the sights she had seen—children poisoned by lead, babies killed with opium, areas so infected by tuberculosis that they were known casually as "lung blocks," naïve immigrants abused by scoundrels without conscience—I saw clear similarities. Both women were fueled by a vision of dignity for all people and true democracy where every human being was valued.

"Not that I can see how we can make any real social progress when women can't even vote," Dr. Hamilton commented as she closed her notebook at the end of the afternoon's work. We were discussing the future of Hull-House and the future of the big cities and by extension the country.

"Women can vote in elections at home," I commented and at her inquisitive look explained, "Wyoming women had the right to vote before the state ever entered the union."

"That's the West for you. The East could take a lesson from their book. I've half a mind to take to the streets at the next feminist demonstration just to protest my inability to speak my mind at the ballot box. It doesn't make sense." As she spoke, she pulled her apron over her head and hung it on a hook by the door, a dark-eyed woman of formidable intelligence without an ounce of vanity who, in the middle of a discourse about women's suffrage, would leave her hair mussed and untidy without a thought to smooth it. "We'll see universal suffrage in our lifetime, though. I'm sure of it." She turned to face me. "I appreciated your help this afternoon, Dr. Davis. How are you settling in?"

"Just fine. I was overwhelmed at first, but I have a routine now and I haven't gotten lost once all week so that's a good sign. And I love working with the nursery and the kindergarteners."

"Yes, I've heard the children look forward to your visits. I don't think this will be a year you'll regret."

"No, I don't think so either."

Mary Smith stopped me as I went into the dining room. "A package was left for you on the table by the front door, Doctor. Did you get it?"

I shook my head and went to find the delivery, curious about what it could be. A small white box lay on the hall table, and when I lifted the cover I gasped at the beautiful flowers inside: hothouse orchids in white and bronze. This must be some mistake, I thought, but the box also held an ivory envelope on which my name was clearly written in bold black script: *Miss Katherine Davis*. The message on the card inside read, *Feel free to spill punch on me anytime. I considered it an honor* and was signed with the same recognizable handwriting. *Douglas Gallagher*.

No one had ever sent me flowers before and I was surprised at how gratified I felt and how secretly flattered and pleased. What a remarkable thing to happen after only a few words and one dance. I left the box on the table when I went in to supper, then picked it up on my way back to my room. During the meal I was as preoccupied as a schoolgirl, wondering about the man and trying to recall everything we had said. Why he should have done such a generous thing I didn't know, but I was thrilled with the gesture and found the flowers beautiful, even if too exotic for my plebeian taste. There was nothing soft or pretty or natural about those exotic orchids, I thought critically, and then scolded myself, as if receiving live flowers was now so commonplace for me that I could fault them for not being my preference.

That evening Petra knocked hesitantly at my door.

"I'm glad you found me," I said to her and meant it. I had watched for her all afternoon and at her continued absence had planned to go in search of her once I finished the letter I was writing. She stood in the doorway.

"You're busy. I can come back."

"I've just finished writing a long overdue letter home," I explained, sealing the envelope with a flourish, "so at least they'll know I'm still alive and well."

"A letter to your mother?"

"To my mother, my father, and my Uncle Billy. Then Mother will pass it to my sister Becca and her family, and they'll pass it along to my brother and his wife and family. If I had to write individual letters to everyone, I'd have no time for anything else, so they've learned over time to be good-natured about sharing. Of course, I still expect separate letters from all of them, but that's only fair. Come in and sit down, Petra. I'm sorry we couldn't talk last night."

The girl sat at the edge of the seat of the one padded chair in my room as if poised for a quick escape, perhaps more likely just a practical posture. She was so petite that if she sat any farther back in the chair, her feet wouldn't touch the floor. As I put down my pen and turned to face her, she noticed the flowers in a bowl on the desk.

"How beautiful! Are they real?"

"Yes. Imagine, real flowers in February."

She looked at me seriously. "I'd guess they're from an

admirer so I was right to say you looked beautiful. Someone else must have thought so, too."

"I don't really know what someone else thought," I said, contemplating the flowers a moment, "but I appreciate the kind gesture, and I'm not sophisticated enough to be complacent about receiving something so beautiful and so unexpected. Anyway, I don't think you came here to admire the flowers or comment on my appearance, did you?"

"No, I wanted to ask you something, wanted to ask you to help me, and it doesn't seem right that I should do that when you've done so much for me already, but it isn't such a great thing and I thought you might be willing." She spoke quickly, all in one sentence and practically all in one breath.

"I'll help you any way I can, Petra, if it's in my power to do so. What are you asking?"

"I'd like you to introduce me to Mr. Sweeney. I've heard him sing and play the piano, and someone told me he's performed on stage, that he's an accomplished musician. I thought he might be willing to listen to me sing and tell me how to improve. I can sing, I know I can, but I need help to get better. I have a lot to learn and I don't know where to go to learn it."

"That's a good idea, Petra, one I thought of myself. I should have done it sooner for you. I wanted to, but I just didn't take the time. Mr. Sweeney is here on Mondays, isn't he?"

"Monday mornings and Wednesday and Friday afternoons. I know he's busy and there's a line of people waiting to take lessons from him, so if he says I haven't any talent or he hasn't the time for me, I won't pester him. I promise."

"That's fair enough, but from the little I've heard, it seems to me you have a lovely voice. However, Mr. Sweeney is the expert and we'll let him decide. I'll talk to him tomorrow morning and see if he can meet with you this week sometime."

"Thank you. If you ask him, I know he'll find the time. I don't think there's anything you can't do," she added, so much trust and admiration in her eyes that I was humbled.

"There's a lot I can't do, Petra. I can't read minds, for example, or know what brought you to Hull-House unless you tell me. Are you ready to do that now?" At my words the animation died from her face, and lines appeared at the corners of her mouth as she pressed her lips together.

"No, I can't."

"You could tell me who hurt you."

"No, I can't," she repeated.

I leaned forward. "Listen Petra, whatever happened isn't going to change our friendship or keep you from living the life you're living now."

"Then why do you need to know?" She asked a good question. What difference would it make after all?

I shrugged. "It's not that I need to know, but I'd like to believe you'd trust me with the information. If you aren't able to, that's all right. It doesn't change things between us." Petra stood to leave, one hand on the back of the chair.

"I do trust you, Dr. Davis, but I don't want to talk about it. I'm sorry."

"There's nothing to be sorry about. You have a mind of your own, and you may choose what and when to speak. Be careful going back to your room. Take the steps. Don't go outside. I think I heard sleet against the window, and the quadrangle can be slippery."

"Goodnight, Dr. Davis." She arranged a shawl around her shoulders with her good arm and gave me a fleeting smile before she left.

I knew Petra was no older than sixteen and that someone had taken a fist to her and that was all I knew for sure.

How could I even be certain that the name she'd given was really hers? But she was right, why did any of that matter? There's more to the human being than names and numbers, and there was certainly more to Petra Stravinsky than her age and her history. To my way of thinking, the only important thing was her future, and that was the one thing I might be able to influence.

In the morning after my rounds in the nursery, I went in search of Patrick Sweeney, tenor extraordinaire, an open-faced, auburn-haired Irishman with a thin mustache, whose twin gifts of laughter and good nature made him popular with everyone.

When I said his name from the doorway of the music room, Mr. Sweeney looked up from the keys of the piano he had been playing and said with a grin, "You don't look like Antonio Silvestri and you're not carrying a violin so I don't think you can be my next pupil."

"I am definitely not here for violin lessons," I agreed, coming into the room and extending a hand. "We haven't been formally introduced but I admit I've stood more than once in the hallway listening to you sing and play. I'm Katherine Davis."

"I know who you are, Dr. Davis, and you should have come in instead of standing out in the hallway. We have no secrets here." He took my hand in a quick, firm grip.

"I've seen your name and face on posters, Mr. Sweeney."

"I told them I'd return the money."

"No, no," I said, laughing, "not *that* kind of poster. Performance advertisements. You're famous."

"Am I? Well, don't tell anyone, will you? I explained to Miss Addams that it was either volunteer here three days a week or accompany the organ grinder in place of his monkey and I've never had a flair for working with animals.

Please sit down, Doctor. It appears that I have a few minutes before Antonio arrives. Is there something I can do for you?"

"Yes, there is. One of our boarders is a young woman who calls herself Petra Stravinsky."

"Calls herself? Do you have reason to believe that's not her real name?"

"No, I think it probably is her name, but I can't say for sure. I don't know much about her except that she came to us one night for medical care and has stayed on. She has a voice."

"Not a deaf mute then."

He made me laugh again. "I'm making a mess of it, aren't I? I mean I think she has more than the average singing voice, but all I've heard her do is croon lullabies and sing nursery rhymes and even I can do that without dogs howling accompaniment—just barely. I wondered if you had any time to listen to her in the near future, share your professional opinion and possibly some pointers on vocal technique. We would both be very grateful."

"Can she read music?"

"I don't know. I'd say it's unlikely, but she is literate so perhaps the written word isn't all she reads." The door opened behind us and we both turned to see a boy standing at the threshold, violin in hand. "I see your next pupil has arrived, so I won't keep you any longer. If you thought you'd have time to consider my request, I could stop in again on Wednesday to talk further."

"Just bring Miss Stravinsky here Wednesday afternoon around one o'clock. I usually arrive at two, but I'll come in early that day." He went over to the desk and said Petra's name aloud as he wrote it in his schedule book.

"Thank you, and I want you to know that if you really were on a wanted poster, I wouldn't turn you in."

"I'm flattered."

"You should be," I said on the way out and heard his chuckle behind me.

I found Petra helping the kindergarten class act out the story of The Ugly Duckling. She had a flair for drama: an animated face, expressive voice, and lively gestures. The teachers there had stepped back and let her do it all.

One of the women said to me, "She really ought to get involved with the Marionettes, Dr. Davis. She's perfect for it." At my blank look, she added, "It's our junior theater and dance group. They put on wonderful productions, and she's such a natural performer."

I waited until Petra finished, then said to her, "Mr. Sweeney will see you in the music room on Wednesday at one o'clock. May I come, too?"

Her face glowed at the news. "Of course. Thank you."

"Petra, he asked if you could read music, and I didn't know how to answer. Can you?"

"I can tell that the music goes the same directions as the notes on the page, but that's all. Does that make a difference to him? I'm quick about music and I know I could learn." I could tell my question had made her anxious and wished I hadn't said anything, had let Mr. Sweeney find out from her instead.

"It doesn't make a bit of difference. Don't give it a thought. If I don't see you before then, I'll meet you Wednesday at one in the music room." She nodded happily, then was pulled away by a child needing help with his shoes.

At that moment Petra looked so different from when I had first seen her huddled in the doorway cradling her arm that I could hardly believe it. Her swollen mouth and eye were back to normal size, and the bruise across her face had gently faded, now just a mottled yellow and dark lilac. Another week and the color would be gone entirely; another month and her arm would be out of its sling and back to normal, too. The girl was spoiling me. I wished all my patients had that same kind of resilience and recovery, not like poor Mr. Pilzner, who had been more tired than either of us had realized and had never had a real chance for improvement. Maybe the old man had never expected to get better, I thought. Maybe he had only wanted the chance to die warm and tended. A small enough request.

The coroner gave inflammation of the lungs as the cause of Mr. Pilzner's death because writing despair or loneliness or poverty on the death certificate was not an acceptable diagnosis. A late February thaw meant the old man would have a speedy burial, with his interment scheduled for Tuesday afternoon. I hoped I could find my way to the cemetery without getting lost. I wanted to go and it would be disrespectful to come late to the ceremony, even one as sparse and simple as that was sure to be.

CHAPTER 4

In the morning I received the necessary directions from Miss Flaherty: "Take the trolley to the elevated train and then take that four stops south. Get off and walk eight blocks west to All Saints Cemetery." The nurse paused periodically to check my attention. "Are you sure you're understanding all this, Doctor? Maybe someone should go with you."

"I'm fine, Nurse, but I wish I could just get on a horse and ride there. That would be easiest for me."

"No doubt you're quite a cowgirl, Dr. Davis, but that won't do here." Then she patiently went over everything with me again. "I'll be that worried until I see you back here this evening." I tucked the directions in my pocket.

"My mother always said that life's an adventure, Miss Flaherty, and I think I'll prove her right today." I crossed the alley that separated our building from the main house and stopped long enough to tell Mary Smith that I might be late for supper.

"We'll save you something warm and nourishing, Katherine. You'll need it after such a trek. Do you know where you're going?"

I buttoned my coat, pulled on gloves, hat, and scarf, then patted my pocket.

"I have the directions in minute detail written down right here and I will guard them with my life. Nurse Flaherty assures me that if I follow her instructions exactly, I will arrive with time to spare. If I don't, I'll only have myself to blame." I went out the front door and down the steps, continuing to fuss with my scarf. I didn't bother to look at the figure who passed me on the steps because a multitude of traffic went in and out of Hull-House on any given day.

From behind me that person said, "Miss Davis?" and I turned to see Douglas Gallagher standing there. I was taken completely by surprise and caught in a dilemma. If I stood and talked with him, even went back inside to greet him more appropriately, I would never make it to the cemetery service on time.

"Mr. Gallagher," I said as I turned and went back up onto the porch. "What a surprise! I don't mean to be presumptuous, but are you here to see me or someone else in the house?" He didn't blink an eye at my abrupt question.

"You."

"In that case, I fear we share a bit of a problem because as you can see I'm on my way out and I'm already late. I'm expected at a funeral at All Saints Cemetery, and I've been told it will take me the better part of an hour to get there. Since it's already past one and the service is scheduled for two o'clock, you see the problem."

"I do, and I have the solution."

I thought Douglas Gallagher was very quick on his feet, and that it would be hard to surprise or discomfit him. He stood looking at me, amused, I think, but with some other more oblique emotion also in his expression. Admiration? Annoyance? I couldn't tell. His eyes glinted black in the cold afternoon sunshine and hid whatever emotion he truly felt. Gallagher waved a gloved hand down the walk toward the curb behind the wrought iron fence.

"I have an automobile waiting there and a driver. I could take you to All Saints Cemetery. I'm sure Fritz knows where it is. He knows everything about the city. It would be a much quicker and more comfortable trip for you."

"I couldn't ask you to do that. Why would you want to attend a funeral for someone you don't know?"

"You misunderstand me, Miss Davis. At the risk of appearing insensitive, I don't care about the funeral, but I do care about spending time with you and this seems to be the only way I'm going to get that opportunity. Besides, you didn't ask me. I offered without instigation. It's not the same thing at all."

One of the volunteers came out the front door and greeted me absently with a "Hello, Dr. Davis" as she passed. At her words, Douglas Gallagher turned deliberately to look from me to the passing person and then back to me.

"Dr. Davis?" he repeated, emphasizing the title and I thought I'd been wrong in my first assessment. The man could be surprised. That greeting had surprised him.

"Yes, *Dr.* Davis. Hull-House resident doctor for the year. I thought you knew. Does that affect your kind offer?"

"Not at all." He lightly tucked my hand under his arm as we turned and went back down the steps together. "It makes it even more important that you accept it. Doctors have notoriously busy schedules, and I need to take advantage of every opportunity."

"You could make an appointment."

"I don't typically make appointments," he told me without a trace of arrogance in his tone. "People usually make them with me. But for you I can see I will have to make an exception." I found Gallagher's self-confidence attractive and thought how pleasant it was to have someone so overtly interested in my company. It might be a flirtation, but there was no reason I couldn't enjoy the experience while it lasted.

"This is an impressive vehicle, Mr. Gallagher. I don't think I've ever seen anything like it." The motorcar was beautiful, a long, shiny black machine with red interior, white wheel rims that appeared immaculate despite the messy streets, and a hood ornament that sparkled gold.

"It's a Pierce Great-Arrow, last year's model I'm afraid, but I've grown fond of it. It can seat seven and go over forty miles an hour, has six cylinders and four speeds plus reverse. A powerful machine." He held a hand out to help me in the back seat, then went around to speak to the driver quietly. I saw the driver nod and Mr. Gallagher, looking satisfied, got in the other side to sit next to me.

"Fritz knows exactly where we're going. The man's worth his weight in gold."

The experience wasn't anything like other automobile rides I had taken, where the constant chugging and the pops of backfires made conversation difficult if not impossible. This vehicle rode quietly and smoothly.

"I haven't a clue as to what anything you said about this automobile meant, but I'm impressed anyway," I remarked, running a hand over the leather interior. Gallagher turned sideways to look at me.

"My guess is that it takes more than an automobile to impress you, Dr. Davis."

"What then?"

"I don't know that yet, but I've just made it one of my priorities to find out. Whose demise am I mourning, by the way?"

"An elderly man named Mr. Pilzner. Mr. Adolph Pilzner."

"How do you know him?"

"He was my patient for forty-eight hours. He came to us dying, but that didn't make it easier for him or for me to let go."

"A stranger?"

"Yes, I suppose he was," I agreed and was quiet.

Gallagher was quiet for a while, too, before asking, "Is it that you feel obligated to go to the burial? I can't imagine that you developed any fondness for Mr. Pilzner over just two days."

"I do few things out of obligation, Mr. Gallagher. I've found doing so only makes me resentful and recalcitrant. I'm going because I want to go, because it's the right thing to do."

"The right thing to do," he repeated as if testing the words on his tongue. "Do you always do the right thing?" The idea made me laugh out loud.

"I would love to tell you yes, but my family and friends would be the first to say otherwise. I think they'd agree, however, that I usually attempt to figure out what the right thing is and then try to do it, with the emphasis on *try*."

"Doing the right thing is very often relative."

This time I turned to look at him, meeting that dark gaze full on. "Is that what you think?"

"Something tells me I'm going to give the wrong answer, but yes, that's what I think. I can tell that you don't."

"I think there are more things absolute in life than we like to admit, and that we use relative ethics to excuse bad behavior."

"Ouch, you struck a blow. You frighten me, Doctor."

"No, I don't, not at all. I doubt that much frightens you, Mr. Gallagher, but that's a judgment based on very little real evidence." After a moment I changed my tone and added, "Forgive me. You must think me very rude. I forgot to thank you for the flowers. How kind of you and what a treat to receive something so beautiful on a dark and wintry February day. I'm not sure what circumstance warranted such generosity, but the mystery was part of the appeal."

"Their colors reminded me of you: white for your porcelain skin and the other as close to the color of your eyes as I could find." Douglas Gallagher's very smooth response made me unaccountably embarrassed, suddenly out of my element and tongue-tied. Perhaps noticing my discomfort, he continued easily, "Our dance was the high point of the evening for me. Most of the night was more business than pleasure so I intended only to thank you for a pleasant interlude."

"What business are you in?"

"A little bit of everything. I own several businesses and two banks, here in Chicago and also in San Francisco. One business you might find interesting as a doctor is pharmaceuticals. One that might interest you as a woman is textiles: Chinese silk and Indian cotton and English wool to name a few."

"I'd rather hear you say American wool. My brother raises sheep and your imports drive his costs up and his profits down."

"You have a head for business, too, Doctor? Is there anything you can't do?" I looked quickly to see if he was mocking me but found only polite interest in his expression.

"I'm a terrible seamstress and a worse cook. All domestic talents were bequeathed to my older sister and missed me entirely. If a person were dependent on me for either of those things, he'd walk around starving and in rags. I'm sadly deficient."

"I have housemaids and a kitchen staff," he commented, "so neither of those talents holds any attraction for me."

We pulled up to a cemetery surrounded by a high black fence.

"All Saints Cemetery, sir," said Fritz, and I stirred to take the written directions from my pocket and reread them quickly.

"We have an area here where we see to the burial of indigent patrons of Hull-House. I've been told where it is and I'm sure I can find it." I put the folded paper away and extended a hand. "Thank you for making the trip here so enjoyable. It really was very kind of you and I'm sure an inconvenience." He ignored my hand and stepped out of the auto and around to my side, opened the door and took me gently by the elbow.

"It was enjoyable," he agreed, "so I think I'd like your company on the trip back as well." To the driver, "We'll be a while, Fritz. Wait for us." He would have placed my hand under his arm again but I wasn't having that, too proprietary a gesture on too short an acquaintance. I gently pulled away.

"It's this way, I believe," I commented, going on ahead, leaving Gallagher to follow. Then, feeling ungrateful, I stopped and waited for him so we could walk along the path side by side, not touching. Only a chilled but patient priest waited by the freshly dug grave, the wind kicking up his black cassock around his feet.

"Are you from Miss Addams?" he asked and at my nod began the reading that committed Mr. Adolph Pilzner's soul to God and his body to the earth. I found it extraordinarily sad that no one but three strangers should be there and two of the three had never even met Mr. Pilzner. At the conclusion, Douglas Gallagher replaced his hat while I thanked the priest, and then the two of us made our way back to Fritz, walking slowly and not speaking.

Fifteen minutes at the most, I thought, and it was as if Adolph Pilzner had never existed. Perhaps the old man's death would make sense to me later, but for the moment I found his obscure passing wasteful and futile. I wished I were home with my family, Lily Kate pulling at my skirts, she and her younger cousin Jack stumbling over the name Katherine and christening me Aunt Kat against my wishes. I had resigned myself to the name because no one can argue with Lily Kate and win. She's like her mother that way, blithely and disarmingly sympathetic but with no intention of giving in or giving up.

Of course, I wasn't home. I was in the middle of Chicago, not a mountain or cowboy in sight, just rundown buildings in a part of the city so negligible that it still bore obvious and ruinous scars from the city's devastating fire forty years earlier. I rode with a stranger in a vehicle that bore no resemblance to a horse and would have sent the sheep—poor dumb creatures that they were—running blindly off the nearest cliff. Many of the decrepit houses we passed showed jagged, broken windows and were fronted by privies that did not offer even an illusion of privacy. My surroundings were so different from those of my childhood that we could have been on another planet.

As I stared out the side of the motorcar, I experienced one of those startling moments when a person asks herself what she's doing there. Shouldn't she be somewhere else? Has she made a terrible mistake? I had them every so often: sudden, unplanned illuminations that clearly showed I didn't fit in and didn't belong, moments that always made me question where I was meant to be and whether I would recognize home when I got there. Sometimes I wondered whether others had similar visions, or was I the only person who experienced such a peculiar mental eccentricity that left me lost and looking for something, yet not even sure what the something was?

"We could stop for refreshments if you like," Gallagher offered. "Perhaps a cup of hot tea? I know just the place." His tone brought me back to the present and I turned to him a little blankly, having almost forgotten he was there.

"Thank you, but I can't. I'm afraid I have commitments that won't wait." He pursed his lips and nodded his head thoughtfully.

"You make it difficult, Dr. Davis. How do you suggest I get on your calendar?"

We had entered familiar surroundings, and I knew we would soon be back at Hull-House. I had mixed feelings about the ride ending, unable to deny a certain relief but feeling a much stronger regret. I had enjoyed this man's company and conversation.

I answered his question with a question of my own. "Have you ever visited Hull-House? Do you know what we do?"

"No and a little."

"Then I suggest you come back when you can spare an hour or two from your demanding enterprises and I'll give you a tour."

"Tell me what day and time."

"Shouldn't you check your appointments first to tell me when you're available?"

"I'll arrange my schedule to fit yours, Dr. Davis. I'm just a beleaguered capitalist, not a humanitarian so it's only right."

We pulled up to the dignified red brick house and as I went to gather up my skirts to step out, he put his hand on my arm and repeated more firmly, "Tell me what day and time."

"If you're serious, make it Sunday at two o'clock."

"I'm very serious, Dr. Davis. More serious than you can imagine." He came around to my side to help me out, then walked me to the front door. "I'll be here Sunday promptly at two o'clock."

"I'll look forward to it, Mr. Gallagher, and thank you again. You were very kind to chauffeur me across town." He touched the brim of his hat very lightly with a well-gloved hand and smiled.

"Kindness had very little to do with it, Doctor, but you're welcome. I'll see you this weekend." I didn't wait to see him leave but slipped in the front door, meeting Mary Smith in the front hallway.

"You made good time, Katherine!" she exclaimed. "I didn't expect to see you for at least another hour."

"Serendipity. As I was leaving I ran into someone I met the other evening at The Rookery, and he volunteered to take me to the cemetery in his auto. I wasn't about to refuse a warmer, faster ride."

"Was it one of our supporters?"

I replied thoughtfully, "No, I don't think so, at least not yet. He'd never been here before and has only the slightest idea what we do, but I wouldn't rule out the idea that he may become one of our supporters. If appearance is any indicator, he has the wherewithal to offer us some kind of financial encouragement."

Her eyes twinkled at me. "You're sounding as devious as Jane. Who is he?"

"His name is Douglas Gallagher. Have you heard of him?" She thought a minute.

"I think I have. Not a Chicago family or Chicago money, if I remember correctly. From someplace out west, perhaps?"

"San Francisco," I supplied. "He said he has businesses and banks here and on the west coast."

"An admirer?"

"That's what he'd like me to believe, but I don't know why. I'm just a cowgirl from the country, you know, still dazzled by the lights of the big city." I met her look with an innocent little smile until she smiled broadly in return.

"Dr. Davis, I can see why Miss Addams has grown so fond of you in such a short time. I'll look forward to meeting your Mr. Gallagher."

"Oh, not mine," I said as I headed toward the side door that led out into the quadrangle, the shortest way to cut through the grounds to the dispensary. "Let's call him ours."

A busy late afternoon with several patients and an early evening visit from Dr. Pasca made me miss supper.

"You've been here almost eight weeks now, Katherine, and I've been negligent. I should come more often to check on you, but Miss Addams is satisfied and Dr. Hamilton appreciative so I must assume you're not finding it too difficult a transition from the hospital in Lawrence. I read your notes about the man who died—was his name Pilzner?—and found nothing remarkable there. Is there anything I should know about his death?"

We sat in the waiting room of the empty dispensary, just the two of us perched on hard wooden chairs.

I shook my head in answer, then added, "I went to Mr. Pilzner's burial today, and it made me sad. I thought his was a wasted life and that poverty killed him."

Dr. Pasca responded firmly, "No, you're wrong, Katherine. Don't make the mistake of considering poverty a disease for which we must find a cure. It is a social condition, not an illness. Poverty does not kill people, but its effects might."

"Angels dancing on a pin, Dr. Pasca?"

"Not at all. Think it through. If we allow people to consider poverty an illness, then they will happily relegate it to the rarified air of laboratories and specialists and asylums instead of keeping it right where it belongs—in their own parlors and sitting rooms. They will expect you and me to find its cure instead of seeing that all of us have the responsibility to rectify the deplorable conditions in which many people live. Never take ownership of poverty, Doctor."

"I hadn't thought about it that way before," I admitted. "Thank you."

As I readied for bed that night I tried to think through that philosophical conversation again, but I was tired and so found my thoughts drifting instead to Douglas Gallagher. I had never met a man like him. I was more used to men like my father and brothers and my friend, Sam Kincaid. They were men without mystery, plain-spoken, honorable, and of unquestioned integrity, who were exactly as they appeared: men I could and would trust with my life. I respected their qualities even if I did find them slightly prosaic and affectionately dull, but as I compared the Davis men to Douglas Gallagher, I realized that I felt a real attraction, even an admiration, for him because he was so different from them. This enigmatic man, who carried with him a barely-sheathed sense of power and a will as strong as my own had the ability to stir me in a new and exciting way, and I looked forward to Sunday afternoon with a shiver that had nothing to do with the cold.

CHAPTER 5

Petra and I met at the door of the music room the next afternoon. She was excited, the pink in her cheeks a becoming contrast to her violet eyes and her rosy, perfect bow lips, a truly beautiful child. When we entered, Mr. Sweeney rose from the piano stool where he had been sitting and came toward Petra.

"I'm Patrick Sweeney. You must be Miss Stravinsky. Dr. Davis has told me about you, and I'm glad to meet you."

Petra responded without any noticeable nervousness. "Please call me Petra, Mr. Sweeney. Thank you for taking the time from your busy schedule to meet with me." He stared at her, entranced for a moment by her face, and then went back to sit at the piano.

"I'm happy to do it. Let's start with some scales, shall we? Sing what I play. I'll keep raising it a half step until we're out of your range." The first few times he played and she faithfully repeated the notes. Soon, however, she moved to the next step at the same time he did, and eventually he dropped the keyboard entirely and it was only Petra's voice trilling up and down the octaves. From my amateur's view, the scales seemed to come naturally to her, no hesitation in her voice that I could hear, and she was so happy to be singing that her face seemed to glow. Eventually Mr. Sweeney held up his hand and she stopped, her face dimming as if she feared she'd done something wrong.

"We will never be out of your range, Petra," he said quietly. "I believe your soprano could climb beyond the piano's ability to play." He was quiet, digesting what he had just heard. Even to my untutored and unmusical ear, her voice was clear and resonant, soaring, beautiful. "What can you sing?" he asked finally. "What songs do you know? Sing whatever you like."

She smiled at him happily and began to sing some of the popular songs of the time: "After the Ball," and "A Bird in a Gilded Cage," and "Shine on Harvest Moon," singing the last tune simply and endearingly, as if she knew what a real harvest moon was, as if she weren't surrounded by skyscrapers and smokestacks that threatened to obscure her moon completely, harvest or not. When Petra sang she was so obviously happy that it gave an observer joy just to watch her, let alone hear that lovely voice.

Sweeney put up his hand and she stopped again but expectantly now and more confidently, understanding that he was not asking her to do so because her singing displeased him.

"Do you know any classical pieces, Petra? Anything more demanding than those popular songs?"

She paused, then nodded hesitantly, a small line of uncertainty furrowing her brow.

"Something like this, do you mean?" she asked and burst into the most amazing song, everything about her as glorious as the music, no longer a girl but rather made a woman by the music.

"*Ah! Je ris de me voir si belle*," she sang, her beautiful voice plaintive and tender and tortured. I didn't understand much of the lyrics because my French was cursory at best, but Patrick Sweeney must have recognized the piece. He had dropped all pretense of light-hearted sophistication and just watched her enthralled, beginning to love her from that moment. At least that's how it seemed to me. As the corners of the room filled with Petra's truly extraordinary voice, his face took on the expression of a man surprised by something precious and beautiful, something he never expected to know in his lifetime, something wonderful beyond his imagination.

When she finished, she just stood there, a child once more and anxious for someone's approval.

"Is that what you meant?" she asked.

He nodded slowly. "Yes, that's exactly what I meant. How do you know the Jewel Song from *Faust*, Petra?"

"When my family came to America we arrived first in New York. I was seven years old and we lived there five years before my father moved us to Chicago. We had a family friend who worked backstage at the Opera and he would take me and let me sit in a corner to hear the performances as often as I wished. I couldn't see the singers from my perch, but I could hear them. I heard Caruso once."

"Did you?" Sweeney sat there on the stool, his hands in his lap, and just watched her.

"I can sing more," Petra volunteered. "I know Wagner's '*Du bist der Lenz*' or Dvorak's '*Song to the Moon*.' I love that. I could sing that."

"No, I don't need to hear more now, Petra. You have—" The Irishman paused, helpless and unable to find the right words, then looked at me, mutely asking me to fill in the blank for him.

"I think Mr. Sweeney is very pleased with what he heard, Petra. It was beautiful. I admit that I'm surprised at how very beautiful it was, and I think he is, too. We weren't expecting such a splendid performance. Am I right, Mr. Sweeney?"

He nodded. "Your voice is a magnificent instrument, Petra, albeit untrained. You have been given a gift that will become only more glorious with time and practice. We need to find you a vocal trainer worthy of your voice."

"No, I want you to be my teacher." He shook his head.

"You're already beyond my abilities to teach, Petra. It should be someone with far greater skill and more classical experience than I."

"No," she repeated and met his gaze firmly, the surprising steel in her showing through. "I want you to be my teacher now. Later, when you've taught me all you know and I've grown older, we can find another teacher. Now I have so much to learn, how to read music, how to use my voice properly without straining, so many basic things that you can teach me. I trust you. Please."

For a moment I wasn't there with them at all as the force of her will reached across the room to him. I knew he stood no chance of refusing her; he finally realized it, too.

"All right. We can start with the simple things. I'm probably capable of that much." Sweeney was slowly regaining his usual amused good nature, slowly escaping the spell of that marvelous voice.

"Good. When can we start?"

I interjected, "Mr. Sweeney is a volunteer, Petra, and has other students. Perhaps you could give him time to arrange his schedule and find a time for you." She looked immediately contrite.

"Of course. I'm sorry. I didn't mean to dictate. I was just excited."

"Petra, why don't you go back to the nursery while I talk to Mr. Sweeney? He and I can figure out a time that will be convenient for you, for him, and for Hull-House."

She smiled shyly at Sweeney, gave me a rare, quick hug and was gone, leaving Patrick Sweeney and me looking at the door through which she exited as if we were mesmerized by the doorknob.

Finally I took a deep breath and said, "I admit I have very little musical ability but even to my amateur ear, she sounded spectacular. Am I right that she has talent and a great potential?" Sweeney stood and went to stare out the window, his hands clasped behind his back.

"Oh yes, she has talent and more than great potential. She has an inevitable potential, Doctor. God did not give her that voice and then intend for her to spend her life in some tenement kitchen. She will be great some day, and famous."

"And are you the man to help her achieve that greatness, Patrick? Petra will need someone to put her on the right path and then stay with her, protect her when she needs protection, teach her more than music, someone who will act honorably with her and on her behalf. She's still a child in many ways, barely sixteen, but gifted and a beauty. I could be afraid for her." He turned from the window to face me, his thin, boyish face serious.

"I have contacts and I can help her, but only if she'll let me, Dr. Davis, only if she'll let me. If she will, you have no reason to be afraid for her."

I studied the man soberly. I didn't know him very well, knew only the charmed look I had seen on his face as he watched Petra sing, as if he saw more than a human, a magical sprite or enchanted princess perhaps. Already in love with her, I thought, after just one meeting, but what could I do about that? She would someday need a champion and perhaps Patrick Sweeney was just the one for the role.

"Good. I'll trust that's so. When will you schedule her lessons?"

"Tuesday and Thursday mornings at 11:00."

"But you aren't here on Tuesdays and Thursdays."

"I am now," he said.

***

Douglas Gallagher arrived at the front door of Hull-House promptly at two o'clock Sunday afternoon, one hand thrust into the pocket of a very fine overcoat and a pristine white box nestled into the crook of his other arm. I took the box as he handed it to me and gasped at the blood-red roses that lay inside.

"They're beautiful," I told him, fingering the velvet blooms that were beginning to unfurl from the warmth of the room, "but you shouldn't have." I looked at him with some mischief. "The tour is free, after all."

"Nothing is free, Doctor. Everything has a price."

"And everyone?"

"And everyone, yes." He paused before adding, "By your expression I can tell I've said the wrong thing again. Will I ever say anything with which you agree?"

"The weather," I murmured, putting the roses into water, "is usually safe."

"Safe is boring. I think even you might agree with that."

"Boring once in a while, perhaps," I answered, even as I understood and sympathized with his meaning, "but I think safe can be comforting, too." As I looked at him, I thought he had little experience with not feeling safe and couldn't possibly know what it was like to be Petra or Mr. Pilzner or a sixteen-year-old first-time mother giving birth in her kitchen. But that was too serious for the conversation and perhaps too accusing. I was becoming Dr. Comstock, socialist tendencies and all, I thought with amusement. It must be an occupational risk that came with the position.

"What was there about that exchange to make you smile?" Douglas Gallagher was sharply observant and a little demanding in his tone. I would need to stay alert and on my toes with him; he inspired neither safe nor comforting feelings in me.

"Nothing. A fleeting thought of my predecessor's legacy is all and only amusing to me in passing. Keep your coat, Mr. Gallagher, since we'll be going in and out."

He put his hand on my arm. "Douglas, please."

"Keep your coat, *Douglas*," I said, smiling at him.

"And may I call you Katherine?"

"Katherine is fine, but I warn you, never Kate. I don't care much for nicknames."

"I'll add that to the list of information I've begun to compile about you."

"I can't imagine that you have much on your list after two relatively brief and innocuous meetings."

"Katherine Davis, third child of prosperous cattleman John and wife Louisa Caldecott Davis of the JL Ranch in Laramie, Wyoming, twenty-three years old, graduated eighth in her class from Kansas Medical School, one sister and two brothers, one niece and two nephews." He paused, appreciating that he had startled me, and then added, "Prefers roses to orchids and doesn't like nicknames. I think that's all I have on the list so far."

"You've been busy. I suppose I should feel flattered but I don't, only a little intruded upon." If I thought my stern tone would remove the challenging gleam from his eyes, I was wrong.

"I have been busy and you should feel flattered." Then he looked around the room and changed the subject. "This is very nice, very welcoming. I compliment whoever is responsible for its design. Would that be the famous Miss Addams?" He was adroit because it would only be bad taste for me to try to reclaim the previous topic after such a compliment.

"Yes, Miss Addams is responsible for everything you'll see today, but we couldn't keep Hull-House going and accomplish all the good we accomplish here if it weren't for our generous donors." Let him chew on that a little so he wouldn't assume I'd invited him for a tour because of some amorous attraction on my part.

Douglas Gallagher was a good audience, careful to listen to everything I said, interested enough to ask appropriate questions, informed enough to comment on Dr. Hamilton's surveys and the latest performance of the Marionettes.

On the last leg of the tour, we stopped at the dispensary where I left him at the door to confer with Miss Flaherty about a patient and stop by the bed of a child who had been brought in undernourished with a hacking cough.

"Your kingdom?" he asked when I rejoined him.

"Kingdom? Hardly. More like my natural habitat." We walked slowly outside as a group of bundled girls exited the Jane Club, laughing and calling their farewells to each other. Crossing the open quadrangle, we entered the main house through the side door. Once back in the front room by the roaring fire, I offered tea and was surprised when he accepted because I thought he might have had his fill of the commonplace by then.

When I came back from the dining room with a tray, he had removed his coat and sat elegantly cross-legged in the big chair by the fire. He rose when I entered and moved the other chair closer to his with a small table between.

"What were your impressions of Hull-House, Douglas?" I asked. He was careful in his reply.

"A noble and foolish experiment to which someone has devoted a great deal of time, money, and energy."

"Foolish? You don't approve, then?" I felt a fleeting disappointment but no surprise.

"I don't disapprove, but I admit to being skeptical about what you believe such a place can accomplish for the kind of people you serve."

"The kind of people we serve," I echoed. "Who would that be exactly?"

"The Irish, the Germans, the Italians, the uneducated, the unwashed, the low, the laboring classes."

"Spoken like a true capitalist."

"I am a capitalist and proud of it. How do you think great cities were built or trains connected the coasts? How do medical discoveries get made even today? Through the energies and fortunes of capitalists, Katherine. If it were up to the masses, nothing would be accomplished but saloons and a continuing plague of too many squalling babies." At my look, he added, "Now I really have said the wrong thing, haven't I, and offended your altruistic nature?"

"Clearly we don't view matters in the same light, Douglas," I responded calmly, "but you have a right to your opinion. Even if it is wrong." He laughed at that and set his cup down to lean toward me and rest a hand on mine.

"You're charming, beautiful, and intelligent, Katherine, and if that weren't enough, you also have the ability to make me laugh. Will you join me for dinner some evening this week?"

I shook my head and pulled my hand away from his touch, hoping my face hadn't given away the little thrill I felt at his closeness. Instinctively, I thought Douglas Gallagher a man with whom I must always be on guard. He would see weakness and pounce, and I found that knowledge both alarming and exciting. I liked the promise of a challenge and the feeling that he was dangerous held a perverse appeal for me.

"There's not a day during the week that I can get away, I'm afraid."

"Saturday, then. Surely you can be spared for dinner. You have to eat, after all."

"Saturday would be fine. I'm not an indentured servant, and I am allowed to leave the premises." He stood when I did, reached into his jacket pocket, and handed me a piece of paper from it.

"I hope you can find a use for this."

"This is very good of you, Douglas," I stammered, startled by the generous amount of the check he had just given me, my voice trembling so that I must have sounded half my age.

"I didn't do it to be good," he answered, "only to see that look on your face, and it was worth every penny." I flushed at his tone, catching something that was more than admiration and uncertain how to respond.

"It's still very generous of you," I said, regaining my composure. "Miss Addams will be pleased."

"The sparkle in your eyes is worth more to me than a year of Miss Addams's pleasure, Katherine. I'll come for you at eight on Saturday, if I may."

"I'll look forward to it."

After Douglas left, I took the check to Miss Addams, who accepted it with a smile.

"Do you think it's a donation because he admires our work here or our doctor?" she asked me.

"Does it matter?"

"Not to me, but it might to you someday." Her answer was more serious than I expected.

"I don't understand what you mean."

"I can see that, and I hope you never do. Be sure to relay my gratitude to Mr. Gallagher."

"We're having dinner Saturday evening. I hope that's all right."

"Of course, it is. Even a doctor is allowed to have a personal life. At the risk of being intrusive, do you have something to wear?"

I hadn't given my wardrobe a thought and answered ruefully, "No, as a matter of fact, I don't, but perhaps I can convince Mary to loan me that green dress again."

"I'm sure we can find something new for you, Katherine. I'll talk to Mary about it. I wouldn't want you to spend the evening with such a selfless supporter in anything shabby or unbecoming. It would be an ill-mannered way to treat such an unselfish gesture on Mr. Gallagher's part." She raised both brows to me in a look of such mock innocence that I had to laugh.

"I do feel a little like a commodity, bought and paid for, but it's probably just my small-town, suspicious mind. Thank you. I'd appreciate it if you could make me fit to be seen in public. I'll have to find time to invest in one good dress so I don't have to keep scavenging room to room for every social occasion. I never expected the necessity."

"You spent too long in the classroom, Katherine, or just didn't bother to take a look in your mirror. Social occasions are bound to come your way but don't spend any of your hard-earned money on dressing. I'm sure we can take care of that for you."

Miss Addams did indeed take care of it for me in her usual thoughtful way, by returning the green gown with a note that invited me to keep it and providing another dress besides, that one in ivory silk, slim-skirted and elegantly tailored to enhance my tall figure.

When I thanked her, her eyes twinkled and she only said, "I do have some contacts in high places, Katherine, so if you don't mind discarded clothing, there are more where those came from."

Probably discarded, I speculated, after being worn once to an afternoon tea and who was I to complain about that? My sister-in-law, Hope, laughed to tell how, when she first came to Wyoming, before she met and married my brother, she had only one small satchel that held all her clothing in the world. As far as she knew, one worn dress, two skirts, one shirtwaist, and an old smock would have to last her a lifetime. Thinking of Hope, how she had set out for the unknown all alone fueled only by her dream of independence, humbled me. I had a family who would risk anything for me, who were eager to do whatever I asked, and I had a place to go where I would always be welcomed open-armed, loved, and completely accepted no matter the circumstances. Why I felt this inexorable urge to go farther away from such a paradise puzzled me and absolutely baffled Hope.

"Chicago?" she had written. "Why would you go to Chicago when the people who love you and everything you need are here in Wyoming? I wish you'd come home, Katherine."

Come home, I thought, how could I when I wasn't sure where or what home was any more? Something else beckoned from the outside and drove from the inside, although I couldn't express that sensibly to anyone, not to Hope, not to my father who trusted my judgment without question, not even to my mother, who sometimes disconcertingly understood me better than I understood myself. There was something about being one of "the Davises" that wasn't enough. I needed to be Katherine Davis, a woman more important than her name.

I knew I had to sort through all those feelings but not dressed in an ivory silk gown with a slit up the back and Douglas Gallagher coming to the door. I would entertain introspection another time. I looked forward to the glitter in his eyes, the promise of a fluttering low in my stomach when he looked at me, the pleasure of flirtation with an attractive man who desired my company, perhaps desired me, a notion that still seemed too farfetched to believe. We had met so fleetingly and on so few occasions that when Douglas looked at me, he couldn't possibly see the true Katherine Davis. He saw only an exterior and interpreted that as he chose, and perhaps that wasn't such a bad thing. Besides the attraction I felt to him, there was that other guarded feeling that said I should not allow him to see too much of my heart, not give him power over me through my emotions. I needed to keep some place inside secret and inviolate from his knowing, speculative gaze.

That was a confusing feeling because it was nothing like the emotion my parents shared and demonstrated, two people who read each other's minds and finished the other's sentences. Nothing between them was hidden or guarded. Such an idea would have startled my mother and made my father laugh out loud. He said often enough that by the time they grew old together, the house would be completely silent because he'd only have to think about what he wanted for supper and Mother would have it on the table. I didn't feel that way with Douglas Gallagher, didn't think I ever could. In fact, I found the idea of being so exposed to him a little disagreeable.

Douglas certainly didn't look disagreeable Saturday evening. He wasn't in tails as I'd first seen him but in a fine, very fashionable double-breasted dark suit and perfectly starched white shirt, a dark silk tie showing the same initial diamond stick pin he had worn earlier. He wore a tailored woolen overcoat and dark, brushed fedora against the weather. A man to make one shiver, I thought, and who'd have thought I would find his brand of polished ruthlessness attractive? I was certainly not my mother's daughter.

When Douglas helped me on with my cape, his hands brushed my shoulders and lingered there long enough that I thought I should say something but not so long that I actually had time to do so. Very practiced with women, I thought, and admitted to myself that I would have been disappointed if it were not so. We made small talk walking to his auto, comments about the weather and the week, everything perfectly innocent so why my anticipatory stomach-tightening that didn't feel innocent at all? I knew I would enjoy the evening more than he and recognized the fact as something only I should know.

"Hello, Fritz," I said from the back seat. "I'm glad to see you again." The driver turned to me, surprised at the greeting.

"Good evening, Miss. It's very nice to see you again as well."

Douglas leaned over to me and commented softly, "Generally, we pretend Fritz is invisible." I looked at him quickly, catching mischief in his eyes.

"But he's not, is he, at least to me? So why should I pretend something that isn't so?"

"It's a social game, Katherine. You should learn the rules."

"I've never been very good at games, Douglas. My brother and I spent some of our childhood in cow-pie contests, and I invariably lost because he always changed the rules at the last minute. You do know what cow pies are, don't you?" I asked deliberately.

"I do," he replied without pause and settled back in the

seat next to me, only the slightest touch of amusement in his voice. "Did I mention I'm in the beef business, too?"

"No, you didn't," I smoothed my skirts and settled back as comfortably as he, "but I'm sure there are many things you haven't told me about yourself." I felt Douglas give me a quick, sideways glance poised to speak. Apparently he changed his mind, however, because we both remained quiet until we reached the hotel where we would dine.

The Palmer House was a fine hotel, renowned for its cuisine and its décor. Named after Potter Palmer, one of Chicago's many millionaires, the hotel housed on its second floor a small but elegant restaurant, one that Douglas Gallagher must have frequented. The staff recognized him immediately, called him by name, quickly and quietly removed our coats, and seated us—all within a few moments.

From across the table, the subdued candlelight put his eyes into shadow, so to warm him a little I commented with a smile, "This is a lovely room, Douglas. Is it a favorite place of yours?"

"Yes. I like both the atmosphere and the chef very much. It's not showy, but I find its elegant simplicity beautiful. Like you." I would have to learn how to respond to those sudden, rich compliments he offered with something other than a blush. Douglas lifted a glass of wine to me. "You get an endearing color in your cheeks when you're flustered, Katherine. I didn't think modern women blushed any more."

"I can't speak for all women, but I blush against my will and better judgment," I said ruefully, "and would stop it if I could. Unfortunately, that's a difficult trick to learn. It's probably physiologically impossible, besides." Douglas laughed, still holding the wine glass forward.

"For which the males of the species are eternally grateful. To you and your charming blush." Over a dinner of many courses that made me feel guilty at its excess, he invited, "Tell me about yourself, Katherine. Why a doctor?"

I shared the early memories of my mother's impromptu doctoring and the tone in her voice when she had spoken of Dr. Frank's excess.

"Being a doctor seemed a very noble profession to me at the time."

"Does it still hold the same appeal for you?"

"Yes, but in a much more realistic and humbling way," I answered thoughtfully. "I know I can't heal all the sick or make everyone better or rescue all children from abuse or keep the old from lonely and undignified deaths. I can only do so much."

"Then why do it at all?"

The question startled, almost shocked, me and I retorted too passionately, "Because it's what I *can* do that matters. We all have a responsibility to do as much as we can for the common good."

"Where did that come from?" Douglas appeared honestly curious about my sudden vehemence.

"From my Grandfather Caldecott, probably. My mother says he was an ardent abolitionist and Kansas free-stater, even at the risk it posed to his own life and family in those years."

"I thought you were from Wyoming."

"Don't worry, your spies didn't get their facts wrong. I am from Wyoming, but my mother was born and raised in Blessing, Kansas, and still pines for the flat Kansas prairie. She always thought she was keeping that longing hidden from the rest of us, but she hasn't got a face able to conceal much, I'm afraid, and there was the ritual planting of the sunflower seeds that gave her away every spring."

"So your parents kept secrets, after all? From your description I wouldn't have thought anything so unwholesome would have been allowed."

He may have been mocking, but I answered honestly, "Only that one, and only because my mother never wanted to distress my father. He brought her as a new bride to Wyoming and would have felt responsible for her homesickness. He's never wanted anything but to make her happy and the same for his children, by extension."

"By extension?" He had caught my ambiguous tone and comment.

I shrugged. "I've always felt that my father loves me mostly because I'm my mother's daughter. She has always been the one ruling passion in his life."

"I can understand and sympathize with his single-mindedness if your mother is anything like you."

There it was again, an unexpected, almost understated compliment that had much more depth and meaning than a social comment about my dress or hair.

"She and I are nothing alike in appearance or temperament." Then to change the subject, I asked, "What about you, Douglas? Have you a family?"

"No ruling passion, or at least not until recently."

"Seriously."

He smiled. "Seriously then. I have a younger brother, Andrew, who also lives in Chicago and leads an outrageously dissolute life, I'm afraid."

"A black sheep?"

"If you saw him, you'd understand why such a description would draw a smile, but I suppose you could call him that. He has no interest in business."

"What then?"

"His chief pastime is spending his inheritance, which he does with great steadfastness of purpose. I wish he would find a more worthwhile occupation and pursue it with the same dedication, but I've given up lecturing."

"He sounds like the prodigal son. Perhaps he'll come to his senses like the boy in the story and all will be well." I'd heard a certain grimness in Douglas's tone that told me he was concerned and upset by his brother's conduct. At his continued silence, I added, "What about your parents?"

"My parents were the Gallaghers of San Francisco. My father was a successful businessman, banker, and real estate tycoon, my mother the mistress of a very fine mansion on Nob Hill. My brother and I were raised by a series of governesses and tutors and eventually sent east to school. I finished Yale with a degree in business. On the other hand, Drew was asked to leave before he ever came close to graduation because of an unfortunate and embarrassing escapade that I won't share with you because of its salacious details."

"I am a doctor," I commented dryly, "so I probably understand a lot more than you give me credit for."

"No doubt but let me keep the illusion I have of you."

"What of your parents now?" I prompted.

"My father died suddenly of heart failure over five years ago and my mother, refusing to leave her mansion, died a year later in the earthquake. The house literally fell down around her and buried her alive."

He said the words so coolly, as if he described a tumble of toy blocks, that I gave a quiet gasp and involuntarily reached across the table to touch his hand.

"I'm so sorry, Douglas. How awful for you to lose them both so suddenly and terribly. Perhaps that explains your brother's immoderate behavior."

"Because of grief over their deaths, you mean? I doubt that. Neither of us knew our parents very well, and we were both shipped off to school as soon as they thought we were old enough, which as it turned out was too young, especially for Drew. Give him an inch, he'd always take the mile, even then. He made life hell for every one of our tutors. It's a wonder one of them didn't strangle him and hang his body in a closet somewhere. Had that happened, I'd have been the only one who would have noticed he was gone." The words may have been intended for humor, but I found them a sad comment, a focus on wealth apparently as destructive to the spirit as poverty.

"My brother and I inherited a great deal of money, as vulgar as it may be to mention it, and while Drew continues to turn on the spigot and watch it flow down the drain of Chicago nightlife, I chose to invest it in a number of enterprises here and in San Francisco. I've done very well, in case you were wondering about my prospects."

"I wasn't wondering about them at all," I retorted indignantly.

"Pity. I wish you were."

Douglas gave me an unsmiling look across the table and I withdrew my hand, which I had allowed to rest over his for too long. Dessert arrived then, something flaming and exotic, and we followed it with an aperitif, making desultory talk, both of us comfortable and reluctant for the evening to end. I had a clearer picture of Douglas Gallagher, a man who'd had little enough of true affection in his life and even less of visionary altruism. No wonder he thought Hull-House and my role in it a foolish experiment.

Helping me into my cape, he said from behind me and against my hair, "I enjoyed the evening very much, Katherine. Thank you." Too intimate and too close, I thought, pulling back, and I stepped slightly away as I turned to face him.

"I enjoyed it, too, Douglas. A lovely dinner in a beautiful setting with good company."

"And not over yet," he said, smiling. He hadn't missed the fact that I'd purposefully put distance between us but the knowledge didn't appear to put him in bad humor.

Fritz brought the auto around and on the trip home Douglas sat closer than before, his shoulder just brushing mine. He would have taken one of my gloved hands in his, but I folded my hands in my lap and made light conversation that didn't fool either of us. A social game, he had called it, and I was rapidly learning the rules.

At the front door he took off his hat and stood for a moment.

"The light caught the gold in your eyes all evening, Katherine." Douglas's voice, husky and low, rattled my composure despite my intention to appear sophisticated. "I don't think I told you how beautiful you looked tonight." He leaned forward as if to kiss me and I, suddenly breathless and as awkward as a schoolgirl, pushed open the door, and stepped slightly over the threshold. A retreat we both recognized but neither acknowledged.

"I believe candlelight has a universally becoming effect on the complexion," I responded prosaically. "Good night, Douglas. Thank you for the evening. I enjoyed it very much and found it a rare treat."

"It doesn't have to be that rare. What about next Saturday?"

"Oh, I don't think—"

"You're afraid of me."

"I am not afraid of you."

"Then why not next Saturday? Are you telling me you have other plans?"

"I don't so I can't."

"You could lie about it. Women seldom feel any real reluctance to do so if it gets them what they want."

"What a sweeping condemnation of my sex, Douglas. I have many faults but lying isn't one of them. All right, next Saturday then." He put on his hat, both satisfaction at my capitulation and laughter in his voice.

"Your tone makes it sound as unpleasant a prospect as a trip to the dentist. I promise it won't be a disagreeable evening." I had to laugh, too.

"I did sound like a pouting child forced to eat her vegetables, didn't I? I'm sorry. I had a lovely evening, and I'll look forward to next Saturday."

"I've made progress, then," he said mildly as he left.

Once inside I leaned against the closed door for a while to catch my emotional breath. My feelings for Douglas Gallagher were a very new sensation, and I enjoyed the experience more than was probably wise. But I found that walking along the edge of a precipice was unexpectedly stimulating and so assured myself—mistakenly, as it turned out—that I didn't have all that much to lose even if I fell over the edge.

CHAPTER 6

The following week flew. The child with the hacking cough recovered enough to be sent home with strict instructions for maintaining his health and an appointment for a return visit. Petra began her voice lessons, everything about her more animated, her happiness so tangible that it warmed any room she inhabited. She went about humming under her breath and smiling for no reason.

I received a letter from my sister telling me to prepare for another niece or nephew. She felt, for no specific reason that it was a boy but wrote with a depth of sincerity that she would be delighted with whatever God sent, as long as the baby was healthy and whole. I was happy for her but concerned, too. Lily Kate's birth had been difficult for Becca, and then she and her husband, Ben, had lost their second child, an infant son, soon after his birth. Although that sad bereavement had happened over eighteen months ago, their grief was still fresh and the danger to my sister's health real. I wished I were closer to oversee the pregnancy, but I was hundreds of miles away and so must rely on my sister's practical sense, Ben's devotion to her, my family's supportive protection, and God's good grace to keep her and the baby safe.

For whatever reason and traceable to no evidence, I did not have a great deal of confidence in the medical community at home. Becca, as perfect for motherhood as anyone I knew, with a heart and home intended for children, had grieved terribly at little Ben's death and for a long time, like Biblical Rachel and her children, would not be comforted. I didn't think she, or any of us, could bear such a painful loss again.

That very evening I penned Becca a return letter and gave her strict maternity instructions—not from your sister, I wrote, underscoring the words, but from Dr. Davis, so pay attention. Becca would laugh when she read the words but would know I was serious and would follow my directions. Some time in the last five years she had ceased being the older sister and I the younger. Now we were just sisters, a much easier relationship for both of us.

Mid-week Alice Hamilton asked me to follow the garbage wagon with her and nab flies in its wake.

"It's too cold for flies," I pointed out. "Shouldn't we wait until it's warm enough to be sure we'll find some specimens?"

"That's one of the issues I want either to prove or disprove," she answered. "I'm not convinced that the little pests don't appear as early as March in the recesses of those nasty wooden garbage boxes. You know they never get emptied properly and it's my theory that their dark, refuse-filled corners are warm and foul enough to be early breeding grounds. Are you game to find out?"

The two of us, dressed like Arctic explorers, spent two consecutive mornings following the rounds of the garbage wagons of the nineteenth ward. We dug out disgusting waste from the sidewalk trash boxes with long-handled spoons and deposited it into small specimen jars. Dr. Hamilton was delighted with the results of our labors and disappeared into her laboratory with an absentminded wave of her hand. I knew it would be several days, if not weeks, before she reappeared and found myself giggling a little during the following days at the picture of the two of us skulking through the streets like grave robbers, furtively stealing other people's rubbish.

One evening I dragged out the solitary good dress I had brought with me, briefly bemoaned its lack of fashion, and the next day took it over to the girls' home education class.

"I have a project for you," I said to Eleanor Terry, who taught housekeeping skills to the neighborhood girls. "Do you think your class could work on this old dress and turn it into something fashionable I could wear by this weekend? I have no ideas and less skill." She held the dress in front of her and eyed it objectively.

"These will have to go," she said pointing to the sleeves. "No one's wearing that style any more, but the fabric is good and the color's not bad. We can put on contrasting sleeves and raise the waist a little, add some lace, and you'll be the belle of the evening."

I patted my hair that as usual was slipping rebelliously out of its net, made several ineffectual motions in the general vicinity of a large spot on my coat where a baby had deposited part of his lunch, and remembered what I had looked like bent over a trash receptacle scraping black, sticky, not-quite-frozen goo from its bottom corners.

"I don't think I'm exactly belle potential, Eleanor, but I'd appreciate whatever you could do."

When I tried on the finished dress, I twirled in front of the mirror in admiration: not of me but of the class, which had turned a well-worn garment into a new and stylish creation.

"We saw one like it in a fashion magazine," one of the girls explained as they crowded around, proud of the results and waiting for my approval.

"It's oriental," another volunteered, although I had figured that out on my own. The transfigured gown definitely had an oriental look, soft and drapey with a short and flowing kimono-like coat in a patterned deep apricot fabric attached to the barely visible pale peach original beneath.

"It's much too grand for me, but I'll wear this proudly. A French designer couldn't have done better. Thank you." I wasn't just being polite, either. The reworked dress was too grand for me and as fashionable as anything I could have found at Marshall Field's.

Petra caught me in my reworked finery on my way out Saturday evening and clapped her hands a little at the sight.

"You look wonderful, Dr. Davis! He must be quite an admirer for you to take such pains with your appearance."

"I don't know how much of an admirer he is, Petra. It's too early for any speculation. I do know, however, that I've used up my supply of evening dresses so this will have to be our last dinner meeting no matter how ardent he might be." We walked together toward the door. "I saw baby Leo today. His mother brought him in for a checkup and she asked about you, if you were still here. Did you know Mrs. Lubchik before you came to Hull-House? I got that impression somehow."

Petra grew quiet. I could see her thinking my question through, her face expressionless except for her eyes that were troubled.

"No," she said finally, relief in her tone. "I know I'd remember if I had seen her before. She's probably mistaken me for someone else." I threw my cloak around my shoulders and prepared to cross the quadrangle to the house.

"Or I may have read too much into her comments. Don't let it bother you." Petra still looked troubled as I left her, fearful even, and I wondered, as I had many times before, who it was she feared, what her real story was, and if I would ever know it.

Douglas took me to a small restaurant called The Berghoff, definitely off the beaten path but very fine with an intimate, friendly dining area and its waiters dressed in waistcoats and bow ties. The staff knew him there, too, greeted him respectfully by name, and quickly showed us to our table.

"Try the grilled fish," he recommended. "It's the best in the city, always fresh and cooked superbly."

I took his advice and at the first bite admitted he was right. "I'm afraid my knowledge of fish is negligible," I told him, laughing. "Wyoming is beef country and landlocked so you see the reason for the gap in my culinary education, but this is delicious. I'm glad I took your advice."

"You may always trust my advice, Katherine. I wouldn't lead you astray," he raised his dark eyes to mine and gave an engaging grin, "although the prospect of leading you astray, especially as you look tonight, is very appealing. That particular color does something remarkable to your skin. Has anyone ever compared you to a peach before? Where did you find a gown that would become you so perfectly?"

"I had it made to order," I answered, "but don't ask for any more details because I'm not sharing them. Women need their secrets." His gaze swept across the bodice but just as he was going to respond, a man came up behind him and put both hands on his shoulders.

"Douglas," the stranger said, "these unplanned meetings are all the more delightful for their unexpectedness."

For a second, Douglas sat completely still. Then he turned in his chair to say, "You're wrinkling my jacket, Drew," and shook off the man's hands.

If I hadn't heard the name, I would never have guessed that the new arrival was Douglas's younger brother; the two men shared little physical resemblance.

"You don't sound glad to see me," Douglas's brother said. He came around to the side of the table to glance over at me. "But I see that I'm interrupting."

He waited expectantly for Douglas, who finally introduced us with a noticeable and rather ungracious reluctance.

"Katherine, this is my brother, Andrew. Drew, Miss Katherine Davis." I extended my hand to the younger Gallagher.

"How do you do? Douglas has recently spoken about you, but I didn't expect to have the pleasure of meeting you so soon."

Drew took my hand and leaned down to whisper in my ear, "You and I both know he's cursing my presence even as we speak," then stood up again and let go of my hand. "I'm delighted to meet you, Miss Davis." He gave a mischievous wink that made me smile in spite of myself.

After a moment of silence, I invited, "Won't you join us, Mr. Gallagher? Or are you with someone?"

Drew sat quickly and answered, "No, I'm alone this evening and was feeling very sorry for myself because I had no friends, but now that I've met you, I can only thank Providence that I am unlovable."

I was reminded of my previous comment about Douglas's brother as I looked at Andrew Gallagher and understood why Douglas had said that describing him as a black sheep would make me smile. He was so its antithesis, blond-white hair, brows, and small mustache, light eyes, very white teeth, fair complexion, all of him golden and his conversation as lighthearted as his appearance. The contrast of the brothers, one so dark and the other so fair, was startling.

Andrew leaned forward toward me again as if we were sharing confidences.

"Douglas is wishing me with the devil right now, but I would much rather be here with an angel like you. Have we met before? I think I would have remembered unless it was after several glasses of wine, and if that's the case, let me apologize now for any indignity you may have suffered at my hands. I can only say I wasn't myself at the time and to prove my regret, I promise to swear off alcohol for the rest of the evening."

I'd realized early on that he had already drunk more than his share of spirits despite the early evening but responded seriously, "I'll share that at the next meeting of the Temperance Society I attend. They'll be glad to know you're feeling a certain alcoholic penitence. We seldom get the chance to experience such gratifying proof of the good of our mission."

For just a moment Drew thought I was serious but then spied the half-filled wine glass in front of me and grinned.

"I do like this woman, Douglas. Why haven't you introduced us sooner?"

"If I ever knew where to find you, I might have done so. Don't you have some place to go?"

"No, I haven't. No place at all."

Drew put an elbow on the table and rested his chin in his hand to stare at me. I suppose I should have been offended at his unblinking gaze, but he was so obviously and purposefully making himself a nuisance—to annoy his brother I guessed, having brothers of my own—that it was impossible to take him seriously. For all his years he reminded me of a little boy who wanted the attention of his elders and would do anything to get it.

I met Drew's look with one of my own, a look known for its ability to settle a room of noisy children, and said, "You're bordering on the rude and foolish, Mr. Gallagher. I tell you so with your best interests at heart, of course. Have you eaten or should we order dinner for you?" He gave a sudden, lopsided, disarming smile and sat back.

"I was being rude and foolish, wasn't I? I beg your pardon. I'd like to join you for dinner, but I'm in the way, and as much as he won't believe it, I am fond of my brother and have no desire to spoil his evening." Drew turned to Douglas, who had remained quiet all this time, observant and unamused. "Miss Davis reminds me of the woman in the portrait that used to hang in the hallway going up the front stairs. Remember? As little boys we called her 'The Warm Woman.' She was dressed in a peach gown with the same honey-colored hair and kind eyes. I wonder what ever happened to that picture. Destroyed with the house, I suppose, buried right along with Mother."

Douglas said his name sharply at that but Andrew looked honestly puzzled at the reproof in his tone. I don't think he had intended his comment to shock me, but it did, much too flippant a remark about his mother's death. I couldn't imagine what lack of natural feeling would prompt him to say such a thing and be completely unaware of its impropriety. He pushed his chair away from the table and stood.

"Someone should paint you, Miss Davis, capture how you look this evening so the resulting image can be enjoyed without forcing a person to appear rude and foolish. Have you had a chance to visit the Art Institute?"

"No, not yet. I'm relatively new to the city."

"I thought you must be or I'd have seen you before this.

Douglas, you should plan an outing for Miss Davis, an afternoon at the Art Institute and a stroll through Grant Park. I'm sure I'd be free if you'd want to invite me, too, but I understand if you choose to omit me entirely." Drew lifted my hand from the table and raised it to his lips. "I am charmed, Miss Davis, and hope I haven't completely ruined your evening. Douglas is wearing his disapproving older brother look, but I don't see similar sentiments in your expression. You really have the kindest face I've ever seen. I hope that doesn't offend you. Anyone can be beautiful, but kindness is much more elusive than beauty and thus it's more valuable. How rare to find a woman who has both. My brother's the lucky one, always has been." As Douglas, with barely disguised impatience, said his brother's name once more, Drew Gallagher gave me that same lop-sided, endearing smile he had used earlier and added, "It really was a pleasure and I do like you. Forgive my idiocy."

With the careful gesture of a man who'd had too much to drink, he pushed his chair back to the table and walked away to take his coat and hat from a man by the door, who had been waiting to hand them over for some time. Drew surprised me by turning to look back at our table once more from the front doorway, a sober look with nothing gay or teasing in his expression. I noticed Drew's serious study out of the corner of my eye; I'm sure he didn't know I caught that last look of his.

"That," said Douglas with a trace of disgust in his tone, "was my little brother." When I made no comment, he added, "I hope he didn't say or do anything that you found too outrageous. Everything Drew does is for effect. He's really harmless."

"I think your brother is a sad young man," I responded finally, "and I felt sorry for him. He seems adrift to me like a little boy lost in a crowd looking for a familiar face."

Douglas and I shared an odd little moment when the sounds of dining around us disappeared, all the people, too, and it was just the two of us looking at each other across the table.

"Drew's right, you know," Douglas said quietly and at my blank look added, "You are 'The Warm Woman,' both kind and beautiful. I'm not sure which one I find more delightful."

Later that night as we stood by the front door of Hull-House, I let him kiss me, nothing passionate, only the lightest of touches, and when he would have had more, I opened the door and stepped inside as I had the Saturday before.

"Good night, Douglas. Thank you. I had a lovely time."

"Perhaps next Saturday—?"

"No," I replied firmly. "I really can't afford to be out every weekend as pleasant as it is. I have a job here and I need to spend more time at it."

"Are you saying you don't wish to see me again?" he asked carefully, no emotion coloring his voice.

"I'm not saying that at all. I would like to see you again, but with some time in between. I have much too limited a wardrobe to do this every Saturday." I tried to make a weak joke, but he was too serious to appreciate my humor.

"When then?"

"A month."

"A month?" He was clearly taken aback.

"It's the end of February now. What about the first weekend after Easter? That's only five weeks. Perhaps the weather will cooperate enough to do what your brother suggested: enjoy the Art Institute and take a walk in the park. I really can't accept these continued extravagant dinners. They're costly for you. I'd be more comfortable doing something simpler."

"I don't know of any better way to spend my money

than in your company, Katherine, and I think a five-week wait is excessive, but I'm quickly finding out that I can't deny you anything and in fact don't want to. Five weeks from today then. Regardless of the weather, I'll pick you up for a visit to the Art Institute and a light supper if that suits you. Don't concern yourself with the cost. You can continue to save the world while I buy and sell it."

Back in my rooms, I was conscious of a vague relief at the imposed month's separation and was confused about the feeling. I only knew my relationship with Douglas Gallagher was moving too fast for me, and I needed somehow to catch a breath and regain a focus on my vocation that I felt I could lose entirely if I wasn't careful. Douglas's closeness and the touch of his lips had panicked me for a moment—not in a fearful or distasteful way—and because I wasn't a naïve innocent to be alarmed by the touch of a man, I needed time to examine exactly why I had such mixed and conflicting feelings about him.

Although my sister-in-law, Hope, was most like me in temperament, even she, when she's with my brother—there's no accounting for some women's tastes, I sometimes tell John Thomas teasingly—is lovingly demonstrative. I could never imagine being that way with Douglas Gallagher, no encircling his waist from behind to give him a quick hug, no gentle pressure on his arm in passing, no kiss dropped on the top of his head as he sat. Those were the easy, unforced gestures I was used to among my family, but they were impossible to imagine with Douglas, and whose shortcoming was it that the picture wouldn't come, his or mine? I welcomed the break from his company.

March forced its way in with a snowstorm, a lion for sure. The wind off the lake was fierce and unrelenting and the cold unusually bitter for so late in the season, I was told. People showed up at the dispensary doors just for shelter, and I never had the heart to turn anyone away. One man carried in a child who had died in his arms en route to us. We all wept. I treated several cases of frostbite, one serious enough to lose toes, which shouldn't have surprised anyone since the boy was sockless and had holes in his boots. So much needless grief, I thought restlessly, so much pain and suffering that could have been avoided.

We saw happy occurrences, too: babies born, lung diseases improved with the available new treatments, an old woman's chronically ulcerated leg completely healed to her excessive and dancing delight, and children leaving healthier than they'd arrived because of better nutrition and the classes offered at Hull-House.

Alice Hamilton and I made another foray into garbage boxes.

"Nothing in the first specimens," she confessed crankily, "but I know the little winged devils are there and I'll find them." Then, looking at me and chuckling a little, she added, "*We'll* find them, I should say. You're the one who said it, Katherine. 'Look for the germ,' you said, and that's what we'll keep doing until we find it."

I was glad to be able to concentrate entirely on my patients and the research contributions I was allowed to make without that uncomfortably exciting, slightly breathless feeling that the presence of Douglas Gallagher always aroused.

Around the middle of March when the Irish exuberantly celebrated St. Patrick, I made a trip downtown to the Carson Pirie Scott department store to find a walking dress suitable both for Easter celebrations and for a stroll through the Art Institute. I couldn't keep on borrowing clothes or assigning myself as a project for the Girls' Home Skills Club. For at least the hundredth time I wished I had paid more attention to my mother all the times she had tried to teach me sewing and knitting skills, but it was too late for that, and she hadn't been very good at them either, for that matter. If my sister-in-law, Hope, were closer, she could turn something out for me in twenty-four hours, something as elegant and lovely as anything I could buy off the rack, but of course distance precluded that as an option. Anything new would have to be store-bought.

I knew Marshall Field's would be out of my price range but hoped I might be able to find something at Carson Pirie Scott. That department store, an impressive downtown building even from the outside, stood twelve stories high with detailed metalwork that started around the heavy glass front doors and extended up two floors. Rows of what were coming to be known as 'Chicago windows' stretched all along the remaining white terra cotta exterior.

As I leisurely strolled by the jewelry displays, I heard my name called and turned to see Drew Gallagher standing before me. He looked very debonair in a light morning suit and carried his coat over his arm. He really had a charming smile—perhaps calculated for just the reaction I was experiencing but charming just the same.

"Miss Davis," Drew said, "how delightful to see you. Are you out looking for a recreational diamond?"

"Is there such a thing? I didn't realize that. No, I'm only enjoying their sparkle en route to the women's floor. I couldn't help but stop, though; they're all so beautiful."

"Be careful you don't start coveting. As I recall from several lectures on the subject, that's one of the seven deadly sins."

"It seems to me there are more than seven, Mr. Gallagher."

"Please call me Drew. I think it's all right since we met earlier and we share my brother as a mutual contact. Have you seen Douglas lately?"

"No. I've been busy as I'm sure he has. We are going to take your advice about the Art Institute at the end of the month, though. I was glad you suggested it. I'm too new to know what's suitable."

"Suitable?"

"A suitable outing, something sensible and pleasant and not excessively costly so it will be within my range of comfort. I have strange sensitivities."

Drew gave me a quick, serious look, at odds with his urbane chatter, and invited, "Could I interest you in a cup of tea? There's a little tea room just a floor away with cream cakes so good you'll want to stuff them in your pockets." I nodded and laughed.

"Now there's a picture I'd want to send home, me sidling toward the door with cream oozing down my coat. My mother would be here in a heartbeat to take me by the ear and drag me home, sure I'd been corrupted by the big city."

"Where is home?"

"Wyoming."

Leaving the elevator, Drew led me with a hand under my elbow to the tea room and settled us both at a small table.

"I'll need to write that down," he said seriously. "You're the first person I've ever met from that state. Are you a cowgirl?"

I had a quick, vivid memory of Becca and me as we galloped full speed across the pastures on horses bred for speed and stamina, both us girls screaming with the pleasure of it, the wind knocking off my hat and streaming my hair like a flag.

"Not exactly," I answered with a smile, "but close enough."

"Really?" He stopped what he was doing and stared at me a moment. "Then you're the first cowgirl I've met, too.

An afternoon of firsts. I don't think I can take the excitement."

"You talk a lot of nonsense, Drew, but I'd guess it's for effect. Were you shopping for something or someone special?"

"Neither. Only a present for a woman of my acquaintance."

"What an unkind thing to say."

"Was it?" He met my look and had the grace to look sheepish. "Yes, it was unkind, wasn't it? But truthful. She's not special, and I only want some small thing to placate her so the object doesn't have to be special either."

I put up a hand. "Stop. Don't tell me any more, please. It's information I neither want nor need to know. Tell me instead what you do all day."

"I couldn't tell you all the details—you'd be shocked."

"I'm not easily shocked."

"You were the other night when I spoke of my mother's death. You thought I didn't notice, but your eyes changed color and you lost your glow for a minute. It was hard for someone to miss, even an insensitive lout like myself."

"I was shocked," I admitted, "and I suppose it showed. I wonder if you're really as blasé about her death as you act."

"You shouldn't try to measure me against your wholesome upbringing, Cowgirl Kate, because it's neither a fair nor accurate comparison."

"I believe in certain absolutes, regardless of upbringing, and don't call me Kate. My name is Katherine."

"What an interesting woman you are. I can't imagine what it is about my brother that would make you want to spend time in his company. He's such a serious stick. Has he ever said anything to make you laugh out loud?" His question brought me up short because its inference was so true. "I rest my case," he added, watching my face, then said, not unkindly, "I didn't mean to make you uncomfortable. Forgive me and have another cake."

I found Drew Gallagher a contradiction in terms—at once a thoughtful conversationalist and an affected dilettante, but I liked him nevertheless. In some respects, in fact, I found him more genuinely likable than Douglas, but I would have to give that concession more thought later, during some quiet evening in front of the fire—if I were fortunate to have such an evening again. They had been few and far between of late.

"And what do *you* do all day, Miss Davis, besides peruse gems and shop? How like a woman."

"This is the first time in my life that I've perused gems, and I'm only shopping out of necessity. I'm a doctor, right now working at Hull-House, which I'm sure you've heard of, so my dress is limited to white coats and smocks. I'm forced to supplement my wardrobe if I don't want to cause a stir at the Art Institute."

"A doctor?" Drew sounded honestly surprised, with nothing artificial in his reaction. "Really? You don't look the type at all."

"What type is that?"

"You know, spectacles and frizzy hair and a serious, furrowed brow."

"Except for the spectacles, you've accurately described me so I think I am the type after all." I put down my napkin and gathered up my purse, adding, "Thank you for the treat, Drew. Your timing was perfect. I do have to go or I'll be late for an evening meeting with my mentor, Dr. Pasca. Do you know the name?" He shook his head, still mentally digesting my vocation. "Dr. Emil Pasca is an internationally noted bacteriologist and should be considered as much a Chicago treasure as The Rookery." I stood and extended a hand. "Thank you again. It was nice to see an unexpected familiar face this afternoon."

He stood and continued to hold my hand but unlike his brother, such a gesture didn't make me feel I must quickly free it and back up a step. Whatever it was about Douglas that caused that reaction in me was not present in his brother.

"You're welcome. It was a treat for me, too. I had no idea that intelligent women could be such good company." His mouth twisted with the words and I realized he intended to mock himself. The words were the first really natural thing he'd said all afternoon. "I wasn't joking earlier about Douglas, Katherine. I really don't know what it is about him that would make you enjoy his company. You have little in common."

"I know," I admitted, "but maybe that's the answer. I can't presume to speak for Douglas, of course, so you might ask him the same question."

"Oh, I understand what he enjoys in you. I understand that very well. We are brothers, you know—although if siblings could divorce, he would have filed with an attorney a long time ago. It's what you see in Douglas that puzzles me." I couldn't respond because truthfully the same question puzzled me even more, so I just shrugged and smiled a good-bye.

I had the vague feeling that Drew Gallagher didn't approve of Douglas seeing me and couldn't decide if I felt insulted or flattered by his reaction. Most of the time it was impossible to tell whether Drew was sincere or simply outrageous, and I knew I should discount everything he said as idle talk and forget it, but I couldn't. There remained the little nagging idea that Drew had tried to tell me something in his own way, something I was either too simple or too dense to understand.

I shopped successfully and went home with a tailored walking suit in a conservative shade of blue and a pretty, high-necked white lace blouse that would soften the suit's effect somewhat. I had decided on a hat, too, one with a fashionably broad and curled brim, ornamented with a small clump of artificial violets and tiny blue feathers. If I was honest with myself, I knew buying the hat was a reaction to Drew's stereotype of women doctors. Glasses and frizzy hair indeed! My purchase was not a woman doctor's hat by his description, and as soon as the salesgirl brought it out, I had to have it. The hat used up the last of my savings, but I could refill the coffers over the next few months so I would have enough money to buy a train ticket home when the time came.

Seated on the elevated train, I watched the winter-dirty landscape slide by and surprised myself by wanting to be home very much at that moment. I pictured my mother's smile or Lily Kate's unruly curls, longed to hear the click of the loom as my sister-in-law wove and gossiped with me at the same time or link an arm with my Uncle Billy and watch his face light up. Where had that little burst of homesickness come from? I wondered. Probably too much winter. I was certain I'd feel much better once the sun reappeared.

CHAPTER 7

The children of the nursery began calling me Dr. Kat out of nowhere and with no prompting that I could uncover. I truly wasn't fond of nicknames but realized after my first few feeble attempts at correction that the name would stick in spite of me.

"My niece and nephew call me Aunt Kat," I shared with Mrs. Teague, "so I suppose *Doctor* Kat was inevitable." She chuckled as she held a little girl in her arms and unconsciously bounced her against her hip.

"They're very fond of you, Dr. Davis. We were just commenting that it seems like you've been with us for years instead of only a few weeks."

"I feel the same way." I looked around at the green decorations of shamrocks and leprechaun hats. "How did the party go?"

"Everyone had a good time. Miss Addams believes in respecting the celebrations of all the neighborhoods, but even if that weren't the case, by March we all feel the need for some kind of festivities. Thank goodness, Easter is early this year and welcome."

"I know. Petra's already made a list of hiding places for the eggs. I can recall being so bundled up I could hardly move as my sister and brothers and I searched for eggs in the barn with snow falling and the wind whistling through the rafters. My poor parents had to blow on their hands for warmth but they were determined we'd have the fun of the hunt. We did, too, even though my older brother always had to find the most and wasn't above snitching eggs out of other people's baskets when we weren't looking." Mrs. Teague gave me an interested look.

"You don't speak of your family often, Dr. Davis, but when you do, it makes me think I'd like them."

"They're a pretty likeable group," I said, gathering up my papers and slipping them into my voluminous pockets, "except my older brother. He's still a brat." But I smiled to myself as I went out the door.

John Thomas had been a husband for nearly five years and was a father twice over, more serious than he used to be but softer, too, and less inclined to boss people around. Not really such a brat at all, if he ever had been. It was usually my influence that had brought out the worst in him so maybe I blamed the wrong person altogether.

That evening after supper Petra and I met at the dispensary. As I made my rounds of the patients there, she chattered about her music lessons, wearing her happiness as if it were a cloak. Her arm had been freed of its splint and to look at her, one would never have matched this cheerful child to the bedraggled, beaten girl, who had huddled in the doorway barely able to raise her head. Petra remained invariably good-natured, always eager to help, and gentle with the children. Destined for fame, too, I thought to myself. I'd listened outside the music room door more than once to her soaring soprano. Well, maybe she'd remember me with front row tickets to a performance in a grand hall one day. It would be fun to point her out on posters and advertisements that announced her performances and say I knew her when—

The bell on the alley door rang that night and we both hurried to it, Petra right behind me as she had done many times before. If it was someone with poor English, her presence as translator could literally be a lifesaver, and she often kept little ones occupied so I could have private time with their mothers.

No woman stood at the door that night, however, but a rough man with a cap pulled over thinning, unkempt, black hair and both hands shoved into his coat pockets. He eyed me and began to speak, then looked behind me to where Petra stood, snapped out her name, and tried to push past me toward her. I heard her gasp and turned to see such a look of terror and shock on her face that I knew instantly that this man was responsible for her miserable condition weeks before. As she backed up, not taking her eyes off him, I quickly stepped between them. He ran up against me and, because I must have seemed only an annoying, negligible obstacle, tried to push me aside to get to her. I adjusted my stance so that once more I stood squarely between the man and Petra.

He shouted something in a language I didn't understand. I recognized only her name in his furious rush of words, but after a moment I put both hands against his chest and spoke in a forceful voice much louder and sterner than his.

"Your conduct is unacceptable here, sir. This is a dispensary and you are disturbing my patients. I will call the authorities if you do not leave immediately."

The intruder didn't leave, but he did stop trying to push

past me and he stopped shouting, too. He simply stood staring at Petra as if I weren't present at all.

"She is my daughter," he said finally in rough English. "You have no right to keep a daughter from her father."

I half-turned toward her. "Petra?"

"Yes," she said, her voice barely above a whisper. She raised frightened, even desperate, eyes to me. "He is my father, but I won't go back with him. Don't make me. I'll just run away again if you do. Please, Dr. Davis, don't make me leave with him." An unspoken—yet clear and unmistakable—message passed from her to me, and I knew there was no way I could send her back to whatever it was that caused such a fearful and pained look on her face. I would do whatever it took to ensure that she was safe.

"I want you to go your room now," I told Petra, but she stood frozen, her face as white as ice and her lips beginning to tremble as if from the cold. I turned back to the man and held both my hands toward him, palms up.

"If you take one more step, sir, I will be forced to call the constable on the beat."

Stepping from the dispensary's waiting area, Mrs. Tabachnik asked, "Is there trouble, Doctor? I just saw Officer Kelly outside, and it won't take a minute for him to be right here." I gauged the man's expression.

"Take Petra to her room please, Mrs. Tabachnik," I said finally. "Come right back and I'll be able to tell you then if we need Officer Kelly's aid."

"I don't like to leave you."

"I'll be fine." I turned to face the man, who stood balanced on the balls of his feet as if ready to spring forward. "Won't I?" Anger and frustration showed so clearly on his face that the words might as well have been written on his forehead, but I could read something else there, too: a calculating awareness that told me he knew he had better move carefully. My initial reading of the man was that he was coarse and violent but no fool.

He didn't speak, only gave a brief nod and stood there with legs akimbo, one hand holding his hat and the other clenched into a fist. With unblinking eyes he watched Petra disappear down the hallway with Mrs. Tabachnik.

"You can't keep a daughter from her father," he growled again in accented English, his voice a rumble and latent violence still showing at the back of his eyes. "It ain't right."

"You beat her, Mr. Stravinsky. It is Stravinsky, isn't it?" He didn't respond to my question, and I went on, "Do you think I'd turn her over to you so you can break her other arm?"

"That wasn't my fault. She don't always do what she's told. A man has a right to make his children listen."

I was so furious I could hardly speak, and my anger must have shown on my face because when I moved toward him, he was the one that backed up hastily, not sure exactly what I intended but suddenly conscious that I was in the mood for action.

"No man has a right to beat a child, father or not. No man has a right to do that. You will have her back when hell freezes over, Mr. Stravinsky, and not a day sooner. Do you understand me?"

"You ain't got a right to break up a family. I'll get a lawyer. He'll make you give her back."

"You get a lawyer, Mr. Stravinsky. Get a hundred lawyers for all I care. Once I describe your daughter's injuries and how she looked the night she came here, you'd be lucky not to spend the next few years in jail. So go do whatever you want except—" I went close enough to tap his chest with my forefinger hard "—don't ever come back here and don't ever bother Petra again. Because if you do, I will use all the force and all the power of my position to make sure it only happens one time. I know many people, Mr. Stravinsky, and I can make your miserable life much worse. Believe me, I don't make idle threats. Do you understand what I'm telling you?" Stravinsky stepped back and shifted his posture—poised to strike me, I thought.

The man was as angry as I, not used to being confronted by a woman and clearly not enjoying the experience, but when he pulled back his arm, I said in a cold and sneering voice I didn't recognize as my own, "Go ahead. Just touch me, just once, and if they don't hang you, you'll spend a lifetime in prison, which might be the best thing for Petra after all."

Mrs. Tabachnik spoke from behind me. "Should I get Officer Kelly, Doctor?"

"Well, should she?" I asked Stravinsky. He shoved on his hat, furious and hating me all the while, and left without a word through the same door he had entered. As soon as he was gone, I locked the door and leaned against it to gaze at Mrs. Tabachnik.

"Have you ever seen him before?" I asked.

She shook her head. "Was that Petra's father?"

The two of us shared a look, I still leaning against the door as if keeping evil at bay on the other side and both of us remembering our first sight of Petra. Finally I straightened, calm once more.

"He may be her father, Mrs. Tabachnik, but for my purpose he was a vagrant up to no good. If he ever comes back we should fetch the constable immediately, and thank you, your help was invaluable." She understood me completely, nodded, and walked past me back to the patients.

"You're welcome, Doctor, but it would have taken a braver man than that one to stand up to you with that look on your face and that tone in your voice. Whoever he was, I don't think he'll come back but if he does, we'll take care of him. You can't be too careful, I always say."

I grabbed an old wool coat from a corner coat tree as I headed down the hall.

"I'll be back, Nurse. I'm going to check on Petra."

I knocked on the girl's door and softly called her name. She opened it immediately, anticipating my arrival I suspected, and stood in the doorway, no tears, just a pale, resolute little face, her lips pressed firmly together and her eyes fierce.

"I won't go back. I meant it. I'll run away again and again, as often as it takes until I'm of age."

"May I come in?"

She pulled open the door and I stepped inside. All the apartments were the same: small, square, and spotless with one simple chair and a bed and bureau. Enough. More, in fact, than most of the lodgers had ever had to themselves before. I thought it must be so for Petra.

"Did you think I would let him take you away against your will, Petra? I promised that you could stay here, and I meant that. This is your home now."

She put one hand over her mouth and sat abruptly on the edge of the bed, her legs appearing to lose the strength to support her. Her face crumpled into tears, but she tried to cry quietly behind her hand, embarrassed, it seemed to me, by the display of emotion. I sat beside her and put an arm around her shoulders.

"Don't cry, Petra. You're safe. I promised you'd be safe here and I meant it. No one will force you to leave while I'm here, not your father, not anyone. He'll never beat you again."

"It wasn't just that." Petra caught her breath, choked back the last tears, and raised her eyes to meet my look fully, ready at last to tell me what for her had long been unspeakable. "It was worse. I could have stood the beatings, Dr. Davis. If it had been only that, I would have stayed for my brothers' sake, but it was worse."

"I don't understand," I said but feared I was beginning to.

"It wasn't so bad before Mama died, before we came to Chicago. He would only hit Mama once in a while, only when he was drunk. When we lived in New York, we even did things like a real family sometimes. Once we went to the harbor to watch the ships and Mama packed a lunch. He was happy then, and Mama was, too. But she died and we came here and he didn't know anyone and he said it was all right. I was the mama now, he said, and it was all right for him to do what he did. He said it would be our secret, and I wasn't to tell anyone." All the terrible words came pouring out of her in a whisper. "The first time I didn't know what to do and he hurt me. I cried and told him to stop, but he said I was the mama now and I'd get used to it, but I never did and I couldn't stand it any more. I took a knife and I planned to kill him this last time, but I couldn't, I couldn't. I was weak."

Her words were a moan of failure and regret that twisted around my heart in a tangible, physical way. For a moment I couldn't breathe for sorrow.

"He beat me and said he'd kill me if I ever tried anything like that again. I didn't know what to do. He wasn't always like that. He was my papa, my papa, and I didn't know what to do and I was so ashamed." We sat very quietly for a long time. I kept one arm around Petra's shoulders, enraged and grieving for lost innocence. I wanted to weep, too.

"There's nothing for you to be ashamed about," I said finally. "You didn't do anything wrong, Petra. You were not the mother; you were just a child. Your father was wrong to treat you so and he knew it. That's why he told you not to tell anyone. Fathers do not treat their daughters in such a way. It's always wrong, but it's not your fault." The girl was like a little sponge, soaking up every word I said, turning to watch my face intently as I spoke.

"Do I disgust you?"

"Disgust me?" My tone was incredulous but calm, the doctor returned to her practice. "No, Petra. You do not, could not ever disgust me. Why would you think such a thing? I admire you. You did a brave thing to risk further injury and run away." Then I added casually, "Tell me, has your monthly cycle been regular since you've been here?"

She looked at me blankly at the abrupt change of subject but nodded, and I felt a huge relief. No child with child then.

"You won't tell Mr. Sweeney, will you?" Petra asked plaintively. "I couldn't bear for him to know. He might not want to be my teacher then."

Standing up I said, "I won't tell a soul, Petra, but I think you wrong Mr. Sweeney if you imagine you could tell him anything that would keep him from giving you your lessons. Sometimes I think he enjoys them more than you do." Then I suggested nonchalantly, "Sometime in the next month, I want you to come to me for a full medical exam, just to be sure you're well and healthy and ready for your musical career. Will you remind me so we can make an appointment?"

She nodded dumbly again, plainly exhausted from emotion, the circles under her eyes more violet than the eyes themselves. I rested a hand against her cheek.

"It's all right, my dear. You can trust me." She reached up a hand to cover mine, almost shy.

"I do trust you, Dr. Davis. I trust you more than anyone in the world." The look in her eyes humbled me.

I said good night and walked slowly back to my apartment, stepped outside for needed air and took the long way home through the quad, slid my key into the dispensary's door, gave a nod to the night nurse in passing, and trudged to my rooms so deep in thought that later I couldn't remember doing any of those things.

Then, Petra-like, I sat down abruptly on the edge of my own bed and put my hand over my mouth, my father's face as clear in front of me as if he stood there, a man who had never once raised a hand or even a voice to any of his children. My father, John Davis, was the most decent and patient man I knew, who protected and cared for his family even at his own risk, read out loud to us from the newspaper, let me beat him at checkers and crow about it later, and after long, cold, physically grueling days always found time to hear our prayers and tuck us into bed at night with a kiss. I never heard a word of complaint from my father about anything. Ever. He remained a formal man, reserved in public and uncomfortable with open displays of emotion but, following my mother's lead, was demonstrative and loving in the privacy of our home. All our lives we had trusted him completely without conscious thought, sure he was never wrong and proud that we were his children. My brothers and sister and I found plenty to argue about as we grew up, but we held one common belief so fundamental it never needed to be voiced: John Davis was the best and bravest father anyone could have.

"I love you, Papa," I said aloud into the room, slipping into the name from my childhood. He had given me what Petra would never know, and I had taken that for granted all my life, as if it were my due, as if all children experienced the kind of love he gave and sacrifices he made. I would never be able to thank him enough.

The Saturday before Easter a box arrived for me, yellow

roses and blue forget-me-nots tied together with a paisley ribbon of the same colors, a bouquet of welcome spring colors. *The longest month of my life will end at two o'clock next Saturday*, Douglas had written in his bold script.

I carried the card in my pocket all that day and took it out to read surreptitiously when I had a moment to do so. Was the man really serious or was it just part of his social game? My heart gave a little turn inside me and somehow ended up in my stomach whenever I considered the weekend to come. Was it normal for a woman to feel this way? How could I know? It wasn't as if I could walk up to Miss Smith and ask, 'By the way, Mary, would you happen to know if it's a typical effect for a man to make a woman slightly breathless and more than a little nervous but not exactly in a bad way?' Hardly a question to inspire confidence in the mature judgment of her resident physician. I would simply have to learn by experience and hope for the best.

Easter weekend remained overcast but mild, a precursor of spring I hoped, and Saturday's egg hunt went off without a hitch. Petra, in charge, had carried out her duties with alarming gusto. Eggs were hidden everywhere for the neighborhood children, under seats in the theater and behind sofa cushions. I had to draw the line when I saw her tuck an egg under a bed pillow in the infirmary. My refusal to participate hardly dimmed her enthusiasm.

"It's not," she pointed out, "as if I picked a bed where someone was resting."

"That fine point did escape me," I replied as I steered her and her basket of eggs to the door, "but it doesn't change my mind. The doctor's rule book says no Easter eggs are allowed to be hidden in hospital rooms. I'll show you chapter and verse sometime. Go to the gymnasium instead. You'll have lots of room for shrieking children there."

The dark circles I had noticed under Petra's eyes had disappeared and she looked herself again, petite and happy, preoccupied only with finding enough egg hiding places for the hordes of tenement children that would descend on us.

The Easter egg hunt turned out to be fun, even for the observers, and I had the unexpected satisfaction of being approached by more than one mother, who wanted to thank me for something I had done for her or her child.

"I've only been here three months," I said as an aside to Mary Smith as we stood on the front lawn and watched the scrambling egg hunters. "I don't remember talking to that many people, let alone assisting them in some way. Was I sleepwalking?"

"There's such a great need, Dr. Davis, so many people to reach, so many new arrivals to the city every week, that I'd be surprised if you could remember most of the people you made contact with." Her eyes followed Petra's movements around the yard. "Your Petra was a find. I've heard her sing. Miss Addams has, too, and she's trying to arrange a scholarship for her to the University's School of Music."

"Really?" I turned to face Mary, pleased at the news. "That's just what Petra needs: an academic setting and taskmasters that will be able to round out her education. Not that Mr. Sweeney doesn't do a fine job. He's a good beginning for her, but Petra will outdistance him soon if she hasn't already. She's a natural for reading music and has an easy ear for the languages. Wouldn't it be wonderful someday to say that the famous Petra Stravinsky was an alumna of Hull-House?"

When I mentioned the scholarship to Jane Addams that evening, she nodded. "It's very feasible, Katherine, but don't say anything about it until I'm certain of all the arrangements. We've offered assistance to other talented young people, and Petra is the most gifted I've heard. It's possible she could start at the university with the fall term."

I thought what a thrill that would be for Petra, a joyful circumstance long overdue considering the tragic, bleak life she had known to date. If nothing else happened the entire year, Petra's progress alone would make my visit worthwhile.

Petra began work with the Hull-House theatrical group the next week on a production of Gilbert and Sullivan's *The Mikado,* with her as the perfect Yum Yum and Patrick Sweeney as her ineffective guardian, Ko-Ko. There was something deliciously ironic in the casting and having read the libretto, I knew the show would be well worth seeing. When Petra pirouetted around the nursery, holding a child in her arms as if they were dancing, all the babies stopped their fussing as if on cue and the toddlers watched her enrapt and wide-eyed. Even Mrs. Teague came to a standstill, smiling at Petra's excitement.

"She'll be in the motion pictures someday," she said to me, "although that would be a shame because then we'd never get to hear that pretty voice."

I thought that Petra possessed unlimited prospects, so talented and pretty and carrying an inner strength one would never have guessed from her petite frame and that delicate, heart-shaped face.

The following Saturday I dressed in my new suit, pleased with its tailored, almost severe lines and unremarkable blue color. The outfit had been just the thing for Easter Sunday, what a doctor should wear, professional, unpretentious, and unaffected. The hat was another thing altogether. At the last minute I'd decided to wear a more modest hat for Easter services, something mundane and unremarkable. Easter Sunday was hardly about me, after all, and I didn't want to draw particular attention to myself.

I still eyed the new hat with misgiving and thought its

purchase a mistake, but by the Saturday after Easter it was too late to consider returning it. Once on, however, the hat looked charming, even on me, the flowers and feathers whimsical and its tilt flirtatious without being showy, a hat my lovely sister Becca would have selected and worn with much more flair than I.

When I opened the door to Douglas Gallagher, I felt a rush of self-indulgent satisfaction that I hadn't returned the hat. I saw undisguised appreciation in his eyes coupled with another emotion hard to name, an emotion that made me feel like a deer suddenly come face-to-face with a mountain lion. Something of the carnivore in Douglas Gallagher, I thought, but instead of fear, I felt only a confusing mixture of gratification and excitement.

Douglas brought flowers again, a bunch of violets that perfectly matched the spray of flowers on my hat. When I commented on the coincidence, he shrugged.

"You shouldn't be so quick to credit coincidence, Katherine. In my experience, it has very little real impact on life." I looked up from pinning the flowers onto my jacket.

"But what else could it be? You couldn't have known I'd wear violets on my hat today."

"No? I suppose you're right."

But I heard something in his tone that made me edgy. I remembered how he had known all about my family and me, how he had recited the facts of my life and how uneasy I'd felt at the time. I didn't like the idea that I was somehow being spied upon. The thought seemed incredible, but the violets were an exact match and he was very pleased with himself.

Douglas handed me another check from his pocket. "Before I forget, please accept this in honor of Easter or spring or just because I'm glad to see you again."

"You're too generous."

"That remains to be seen." I detected the same enigmatic tone that had caused me earlier disquiet, but then he smiled and said, "I'm sure you can find a use for it that will benefit the people you care so passionately about. That's my only motivation, Katherine." I put the check carefully in the hall bureau drawer and turned a thankful smile to him.

"Of course, we can put your kind donation to good use. Thank you, Douglas."

The weather was perfect, sunny and as warm as June, and the day was nearly perfect, too. Douglas knew a great deal more about art than I and was an informative guide through the Art Institute.

"For a man of business, you seem very comfortable in the arts," I told him. "I think I'm surprised."

"You shouldn't be. Chicago capitalists bought every painting in this place. I know each one's history and can appreciate it for its material worth even if its aesthetic appeal sometimes escapes me."

I lingered in front of one of the museum's new acquisitions: a portrait of a woman in a striped dress carefully bathing her child, both dark heads bent to the water, something natural and endearing in the shared, common activity.

"Mary Cassatt," Douglas read, "*The Child's Bath.* From the look on your face you must like it."

"I do, very much. I thought the El Greco was grand and its colors magnificent, but I'd never hang it in my parlor." I looked at the Cassatt again, caught how trustingly the chubby child relaxed in her mother's arms and how tenderly intent the woman was on so prosaic a purpose. The mother's strong hands that protectively supported the child reminded me of my own mother's hands. "This one, though, takes me back to my childhood. I could look at it every day, I think, and be comforted by its message of home and family."

"I didn't expect you to have a turn for such domesticity."

"Domesticity—is that what it's called? More like the ordinary affection of day-to-day life, which anyone can appreciate. Why would it surprise you that I can be as charmed by such tenderness as the next person?"

Later, among the sculpture, Douglas commented, "Now you really do surprise me. Not a blush."

At first I didn't understand what he meant but then realized I was giving a statue of a nude man the same scrutiny I gave patients.

"I'm a doctor, Douglas. I don't think the human form holds many surprises for me any more. In my first year of medical school the professor wanted all the women students to leave the room so he could set up a screen behind which we would dutifully stand so we wouldn't be exposed to the naked male body." I gave an undignified snort. "As if that would have done at all! We women just refused to leave. Period. It was either continue in front of our maidenly eyes or cancel the class and fall behind, so the professor gave in. Very ungracefully, I might add, and with constant pointed asides about how progress had ruined women."

"You're a woman of the new century, Dr. Davis." I couldn't decipher Douglas's tone and chose to respond lightly.

"Not so new any more with the first decade behind us, but times are changing. I predict female suffrage in America by the end of the next decade."

"Women will never have the vote," he said to goad me, and we spent the next hour in sporadic, pleasant argument.

We walked through Grant Park, most of its classic gardens just beginning to green while a few early daffodils lined the paths and brightened the shadowy spots under trees. Without quite knowing when or how, I found my hand tucked under Douglas's arm and my shoulder pressed against him. The tilt of my hat's brim forced me to come closer still to speak to him so that I caught his fragrance, something clean with a touch of spice, very pleasant.

As we sat on a park bench together, the warmth of the sun made me lethargic, almost sleepy, and I felt like resting my head against his shoulder to take a quick nap. I was that comfortable. We both stopped speaking and just sat there very close in the sun. As if from far away I could hear the persistent buzzing of a bee, a murmur of laughter, a baby's cry, almost as if there were two worlds, Douglas and I the sole inhabitants of ours.

He brought his mouth to my ear and said quietly, "I find myself thinking about you most of the time, Katherine, picturing you with your hair down, wanting to see the gold flecks in your eyes catch the candlelight again, my own enchanting Warm Woman, everything about you honey and velvet. Is it too much to hope that you give a passing thought to me now and then?"

I liked the whisper of his voice in my ear and his breath against my cheek. Combined with the languid warmth of the early spring sun the moment seemed very seductive, and when I turned my face to respond, he kissed me. A practiced, possessive kiss but very enjoyable, nevertheless, even if it unsettled me. Nothing like the fumblings of adolescents but something else entirely. You're not a child anymore, I thought, and reacted to his kiss on a level that was definitely not childlike: instinctive, passionate, lingering.

The laughter of a real child invaded our world, and I snapped away from Douglas, hoping no one I knew was enjoying the park around us. How would I ever explain my conduct? Being kissed on a park bench would not become Hull-House or enhance the professional image I wanted to cultivate. Douglas stood up and raised me with a hand under my elbow.

"It's all right." His eyes glinted and I detected humor in his voice. "No one saw us." Then, as if nothing had happened, he began to talk about something completely inconsequential and guided me along the pathway to the curb where Fritz waited. "I thought something light for supper. Sandwiches and fruit, perhaps. Fritz, we'll go to *Leonie's*."

Inside the motorcar I sat quietly, not interested in supper. Instead, I scrambled for my composure as I mentally examined my unexpected response to his kiss with the same scrutiny I might give a specimen under a microscope.

"You didn't answer my question, Katherine, although I admit I didn't give you much opportunity to reply. Is it too much to hope?"

I turned my head toward him, remembering his question very well. "I do think of you, Douglas, but to be truthful only now and then. I have a full schedule and a busy life." If my response disappointed or annoyed him, the emotion didn't show on his face.

"Perhaps that will change. Perhaps I've given you more to think about."

I turned away and settled myself more comfortably in my seat, repeating the thought I'd had before: Douglas Gallagher was very practiced with women and had demonstrated more technique than real emotion in his kiss. Just the opposite from me, I thought candidly, and smiled at the humbling realization.

"Perhaps," I agreed before casually changing the subject. "Sandwiches and fruit sound perfect."

Before I said good-bye at the door, Douglas asked, "Will you make me wait another month, Katherine?"

"I don't believe I have the power to make you do anything, Douglas."

"You may be a degreed physician, but you're an innocent when it comes to men and women. You, like all women, hold the real power." I gave an unladylike hoot.

"Look around you, Douglas. Who holds office? Who leads armies? Who are the industrialists? Who holds the monopolies? It's not women in those positions, so don't try to persuade me that women have any real authority or control. We have none—at least not yet—only crumbs thrown us from the male largesse. Commenting on the attraction that men feel for women is a standard response from those who have neither the intention nor the desire to share their power and possessions, as if we poor fluttering females should agree that it is our physiology that gives us worth and nothing more."

I thought my response surprised and annoyed him, and he did not immediately reply.

"I think you underestimate the appeal that female physiology holds for the male," he stated finally.

"I doubt it. I have a general understanding of commodity trading and supply and demand." Then, because I knew my words bordered on spite, I added, "Forgive me if I sound ungrateful and unkind. I liked the Art Institute very much and supper, too. Thank you."

"I think I must have enjoyed our time in the park more than you," he said obliquely, then changed his tone. "I have tickets to the theater in two weeks. Probably something too melodramatic for you, but dissecting it with your dispassionate scientific mind might hold some small interest for you. Would you attend with me?" From his manner I was certain I'd irritated him and regretted my earlier diatribe, especially after he'd been so agreeable and generous.

"Don't be annoyed with me, Douglas. I've been told

I'm outspoken to a fault, but I don't speak my mind to be purposefully disagreeable."

He lifted my hand to his lips, then gave me a glittering smile that lit his black eyes. "I'm not annoyed with you and you're not disagreeable, purposefully or not." I reclaimed my hand.

"I'm glad. It would be poor manners on my part to exchange your kindness for my bad temper. I'd enjoy the theater, whatever's playing. I've never been to anything bigger than the college production of *As You Like It*, so it will be a treat."

With more technique than real emotion, I mollified him back into a good humor and thought as I watched him leave that doing so made us even.

April seemed a perfect month. The days warmed so that the children could go out on their playground—the first such area set aside specifically for children's activities in all of Chicago, if not the entire country. Dr. Hamilton and I made another early morning trip behind the garbage wagons. Petra sang everywhere she went.

"Three little maids from school are we / Pert as a schoolgirl well can be / Filled to the brim with girlish glee / Three little maids from school," she'd trill, then put both palms together and bow in front of me lost in giggles, making me giggle, too.

I attended the theater with Douglas Gallagher and enjoyed the production very much. The Auditorium Theater, which could seat over four thousand, was part of a seventeen-story building that also held four-hundred hotel rooms. The interior of the theater was very grand, with gold trim and plush seats and rich red carpeting. I was openly impressed, and Douglas was pleased. Sometimes, because he knew my rural background, I believed he expected me to feel more awed and overwhelmed by the big city and its cultural offerings than I actually was. He couldn't know that my father had entertained us as children by reciting Shakespearean sonnets and my mother had taught us to read by using classical literature, mature in themes and content but possessed of rich vocabulary and consummate grammar. I didn't have the heart to spoil the treat that Douglas intended an evening at the theater to be, and because I had never seen a building so formally grand as The Auditorium, it was easy to be sincerely impressed with the setting.

We saw *Salvation Nell* with the graceful and talented actress Minnie Maddern Fiske in the lead role, and if the fictional Nell wasn't anything like the women I saw at Hull-House on a daily basis, who was I to criticize? The theater should entertain, I told myself, and create a world of its own, and if it romanticized life and the effects of poverty, I supposed that was all right. Wasn't there enough grief and pain and despair in the real world as it was? When the lights dimmed and the play began I sat spellbound, startled when the first act came to an end, consciously and almost physically having to force myself back to the present. I turned to catch Douglas watching me.

"It's wonderful!" I exclaimed. "I never thought I'd have the opportunity to see an actress like Mrs. Fiske. She's everything the papers said about her! How did you ever get tickets? When I mentioned to someone that I would be coming, they said the production had been sold out for weeks." The theater was packed with not an empty seat in sight.

"Everything's available at the right price." He smiled, genuinely pleased at my transparent enthusiasm. "I'm glad you're enjoying it."

We stood and walked a little, my hand lightly on his arm, surrounded by a great deal of chatter and laughter. I wore the green gown from weeks before but still felt underdressed with so much finery around me, the lights twinkling off the women's jewelry and reflecting again in the huge mirrors on the lobby walls.

In honor of the special evening, Petra had appeared at my door as I dressed for the theater and volunteered to arrange my hair in a current popular style.

"You'll look just like a Gibson Girl," she said grimly as she wrestled with the weight and willfulness of my hair. I heard an implied "or else" at the end of her sentence.

When I caught a glimpse of myself in the lobby mirrors that evening, I was surprised at how well Petra had made good on her promise—or threat, whichever it was. My hair had the same soft look of the famously elegant but unrealistic Gibson woman, on a similarly slender neck, one John Thomas had matter-of-factly called a gooseneck. I recalled crying from hurt feelings and my mother telling me not to worry, that I had a beautiful neck and the rest of me would one day grow into it. From my reflection, my mother had been right—but just barely.

Petra had finished her efforts by pushing a curved, sweeping feather through the pompadour saying, "There. Anyone can wear jewelry, it's so common,"—I had to laugh at that because she didn't have a jewel to her name and I had one small and simple bracelet—"but this will set you apart as someone with more than common taste." The girl possessed an unerring eye for what worked when it came to appearance, a gift that would prove helpful once she began her performing career.

"What did you do this week, Douglas?" I asked, honestly curious about his day. From my background I was familiar with dawn-to-dusk physical labor, but I couldn't visualize what he did from hour to hour, day after day.

"Bought an apartment building, met a man with interests

in China to discuss raw silk, made an arrangement to ship beef in refrigerated cars to a group of butchers in Detroit, approved several loans on behalf of my bank in San Francisco. Thought of you."

I wished he wouldn't do that, I thought crossly—toss in some compliment that invariably caught me unawares. I did what I usually did—ignored the remark—and said, "You must have a great many contacts."

"They were the most significant part of my inheritance. My father was well known for his shrewd business sense, and he was very proud of his name and reputation. After he died, his business associates had no qualms about doing business with me and one contact always led to another."

We were stopped in our lobby stroll by a man who knew Douglas.

"I wouldn't have guessed you took time for the arts, Gallagher." Douglas introduced us and I nodded, smiling but saying nothing. The man looked at me, then added to Douglas, "But I can see the theater may not be the primary attraction here. I'm delighted to meet you, Miss Davis."

I waited for Douglas to correct him, to say, "*Doctor* Davis," and was surprised and disappointed when he didn't.

The man concluded, "This fellow's been all work and no play for as long as I've known him, Miss Davis, so I'm glad to see him out in the world enjoying the softer side of life." After he was gone, we turned to go back to our seats.

"Are you embarrassed that I'm a doctor, Douglas?"

He answered without pausing to reflect on my question, as if he had already thought the matter through and come to his own conclusion.

"When we're together, you're not a doctor. You're a beautiful woman I have the good fortune to be with at the time."

I considered his remark well into the last act. Evidently

he could separate the two, woman and doctor, and apparently preferred one over the other, maybe even found the doctor part to be some sort of obstacle. I, on the other hand, was unable to differentiate. It wasn't as if I had two natures and brought one out in the morning, then stored it in a box under the bed when I put on the other. If there was any kind of a future for us—and I found it impossible to consider that without feeling curiously confused, excited, and apprehensive—he would have to adjust to who and what I was. He would have to be as proud of saying "This is Dr. Davis" as he was of my appearance. Even prouder, since one was the real package and the other just the outside of the box.

We shared a late dinner at the restaurant on the tenth floor of the same building. I was hardly hungry, interested only in something light and sweet, and we lingered over coffee to discuss the play and politics and argue haphazardly over the right of workers to organize. Of course we disagreed, but I was careful to do so moderately and he was tolerant.

"Have you always been so opinionated?" he asked, placing my shawl around my shoulders and resting his hands there for a moment.

"Those long Wyoming winters and all that western air must breed opinionated women," I replied complacently. "It runs in my family. I've always been encouraged to think for myself."

He kissed me that night, surprised me really—we were still in the back of the motorcar. At first I was hotly embarrassed because Fritz sat in front of us, and I am my father's daughter. One's private moments are not for spectators. But it didn't take long for Douglas's insistent mouth to make me forget that someone else was present. He tilted my face with a palm against each cheek and his thumbs fixed under my chin so that I was immobile and would have had to jerk away awkwardly to escape him. Not that I ever gave a thought to do so. Clearly my longstanding suspicion that I had a cool, dispassionate, and unresponsive nature was groundless. He kissed me again by the front door, murmured my name and put both arms around me to pull me close, his hands and his mouth both so persistent that I finally had to push away, no longer comfortable with his touch.

"Are you going to reach for the doorknob and run away again?" he asked, still not freeing me despite my clear desire to be released. For a minute I felt a frisson of fear and thought that he was stronger than I and why should he stop if he didn't want to? But that was a quick and passing thought because he did release me, and I scolded myself for schoolgirl imaginings. The problem was that Douglas Gallagher was nothing like the young men I'd grown up with, who had handled me respectfully and cautiously, no doubt with the image of my father and older brother in their minds. No one had wanted either of the John Davises, senior or junior, to show up on his doorstep. Douglas was a different type of man altogether, a man new to me, with his own rules, used to his own way, and it was his commanding confidence that I found so intriguing. I couldn't account for why I had felt almost frightened. I stood on an open front porch with assistance just a call away if it came to that, which of course it didn't and wouldn't.

I took a breath to be sure my voice was steady, still disconcerted by that momentary intense panic, and said softly, "I don't think of it as running away. I think of it as a calculated retreat for the protection of the troops."

Douglas said my name and would have reached for me again, but I did exactly what he had said: turned the knob, opened the door, and backed inside, speaking as I did so.

"As usual I had a wonderful time this evening, but it's

my turn to extend an invitation. On May 14 we're putting on a production of *The Mikado* in good-natured challenge to the appearance of Halley's Comet that has everyone so worried. Will you come as my guest? I'll arrange an early dinner on the quad for us. I'm excited to show off a new talent who's dear to me, and I think it will be fun." Douglas stood just across the threshold from me, in shadow so that I couldn't see his face clearly.

"Is that the next time I'm allowed to see you?"

I said as sincerely and as kindly as I could, "Douglas, I have work here that means a great deal to me and only a year to learn as much as I can. If my schedule doesn't suit you, I understand." My tone expressed more than my words and he didn't miss the message.

"Your schedule doesn't suit me," he admitted, "but you suit me very well, so if May 14th is the next opportunity I have to be with you, I accept with pleasure." Then he brushed my cheek with the back of his hand, the only tender gesture I could remember him doing in all the weeks I'd known him. I saw him as the little boy he must have been, unaccustomed to affection, raised by strangers, and sent away by parents with priorities that did not include him. "You really have no idea what's going on here, do you?" he asked, and then added, "Good night, Katherine. I was very proud to be seen with you this evening."

I thought of both his departing comments for days afterward, his question and his statement. I had to confess that he was right: I didn't know what was going on. I didn't know how I felt about him or how I could be both attracted to him and still experience a moment of fear in his arms. The two emotions should not have been able to coexist.

I couldn't even decide what it was about Douglas Gallagher that I found attractive. Was I so superficial that the fact that he was a wealthy and handsome man, who dressed impeccably and found me desirable, was all I needed to cause my heart to pound fast and hard in my chest? Was it pity I felt, for a man who had never known a true family or home, and if so, how reliable was pity? I knew I had reacted physically to his kiss with no certainty that I felt any true or abiding affection for him and what did that make me? Something not very nice, I thought, having more in common with the Levy's working girls than I would ever admit out loud.

I didn't understand what Douglas saw when he looked at me, either. Why would he be loath to share with others that I was a doctor, why say he was proud to be seen with me—not proud or happy to be with me but to be *seen* with me? Douglas had been exactly right in one respect: I didn't know what was going on, not in him or in me. *Doctor* Davis knew disease, recognized infection, and confronted illness with assertive action, but *Katherine* Davis didn't seem to share that same level of confidence when it came to her personal life. I didn't like the idea, but perhaps I possessed two natures after all.

CHAPTER 8

With summer's arrival, the rhythms of Hull-House increased in variety and tempo. English and citizenship classes multiplied; the nursery and kindergarten flourished; reading groups proliferated with animated discussions about Edith Wharton and Henry James that continued into the hallways. Boys' and girls' clubs met day and evening, packed classes learned basic household arts and cookery, and renowned volunteers led sessions on art and theater. I thought the house resembled a great beehive. People buzzed everywhere and all the buildings in the complex overflowed with energy. It was wonderfully satisfying to be a part of it.

Petra became more animated as the date of her performance grew closer, but to her credit she never forgot her responsibilities in the nursery and the dispensary.

When I told her she could take a break from work the week before the performance, she told me, "No, I can't. I owe everything to you and Miss Addams and Hull-House, and I'd never let you down." I was touched by her trusting affection and thought if nothing else came of my time in Chicago, Petra's friendship alone would make the year worthwhile.

May 14 dawned bright, cloudless, and breezy, but not so windy that the weather would upset the day. In the quadrangle, which offered protection from the wind surrounded as it was by buildings, we set up small café tables that the household arts class covered with pretty pink tablecloths and bunches of delicate flowers: pansies—some of them the color of Petra's eyes—and forget-me-nots.

I ran late the whole day, spent too long with the baby care class and took more time than I could afford with an elderly woman who came to the dispensary with both eyes infected. More than once I hoped someone was researching that *penicillium* I had read about earlier because we needed an effective weapon against infections like the one she had. I hated that all I could do for this woman, who fatalistically anticipated blindness, was instruct her to wash her hands before touching her eyes and rest until she felt better. My simple directions seemed inadequate at best and her expression hinted that she agreed.

The day before the matinee I presented a bouquet of flowers to Petra, something simple and in my budget, but she was so appreciative she threw her arms around me in a rare, emotional hug.

"No one's ever done such a thing for me before," she cried, the posies now crushed between us in the hug. "Thank you, thank you."

"I predict many more proffered bouquets in your future, Petra, and much finer than these little daisies."

"But none will ever mean as much to me as these," she answered, blithely taking her future fame for granted. She went off to dress for the afternoon's production as I changed.

With no Petra to help with my unruly hair and out of primping time completely, I let my hair down and pulled it back with side barrettes, a style too youthful for me but all I could do on my own. I wore something as light as the day, a dress I'd had for years, white with unidentifiable lavender flowers scattered across it. Its scoop neck and puff sleeves declared it completely out of style, but this isn't my debut, I thought, so it doesn't matter. I borrowed an amethyst shawl from Mary Smith to cover all my fashion flaws and met Douglas at the door, breathless and feeling slightly disheveled because I'd had to rush.

I was surprised at how glad I was to see him and my happiness must have shown on my face because his expression lightened, and he gave me a smile that didn't appear to have any ulterior motives. Douglas looked more springlike than usual himself, dressed in a single-breasted suit the color of fine pewter, white shirt, soft gray silk tie, and—unusual for him—hatless. Putting a hand on his arm, I stepped outside to join him on the porch.

"I'm glad to see you," I told him gaily, the words spoken from the heart, my usual caution forgotten in my excitement for Petra. "We can walk the long way around to the theater if you'd like, down Halsted and onto Polk." I tucked my hand under his arm without thinking and drew him down the steps, chattering too much about Petra and the production until I realized he hadn't said one word since his hello at the front door. "I'll be quiet," I said finally, laughing at myself, "and let you speak. You can tell I'm excited for Petra but that doesn't excuse my babbling."

"I don't know how many women you are or who to expect at any given moment: sophisticated beauty, professional doctor, ingénue as you look today, anarchist—"

"Anarchist! That's a little strong."

"Are you telling me you have no anarchist sympathies?" When I hesitated, he laughed. "I rest my case. I think a man could never grow tired of you, Katherine."

"More to the point is if I'd grow tired of the man," I retorted and at his expression added, "I just said it to tease, Douglas, so don't look so disapproving."

By then we had come to the 750-seat auditorium where all the Hull-House theatricals were performed. I had begged some of the best seats in the house so we could sit close enough to hear every note and see every expression. I was as nervous and excited as if I were the one performing. Finally, probably tired of my restless fidgeting, Douglas took one of my hands in his and held it in his warm, firm grasp until the opening chords.

From the very beginning, from her first appearance on stage, the performance was Petra's triumph. She was a flawless Yum-Yum, an ingenuous foil to Mr. Sweeney's pompous older Ko-Ko and ardently enamored of Nanki-Poo. Petra spoke every line to its greatest effect, so huge a laugh following her perfectly-delivered "Sometimes I sit and wonder in my artless Japanese way why I am so much more attractive than anybody in the world" that the audience broke into spontaneous applause. Even Douglas laughed out loud, and from what I knew of him that was rare indeed.

Petra's voice carried every song to the rafters and bounced it back to the audience. Despite our close friendship, I had not truly realized what a powerful instrument she possessed, how pure and clear a voice until I heard it soar from the stage. She was so happy, I thought, watching her, so obviously, unambiguously, endearingly happy up on that stage, and she deserved it, deserved every moment of happiness she could get. Clearly I was not alone in my admiration. Petra received three ovations and for a while the audience wouldn't let her leave. I was as proud of her as if I were her mother.

Walking to the little table I had reserved for us, I couldn't help but talk about her and later as Douglas and I finished our light meal—served al fresco by the Household Arts class—Petra joined us. I put both hands on her shoulders and tried to say how proud I was of her, but I couldn't—I felt too emotional. Because I was unaccustomed to such helplessness, Petra had to take charge of the moment.

"Fiddle tears, Dr. Davis?" She hugged me, able to hear what I wanted to say without my speaking a word.

"Petra, this is my friend, Douglas Gallagher. Douglas, meet Yum-Yum, better known as Petra Stravinsky and my dear friend."

She put out her hand to him as he rose and said simply, "How do you do? If you're Dr. Davis's friend, then I hope you'll be mine, too."

Douglas raised both her hands to his lips in a theatrical gesture that surprised me and said, "Miss Stravinsky, you have an extraordinary talent. I'll always remember that I had the opportunity to see and hear you before you took the country by storm."

Watching Douglas, I didn't see Petra's face, but I sensed an unexpected reticence as she withdrew her hand and answered, "Thank you."

When I looked at her, I thought she lost her smile for a moment but then decided I was imagining things. Petra appeared the same after all, pleased with the day, smiling and happy. I watched her drift away to other groups, like a butterfly going from flower to flower, just that delicate and lovely. When I turned back, Douglas was watching me.

"Where did you find her?" he asked. "I wasn't just being polite. She could very well take the country by storm with that talent, face, and figure, another Geraldine Farrar." His words made me frown.

"Miss Farrar is nearly thirty, and Petra is still a child with a number of years before she's ready for the national stage, Douglas. I won't let her be rushed. She came to us through the dispensary and stayed on." He pressed to know more, but I changed the subject. Petra's past was just that and her future still needed to be carefully planned. For the time being only her present mattered.

Miss Addams stopped by our table to comment on Petra's success and to thank Douglas for his generous donations. She looked stronger and in better color.

"Mary and I leave next month to spend the summer in Maine," she informed me, "but Dr. Pasca will still be here to mentor you, Katherine, and I'll have a chain of command in place in my absence. Not that we really need it. By now the House runs itself."

In one way she was right because all the activities were delegated to competent hands who knew exactly what to do, but in another way she was completely wrong. Jane Addams underestimated the effect of her own energy, vision, and commitment that no one could replicate. The publication of her most recent book, *Twenty Years at Hull-House*, had just been announced and was in demand even before it became available to the public. I wondered if Hull-House would be able to survive without her someday. I couldn't imagine it.

By early evening, Douglas and I walked leisurely hand in hand to the curb where Fritz waited.

"We could go for a drive," he offered. I thought he made the suggestion so he could capture me in the back seat again and because I wasn't in the mood to repeat that experience, I declined. "Tomorrow, then?"

I shook my head again. "Tomorrow Dr. Hamilton and I

are examining flies' eggs." At his look, I patted his hand. "It is disgusting, isn't it? Please don't misunderstand that I prefer flies' eggs to your company, but we're concluding a study on a very strict timeline and I promised my help."

"Flies' eggs are very humbling to a man. It appears I must add scientist to the list of women who inhabit your body." He kissed me lightly on the cheek, a brotherly caress. "It's my turn to thank you, Katherine, for a pleasant afternoon. I think I could learn to love you very easily, every one of you."

As I stood startled and speechless, Fritz drove him away. Love was a word I hadn't expected to hear from Douglas Gallagher and one that I was not ready to use myself. He didn't fight fairly, I thought, and he was too fond of having the last word.

May was my birthday month. My mother told me that I was the first wildflower she saw in the spring of 1887, a spring that followed the worst winter in recorded Wyoming history. Snow still covered the ground at the end of May when I was born and only after my arrival, she said, did spring and then summer finally make an appearance.

When I was a very little girl Mother would smile at me and say, "God and your papa and I were all waiting for you, Katherine. You were the very first flower of the season. We knew that when you finally showed, that terrible winter would be over."

When I proudly shared the comment with my older brother, he gave a snort and said that was the stupidest thing he ever heard, that they would have named me Indian Paintbrush if they expected a flower. I shrugged off his teasing words and for years clung to the picture of my parents standing out in the snow, arms wide open, waiting for God to drop me down to them from heaven. How else would I have gotten there, after all, with the roads snowed shut and everyone housebound from October on?

So my birthday at the end of May saw several packages arrive from my family: a new shirtwaist and skirt from my parents along with some spending money—my parents still supporting me at my age, I thought, with shame that lasted as long as it took me to slide the bills happily into my journal for safekeeping—the latest Mary Roberts Rinehart novel ostensibly from both my brother and sister-in-law but with Hope's love of reading all over the selection, and kid gloves and sparkling hair combs from my sister.

"I think you must be able to use these," Becca wrote, "with the social schedule you're cultivating," but her tone was teasing, even in a letter. My sister doesn't have a spiteful or mean bone in her body.

My younger brother, Gus, at the time away at the University and studying for the bar, sent me a pretty card. I sat in my room surrounded by the birthday gifts, a little happy, a little sad, gratified to be remembered and thankful to be loved. How did Petra manage with no family for comfort and encouragement?

I found another package waiting for me the evening of my birthday when I walked across to supper: an elegant box in which, between layers of delicate parchment-like paper, lay a large, dazzling square of silk in shimmering black. Woven through the black silk was a paisley print in gemstone shades of emerald and sapphire and ruby, vivid and startlingly beautiful. It would make a wonderful summer shawl. I should have been delighted with the gift, and there was certainly no denying its extraordinary beauty, but I knew before I read the card that the giver was Douglas and because of that, I felt a nagging unease. I stroked the cool, smooth fabric as I asked myself the important question: How had Douglas known it was my birthday? I had purposefully kept the date to myself, hadn't mentioned it to anyone, not Petra or Mary Smith or any of the nurses I worked with on a daily basis. There was no way to bring it up without appearing self-serving, and birthdays should be spent with family, anyway. Since mine was half a continent away, I had chosen not to mention the occasion at all. How could Douglas have known it was my birthday when no one at Hull-House knew, and I was positive I hadn't said a word to him or anyone else?

I recalled the serendipitous violets that matched my Easter hat and his ready knowledge of my family the day he first visited Hull-House. "I have been busy," he had said without embarrassment when I had attempted to chide him for being intrusive. Now I wondered what else he knew, or thought he knew, about me and my family and how he obtained the information. Did spies hop off the train in Laramie or skulk outside my window? I didn't like the thought and while I tried to scold myself for being unjustly suspicious, the idea still seemed vaguely ominous and took some of the pleasure from his gift and from the day.

I scribbled off a thank you to Douglas and intended to spend more time considering the details of his gift, would even have spoken to him about it, except for the June emergency. During the first week of June, the very day after Miss Addams and Mary Smith left for their summer holiday in Bar Harbor, a woman carrying a feverish, coughing child appeared at the dispensary door. Miss Flaherty had the mother place the girl on the examining table and as I started to remove the child's clothing, I saw something that made my heart momentarily stop. A flat rash of rose-colored spots covered the girl's abdomen.

Nurse Flaherty and I stared at each other across the table before I said to her calmly, "We'll need cool compresses for the child and boiling water for the rest of us all the time. We have to be sure to wash our hands constantly and don't handle any food or water." I led the mother to the waiting room and told her to wait for us there.

Back with the now-unconscious child, I stated, "I'm almost positive it's typhoid, Nurse. Use the hall phone to call Dr. Pasca. He'll notify the Board of Health. There's not much we can do for this girl now except watch and pray that she's strong enough to resist the disease. Wash your hands all the time, Miss Flaherty. I can't stress it enough, and have the mother wash, too. I'm going to find out where she lives and make a visit to see if others with the same complaint live there. With any luck, this is just an isolated case."

But I knew that was unlikely. Cholera and typhoid fever were regular killers that swept through congested, unsanitary areas and usually took the very young and the very old with them when they left. The cause of the disease was seldom confined to one person.

"I don't think you should go by yourself, Dr. Davis."

"Someone has to stay with the patients and wait for Dr. Pasca. I'll be all right."

I followed the woman's directions to the apartment building where she lived and went door to door, asking if there were others with the symptoms of typhoid fever. The response was grim. There were several. I examined as many people as I could into the night and stressed the same instructions over and over: wash your hands with hot water and soap, boil all water before you use it, handle soiled garments carefully, discard them and if you don't discard them, wash them in boiling water with strong lye soap. It was all I knew to do. There was no effective antidote or treatment for the disease once you had it so all I could do was stress its prevention.

Sometime late that night I wearily walked home, too tired to enjoy the big, white moon that illuminated the way. The lukewarm summer breeze did nothing but carry the smells of garbage and human waste throughout the neighborhood. None of the children here had ever known anything but this, didn't know what it was like to see moonlight reflect off snowy mountaintops or sit on the front porch with the rich fragrance of summer roses your only companion. I felt disheartened and desperate. Some of the people I had seen would die of typhoid fever, and there wasn't a thing I could do for them.

Mrs. Tabachnik had replaced Miss Flaherty by the time I got back, and she met me at the door.

"We were worried about you, Dr. Davis. You shouldn't have gone by yourself."

I brushed her comments off, smiled at Petra who hovered behind her, and said, "I'm fine, but there are more people sick than I expected. Did someone reach Dr. Pasca?"

"Yes. He said the Board of Health will visit here tomorrow morning for information and then try to contain the area."

The child's mother sat in a chair next to the girl's bed, a bandana still around her head, her worn face too pale and one hand occasionally rubbing her temple. I put a hand to her forehead.

"You're ill, too. We need to find you a bed."

"Can't leave my girl," the woman said. Her voice slurred with fever and fatigue and headache.

"I know," I answered gently, crouching to untie her scarf and put a hand to her cheek, "but you're no good to her if you're ill. We'll put your bed right next to hers." She nodded and her eyes filled with sudden tears, relief or fear or pain I couldn't tell.

Later, both of them settled, I caught a few hours of sleep before Dr. Pasca arrived, and that's the last I remember sleeping for several days. All the following week I refused to let Petra come to the dispensary, and I stopped contact with the nursery, the kindergarten, and the baby classes. The mother and daughter who had come to us for help both lived, but I can't say the same for a number of the people in their tenement building.

Dr. Pasca told me the typhoid had been traced to a family who from desperation had used river water—as filthy and full of stockyard offal as it was—to bathe in and wash their clothes. One had grown ill and from there, because they didn't know and so didn't take the necessary sanitary precautions, the sickness spread quickly to others in contaminated water and food. All the month of June I made regular visits to those who were ill, not taking the time for much of anything else except to change my clothes and try to nap whenever I could. I don't remember eating but of course I must have. Dr. Pasca made daily visits to bring me up to date on the city's precautions and to check on the patients in the dispensary. Perhaps he was checking on me, too. It didn't matter and I had no conceit about it. I could use all the help I could get. That June was the fastest month of my life.

By the end of the month I thought I could try to resume my normal life—whatever that had been, pick up childcare classes again and make my regular visits to the nursery.

"You look thinner," observed Mrs. Teague critically at my first day back in a month. "I heard it was very bad."

"It was, but I know it could have been worse. I just wish there was something to give people once they contract the disease. It makes me so angry to be helpless and at the mercy of such a plague!" I was beginning to understand Dr. Hamilton's personal vendetta against disease, why she treated it as if it were actually a person with whom she engaged in fierce and merciless battle.

"Maybe someday there will be a cure, Dr. Davis."

I agreed. "We're making exciting strides in medicine almost daily. A decade ago we didn't know how yellow fever was transmitted and now we know what to blame. Eighteen months ago people couldn't believe we could save lives through a blood transfusion and now the future for such a procedure is limitless. I hope you're right, Mrs. Teague, and that sooner rather than later we find a cure for typhoid fever and tuberculosis and cholera. But that doesn't help the victims today, does it?" She patted my hand in comfort.

"You can only do what you can do, Doctor."

"I know, but it's not enough when people are dying."

A boy at the door interrupted our conversation. "There's someone at the big house asking for you."

When I went over I found Douglas standing by the now unlit fireplace in the front room. I was dressed in a plain smock, my hair held back with a bandana much like the woman who had brought her sick child to us a month ago, as inelegant as he had ever seen me. But if he noted my appearance, it didn't show on his face. I realized with a small pang of conscience that I had not given him one thought the whole month of June. Not one.

He examined me as critically as Mrs. Teague had earlier. "You look worn, Katherine. It must have been worse than they told me."

I sat down—sank really—onto the closest chair and answered, "Did you come by before, then? I didn't know." Douglas sat, too, but leaned forward so that he could have reached out a hand to mine if he chose.

"I told them not to bother you. I received your thank you and sent you a note in return. Did you get that?"

I shook my head, then confessed guiltily, "It may be in that stack of mail on my desk. I haven't had either the time or the opportunity to look at much except patients lately."

"They expect too much from you," he said tersely and accompanied his words with a frown.

"Nonsense. It's exactly what Dr. Pasca described when he offered the opportunity, and I wouldn't have it any other way. I have a lot to offer."

"Yes, I agree you do," he responded, but I didn't believe he was thinking about medicine when he said it. To fill the sudden silence, he asked, "Did I ever mention that I was building a home?"

"No."

"On Prairie Avenue." At my blank look, he explained, "The street of the Armours, the Fields, the McCormicks, the Palmers, and the Pullmans."

"With those neighbors, it must be a very grand home."

"It is grand, I suppose, but not in their style, which is too old-fashioned, too dark and bulky and outdated. You'll see."

"I'd like to. I'm sure it's lovely."

"I hope you like it." He leaned forward to place a hand over mine. "I want you to." I didn't know how to respond, something unspoken but evocative in his tone. "I'm having a party to celebrate the Fourth of July. Will you come and see it then?"

"I must have lost track of time. Can it really be Independence Day already?"

"On Monday, Katherine. Do you think you could spare me an afternoon?"

He sounded good-humored about the invitation and I smiled in return, happy to be sitting down, as relaxed as I supposed I would ever be in his company. I felt the familiar edge of anticipatory excitement I often experienced when I was with him.

"Yes, I think I can. It sounds pleasant."

"I'll have Fritz pick you up Monday around three. I

hope you won't be disappointed in the house." I retrieved my hand and stood, which forced him to do the same.

"I'm sure I won't be. You have excellent taste." He put a hand under my chin and bent to kiss me lightly on the mouth.

"You're proof of that, I think." I didn't appreciate a comment that made me feel much like his house or his motorcar or any object he had acquired, something that validated his good taste and impressed his friends.

I didn't know what had come over me lately, why I found fault with Douglas when he was so generous and complimentary. To make up for my critical thoughts, of which he was completely unaware, I returned his kiss more eagerly than he expected or I intended. Surprise showed momentarily on his face before his arms tightened around me and his kiss deepened, clearly pleased with my passionate response. Embarrassed, I finally slipped from his embrace and murmured a hasty good-bye.

I knew that feeling guilty about unflattering thoughts was not the proper motivation for passionate kisses, yet that's exactly why I had practically thrown myself into his arms and so given the opposite impression of my feelings at the time. I had never been as transparent as my sister, had always been compared more to my reserved father, but I had always claimed Father's integrity, too. Sad to say, that did not seem to be the case. I lacked his honesty and perhaps his courage, which was nothing I admitted with pride.

I told myself that I was still tired and too worn out from my role in the typhoid epidemic to engage Douglas verbally about considering me an inanimate object. And to question him about how he had known the date of my birthday after I'd accepted his gift and allowed a full month to pass without another word seemed petty and ungrateful. Neither rationale rang true, even as I put them forward.

I would take the weekend and rest, and perhaps things would right themselves by Monday. Douglas hadn't changed after all, still dark and handsome with the same latent, powerful energy that he wore like a suit coat. I seemed to be the one who had changed, and what could possibly have caused that except the stress and fatigue of the last month? I was sure I would see the situation differently by Monday.

CHAPTER 9

Petra came to see me as I dressed to leave Monday afternoon.

"I thought you might like to come with us to see the fireworks this evening," she said, and when I told her of my other plans, she grew serious. "You must think highly of Mr. Gallagher to spend so much time in his company."

I paused in the middle of putting on my hat, both arms still extended up, and soberly considered her words. I didn't know if I thought highly of him. I liked being with him, liked the verbal sparring, liked his commanding presence, and if I admitted the truth, particularly liked being admired by a handsome, influential man about town. But think highly of him? I held my father and my sister's husband, Ben, and Dr. Pasca and former President Roosevelt and sometimes—against my better judgment—my older brother John Thomas in the highest possible regard, but Douglas Gallagher? It was much too early to put him in such august company.

I made a noncommittal response: "I enjoy spending time with him now and then, Petra."

"Will you marry him, do you think?" she asked persistently.

"The subject has never come up," I answered, surprised that she would ask the question. "I've only just met him and we're just friends." She gave me a clear, unblinking look as if trying to look into my heart and then smiled.

"We'll miss you tonight. Mr. Sweeney is taking me and some of his other music students to the fireworks. We're going to pack a picnic, too. I wish you were coming with us." Looking at her, I suddenly wished I were going with them, too, instead of spending the afternoon with a group of strangers with whom I'd have nothing in common but Douglas Gallagher. The hot, sunny day was perfect for a casual picnic surrounded by laughing young people and the good nature of Patrick Sweeney. Even the few faint thunderclouds along the horizon could not spoil the prospect.

"I wish I was too," I admitted, "but I've already accepted Douglas's invitation and it wouldn't be right to cancel at this late date to accept an invitation I liked better."

"You could say you were sick. He'd never know and I'd never tell."

"So I should add lying on top of bad manners? I don't think that's a very good idea." I stuffed my new kid gloves into my purse and kissed her on the cheek on my way out the door. "Say hello to Mr. Sweeney and have a wonderful time." A little vertical line formed between her brows, her expression too serious for a holiday. "Petra, is everything all right?" She gave a laugh, herself again.

"Yes, everything's fine," but somehow I didn't think so. I'd have to talk to her more seriously later.

"Hello, Fritz," I said, coming down the walk to where he stood by the auto. "Are you well?"

He nodded. "Yes, Miss," holding open a rear door for me, but I stopped next to him to ask, "Is there some rule that says I can't sit in the front next to you?" He looked scandalized at the idea as I continued, "We can stop before we get to our destination and I'll jump in the back so no one will ever know, but it seems silly to have you up there and me back here. Besides, I want to watch you drive. I expect there will be an automobile in my future someday, and I can use the instruction."

He grinned, then closed one door and opened another so I could sit next to him during the trip. I asked him questions about gears and pedals and the whole concept behind the working of the engine, which continued to elude me despite my scientific and medical background. It had almost begun to make sense when he pulled to the side.

"You should get into the back now, Miss. Mr. Gallagher wouldn't approve of our sitting side by side." I gave him a quick glance to see if he was serious and when I realized he was, I didn't argue.

Prairie Avenue was something to see, lined with huge, imposing homes, landscaped lawns, front walks that looked as long as the street itself, porches filled with enormous planters of colorful flowers, everything exactly right, no curtain, no blade of grass out of place. No little children could live here, I thought, because Lily Kate would have made short work of all those potted flowers, had them picked and pulled and beribboned into bouquets for her favorite people.

Douglas's house, still new enough that the lawn was sparse and flowers hardly visible, was noticeably different from all the others. No roof peaks and turrets and narrow windows but a home built of light, rosy-white brick, with stark, geometric lines unencumbered by ornament, and large Chicago-style windows everywhere.

He must have been watching for me because as soon as the auto pulled up to the curb, Douglas came down the walk. He wore an informal fawn-colored flannel suit and looked as contemporary and stylish as the house behind him. I was conscious of my plain blue dress that I had worn five years ago during my first year at school, an unremarkable garment. I thought I could get away with so ordinary a dress, though, because I had draped the brilliant paisley silk shawl across my shoulders and tied it to the side almost like a sash and replaced the prim violets on my hat with a splashy red flower. People's eyes would be drawn to those items and not to the dress beneath.

"Douglas, your home is striking. It has such flair."

"Wright was the consulting architect," he said, knowing I would recognize the name. "I told him what I wanted and he sketched it out immediately. Come inside and let me give you a tour."

I could tell he was very pleased with it and rightfully so. The windows let in natural light and a soft breeze to every room. All the wood trim was blonde with nothing dark or heavy anywhere in the house, no thick satins or brocades, only the most minimal of coverings over the windows, the furniture streamlined in lightly-textured, plain-colored fabrics. The paintings on the walls were airy and light, too, some from the Impressionist school, all gardens and sunshine.

"Douglas, it's so beautiful! So much light! How could anyone be unhappy living in this house?"

He took me by the hand and led me outside through the double doors off the library onto a veranda that covered the entire length of the back of the house, then down some steps into the gardens. Round tables dotted the yard, each with an umbrella striped red, white and blue that shadowed the ample refreshments. Pots of flowers in the same patriotic colors sat in haphazard arrangement around the lawn, giving a festive and cheerful effect. I knew he must have spent a fortune, but I was raised poor so I couldn't help such a proletarian reflection. The house and the yard were beautiful, everything perfect, and I thought he deserved to be proud.

Douglas unashamedly watched my reaction, and when I turned to him to say warmly, "What a wonderful scene! Your guests can't help but be charmed," he gave the most sincere smile I had ever seen from him, one that reminded me of his brother's boyish grin.

"I'm glad you like it, Katherine. When I selected all the furnishings, I was thinking of you. Everything about you is bright and beautiful. There's nothing dark in you anywhere, and I wanted the house to reflect that."

No one had ever paid me such a generous compliment before and I was speechless. Then the bell to the front door rang, able to be heard clearly through the open library doors, and he left to welcome the first of his guests. By late afternoon people crowded the lawn. The weather had turned hot and humid, and I stood on the veranda under the overhanging roof looking apprehensively at the graying sky when Drew Gallagher, resplendent in a white suit and white shoes, came toward me, carrying a glass in each hand.

"I haven't had a chance to say hello," he greeted cheerfully, handing over one of the glasses of lemonade. "I'm glad to see you again, Katherine. What do you think of my brother's castle?" Drew looked like summer itself, all gold and white.

"I think it's beautiful, don't you?"

"I think it's the showcase he always wanted and it makes him happy, or as happy as Douglas is capable of being."

"What does that mean?"

"Nothing. Only that my brother enjoys making a profit and letting people know that he's done so. It's the American way."

"He works hard. Why shouldn't he enjoy the fruits of his labor?"

"I think that was a veiled jab at his immoral and profligate brother, wasn't it?"

He made me laugh. "Not at all. If I wanted to jab his immoral and profligate brother, I'd do so to his face without a veil in sight."

We sat down at a table under the shade of one of the umbrellas.

"Were you looking at the sky and worrying about rain spoiling your pretty hat?"

"I wasn't worrying exactly, but some of my young friends from Hull-House are enjoying the lakefront today on a rare outing, and I'd hate for rain to spoil their fun."

"That reminds me, I read about you in the *News.* Did you know you made the papers?"

"No. I can't imagine why. Are you sure it was me? It must have been someone else."

"The article didn't mention your name, but it had to be you. A woman doctor working with the poor at Hull-House, it said, almost single-handedly prevailing over an outbreak of typhoid. It was a glowing tribute to the new woman of the new century, which apparently you personify. I knew immediately it had to be you."

"I am a woman doctor and I do work at Hull-House and we did have a recent outbreak of typhoid fever, but there was nothing single-handed about it, and I'm hardly an emblem of the new century or the new woman, whatever that means. Thirty years ago my mother left everything familiar and comfortable to move with my father to Wyoming. Just the two of them, no other family in the world, and no one around for miles. That's more daring than anything I've ever done."

"Tell me about your family."

I did, hesitant at first, then warmed to the subject, making him laugh with stories, making me laugh, too, at the memories.

"I think you miss them," he commented. I responded without thinking about the effect of my words.

"Truthfully, I miss them more than I ever expected. It gets lonely sometimes. After all, without family how can you have a home?" Then I stopped abruptly and put a hand over his. "I'm sorry. That was thoughtless of me. I know you lost your parents. I didn't mean to be unkind or sound so smug."

"Katherine, even if both my parents were still alive we wouldn't be a family, not the kind you describe, not the way it should be. To them Douglas and I were just an investment with a purpose: to help run the business and marry money in order to increase the family holdings. They were blind to us as individual human beings. I don't believe either of them ever did a single act in their lives that was simply for kindness or for generosity's sake."

"Sometimes children can feel a little excluded when their parents love each other a great deal," I remarked, my own childhood in mind.

"What a kind innocent you are, always trying to find the right thing to say. Let me assure you that my father found my mother unattractive, if not distasteful, and if my mother hadn't known it was her duty to have a child or two, I doubt she would have let him touch her. Even now the fact that she conceived two sons borders on the miraculous. I can't imagine the two of them consorting in the normal way that men and women make babies."

"Stop. Don't be crude, Drew. It really isn't necessary

for you to act that way with me. I'm seldom shocked and never impressed by risqué conversation."

He put both elbows on the table and looked at me over his folded hands.

"You," he said quietly, "are a very nice woman, much too good for my brother, and I encourage you to look around for other suitors."

"Douglas is not a suitor," I began disingenuously and then at the look in Drew's eyes added, "At least I don't think of him in that way. I don't think I do." I gave Drew a slight smile to apologize for my ambivalence. "It's a confusing relationship, Drew, and I'm generally too busy to try to sort it out."

"You know as well as I do that he's a suitor. He's more serious about you than I've ever known him to be about anyone or anything in his life, even his work. If you knew my brother as well as I do, you'd realize that when Douglas wants something, he'll do whatever it takes to get it, and he definitely wants you, Katherine. Sooner or later you'll be forced to consider his attentions seriously, whether doing so is convenient or not. Will you promise me that when Douglas decides the time is right to discuss his place in your future, you'll talk to me before making any decisions?" Drew's grave words troubled me.

"Why would I need your advice?"

"Because I believe it would be for your good. I do possess some sense, Katherine. I'm not the complete ass that I act or that my brother describes. I hope you realize that."

"I do," I said in return, "although I'm baffled by your compulsion to speak and act in the outrageous way you do. I'm sure Douglas would be so proud of you if you settled down a little." Drew stood, smiling down at me. "You might be right," he acknowledged, "and speaking of Douglas, here he comes. I think I'll leave before he has a chance to look disapprovingly at me. You'll remember your promise, won't you?"

From behind me, Douglas asked, "What promise would that be?" and I answered lightly, "I promised Drew I'd stop scolding him as if he were a little boy. It comes from working with children all day." I turned toward Douglas as he rested a hand on my shoulder. "Come and sit down a while, Douglas."

"Take my chair," Drew offered and drifted off to talk to someone else.

"I hope he wasn't being too idiotic," Douglas said, joining me at the table. He set another glass of fresh, cold lemonade in front of me.

"No. I like your brother."

"Drew has a strange and inventive imagination. Because he really doesn't understand what I do, he tends to make things up. I hope you won't believe everything he says."

How odd, I thought, that each brother seemed to feel a need to caution me about the other. What was that about? I made a trivial response and moved the conversation to another topic.

Later, after the guests had gone and the servants were busy cleaning up the yard, I heard a distant roll of thunder.

"I should go home before it storms."

Douglas and I had strolled into the library from the veranda and I had turned to look outside when he pulled me into his arms, almost too rough in his touch and certainly surprising me. I said his name with annoyance and tried to extricate myself, feeling undignified and a little manhandled, but he held me by the wrist and wouldn't let go.

"That silk becomes you, but the hat only gets in the way." He reached up to remove it, but I pulled loose and stepped back quickly.

"I don't like it when you do that," I told him crossly.

"Do what?"

"Surprise me with your attentions," I answered but wanted to add more. Touch me as if you owned me. Think that a compliment confers some sort of privilege. Ignore my clear wishes. I didn't like those things either.

"You didn't seem to mind my attentions last Wednesday."

"It had been a long week, a long month, really, and I wasn't myself. I'm sorry if I gave the wrong impression."

"You gave the right impression, at least the one I was looking for." Douglas stood before me, hands in his pockets and his black eyes narrowed as he searched my face for something, an indication of my feelings, a glimpse into my heart. Finally he spoke very seriously. "This could all be yours, Katherine."

I didn't pretend to misunderstand him.

"Douglas, I have known you less than six months and wouldn't need two hands to count the number of times we've been together. It's much too soon to talk like that, if there will ever be a right time." I thought I had made him angry and found myself tensing, but he went past me to open the door and call Fritz's name.

When he turned back to me, he said in a cutting voice, "I accept that because I have no choice in the matter, but I hadn't thought you were the kind of woman to pretend to be coy."

I retorted, angry at his words and tone, "You're the one who told me to learn to play the social game, Douglas. I recall the words quite clearly. You just underestimated how quickly I'd learn the rules. Let that be a lesson to you."

If Fritz hadn't come to the door, I think Douglas would have said something he would have regretted later, something we both would have regretted. Anger darkened his expression and I thought at first he would shut the door in Fritz's face to finish the conversation with me.

Instead he said smoothly, "Will you drive Miss Davis"—not *Doctor* Davis on purpose, I thought, "—home, Fritz? The storm is making her uneasy."

It wasn't the storm that made me uneasy, I thought but said aloud, more for Fritz's benefit than anything else, "Thank you, Douglas. Everything was perfect. You must be very proud of your new home." I walked past him close enough to catch his scent and followed Fritz down the central hallway and out the front door to the waiting vehicle.

During the trip home I replayed the altercation in my head. I knew he found me puzzling and frustrating, and I couldn't blame him for that. I was not always proud of my behavior when we were together, but I thought he should know me well enough by then to realize that I was not a coquette, who teased and purposefully misled. Douglas Gallagher interfered with my desire to concentrate fully on my work, and I didn't know what to do about the physical and emotional way he affected me. I wished he would see that I was as confused as I was confusing. And, of course, he must learn to read me so that he would never again surprise me with force, even if it were unintentional. I knew I would eventually forgive the entire exchange, but that particular offense I could not forget.

The next day I received flowers from Douglas with a note. *I'm sorry* was all he wrote on the card, which should have been enough, I suppose, but wasn't.

Douglas kept his distance for two weeks, then one Saturday afternoon appeared, of all places, at the dispensary's alley door. I was totally flabbergasted to see him there and could tell he enjoyed my discomfiture.

"I thought if I announced myself first, you might still be angry and not see me. This was the only way I knew to get your attention." We moved into the empty waiting room. "Katherine, I'm sorry. I treated you unkindly and spoke to you unfairly. Please forgive me. You were absolutely right. You hardly know me and I was presumptuous. I shouldn't expect you to be at the same place I am. Women have a different pace than men and I'm sorry." He apologized quietly, hat in hand, not a trace of artifice, his whole demeanor sincere and endearingly humble. My defenses were no protection against such contrition.

"I didn't come off very well in the exchange, either," I admitted. "I shouldn't have been such a shrew."

We smiled at each other until behind me someone said, "Dr. Davis?" Petra stood hesitantly in the doorway.

"Petra, you remember Mr. Gallagher, don't you?" She nodded, her eyes slipping away from his face and coming back to me.

"Our songbird," Douglas acknowledged pleasantly. "Do you have any future performances planned, Miss Stravinsky?"

"No, I'm busy with lessons now. Mr. Sweeney says I have too much to learn about technique to consider performing again for a while." She answered Douglas but looked at me, giving an odd effect.

"Your timing is perfect, Miss Stravinsky, because I came to invite Dr. Davis to hear Caruso sing. He'll be performing Verdi's *Macbeth* at the Auditorium Theater the last week of July. I don't pretend to know much about opera, but I'm told this is a rare opportunity and it just so happens I have three tickets. I thought you might like to join us."

"How wonderful!" I exclaimed. I turned to Petra and expected to see an excited, pleased look on her face, but instead she wore a cautious expression.

"I don't believe I can go. I practice every day now and have responsibilities in the nursery and with the kindergarten.

Dr. Davis should go, and I'll stay with the patients while she's gone."

"Nonsense, Petra. It will be fun, and what an exciting experience for us both!" I turned to Douglas, my bad humor with him forgotten, and said warmly, "Thank you, Douglas. How generous of you! Of course, we'll both be delighted to attend."

Petra gave a small smile and said to me, "All right, if that's what you want," then excused herself.

"I thought she would be more excited," I admitted to Douglas, "but she may just be worried that she hasn't anything to wear. It's perfect for her to see someone as famous and accomplished as Caruso. How very thoughtful of you to include her." He was on good behavior, pleased with my response and I think sincerely sorry for the harsh words we'd had.

That evening I sought Petra and found her in the music room, heard her trilling up and down the scales before I even reached the door. She never seemed to tire of the musical exercise. I slid in the door and sat down on a stuffed chair, curled my legs beneath me and simply enjoyed the sound. Petra's voice was so heavenly it made even the drills a pleasure to hear.

After a while she turned her head slightly and saw me there, stopped mid-scale and asked, "How long have you been here, Dr. Davis? You should have said something." She looked curiously grown up to me at that moment, a motherly tone in her voice almost as if our roles had reversed and she had become my protector.

"I didn't want to interrupt. It was too lovely." Petra rolled the piano stool close to my chair and sat down on it.

"You still look tired." Roles definitely reversed. She was the doctor, too.

"I must look more tired than I am, then, because I feel

just fine. Did you come to see me earlier for a reason? I felt there was something you wanted to share, but then we got sidetracked considering Caruso." Her face lit up.

"Mr. Sweeney stopped by to tell me that Miss Addams has arranged a year's scholarship at the University's Music School. Everything's approved and I'm accepted. I'm to start in the fall."

"I'm so pleased, Petra! I knew Jane was working on the opportunity for you but was afraid to say anything until it was certain."

"I've been thinking about how I can attend the classes and still meet my responsibilities here. I know I work for my room and board and—"

"You don't have to keep doing that," I interrupted. "You should concentrate on your studies." Her lips pressed together in a stubborn line.

"I won't take charity, so until I can support myself through my music I want to keep working here. Besides, I'd miss the children."

"But you might have class during the day."

"Then I can help in the dispensary at night or the kitchen at breakfast. I want to keep my apartment and my work here. I don't see why I can't."

When I said I thought it would be too much for her, she retorted, "Did you find anything to be too much when you were studying to be a doctor?"

She made a point well taken. I had had one goal and I did whatever it took to reach it. Nothing had seemed insurmountable, no workload too heavy, no sacrifice too dear. Every step, every effort, moved me closer to my dream.

"No. You're right. When you want something very badly, everything that helps you reach your ambition is a joy. I just don't want you to make yourself ill along the way. I expect front row tickets to a performance someday." After a comfortable silence, with street sounds from the open window slowly lessening and the light fading, I said, "Petra, I know just the thing for you to wear to the opera, so if you were troubled about that, don't be. Mary Smith passed along a dress much too graceful for a woman my size and too youthful for a woman my age. It's a pretty shade of purple to match your eyes."

"Thank you," she responded calmly, "but I think one of the dresses from the operetta will be just fine. I wasn't worried about it."

"You were worried about something it seemed to me. You aren't uncomfortable with Douglas, are you? He can be intimidating, I know, but he's not unlikable."

"You like him. I can tell that."

"I do," I admitted, suddenly shy—and with Petra of all people! "I do like him, more on some days than others, but I don't think that's unusual for a new friendship." I gave a shrug and changed the subject. "Anyway, you seemed less than enthusiastic about seeing Caruso and I thought—" I met her clear gaze and concluded, "It doesn't matter what I thought because obviously I was wrong."

"I was too caught up in the excitement of the scholarship," she explained. "I didn't mean to appear ungrateful. I'm sure we'll have an enjoyable evening, and it was kind of Mr. Gallagher to include me."

"It was, wasn't it?" I said, smiling a little to myself at the thought. "I think sometimes I don't give him credit for his kinder side." On my way out I stopped at the door to say to her, "I hope you know I'm your friend, Petra. If something was troubling you, you'd tell me, wouldn't you?"

She returned my look soberly, her violet eyes calm and direct.

"Of course I would. There's nothing troubling me."

***

The dispensary stayed busy with a steady stream of wounds and coughs and fevers. One man lost two fingers in an accident at one of the meat packing plants and came straight to me, his hand wrapped in bloody bandages.

"You saved my boy's life," he grunted in accented English through the pain. "Only want you."

"He's little Leo's father," I told Miss Flaherty later, "who finally found work only to lose half of his hand at the job. Talk about a mixed blessing." I kept Mr. Lubchik overnight and gave him laudanum for the pain, then sent him home the next day with strict orders about cleanliness.

"I must work. Can't stay home."

"If you try to work with your hand in that shape, you'll either bleed to death or infect it so badly you'll lose the whole arm."

"If I not work, I lose my job."

"They can't expect you to work with your hand like that."

"If I not work, I lose my job," he repeated and went to work the very next day, returning at its end and at the end of each day for the next two weeks to ask me to rewrap the wound for work the following workday. The necessity of the task infuriated me.

"I have half a mind to go talk to Mr. Armour myself," I fumed. "A man loses two fingers in an accident and then faces losing his job as well?! It's inhuman."

Miss Flaherty said stoically, "Even being a doctor wouldn't keep you from being sick to your stomach at what goes on in those plants. Sometimes you can hear the sounds of the pigs squealing a block away. Makes a person consider going off meat altogether. And they don't treat the humans that work there any better. I've seen some terrible things."

"The world is full of terrible things," I agreed, "but not only terrible things. Think about little Leo or Petra or Mrs. Tancheck and her daughter, our first two typhoid patients, or even Mr. Pilzner, who didn't die abandoned in a doorway somewhere but ended his days in warmth and light with people around to care for him. My mother says life's a balance, good and bad, joy and grief."

"Your mother is a wise woman, then."

"To tell you the truth, Miss Flaherty, I never appreciated that fact when I was home. It's taken time and experience—and distance, too, I guess—to see how special she is."

"You should write and tell her so."

"You're right. I don't think I take the time to say the important things often enough." The nurse patted my shoulder on her way past me.

"None of us do, Doctor, until it's too late to say them. Then we wish we could turn back the clock. That's human nature."

She was right, I thought. We wasted so much time in unimportant, even harmful, talk, and neglected to say what was really in our hearts. Sometimes it seemed life just hung by a thread so why not skip the frivolous and go straight to what really mattered?

I wrote home that very evening. A letter had been long overdue.

CHAPTER 10

The last weekend in July was sultry and humid; the city steamed. When Petra appeared dressed for our evening at the opera, however, she looked as cool as snow, dressed all in white, her black hair pulled back with the sparkling hair combs I had loaned her.

"You look like Snow White," I exclaimed, "and very pretty!" Besides wanting to compliment, my words had a literal turn, too, because she looked somewhat pale and not as animated as I had expected, a thought I didn't voice. When she returned a compliment, I laughed.

"I wear evening clothes in sequence and tonight it's time for the ivory dress again. I'm not wearing one new thing except this feather in my hair."

The three of us fit into the back of the motorcar, Petra between Douglas and me. When I said I could sit up front by Fritz, the driver turned with a slight smile on his face at my words, but Petra took my arm.

"No, stay here. We can't talk if you're that far away."

Her tone had a touch of urgency in it so I stayed crowded in the back with her and Douglas. It crossed my mind that she must be more nervous about the rare evening out than I thought, or perhaps she found Douglas especially daunting. I couldn't blame her for that. Even I, as used to his perfectly turned-out appearance as I was, thought Douglas especially impressive that evening. From his starched white shirt to the shine on his black shoes, he looked every inch the successful and handsome businessman, nothing garish, everything tastefully ostentatious. The lights caught the diamond on his finger and the same stickpin on his lapel that I had seen before. The diamonds in the *G* sparkled as if lit from within.

As we walked through the doors of the theater, I linked arms with Petra and whispered, "Some day I'll come to see you here. You'll be as famous as Caruso only much prettier." The Auditorium Theater held no private boxes, but our seats were better than any box could have been. Ten rows back and dead center. I had a perfect seat, with Douglas on my left and Petra to the right.

"You've outdone yourself, Douglas," I murmured into his ear. "This is perfect for her," and remained in such charity with him that I let him hold my gloved hand during the entire first act. Once the overture began, Petra, who had been subdued, brightened perceptibly, leaned forward and as far as I could tell, never took her gaze from the stage.

"Does she speak Italian?" Douglas asked low-voiced, noticing how enrapt Petra was.

"I don't think so," I whispered back, "but she has a real ear for languages so perhaps she knows enough to understand some of what's being sung. More than I, I'm sure, which isn't saying much."

"Next time I'll pick something that you'll enjoy more. What language should it be?"

"Medicinal German," I replied before settling back in my chair and was gratified to get a low, spontaneous laugh from him. He was at his most charming when he was like that, natural and pleasant, and it was at those moments that I thought I might be able to care for him in the way I thought he deserved. Because of his kindness to Petra, he was more attractive to me that night than he had ever been. That he had thought to include her touched me a great deal and was more important than the size of his house or the diamonds on his lapel. In that way I was truly the daughter of Lou Davis, who had given up her comfortable life to marry a man whose total worldly goods consisted of one horse and a small plot of land along the foothills of the Laramie Mountains. They'd worked hard and had come to own at least half the county, could be considered wealthy in their own right, but I didn't think that meant any more to my mother at the present than it had thirty years before.

Later in the evening, after the opera was over, Douglas suggested something to eat in the restaurant there, but Petra pleaded a headache.

"I haven't known you to be ill before," I told her. "I hope it's nothing more serious than the excitement."

"I'm sure it's nothing serious, and I'm so sorry to spoil things. Couldn't I go home by myself and the two of you come later? There's no reason you shouldn't enjoy what's left of the evening."

But I wouldn't hear of it, so we went back together, Douglas gracious and concerned about Petra. I had expected him to be a little miffed at the early end to the evening but he wasn't at all, and I chided myself for my thoughts. Perhaps he was changing, or I was.

After Petra offered her thanks and said her good night, Douglas and I sat on the sofa in the front room. Mary Smith and Miss Addams were gone and the house seemed empty and sterile. They both brought a great deal of energy to Hull-House, and it seemed to me the house knew they were gone and reflected their absence.

When I said as much to Douglas, he responded, "I might have disagreed with you at one time, but now I think you're right. My house never seemed as alive as when you were there, and it hasn't been the same since."

"Do I hear a touch of the metaphysical? I wouldn't have expected that from such a staunch capitalist. I thought your credo was trust only your senses." He turned and brought his face close to mine.

"When it comes to you, I've taken complete leave of my senses," he said and kissed me, leaning against me so that I was pressed against the sofa back. I felt suffocated by his weight and by the confusion of emotions that roiled inside my head and heart. In an irrational and fictionalized way, I wanted the experience of being deeply and passionately kissed to make me forget everything else around me, but with Douglas it was never so. Almost always I experienced a queer sense of detachment, as if part of me felt I must be ready to run. I thought it shouldn't be like that and felt a private shame at my inability to be the woman Douglas so obviously desired. After a moment he pulled back.

"Is something wrong? I'm sorry if I overstepped again." He placed his hand around my neck and under my chin so that I had to look at him. "Are you toying with me, Miss Davis?" He was only half teasing.

"I'm supposed to be the one who asks if your intentions are honorable," I retorted, not pulling away, "and it's *Doctor* Davis."

"You wouldn't need to work for a living if you found a rich husband."

His hand dropped and I did move away then, scooting down on the sofa to put some distance between us.

"I don't work because I need to. I love my work and I'll practice medicine if I marry or if I remain a spinster. Will you stop working if you marry?"

"I won't be giving birth."

"I can hardly argue with that observation, Douglas, but I'm not sure what your point is. Women continue to work inside their homes after they have children, don't they?"

"Not smart or beautiful women, who marry well and whose husbands can afford servants for all the mundane household chores."

"Douglas, smart women don't marry to avoid housework. That would simply exchange one drudgery for another."

"Pleasing your husband and enjoying the finer things in life don't have to be drudgery."

I thought as he spoke that he would never understand me. Perhaps he had been too affected as a boy by his parents' need for material wealth to grasp what I was trying to say.

"I only meant that it doesn't have to be exclusive. A woman can care for her family and love her husband and enjoy her work, whatever it is. There's room here—" I put my hand over my heart "—for all of that, if it's the right man and the right work."

"Will you know when it's the right man?"

He posed the same question I had been asking myself for quite some time and I answered carefully, "I think so."

"And have you met him yet?" He watched my face without blinking, his eyes fixed on my expression.

I felt an honest sympathy that I couldn't say what he wished to hear, that I could only answer helplessly, "I don't know. I honestly don't know." He stood abruptly but didn't appear angry or upset.

"At least you didn't say no, didn't say you were still

waiting for the right man to come along. That's something."

I wanted to ask him if he loved me or thought he did. The words would have made a difference to me, but Douglas never spoke of affection for me. Instead it was about what he could give me, about the things I could possess or how easy my life might be. He worked in commerce all day and so made even such an intimate relationship as husband and wife sound like a business transaction. Maybe he couldn't help it, but it wasn't how I had been raised to think of marriage.

In August I received a telegram in the middle of the day and opened it with misgiving. Miss Flaherty lingered in the background, worried about bad news, too, but the tidings were just the opposite.

Congratulations, Aunt Kat, the message read. *Baby Blessing Rebecca born Tuesday. Daughter well, mother ecstatic, father thankful.*

"I'm an aunt again," I announced happily and grinned at Miss Flaherty. "My sister's had a little girl and everyone's well." One concern I could set aside, and a second piece of good news came the same month.

"You look happy," observed Petra, plopping into a chair in my study one evening.

"I am," I replied as I waved a letter in the air. "My parents are coming for a visit in September. They plan to take the train and will arrive exactly one month from today. They have a meeting with someone about a business arrangement."

"Will I get to meet them?"

"I hope so, and I hope Miss Addams is back by then, too, because I'd like her to meet them."

I tried to picture my parents in Chicago and had to give up. The vision wouldn't come. My mother was more at home in men's pants and my father on horseback, and the thought of the two of them among the skyscrapers made me uneasy. They were full-grown adults, of course, but Chicago would be something they had never seen the likes of before. They had taken an anniversary trip to San Francisco a few years before but even that would not prepare them for the sights, sounds, and smells of this huge metropolis on the lake.

When I mentioned to Douglas that my parents would visit, he said, "I'd like them to join us for dinner one evening. Will you extend an invitation on my behalf?" I felt an odd reluctance, which must have shown on my face. "I know they may be out of their element, Katherine, but I assure you it won't matter to me."

For a moment his presumption that I was ashamed of them so outraged me that I wanted to shout at him, 'It's you! I don't want them to meet you!' I had the strangest feeling they wouldn't approve of him.

Instead of shouting, however, I managed to reply carefully, "I'll see if they have an evening free. They've been invited by one of the Swifts to discuss a beef partnership so their schedule might be filled."

"If your father is preoccupied with business, perhaps your mother would want to join us for dinner." I laughed at the thought.

"Douglas, my father doesn't make business decisions without my mother's full understanding and agreement. If there's a business meeting with Mr. Swift, believe me, both my parents will be there."

Douglas said nothing, but his mouth gave a little twist and I could almost read his mind: hen-pecked husband, domineering wife. He was so very wrong about them, but there was no way to explain so I didn't try. He would have to meet my parents to understand.

Miss Addams returned to Hull-House the first week in September. She looked rested and healthy, her face browned by the sun, and surprised me with a vigorous hug when she first saw me.

"I'm so proud of you, Katherine! More than one person wrote me of your dedication during the typhoid outbreak. I understand it even made the newspapers." I felt myself flush.

"Someone mentioned that to me, too. It's just a shame that not everyone shared in the public credit. Both Miss Flaherty and Mrs. Tabachnik were invaluable, and Dr. Pasca and the Health Department really orchestrated everything. I only did what I could, and more often than I care to remember it wasn't enough."

"That's not the way the epidemic was described to me, but I appreciate your modesty and understand your disappointment that you couldn't save everyone. I feel the same way sometimes."

When I thanked her for arranging Petra's scholarship, she grinned.

"Too often my life is all about knowing the right people, Katherine, so when I have the chance, I like to use that to the advantage of someone who is as talented and deserving as our Petra."

It was wonderful to have Jane Addams back. She brought with her an almost tangible energy and sense of purpose. I hadn't realized how barren Hull-House seemed to have become in her absence. Perhaps it was that she loved it so, loved everything that was accomplished there, and it was that love that filled the corners and once again made people smile for no reason.

Even Douglas noticed the change and commented. We had returned from a Sunday afternoon excursion to the Field Museum and sat on front porch chairs observing the sky darken in preparation for a storm. A steady stream of people moved in and out of the house.

"I don't remember it being this busy," he remarked.

"Miss Addams is back and all's right with the world. I'm so glad my parents will get to meet her."

"You haven't forgotten my invitation, have you?"

"No. They're staying at the Palmer House, as a matter of fact, so I thought we could just meet them there."

"Do you favor either of your parents?"

"Not my mother at all and only a little resemblance to my father. If you saw my sister and brothers and me all in a row, you could easily tell that I'm the odd child out. My older brother always tried to make me cry by telling me I had been found in a box by the side of the road."

"And did you cry?"

"Let my brother make me cry?! Not on your life! If I had allowed that, it would have given him power over me. I always gave as good as I got, much to my poor mother's despair."

"You're on speaking terms with your brother now, I presume." A question, not a statement.

Douglas's query brought to mind my last look at John Thomas. The whole family stood on the train platform waving and watching me leave. My brother had one arm around Hope's shoulders and held little Jack in the other, so obviously proud of his little family that I thought he might burst.

"He had the good fortune to be domesticated by a wonderful woman and is the happiest I've ever seen him. We get along quite well now. I'd like to think he's the one who changed, but I'm sure it's both of us. John Thomas is a page from my father's book, a good husband and father and brother, but don't tell him I said that. It would go straight to his head." Rain began to splatter, nothing heavy and no wind, just a gentle summer shower that tapped against the porch roof.

"Being domesticated by a wonderful woman is something I never had an interest in until recently," Douglas remarked. He had been circumspect and noncommittal since the night of the opera, a pleasant companion and nothing more, and I enjoyed that Douglas, even as I missed the edge his company usually afforded. As usual, I didn't know what to make of the emotional contradiction.

"It's not all sweetness," I cautioned, "and I know it's not always easy, either. Maybe you have an idealized version of what domestic life is like. My parents never shouted, but I do recall a few sharp disagreements and times when our house was uncomfortably quiet. John Thomas and Hope have words every now and then, and even my sister and her husband, who's the most charitable and even-tempered man I know, get out of temper with each other."

"I'd guess the good must outweigh the bad."

"You know," I said, turning to look at him with a smile, "my mother, my sister, and my sister-in-law have all said exactly that on more than one occasion."

"I'd probably fit right in."

I looked at him dispassionately and thought just the opposite, thought Douglas Gallagher wouldn't know what to make of the Davis clan as it thronged the kitchen and snitched supper from the stove. He would find us inelegant and rowdy, and my dear, simple Uncle Billy would cause Douglas to back up a step in distaste.

So I smiled again and said nothing. Douglas in Wyoming was a picture that wouldn't come any more easily to mind than my parents among skyscrapers.

CHAPTER 11

"You have company at the House," announced Petra excitedly from the dispensary doorway. "They're waiting for you in the reception room."

I had just set a boy's broken leg and he hobbled on the other leg, crutch under his arm, toward the door, holding on to his mother as he did so. The boy had been lucky with just a break, and his mother realized it. Had he fallen another six inches closer the streetcar could have severed his leg, but instead he bounced off its side and landed on the street with a broken leg and a big purple bruise on his hip.

"I'll clean up," volunteered Miss Flaherty, taking over and pushing me toward the door. "They've been waiting to see you for months, and it isn't right to make them wait any longer."

Petra looked as happy as I felt. "Your mother's so pretty!" she exclaimed. "You never told me that."

I pulled my smock over my head, suddenly anxious and eager to see the two people who, despite our differences, I loved most in the world.

Until that day September had been warm with no hint of autumn at all, but as I crossed the quadrangle I felt the cool tease of fall in the air. Not long before winter again, I thought, and my year in Chicago will be over. Then I'd return home, I supposed, and felt saddened at the thought of the end of this great adventure. But I was contrarily and inexplicably cheered, too, as I considered going back to Wyoming, seeing the new baby, and being home for a while.

My father stood by the fireplace that was lit for the first time in weeks, and my mother sat in the chair nearest him. When I came in calling "Hello," Mother stood and came toward me, both arms outstretched as I used to picture her waiting for me to drop out of the heavens.

"Oh, Katherine," she said and hugged me, "we have missed you so much. Everyone sends their love, and I've brought a picture of Blessing."

Her eyes were unnaturally bright and I asked teasingly, "Are those fiddle tears?"

"No, they're Katherine tears!" she retorted with spirit, making me laugh.

My father, less demonstrative but still glad to see me, gave me a kiss on the cheek. Then as if he couldn't help himself, he put an arm around my shoulders and drew me to him to kiss the top of my head as he used to when I was a little girl and needed to be held and comforted.

"Did we take you away from your patients?" he asked.

I could never tell if he approved of my vocation or just tolerated it, but from the start he'd always been respectful, never one to denigrate or question my ambitions.

"No, but I just treated a young man with a broken leg. If he'd fallen any closer to the trolley, he could have lost the leg entirely, so I was happy to be setting a limb that might have been completely cut off instead."

Keeping one hand on my arm, my mother sat and pulled me down next to her. Her face glowed in the way she always had about her when she was happy, the way that made her beautiful. She was dressed in a stylish walking dress of dark gray linen and a tailored overcoat a shade darker. The high neck of a white silk blouse and the small aquamarine brooch she'd worn for years showed at her throat. Her hat of gray straw was fashionably large and ornamented with a white plume that gently brushed the faint scar that ran along her hairline. The scar showed white against her chestnut hair and had been there as long as I could remember.

"You look wonderful," I said.

"We didn't want to embarrass you," she answered, giving a quick, smiling look up at my father. "That's why John was willing to wear a suit. You can appreciate the sacrifice, I know. Isn't he handsome?"

My silver-haired and lightly bearded father wasn't handsome and never had been. Once he reached sixty, however, he had become something more than handsome: distinguished, I thought. But before age had granted him that dignity, he had been lean and austere, his thin face lined by hard work and weather, a quiet man with remarkably blue eyes and a rich, rare smile. Father wore a dark tweed overcoat over a light-weight black suit pin-striped in gray and a gray tie. As fashionable as Mother and surely due to her touch. Only his hat displayed his visitor's status: a very fine, flat-crowned Stetson that belonged out west.

"Yes. You both look wonderful. I've been making everyone's life miserable anticipating your visit, so if you'd come dressed in sackcloth, you'd still be beautiful to me. Let me see my new niece."

In her photograph Blessing was on the verge of fussing,

eyes beginning to squint and lower lip stretched out, but you could tell she was a beautiful child with lots of hair and a perfectly-shaped head. I couldn't stop looking at her.

"And Becca's well?"

"She's fine," Mother said. "She had an easy labor and Blessing made her appearance before anyone expected her, including the doctor. We wished you had been there, though, Katherine. I can't say Dr. Jeske inspires a lot of confidence." She wouldn't elaborate despite my questions, only added, "Hope is counting on you being home for her next one so we won't have to bother with Dr. Jeske at all."

"Is there going to be a third for Hope and John Thomas? She hasn't said anything."

"We only just found out ourselves. Hope probably shared it in her letter. I've brought a whole sack of letters for you, from Hope and Becca, and even Sam sent along something."

"Really?" I was surprised and pleased.

Sam Kincaid, who had come to work for my father on my twelfth birthday and was still there eleven years later, was an old and trusted friend, but letters from him were rare. Sometimes I wished that weren't the case, but it seemed presumptuous to tell him so. He was busy and so was I.

"I'll save them all to read after you leave. It will be a treat. How's Uncle Billy?" Mother hesitated a moment.

"I don't know. That's another reason we'll be glad to have you home. Billy hasn't been feeling himself and Dr. Jeske is treating him, but I think he's getting worse instead of better. That's probably my imagination, but Billy doesn't complain and it's hard to tell how he really feels. You'll see when you get home." I stood up and pulled her up with me.

"Are you ready for a tour of Hull-House? I have so much to show you."

My mother has always been an animated woman, but she was particularly enthralled by Hull-House and its activities. In some respects she and Jane Addams were very much alike, both kind women with a passion for protecting the vulnerable and needy. If Louisa Caldecott Davis hadn't met, loved, and married my father, I could picture her in a similar setting, perfectly happy to spend her life on behalf of others.

"Even from your letters, Katherine, I had no idea." Mother's voice carried awe. People buzzed everywhere: in music lessons and book study groups and citizenship classes, learning English, rehearsing a play, baking a cake, reciting Shakespeare, cuddling a baby. When we stopped by the Labor Museum she remarked, "Hope would love to see all these looms and fabrics. She's never still. You should see the blanket she wove for our anniversary this year."

My father found the displays of different nationalities and their native work—from carpentry to glass blowing—interesting and asked about it.

"We're surrounded by more people in the nineteenth ward of Chicago than in the entire state of Wyoming," I told him, "and they all bring with them the customs and culture of their native countries. Miss Addams believes in respecting all of them as individuals, whose backgrounds are as valuable to them as ours is to us. It's a great experiment in democracy." I could see him thinking the idea through, always quieter than my mother, but he made no comment.

We met Mrs. Teague in the nursery, who caught one of my mother's hands in both of hers and said, "I am that happy to meet you, Mrs. Davis! The doctor speaks of you so warmly that I feel I know both of you. We love Dr. Davis and I've been waiting to thank you for letting her come to us."

"We love her, too," my mother returned, "but we can't take any credit for letting her come. She made that decision on her own. We learned a long time ago that when Katherine sets her mind on something, we should simply nod and say, 'Yes, dear.' Katherine's instincts are never wrong."

I felt proudest showing off the dispensary, my territory and the place where I felt most at home. I left my parents at the door long enough to stop by the bed of an elderly woman patient, who had arrived with complaints of pain in her stomach. I had felt a growth there and diagnosed cancer. All we could do was wait for permission to send her to the local hospital. I turned to leave, but the old woman grabbed my hand and pulled me back to her.

"I'm bad off, Doctor. I can tell."

"Mrs. Grundwald," I said, smoothing back her hair and bending down to her so she could hear me, "I won't lie to you. You are ill, but we're going to send you to the hospital where you can get better treatment."

"I'd rather die here. No one's got as kind a face as you, and I wouldn't mind if it was the last face I saw."

"You're not going to die here, and you may have many years left if you listen to the doctors at the hospital."

"A kind face," she repeated as if I hadn't spoken and drifted back to sleep.

When I went back to my parents, they both stared at me as if I were a stranger. I realized it was the first time they'd actually seen me in a doctor's role. They had visited me at school and had come to Lawrence for graduation but watching me in the active role of a physician was new for them.

As if they had spoken, I said, "I've grown up."

My father answered, "We can see that." I knew he loved me, but the pride I heard in his voice was something more elusive and rare, and his few words made me flush with pleasure.

When we concluded the tour at my rooms, Petra waited by the door with an invitation. "Dr. Davis, Miss Addams wondered if your parents would like to join her, Dr. Hamilton, and Miss Smith for tea in her study."

I pulled Petra closer and introduced her.

"Katherine has written nothing but glowing compliments about you, Miss Stravinsky," Mother said, always at her best greeting people and putting them at ease. "I can't tell you how pleased I am to finally meet you!" My mother possessed a very warm, unpretentious, and true nature that people recognized as genuine. Because of that, they were always drawn to her in the same way one is drawn to a patch of light on a gloomy day. Even if my sister Becca did inherit all our mother's finest qualities leaving none for me, I could still appreciate those gifts because of the expression on Petra's face, who looked as if she had just met royalty.

I expected my father to feel out of place surrounded by women, a man used to bawling cattle and the company of cowboys, but he surprised me by acting very comfortable and courtly. He charmed them all as he brought up flies' eggs with a perfectly straight face and listened attentively to Dr. Hamilton speak about her new enemy: lead poisoning.

Miss Addams, who I'm sure liked my mother well enough, seemed to take to Father immediately.

"We appreciate you loaning us your daughter for a year, Mr. Davis," she told him. "Katherine has brought both competence and compassion to our work and our people here."

"Her mother and I brought Katherine into the world," Father replied, "but we don't consider her ours. She's her own woman and makes her own decisions." His response was exactly right, and I shared a smile with my mother across the room, both of us proud of him. I was surprised by Father's easy manners, but my mother was complacent. Apparently his ability to charm was no surprise to her, so how had I missed it for all these years?

My parents returned to their hotel in an automobile sent by Mr. Swift, the man with whom they would be meeting the next day.

"We'll be busy most of tomorrow, I'm afraid," Mother explained before they departed, "and there's an evening dinner planned somewhere." She sent a questioning look to my father but he shrugged, not having any more specifics than she. "But Friday morning your father has an appointment somewhere, and I hoped you and I could spend some time together then. I know you're busy and I don't want to get in the way, so I could come back here or meet you someplace else, whatever you thought best."

"I have just the idea. We can go to the Newberry Library right off Washington Park. You'll love the place. It has rare editions and old maps and a wonderful marble staircase. I'll meet you at your hotel Friday morning and we can go from there." Then belatedly remembering, I added, "I almost forgot that my friend, Douglas Gallagher, has invited all of us to supper Friday there at the restaurant in the Palmer House. It's very nice. I've been there myself. Is that all right?"

Without missing a beat or blinking an eye, my mother responded, "That would be lovely. We hoped we would have the opportunity to meet your friend," and gave me a bland smile.

Too smooth, Mother, I thought, and suddenly wondered what kind of business had really brought my parents to Chicago. She met my look with a perfectly innocent one of her own, gathered up her gloves and purse, and kissed me good-bye.

"We're very proud of you, Katherine," she said in my ear, and I thought that it didn't matter if they had come to Chicago to check up on me. If that were the case, it only meant they loved me, not that they didn't trust me. Five years ago I would have had difficulty seeing the difference but no longer.

That night Petra came to the dispensary. She stood silently in the doorway while I completed paperwork at my old wooden desk oblivious to her presence. Finally I raised my head and saw her.

"Why are you standing there? Come in and sit down and keep me company. Mrs. Grundwald is sleeping soundly so we won't wake her. She's transferring to the hospital tomorrow." Petra settled herself onto one of the empty beds.

"I liked your parents very much. Will they be back here?" When I shook my head she looked disappointed. "Your mother is so—" Petra paused to search for the right word and then gave up. "She shines is what I want to say, but I don't know how to say it. She makes you feel like you're the most special person she's ever met, so friendly and kind. My mother always looked tired, and she didn't smile very often." Petra hesitated, then continued, "If I ask you something will you tell me the truth?"

She sounded so serious I put down my pen and answered, "If it doesn't involve breaking a confidence, of course, I will. I promised to always tell you the truth, Petra."

Her question came out of the blue: "Has your father ever hit your mother, even just once?"

"Hit my mother?" I repeated blankly, the horrible words literally impossible to picture. I shook my head, both to emphasize my answer and to banish the appalling notion. "Oh, no, Petra. No. My father is devoted to my mother.

He'd never do anything to hurt her. I believe he'd die first. My father is a quiet man so he's not one to say it very often, but he loves my mother with a passion and he would never hurt her. Never." I thought I understood where that question had come from, however, and so continued, "I wish the way your father treated your mother wasn't as common as it is, but you must not think that's how it always is or has to be or was meant to be. Men of integrity do not strike women or mistreat children."

"But how do you know if it's a man of integrity?" she asked, parroting my phrase. "How can you tell?" That was a question I hadn't quite figured an answer to yet myself.

"You just know, I guess," I said, struggling to say the right thing. "My mother would say that you know when you meet him because you feel it here." I put my hand over my heart. "She'd say listen to your inner voice and don't settle for less."

"I don't think I have an inner voice."

"Now that's one thing I am sure of, or you wouldn't have ended up on our doorstep looking for a new way of life. I know that Petra Stravinsky's inner voice is loud and lively." I wished I could say the same of mine, I thought later as I said good night and watched her leave. When it came to Douglas Gallagher, my inner voice seemed mysteriously quiet.

I sent a note to Douglas the next day to confirm Friday's supper with my parents, rushed through Thursday, and took the elevated train to meet my mother at her hotel Friday morning.

"How was yesterday's meeting?" I asked.

She gave a quick grimace and said, "I don't think it's a business arrangement we feel comfortable with."

"Sounds to me like it's the people you don't feel comfortable with."

"That, too. We didn't like the attitudes we heard expressed about the workers in the packing plants. Your father and I aren't anarchists, but we believe everyone has the right to a fair wage and a safe working place. We couldn't find any common ground on the topic, and by lunch we all realized we would not make good business partners, which made last night's dinner a little awkward. We made it through, though, and I don't think we would have embarrassed you too much." We were entering the library as she concluded and I stopped so abruptly she almost collided with me.

"You've made a similar comment at least twice, Mother, and I wish you'd stop it. You could never embarrass me, and I would never be ashamed of you." She had the grace to look sheepish.

"It's just that you're so grown up, Katherine, a professional woman with prestigious friends, and we're still just cattle ranchers from Wyoming. I told John this morning that if I had to wear a corset one more day, I'd either fall over in a dead faint from constricted breathing or start weeping from the discomfort."

"Not as comfortable as men's pants, I bet," I said with a grin, and she gave me a poke with her hand, grinning in return.

"That's enough from you, young lady, but you're right. I've been spoiled with freedom and I don't like giving it up, even for a few days. I'll wear a corset this evening so I look a little more fashionable and not quite so stout to your Mr. Gallagher, but after that I'm throwing it out with the trash. I'm too old for the discomforts of fashion, thank the Lord."

Mother didn't look old as she spoke, dressed in a suit the color of faded raspberries and a large straw hat trimmed in the same hue that shaded her gray eyes. Only a small, dramatic silver streak in her chestnut hair betrayed her age—and even that held a certain striking appeal. I saw what my sister would look like in thirty years, she was so like Mother in appearance, and the thought of Becca made me think of the new baby, which sent us off onto another subject. We chattered as we walked and at one time had to be shushed by the librarian because Mother reminded me of a memory so ridiculously funny it brought me to tears of laughter I simply could not restrain.

Mid-afternoon I took the elevated as close to home as I could get and finished the trip on the trolley, checked patients, stopped in at the nursery, bathed, then dressed in the soft, draped, oriental dress of apricot silk created for me by the Hull-House Home Skills Club. Miraculously, I was ready right on time when Fritz pulled up to the curb.

In the auto, I shared the day with Douglas, who said with obvious sincerity, "I'm looking forward to meeting your parents."

I responded, "They're looking forward to meeting you, too. Will you be very embarrassed if my mother's wearing men's pants?" and laughed at the look on his face.

Of course, she wasn't wearing men's pants. Mother entered the dining room dressed in a slim-skirted gown with cap sleeves, draped neckline, and a pinched-in waist that showed off her slender figure. The gown's black silk had a sheen that caught the light from the sconces on the wall. She trailed a vivid red, fringed shawl over her shoulders and was hatless, her hair parted down the middle, woven into two gleaming braids, and caught at the back of her neck. No jewelry adorned her throat or ears, and only the silver streak over her temple showed as ornament, an elegant and pleasing contrast to the frilled and flounced women who sat around us. Even with my bias my mother was a stunning woman, not beautiful in any traditional sense of the word and certainly past her youth but in her own distinctive style breathtaking. From his first sight of her, I watched Douglas hastily rearrange all his preconceived ideas about my parents.

Father was stylish in his own way, as well. The slight hint of red that threaded through the waistcoat he wore under a well-tailored, coal-black suit matched the color of my mother's shawl, and no other man in the room could have worn a similar string tie with his same dignity and style. With a literary turn of mind, I thought that with his lean, brown face, silver hair and beard, and sky-blue eyes my father could have stepped out of an Owen Wister story.

"Mr. Gallagher," my mother said at her friendliest, "I'm so happy to meet you. How kind of you to include us in your supper plans!"

I watched Douglas's face, amused. When my mother chose to charm, she couldn't be matched, and she was at her finest that evening. How many men did I see walk past our table and turn for a quick, surreptitious second look at her, while she, unaware as usual of her effect, had eyes only for my father as if no other man lived on the planet? I had observed similar scenes before—at one time had even felt a secret resentment at the attention she so effortlessly received—but I was glad to discover that nasty little feeling completely gone. I felt proud of her, proud of them both. Perhaps it was the recollection of Douglas's and Drew's parents and the sad legacy they had left. Perhaps it was Petra's story and her innocent question, 'Has your father ever hit your mother, even just once?' as if she believed such violence common, even necessary, to a normal relationship between husband and wife. Perhaps it was just that I'd grown up at last. Whatever the reason, that night I was filled with a pride for who and what my parents were that has never diminished since.

I couldn't claim the evening an unqualified success but

most of it was enjoyable. My mother came to dinner wanting to like Douglas and did her best at quizzing him without appearing to do so, a skill at which she excelled. On the other hand, from the start I could tell that my father didn't take to him so the men's discussions about general topics of business and geography were less easy. Douglas's impeccable manners displayed well: respectful and solicitous, urbane in his usual way, never showy or condescending. I thought he looked very handsome, besides, at home in the role of attentive, interested host, and I appreciated the way he went out of his way to make all of us comfortable. He made only two missteps, but unfortunately they affected the evening's success. The first gaffe he recovered from quickly, but the second brought a chill to my father's blue eyes that didn't thaw for the rest of the night.

Early in the evening, still on the fruit course so hardly into supper at all, Douglas remarked, "I ran into a man who recognized your name from some years ago, Mr. Davis." My mother sent a quick glance to my father, telling him something with that look although I couldn't interpret the message.

My father's gaze rested thoughtfully on Douglas's face before he said, using the mild tone he saved for reprimand and that under certain circumstances had been known to send chills down his children's spines, "Is that right?"

I tried to communicate my own silent message to Douglas to advise him to move to another topic, but he, trying too hard to make conversation and intending to compliment, continued, "John Rock Davis, isn't it?" He put gentle stress on the middle name. "The man I was talking to came from Denver, and he told me that something of a legend had grown up around your name out west. Thirty years later they still talk about your prowess."

My father deliberately resumed his meal as if Douglas's

words had not occurred, and my mother bravely leaped into the gap.

"John is often confused with that man," she remarked with an innocent smile, "but that was a long time ago and someone else entirely." Then she complimented the fresh strawberries and I joined in, my father added a cordial comment, and the moment passed.

Poor Douglas, I thought, and caught his eye with a faint but commiserating smile. He could hardly have been expected to recognize my father's quelling tone or know that he spoke infrequently and unwillingly of his life before he met Mother, as if that life were of no consequence compared to his role as husband and father. I knew little of those years, only that he and his brother had fought in the Civil War in which his brother had died. The immediate years that followed the war were unaccounted for until he met and married my mother later in life. For my father all that mattered began on his wedding day. I'd never given much thought to his reticence before—he was always there for us and that was all that had seemed important—but decided to ask him about those early years sometime in the near future. Douglas's comment and my father's reaction had made me curious.

That exchange was a slight tactical error on Douglas's part, a little endearing and entirely forgivable because I thought he had made it out of pure intentions. The chill that swept the table just before coffee was caused by a misstep that damaged him much more severely.

As the waiter brought breads and pastries to the table, set down small cups for coffee, and brought fresh cream, Douglas observed, "You're wearing a beautiful ring, Mrs. Davis. I don't think I've ever seen anything like it before."

His comment drew my attention to her left hand, which she held out palm down so we could view the ring. Six diamonds sparkled in a setting of blush gold: one large, round central gem surrounded by five smaller marquis stones each set at an angle. I'd never seen my mother wear any ring except her wedding band and certainly nothing as grand and magnificent as what she held out in front of us, but the ring was perfect for her strong, brown, long-fingered hands. Like the wearer, not showy but striking. The stones themselves were clearly of the finest quality and their setting unique.

"I've never seen that before, Mother. How lovely! I can tell it's meant to resemble a sunflower. Is it new?"

"Yes," she answered in a small voice, "it is new. I wish I had prettier hands to do it justice, but I'm afraid they're irredeemable, too many years of house work and ranch work and children."

"You weren't wearing it this morning or on Wednesday, either," I pointed out. "I'm sure I would have noticed it."

Mother looked down at the ring without speaking and I realized she couldn't speak, that she had to compose herself first because something about the ring had stirred emotion.

Finally she lifted her head and explained, "That was your father's secret appointment this morning while you and I visited the library. He surprised me with the ring just before we came down to supper tonight. A belated anniversary gift, he said, the central stone for him and the five stones for you children, all in the shape of a Kansas sunflower because that's where we met." She took a shaky breath and gave the kind of smile you give when you're trying not to cry. "Your father told me—" she continued, and then, remarkably, my mother began to blush. The color crept up her cheeks to her temples as if her face were reflecting the brilliant red of the shawl tossed across the back of her chair.

Mother's loss of composure was an amazing sight. In

all my years, I had never seen her blush like that and could only stare. There was never a social situation my mother couldn't handle, and I knew of nothing that ever caused her to lose her self-possession. Nothing. Ever. She always knew what to do, said the right thing at the right time, acted the peacemaker, gave needed encouragement, quashed bad behavior, read minds, and soothed hurt feelings. The family counted on her for that. I should have had pity on her and moved the conversation on to another topic—she would have done that for me had the roles been reversed—but at the time I didn't. I couldn't. I was so astounded by her speechless confusion that I sat mute.

My father finished her sentence, speaking quietly to her, to all of us. "I told her that I never expected to have much in life and what I have I don't deserve. But thirty years ago I happened on a treasure and she's the one who makes me rich, always has, and always will. I told her that she deserved something more than that worn wedding band she's been wearing for the last thirty years, and I told her it's still not near enough. Nothing ever could be."

Well, I thought completely dumbfounded, my mother blushing and my father giving an emotional speech in public. Was the moon turning to blood as well and the stars falling from the sky?

We could have maneuvered through that odd little time, though. Mother's blush had already faded and I had regained my wits enough to comment about the dessert cakes that dominated the center of our table. Father sipped coffee as if nothing out of the ordinary had occurred, his faint smile the only sign that he was pleased.

So we had reclaimed our conversational equilibrium when Douglas, not knowing my parents and perhaps incapable of understanding them raised his glass of wine specifically to my father and said, "You have very good taste."

Whether he meant the gesture or the ring or my mother, it was impossible to tell. The remark should have sounded innocent enough, I suppose, but it didn't, Douglas's tone a masculine purr, his look to my father one of a shared and subtle male secret. The message he sent was clear to all of us at the table: *Good work. You've recognized your wife's contributions and this should keep her mollified for a while.* As if she were a dog that needed a periodic pat on the head, as if my father had condescended to favor his wife with some obligatory, patronizing attention and now should be feted for the gesture. All of that was in Douglas's tone and look, and my heart sank. His comment was so inappropriate, he had missed the point of my father's words so completely that I physically winced and then hastily made another comment about the little frosted dessert cakes. My mother, back to her normal self, recognized the mistake, too, and made a similarly innocuous remark. But the damage was done.

Father gave Douglas a long, unblinking look from eyes suddenly the color of aquamarine and then purposely turned to me to ask a question about Hull-House. The temperature at the table fell several degrees and poor Douglas didn't even feel it plummet.

Later, we said good night outside the restaurant.

"I'll come to the train station and see you off tomorrow," I told my parents, already melancholy at the thought of their departure.

I reached up to kiss my father on the cheek so I could whisper, "You made her very happy, Father. You're an old fox to keep such a secret." He just smiled, still pleased with himself, I think, although with him it was hard to tell.

Mother, remembering her manners and always kind, put out a hand to Douglas.

"We had a delightful evening, Douglas. Thank you.

Everything was lovely. I hope I didn't embarrass you too much with my little display of emotion."

"Not at all, Mrs. Davis. Thirty years of a happy marriage calls for it." The diplomatic response might have redeemed him in her eyes, but clearly it would take much more than a well-turned phrase to put him back in my father's good graces.

On the ride home Douglas said, "I'll tell you honestly, Katherine, your parents are nothing like I expected."

"I know. I could tell. That will teach you to form advance opinions." But he knew I meant to tease.

In a hesitant voice, nothing like his usual firm, self-confident tone, he asked, "Do you think they liked me?" My heart went out to the little boy in his tone. A grown up man with a life and business of his own but still unsure if he had said or done the right thing, wanting very much to be liked but not really confident that he was at all likeable.

"You were an attentive host this evening, Douglas, thoughtful and generous and I'm sure they both noticed that. My mother wanted to like you from the beginning, so I wouldn't spend any time worrying about the evening." He was quiet, digesting what I had—and had not—said.

As the auto pulled up to the front gate, he turned to look at me and say, "You're like your father, hard to read and not one to give much away. I couldn't really tell where I stood with him."

I could, I thought, but didn't say it. What would have been the point? Instead I replied, "You're not the first person to notice a resemblance. I'll take it as a compliment."

"I meant it as one." He got out, came around to my side, and extended a hand to help me out. "Meeting them helped me understand you better. You come by that idealistic streak naturally."

I wanted to tell him that the four of us together had

helped me see him differently, too, but because I wouldn't have known how to explain further, I was quiet. Maybe there would be a time for that later—after I had sorted through my feelings.

***

I had been away from home for five years, had said any number of good-byes, had waved farewell, and never given the departures a thought once my family was out of sight, but the next day at the train station was different.

"I wish you could stay longer," I said to my parents. The train was boarding but we all continued to stand on the platform reluctant to part. My mother pressed something into my hand and when I looked at it closely saw it was a check.

"This is our contribution to the valuable work that's done at Hull-House. We talked about it last night. John knows I treasure the ring he gave me, more for the thought and the love behind it than anything else, but it cost a great deal of money. We decided to match the cost of the ring as a gift for Miss Addams to use as she thinks best."

"I'm glad you had the chance to see what we do there because now you understand how really valuable the work is. There's always more need than there is money, and I know we'll put your contribution to good use. Thank you. Miss Addams will send you a personal letter. She always does."

Behind us my father said, "Lou, we need to go," and Mother gave me a last hug.

"Will you be home for Christmas?" she asked, and I shook my head.

"Not until January," I told her, sad to miss another Christmas with my family, "but it's not that far away, and

I'm happy in my work here. It really means something."

"*You* mean something to us," Mother responded fiercely, "and home isn't the same without you," then added, blinking back tears, "but we want you to be happy, Katherine. Your father and I love you and we want you to be happy." Father helped her up the steps into the car, then turned to me before he boarded.

"You'll grieve your mother if you don't come home, at least for a while, Katherine," he told me gravely. I had the sense that he wanted to say more, something between just the two of us, but he only leaned to kiss me on the cheek. "You'll grieve me, too," he added and hopped up into the car as the porter removed the wooden steps. I watched the train pull out slowly and continued to wave even when I couldn't see them any longer and there wasn't a chance they could still see me.

I didn't know when or how I changed but I had. I'd never given their feelings a second thought when I agreed to the opportunity in Chicago, hadn't asked their opinion or even believed they had a right to any input. My life, after all, and my choice. I never considered that my mother might worry about me, my father miss me, or my family need me. How relieved I had felt not to have to return to Wyoming, to a life full of the common, prosaic, and unexciting activities that filled the days and weeks and months of life at home, year after year after year! If I were honest with myself, I could recall my vague scorn for the familiar routine and a more pronounced disdain for my roots, my ordinary, unglamorous roots. But sometime in the last several months those self-indulgent feelings had been replaced by warm affection and pride and a sharp pang of longing to be on that train with my parents, going back to the people I loved and who loved me.

I stood on the train platform too long, lost in thought,

then had to ask the hour from a passing gentleman. By the time I was back at the dispensary, I had shaken off my little bout of homesickness and was myself again. The last weeks of the year would pass as quickly as the first and I would be home soon enough. No use wishing my life away.

CHAPTER 12

I enjoyed a wonderful feast of reading the next few days. I rationed the letters out as if I were Robinson Crusoe and they were the crumbs that must nourish me for weeks. Becca's letter came first, with the picture of baby Blessing propped on my desk in front of me as I read. My sister had longed for children her whole life, wanted to be nothing but a wife and mother since she was old enough to play with dolls, had hummed baby lullabies when she was hardly more than a baby herself. While I ran around collecting worms and flower petals and making detailed notes as the barn cat gave birth to kittens, Becca stayed busy learning to cook and sew and started a list of names for the children she would one day have. With her second daughter, she had what she'd always dreamed of. Different as night and day, someone had once observed about the two of us, but I knew better. We shared a common birthright, the same parents, the same values. Not so different after all.

Hope, my brother's wife, only five years in the family

but so at home with us you'd think she had been born a Davis, wanted me to come home. She said it more than once in her letter.

Lou probably told you I'm expecting again, she wrote. *John Thomas has put in his order for a girl, but I don't care as long as the baby's healthy. I can tell this one's different from the boys. I can't explain it, but I don't feel easy about this baby. Will you be home by February? I can't say I have a lot of confidence in Dr. Jeske. When I try to tell him I think something's not right, he pats my hand and says he's surprised I'm still having jitters after already having two babies. Jitters he says, as if I don't know what I really feel. I wish you'd come home for the birth of this baby, Katherine. I'd feel a lot better.*

Hope was not a woman prone to exaggeration or hysterics. She had a steady hand, a level head, a quiet sense of humor, and a highly developed sense of purpose. Certainly savvy enough to know when something was not right. For the doctor to discount her instincts was patronizing and dangerous.

I'll be there in February, I wrote back, and remembering Petra's and my conversation added as a postscript—Just trust your inner voice.

I saved the letter from my friend Sam Kincaid until last. His writing was a rare occurrence and something to be treasured, reread, and brought out for comfort now and then. For a man with no formal education, he wrote a fine letter, describing the cycle of the seasons so clearly I felt I was there with him despite the miles between. Sam had a gift for the comical, able to laugh at himself and to paint a word picture that was clearer than a photograph. Sam closed his letter by writing, *I told Uncle Billy I was writing to you and now he's standing right next to me insisting I tell you to come home. You know he'd write if he could, but he wants me to write his words exactly: "It ain't the same without Katherine." I can't but agree with him. Your friend, Sam Kincaid.*

Well, I thought, conscious of a small kindling warmth I couldn't recall feeling before, wasn't that nice? For a reason no one could figure out, I was always my Uncle Billy's favorite, and I had known Sam Kincaid for so long he was like another brother. He'd been a scrawny young man, eighteen at most, when he turned up at our ranch carrying his saddle and asking for work. He didn't talk of his past, didn't talk about much of anything really, but my father took to him right away and hired him and because he was the same age as John Thomas, they became best friends before the year was out. My mother added Sam to the family from the start and spent enough time with him to learn his secrets—whatever they were. He grew right along with the ranch over the years and never forgot that my father took him on without question and my mother treated him like a third son. I knew he'd do anything for them, for all of us, really.

A few weeks before I left for school in Lawrence, Sam and I rode out on a clear August day. The white peaks of the mountains shone and the sky stretched blue and cloudless, not too hot, the kind of rare, perfect day I still believe happens only in Wyoming.

"If you're ever in any trouble, Katherine, you know you only have to send word and I could be right there. Lawrence isn't that far. Send me a telegram and tell me to come and I'll be there. No questions asked."

Sam was too serious for me at the time. Nearly eighteen and full of a great adventure, I was so focused on becoming a physician that I couldn't think of anything else, and I treated his offer lightly.

"I can take care of myself," I said and didn't bother to

thank him. “You don’t need to baby me. I’ve got enough people doing that already.”

“What *do* you need then?” Sam looked at me soberly, no longer a boy but suddenly a grown man, something about him at the moment that made him seem like a stranger. The horses shifted restlessly under us and I felt restless, too, eager to get away and leave the familiar behind, to see the world and make something of myself, to follow my lifelong dream. I was in no mood for serious talk.

“I can always use a friend,” I answered and laughed out loud, “but he’s got to be a better rider than I am,” and without warning took off across the flatlands, leaving Sam behind. I recalled that he caught up with me. There was never any doubt he was the better rider. We hadn’t had very many opportunities for conversation since that day, but he seemed to take my words to heart and ended each letter the same: *Your friend, Sam Kincaid.*

The month of October stayed beautiful and crisp. Dr. Pasca came early in the month to say he thought he had already found next year’s intern, who would arrive the last week of December, and could I stay long enough to show him around? When I said of course, he followed up with a question about my own plans.

“I still want to be a family doctor with my own practice, someone who’s part of the community and grows right along with it, brings babies into the world and watches them grow up and have babies of their own. That’s what I want so I’m going back to Laramie.”

“Going home, then?”

“Yes,” I said, surprised that the thought brought such satisfaction, “I’m going home.”

Petra began her studies with several music instructors and took a classical language course along with basic courses in English and history. She would come to the dispensary in the evening loaded down with books and papers and spread them across my desk, a serious and intent Petra, who allowed herself to be interrupted only by an emergency at the dispensary door.

I sought out Patrick Sweeney one afternoon.

"How is your star pupil taking to university life?" I asked. He turned on the piano stool where he had been plunking something out on the keys to smile at me.

"Like a fish to water. I taught her everything I knew in twelve weeks so it was past time to move her along to the real experts."

"But none of them is her friend, not like you are, Patrick. You haven't washed your hands of her entirely, have you?"

"Washed my hands of Petra?" he repeated quietly, met my grave look with one equally as serious, and shook his head. "I'll be able to do that when the earth stops turning and the sun stops shining and not a moment before." He told me quite a lot with those words.

"I'll only be here another ten weeks, Patrick. After I'm gone Petra will need someone to continue to stand by her and help her make good decisions, someone who won't take advantage of her youth and innocence. I'd like to think that's you."

"She'll miss you, Katherine, and I could never take your place with her. It's always 'Dr. Davis this' or "Dr. Davis that,' but I'm not sure I'd want to do that anyway. I'd rather carve out a place in her life for me alone."

"She's still young and I think more vulnerable than either of us really understands. You'll need to be respectful and careful with her." I eyed him and waited for his response, didn't want to prompt or suggest.

"I'm a patient man, Doctor. Right now it's enough to be

her confidant, advise her when she asks, and be there if she needs me."

"I can't imagine that will always be enough for you."

"She won't always be sixteen, so it may not have to be, but I'll take my chances." He paused, then said with intent, "Petra will always be safe with me, Katherine." I stood.

"I won't interrupt you any longer then. I found what I came for."

Whatever happened in Petra's future, she would always have two true friends: one a Wyoming country doctor and the other a man of integrity—a man she would recognize if she listened to her inner voice. How that story would end remained to be seen, but I knew I left her in good hands, hands that would help mold her into the woman she was destined to become. Petra needed direction, of course, but she already possessed a reservoir of strength and dignity. How else had she survived as bright and beautiful as she was?

I saw Douglas every weekend and sometimes during the week. The frequency was sometimes against my better judgment, but he was insistent, as if my one-year assignment was new to him, as if I hadn't explained the arrangement from the beginning. He remained generous with me, took me to theatrical events and to the Chicago Symphony, spent Sunday afternoons at local museums and parks, enjoyed candlelit dinners in fine restaurants. I felt unable to stop the momentum and didn't want to appear ungrateful. Infrequently I worried about his feelings, but when we were together I couldn't seem to recall the reason for my worry because he balanced his attentions with just the right level of affectionate regard.

One evening as we came home in the cold October night, he draped something wool across my shoulders as we rode and then instead of removing his arm pulled me closer to him instead.

"You're not really going away, Katherine, are you?" His voice a whisper. "You don't have to. You have a life here now."

"I need to go home, Douglas. I haven't been there for any time to speak of in two years. My family's there, a nephew and a niece I haven't ever met and another baby on the way. I need to go home."

"I understand you need to *visit* your family, but that's not home for you any more. Why can't Chicago be your home? Why can't I give you a home here? I can do more for you than you can imagine," and he kissed me hard, something heartfelt in that kiss, something suppressed that he couldn't talk about because he never spoke of deep feelings or of love. Caught up in his embrace, I thought it was that he didn't know how to say the words and felt a deep compassion for him, a deep love for him, perhaps. One emotion seemed to overlap the other.

I couldn't give the answer he wanted that night, could only repeat that I needed to go home. How many times had I longed to tell him what he longed to hear and yet didn't? More often than he knew, certainly. As the year began to wind down I felt a more frequent compulsion to say yes to the Douglas who could be so likable and so unconsciously vulnerable, to the little boy, who yearned for his parents' approval and affection, to the Douglas unloved.

The voice that usually drew me back, that counseled caution and urged independence, that was reluctant to give anything away became quieter and quieter. Something inevitable approached.

Early in November the noted activist Ida B. Wells-Barnett was scheduled to give a lecture in the Smith Building, a comfortably intimate meeting area off the Hull-House Theater. Earlier that year she had helped to found a new organization called the National Association for the Advancement for Colored People, over which there was enough debate to draw a sizable crowd to her presentation. I admired the woman for her confrontational articles in the *Chicago Conservator* and for her history of speaking the unspeakable and arrived early enough to find a seat toward the front of the room. Someone sat down next to me and nudged my shoulder.

"I imagine if you were asked to name the person you least expected to see here this evening, my name would have been number two on the list, right behind President Taft," said Drew Gallagher.

"No. Number three. Behind the President and King George of England."

"Still in appropriate company, then," Drew murmured, and I had to choke a giggle.

"What are you doing here, Drew? Don't tell me you have a social conscience."

"You really think me a worthless man, don't you? In fact, I do have such a conscience, although I wouldn't let just anyone know that. It would ruin my image. I'll trust you to keep the knowledge to yourself."

We settled comfortably side by side until Mrs. Wells-Barnett took the podium and then we were caught up in the passion of her ideals and her rhetoric for over an hour. When she finished and the applause finally died down, people began to leave, but Drew and I remained in seated conversation as people climbed over and around us.

"What did you think?" he asked.

My answer came out in an outraged rush. "I think it's a blot on our land that she has to talk about these issues at all, that we don't just do the right thing without needing some-one to stir our consciences and our hearts. It's unthinkable that we still have lynchings in the twentieth century and that she should be told to give up her seat on a train to someone just because of the color of her skin. It's not American."

"You're wrong, Katherine. You've spent too much time in the rarified air of Hull-House and not enough in the world outside its doors. That conduct is more American than not, unfortunately, and it will take more than one impassioned person—whether Mrs. Barnett or Jane Addams or you—to change what we are."

"I didn't expect you to be so serious or so negative, Drew."

"I am seriously realistic, not negative, Doctor, and I didn't say the situation was hopeless." He stood, took my hand, and drew me to my feet. "Show me your place here. Do you have the time?"

"Of course. I'm happy to tote." Drew shot me a puzzled glance and I explained, "It's a Hull-House term. Toting means to take people on a tour. During the day we have official toters, but it's too late for that now. I can still give you a quick look around, though."

I took Drew up one floor for a view of the theater, then through the house kitchens into the dining room, down stairs and outside across the quadrangle, and into the long apartment building that housed the dispensary at its far west end.

"I'm afraid it's too late to show you the club rooms, the nursery, or the playground, and you should really come on Saturday to get the full effect of the Labor Museum. It's already lights out in the boarding room apartments, too, so I can't show you them, either, but I can show you my home away from home." We went into the dispensary's waiting room where Mrs. Tabachnick met us in the doorway.

"Is everything quiet?" I asked her.

"Yes, Doctor. You might want to take a look at the

woman who came in this afternoon, though. I think she's looking better, but that might be wishful thinking on my part."

I left Drew behind to go place a hand on the woman's forehead. She slept soundly and snored a little. Her worn face relaxed in sleep to make her younger than I had originally thought. The woman was a prostitute, who had heard of a woman doctor and come to me about an infection from her work that caused her to run a fever, caused her some pain and some embarrassment, too. Her most prominent fear, though, was that the condition would affect her ability to earn a living. I couldn't offer much help as long as she worked the streets, I told her, could alleviate some symptoms for a while but she would not get better and after a time would certainly get worse.

"Make a note for Miss Flaherty to release her tomorrow," I told Nurse Tabachnik. "She's as good as she'll get if she doesn't change her line of work."

"You look very at home here," Drew observed after Mrs. Tabachnick left.

"The dispensary is my home. Or was. I'll be gone in eight weeks, and then it will be someone else's home."

We had started down the hallway to the door that would take us back to the main house when he stopped suddenly at my words.

"I don't think I knew that, Katherine."

"I'm sure I must have mentioned that this was just a one-year opportunity for me. And now my year is almost over." Once outside we didn't speak until we crossed the quadrangle and entered the warmth of the house. Drew immediately picked up the conversation where it had left off.

"Are you really leaving then? I can't imagine my brother will allow that."

I raised both eyebrows at his comment. "Allow is a strong word. Why would you think I need his permission?"

Drew stood with his back to the fireplace in the front room, dressed for winter in a beautiful, dark, woolen coat and fashionable trilby hat that contrasted handsomely with his fair hair and complexion, every inch the cosmopolitan man.

"My brother has quite a proprietary interest in you, Katherine. You know that. He speaks of you as if you already had an understanding, although I'd be disappointed if that were the case because you promised you'd talk to me first before you made him any kind of commitment."

"Douglas and I are good friends, Drew, but besides that I don't know. For a man who admittedly spends very little time with his brother, you seem unnaturally interested in his private life. Are you worried that I'm not good enough for him? Is Cowgirl Kate not quite the woman you think should grace his home?" I didn't speak with either vindictiveness or meekness but felt an honest curiosity about his veiled comments.

"I believe Douglas would make you very unhappy, and I would like to spare you that if I could. I like you, you know."

"What an odd thing for one brother to say of another! Not very kind and much too mysterious."

He shrugged, buttoned his coat, and headed for the front door.

"I'm a mysterious man by nature. It adds to my appeal with the ladies. I need to walk a few blocks to find a ride so I can't stay any longer, but I'm very serious that you talk to me before you make any kind of life-changing decision. You won't forget your promise, will you?"

"No, I won't forget. I am leaving at the end of December, Drew, and I'm going home, at least for a while, so if I don't see you again, I wish you well. I like you, too, you know." I gently mimicked his drawling tone and he gave me that lopsided grin of his, intended to charm as it always did.

"Thank you. That's high praise coming from you." He came back from the door to where I stood and kissed me lightly on the forehead. "You should go home as soon as you can. You'll be happier there than you could ever be here. Trust me, Katherine." After he left, I thought through all he had said but was more troubled by what he had left unsaid.

Hull-House celebrated Thanksgiving with reverence, read and told stories of the first Thanksgiving, arranged special music and an ecumenical worship service, and ended with a festive meal, all for the benefit of the neighborhood. Douglas had invited me to his home where he would host a dinner for a few business associates and their families, but I knew a secret relief that I had already committed the day to Miss Addams. The idea of having to be on formally good behavior was too daunting, and there would be another persistent conversation with Douglas about my imminent departure for which I was not in the mood. I preferred to sit comfortably and listen to Petra sing. Outside the day drizzled wet and cold, but inside I relaxed warm and cozy with the people for whom I had developed a sincere affection. I remember that Thursday as the last uncomplicated and happy time I spent in Chicago.

The following Saturday after dinner at his favorite Palmer House with both of us seated at the private corner table he requested, Douglas placed a small box next to my coffee cup.

"This is for you." He watched me closely and smiled with his mouth, but none of the smile reached those sharp, black eyes. Something still and expectant rested there instead.

I didn't touch the box, said only, "What is it?" But I already knew.

"Open it, please, Katherine." The small black box that sat between us on the table sent a message with its velvet cover and the gold initial scrawled across its top.

"Douglas, I don't want—"

"Open it, please, Katherine," he repeated and so I did. I stared at a diamond ring, its sole stone set in an intricate gold filigree, perfectly proportioned, and faceted so that it flashed the light. A gorgeous thing. I took a deep breath, then purposefully closed the cover over the ring. Douglas took my hand in so tight a grip that my fingers felt crushed.

"It's beautiful, Douglas, but you know I can't accept it." I spoke with a calm I didn't feel and felt his grip tighten.

"You don't have to give me an answer now, Katherine. I don't expect that, but surely my feelings can't come as a surprise. We've known each other almost a year now, and I don't understand why that isn't enough time for you." When I didn't respond, he added in a low voice, "I've thought of you constantly for months now, Katherine, how you'll grace my table, and the light and life you'll bring into my home. You and I fit together. I knew it from the first moment I saw you, and I can't believe you don't see it, too." I finally pulled my hand free.

"I can't accept this," I said again because I had no idea what else to say. My fault entirely. Of course, I had known it would come to this, and still I was speechless despite my foreknowledge. What kind of woman had I become?

"I am making you an offer of marriage," he said quietly but firmly, "and I want to know whether you are refusing me outright. I have never been anything but honest about my intentions, and I deserve to know that at least."

"I'm not refusing you outright, but I'm not accepting

you either. I'm simply not sure, and I resent being forced into a response." He held my gaze for a long moment before he finally put the box back into his pocket.

"I believe you, Katherine, but I don't understand you. I don't understand you at all. I know you well enough to recognize that you're incapable of deceit or manipulation. If there were someone else, I think I'd know."

"There's no one else."

"Then what is it that holds you back?"

If he had paused then, I might have tried to fumble through an answer, but he was propelled on by emotion. I thought my cool reaction had hurt him deeply.

"Take some time," he continued. "Take the next two weeks and think about my offer, think about us. You know I can't deny you anything so you would want for nothing all your life. Think about it seriously, Katherine, about the future we could have together. I won't trouble you for the next two weeks and then two weeks from tonight, I'll send Fritz for you. I've invited some friends and colleagues for a holiday dinner that evening, and I want you to join us. I have every confidence that you'll make me a happy man that night."

"And if I don't?"

He didn't miss a beat.

"Then I'll accept your refusal with all the grace I can muster and not bother you anymore. I won't like it but I'll accept it." His forceful tone flickered for one imperceptible moment before he concluded, "But I know that won't happen. I understand that you want to visit your family, but I don't want you to leave without promising you'll return to be my wife. You and I were meant to be together."

Douglas sounded so confident that I almost said yes right then. His powerful magnetism reached across the table and pulled me to him in a way that was nearly irresistible. When would I ever have such an opportunity again? I asked myself. Surely the passion of his request spoke of love even if he didn't actually say the words, and I believed us evenly matched in temperament and will. Life with Douglas would always be exciting; I would never be bored. And I could do a great deal of good with his wealth, even set up a dispensary of my own to serve the poor and needy.

But instead of the *yes* that began to beat in my heart, some other voice—from my head perhaps—replied calmly, "All right. Two weeks then, Douglas, and we'll settle the matter." To me, the words sounded like a business dealing.

He was so sure of success that he must have heard those words as capitulation because he took my hand again, this time more gently, and lifted it to his lips.

"Good." He smiled at me across the table, a genuine smile this time that warmed his expression. "We can enjoy a wonderful life together, Katherine, and make a wonderful home."

CHAPTER 13

The next two weeks I planned my departure from Hull-House. I put all the dispensary's paperwork in order, readied patients, the staff, and the children for my successor, arranged a train ticket home, and all the while struggled with my answer to Douglas Gallagher. It made no sense to me that a woman who had single-mindedly pursued one goal for as long as she could remember could not give a simple yes or no to a marriage proposal. But I realized that with Douglas *No* would be irrefutably and irrevocably No—with no second chance—and how could I tell whether never seeing Douglas again would be bearable? Make knowledgeable choices and be prepared to live with them, my mother always advised, but how could I do so in this situation? Much of what I needed to know would be available only after I made the decision.

I still remained undecided the Thursday before Douglas's holiday dinner, despite the fact that I seemed to edge closer to an answer and a vague measure of relief as the days passed. A feeling not unlike being lost in the darkness, spying a distant pinprick of light, and recognizing that light, however faint, as the place I needed to be. Certain, too, that I would reach it.

But the impetus of circumstance unexpectedly intruded and made my decision for me. Out of the blue and going about my regular business, my future suddenly took form—because of fate or the confluence of planets or divine intervention, whatever one chooses to credit. With 'God bless Aunt Kat' dutifully repeated twice an evening in bedtime prayers, I know what I believe.

We began December with an empty dispensary and because Petra was with me, I gave Mrs. Tabachnik the night to herself. She had plenty to do at home with Christmas around the corner, she said, and was grateful for the time. The bell at the dispensary's alley door startled both Petra and me as she sat in the corner intent on her studies and I attempted to organize the contents of the dispensary desk. The bell rang again, desperation and urgency in its tone, and Petra and I stood simultaneously. I reached the door first and pulled it open.

A young woman waited there, not that much older than Petra, plump and round-faced, leaning against the door jamb, her short gasps of breath visible in the frigid December night. Blood flowed from her nose; her entire face was a bruised mess. She clasped both arms to her stomach as if she had pain there.

"Can you help me?" she asked, her voice jerky and rough. "You helped a friend of mine the other day. She said there was a lady doctor here, who took care of her and didn't judge. Can you help me?"

Petra and I brought the young woman inside and strained to get her up on the examination table. She allowed a low moan to escape, then gasped out an apology and clamped her lips shut. I sent Petra for warm water and cloths as I tried to unwrap the woman's clothes for a look at her injuries. Under her ragged coat she wore a low cut, frilly dress in bright pink, not the sort of thing a woman from the tenements would wear. She was something else, then, not that it mattered.

The girl had clearly received a ferocious beating around her face for sure and had almost certainly been punched in the stomach, besides. I feared something might have ruptured internally because she gasped in pain as I examined her, my touch gentle but not gentle enough to keep her from wincing. Petra hovered in the background as I washed the woman's face and cleaned the blood from her broken nose and out of her right eye, which had begun to turn a deep and ugly purple-black. One tooth was lost, and her whole face looked swollen and distorted. She must have been fair and pretty once, but she was anything but pretty as she lay on the table. Through all my ministrations she kept one hand tightly clenched, and when I tried to loosen her fingers, she muttered, "No, mine," with such vehemence that I decided something other than an injury to her hand caused her distress at my efforts.

"Can you breathe comfortably?" I asked, afraid that the swelling might interfere with her ability to catch a breath, but she whispered "Yes" out of her bruised mouth. The poor child was an awful, awful sight.

After a while, when she didn't vomit blood and when the pain in her stomach seemed to subside, I decided she wouldn't need to go to the hospital.

"You can stay here tonight and as long as you'd like," I explained, "but you need to tell me what happened so I can file a report with the constable. No one should be allowed to abuse you like this." The girl tried to shake her head but flinched at the pain.

"Don't do that. I'm the one they'll lock up. Women like me, we're the ones they punish."

She was right so I didn't pursue the subject, asking only, "What happened?"

"He come to see the vaudeville show at the Haymarket Theater over on Madison Street. That's where I work. I dance and sing and I can act pretty good, too. I was Bertha the Sewing Machine Girl, once, and Mr. Flannigan said I sure knew how to make the crowd cry." From her expression, I could tell she recalled the compliment to her performance with pride. "I dress to please the gentlemen but that's just the show. Mr. Flannigan says a pretty girl keeps the audience happy. It's a living and I don't mind it."

She still lay on the examining table, slowly relaxing with the warmth of the room as I stroked her fair hair and continued to bathe her poor, ruined face. Her voice was halting and weak so that sometimes I had to lean forward to hear her. Petra brought a blanket and tucked it gently around the woman.

"He was in the audience," she continued. "Sent someone back to tell me he liked me and could we meet after the show. I knew what that meant and I ain't proud of it, but it's money in my pocket and a girl's got to eat. He come to my room there at the back of the theater, everyone gone home but us. A gent. Dressed fine and he starts with me, but after a while I get scared. He scared me bad. He was rough and he wouldn't stop. I tell him I'm done and I want to leave, but he won't let me go. I ask for my money and he laughs at me. Tells me *he* ain't done, and if I want the money I ain't done either. I got real scared then, so scared I hit him, just in his chest but hard, trying to push him away from me. That made him mad. I thought he'd kill me—he was so mad! He wouldn't stop hitting me. Told me who did I think I was to lay a hand on him. Oh, he was crazy, crazy, and I thought he'd kill me."

Tears slipped from both eyes, even the one swollen shut, and I wiped them away, outraged and grieved for this girl in her bright pink dress, once pretty, perhaps happy, singing and dancing her way through life, a working girl trying to get by the best way she knew how, right or wrong. But not deserving this. Never this.

"He never did pay me, neither. Not a cent." Then from under the blanket she brought out her clenched fist and slowly unfurled her fingers as if displaying something rare and precious. "But he dropped this, left this behind on the floor. It shone so bright I could see it sparkling, even with one eye. It's worth something, ain't it? Don't you think it's worth something?"

Behind me Petra made a sound and then was still, not speaking, not moving, and I was still, too, seeing how the lights of our modest little dispensary made the diamonds in the stick pin sparkle. A brilliant and unmistakable *G.*

For a moment I was unable to breathe or move or make a sound, saw only what she held out in the palm of her hand, and then I said, someone else speaking although the words came out of my throat, "Yes. I think it's worth something. Now let's get you into bed. You're safe here and you can rest easy." After Petra and I dressed her in a plain gown and settled her for the night, I sat down in a chair next to her bed.

"You don't need to stay here with me," the girl said. The laudanum I had given her for pain had finally begun to take effect, and she was almost asleep.

"I know I don't, but I can't sleep so I might as well keep you company for a while," I answered. She drifted asleep, still clutching the diamond pin.

"Dr. Davis, I can sit with her. You should go to bed," said Petra, poor child, not sure what to say or do.

"I will but not now."

"You should—"

"Petra, I want to sit here by myself for a while. I'll be fine."

She was wise not to argue because I wouldn't have heard a word she said. As it was, I sat there until Miss Flaherty arrived the next morning, sat there silent as a stone, stunned and stupefied yet knowing the story was as true as the earth circling the sun, knowing it all along in the crush of fingers and the bruising grip and that perversely exciting, uncomfortably breathless feeling of being momentarily trapped and panicked. I felt ashamed, encased in shame, that I had been touched by the same hands that had done this violent act, that I had allowed caresses from a man who would be so rough and would not stop and would taunt this poor, powerless girl for being afraid and then punish her for protecting herself. It was all I could do not to drop on my knees beside her bed and beg forgiveness from that terribly beaten girl—although how her circumstance was my fault I couldn't have expressed.

By habit I soothed the young woman as she cried out in her sleep, as she turned a little and whimpered from the pain, inhaled harshly and relaxed again with a trembling breath. All the while I told myself over and over again that I had disregarded my inner voice and for what? For lavish attention and the vanity of undisguised admiration, for candlelight dinners and front row seats, for whispered words and passionate kisses, for the thrill of the company of a handsome man, who excited me for all the wrong reasons.

A passage from a book I'd recently read came to mind, a book nearly banned and still hard to come by. I hadn't been able to forget the words and their cadence: "*For the odor-yielding, insect-drawing, insect-infected rose of pleasure.*" The author wanted to describe the seductive conceit of wealth and vanity, and I suppose I could not forget the phrase because I somehow recognized that it depicted my state of mind over the past months. Rose of pleasure, indeed. I had been a fool, a vain and ingenuous fool, scorning the familiar rightness of home and family—in fact, running away from all that—so I could prove myself part of a new and progressive generation, a harbinger of a new century set free from an old-fashioned, outdated past. How foolish I had been! As if the affection between my parents was not timeless and their commitment to doing what was right, anything but absolute and enduring.

Wanting to escape the values of my childhood—what had I been thinking?! I had made very bad decisions, I told myself, and how close I had come to making an even worse choice! The picture of what that choice might have brought me caused a physical shudder that briefly shook me head to toe. I sat there through the night, humiliated and horrified, berating myself, mortified at my lack of good judgment yet conscious of a distant relief and a much more immediate anger.

A feverish baby arrived early in the morning and then it was time to stop by the nursery, so it was almost noon before I made it back to my room, closed the door and lay down, mistakenly thinking sleep wouldn't come. When I awoke a few hours later, I gathered up the shirtwaist and skirt I had received for my birthday and took them down to the young woman.

The girl was awake and looked worse than the night before, the way those injuries sometimes progress, the bruises swollen and black and her eye and lip grown so big one would think they must burst. But her stomach, besides being bruised, wasn't distended, and when I applied pressure, she hardly complained about pain or tenderness so I knew there was no life-threatening injury there. Thank God, thank God.

She told me she was called Mary Fay.

"A pretty name," I commented, and she tried to smile.

"My ma said she read it in a book and planned right then to name her baby Mary Fay if it was a girl. Picked it right out of a book, she did." After a pause she said reluctantly, "I guess I need to get going. You'll want your bed for someone else."

"No, we have other beds, Mary Fay. You should stay another day at least."

"I need to tell Mr. Flannigan where I am. He ain't a bad man, but he's the manager and he'll give my job to someone else if he thinks I've run off. I need to get going."

"I'll go myself and explain."

"You can't go there!" Her tone scandalized. "What would people think, a woman like yourself going there?"

"It doesn't matter what people think, and I wouldn't care even if it did matter."

She gave me directions along with the name of a man to talk to, and I bundled up against the wind and went out. The frigid cold was bracing. I relished the opportunity to move around vigorously, to stride and swing my arms and take deep, deep breaths. Fueled by emotions I was still trying to get under control, I had energy to burn.

I talked to Mr. Flannigan himself, a balding man in a dirty shirt and baggy pants held up by bright blue suspenders. He put out his cigar when I told him who I was, then wiped his hands on his pants before he reached out a hand to shake mine.

"I'm pleased to make your acquaintance, Dr. Davis. I've heard your name and it's all been good. You set my grandson's leg when he ran into a trolley. Did a good job, too. It healed straight as an arrow."

"I'm glad to hear it. Tell him to be more careful next

time. He came very close to going through life with one leg." I told Flannigan about Mary Fay, said she needed quiet for a while but worried about losing her livelihood.

He shrugged. "People come expecting a show, Doc. Don't see how I can use a girl that's all banged up,"

I fixed a stern eye on him and responded, "Mr. Flannigan, I am asking you as a personal favor to find something for Mary Fay until she heals, and then to give her back her job. She's suffered enough." He conceded easily.

"Since it's you asking, all right. You tell her to come back here as soon as she's able. She can help with the costumes and clean-up until the bruises fade. Mary Fay's a good sort, anyway, got a pretty way with herself on stage, always makes the men come back." I couldn't argue or ask for anything more. Mary Fay would go back and pick up right where she left off, and no one would have learned a lesson from all this but me.

Friday evening someone knocked timidly on my door; I knew it was Petra before I saw her. I had been rereading Sam Kincaid's letter, lingering over his description of the sheep he'd recently been asked to run along with cattle. Sam wrote with humor and some disdain, a true cattleman but not one to disregard progress for the sake of tradition.

I believe they are the stupidest creature I have ever seen, he wrote. *One nearly drowned by looking up as it was raining and forgetting to close her mouth. You'll think I'm making that up but I swear I'm not. John Thomas will tell you the same.*

It would be just like the two of them to try to pull my leg, but from what I knew of sheep, I felt he might be telling a true story.

"Are you all right?" Petra asked without preamble. She stood in the doorway until I motioned her to come in and shut the door.

"I think so. If it takes some time and hurts a little, it's nothing worse than I deserve."

She came forward and said quickly, "That's not true. Why would you blame yourself? You always look at the good side of things. How could you have guessed?"

"Oh, Petra, don't you see? I shouldn't have had to guess. I should have known, should have paid more attention to that inner voice we talked about, but I was too busy enjoying myself. I feel that I'm to blame somehow for poor Mary Fay. I was a fool." In spite of my efforts, tears formed in my eyes and trickled down my cheeks, sorrowful tears of shame and regret.

Petra slid to her knees in front of me and said with passionate sincerity, "He was never worthy of you. Never. He was a bad man from the beginning, never what you told me that night, never a man of integrity, but he hid it from you like a man wearing a mask. He was bad from the beginning."

I was taken aback by the fierce loathing in her tone, knew it came from something more, caught her chin with my finger, and lifted her face to look up at me.

"Tell me, Petra." At first she didn't speak, but a soft color started at her neck and rose up into her face.

Finally she said, "I can't. I told myself I would never tell you. I'd lose your good will and your friendship, and I couldn't bear that."

Something in her tone chilled me, slowed my heartbeat so that I had to take a breath before I could gently say, "There is nothing you can't tell me, and we will always be friends, miles and years apart, we will always be friends. I promise. Now tell me, what did Douglas do?"

"He came to me after the operetta during the typhoid outbreak last June. At first he said he came to see you, but when I told him you couldn't be disturbed, that you had too many sick people, it was like he was angry, angry with you for not being there when he wanted you. He said he thought I was pretty and that I'd be famous someday. He said he could help me—he had lots of money, he said. I told him that was kind of him and he said it wasn't kindness he wanted from me. He touched me in a way I remembered from my father."

"You should have told me." I felt cold as death.

"You were so busy going out to the tenements and when you were here, too many people needed you. I couldn't tell you anyway because I knew it would hurt you. I thought you cared for him and you'd think it was me that had betrayed you—after all you'd done for me! I thought I was the bad one. First my father and then him. I thought it had to be something bad in me."

"Is there more to it?"

"He came back again and asked if we could strike a bargain—that's what he called it. And the night we went to the opera it was like a game to him, touching me as we rode in the automobile, whispering to me when he thought you wouldn't notice. All a game to him. He knew I'd never say anything to you, and he liked having that power over me. Over you, too, in a way."

I stood and began to pace, so furious I believed I could have killed Douglas Gallagher at that moment, taken a bead through the sight of a rifle and pulled the trigger without compunction, stepped over his body on my way down to dinner and hummed a Christmas carol as his blood soaked into the carpet, the cleaning bill my only regret. Angrier at that moment than I had ever been before or have ever been since.

"Do you hate me? I couldn't bear it," Petra's voice a whisper as she watched me roam the room. I went back to take both of her hands in mine and pull her to her feet.

"Listen to me, Petra. You are not the bad one and this is not your fault. You've done nothing that I should hate you for and you are never to suggest such a thing again. I gave you my word that you would be safe here, and then I stupidly and selfishly brought a terrible man into our midst, let him prey on you because I was so caught up in my own attractions I thought he wouldn't look at anyone else but me. Oh, Petra, I forced you to go to the opera when you told me you didn't want to go. I ignored your wishes because I was so sure I knew what was best for you. I'm so sorry. You were the adult and I was the child, vain and foolish. I compromised you and it's you who must forgive me. I hope you can find it in your heart to do so." She opened her mouth to speak, but I held up a hand. "Right now I need to be alone. I promise we'll talk later, but I need you to leave me alone for a while."

After she left I sat there and held Sam's letter with both hands in my lap as if his sane good humor and his familiar affection could flow from the page into my fingers, leach through my skin, course through my veins, cleanse my heart, rid my conscience of the guilt I felt, and wash away the pictures that crowded my mind's eye. Last night I'd thought it couldn't be worse, but I had been wrong.

Saturday morning I found Mary Fay sitting at the edge of her bed, youth and a naturally cheerful disposition already putting her on the road to recovery. I told her I had talked to Flannigan, then laid out the shirtwaist and skirt for her.

"I meant it when I said you could stay as long as you like, but when you're ready to leave, you'll need clothes. We washed the dress you had on , but it's hardly the thing to wear outside in this weather. You can have these. They might not be a perfect fit, but they're warm."

"Why would you do that for me?" she whispered as she

gave the clothes a respectful stroke. I couldn't tell her why, couldn't say that—sensibly or not—I felt I had contributed to what happened to her. Instead of answering her question, I put a hand on her shoulder.

"Mary Fay, you're in a dangerous line of work. Can't you find something else?"

"What? Work in a factory, earn $4.00 a week, and then have to pay for the machine I'm working on out of that? My ma sewed in a factory for years, scraped by, was charged for the oil her machine used and for every broken needle. Sometimes there weren't even a dollar left for her to take home at the end of the week and how could she feed us kids on that?"

I knew Mary Fay spoke the truth. All the needle-trade industries of Chicago were on strike even as she spoke because the conditions her mother had worked under had grown more deplorable over time. The strikers were threatened with violence and from what I heard from the women who visited Hull-House, it was only a matter of time before someone would die as a result of the strike.

"I should be ashamed, I guess," Mary Fay continued, "but I ain't. I can make good money and I guess I'll just take my chances." She reached over and took my hand in hers, turned my palm up, and opened my fingers. "Here, you take this. I can't pay for what you done for me but you can have this." She placed the diamond stickpin into my hand. Because it scorched my skin, I shoved the pin back at her.

"I can't take this. You sell it. It will keep you warm through the winter."

But for all its seductive sparkle, Mary Fay wouldn't take the pin back, saying with sparse nobility, "I don't want it. A man like that, who knows what he did to get it. You take it, Doctor. Use the money to help people. Spend it on this place. Do whatever you think is right. I don't want the thing." Then she lay back down, her round, discolored face a study in dignity.

Petra knocked on my door as I dressed for Douglas's party that evening. Her eyes widened when she saw me.

"You're not going to be with him after all this, are you?" I looked in the mirror in order to pull my hair back from my face and spoke to her reflection.

"Oh yes," I replied grimly, "but it will be a short evening. I have some things to return to him."

"You shouldn't go. What if he hurts you?"

I turned to face her, my hair up and toilette complete, very fine in kid gloves and silk hose and a deep red dress the color of wine. A woman pretending to be what she was not, never could be, and never wanted to be again.

"The house will be full of people, Petra, people whose good will is very important to Douglas Gallagher. He wouldn't do anything to jeopardize his reputation so he won't make a scene any more than I will." I threw my cloak over everything, picked up my package, and kissed her on the cheek as I passed her in the doorway. "I'll be home soon, and then we'll both try to put this sad and demeaning time out of our memories."

"I still don't think you should go."

"I know, but it's like the words The End at the close of the moving picture. They have to be said so you know the story's over."

I rode in the seat next to Fritz, my usual place when it was just the two of us.

"It's dark," I told him. "You can take me straight to the door like this. No one will see us and you won't get into trouble," but he couldn't bring himself to do that, still had to stop and I had to get into the back so Douglas would never know I sat next to his chauffeur and talked to him, one human being to another. Shouldn't that have told me something a long time ago?

When I got out of the motorcar, I turned to say, "Fritz, I don't believe I'll be staying very long this evening, and if I'm allowed, I may ask you to take me back home within the hour. If you wouldn't mind."

"Are you feeling ill, Miss?" I thought about it a moment.

"Yes, as a matter of fact, I am. Quite ill."

A few steps up the walk, the door opened and Douglas stepped outside to wait for me. It was a good thing I didn't have a gun with me, I thought, because I was a good shot, had been taught at an early age by the best, and his silhouette made such an inviting target.

When he lifted my cloak from my shoulders, I reached to take it from him, draped it over my arms, and said calmly, "I'd like to keep it with me since I won't be staying. Is there a place we can talk?" His eyes narrowed and I know he expected that I wanted to discuss his proposal, perhaps from my tone and words even thought he knew what I would say.

"I have guests, Katherine. Can't we wait until the end of the evening?" I glanced through the graceful doorway to the large room, one corner filled by a huge, beautifully decorated Christmas tree draped in sparkling red and green. The rising murmur of voices from the guests mingled with the clink of glasses, everyone busy with conversation and refreshment.

"No. I'll wait for you in the library if you feel you must act the host for a while." As I passed the wide doorway, I noticed Drew in the other room with the guests, saw him raise his head to follow my arrival. He gave me a hard look with nothing flippant or affected about him. Somehow I believed he knew—just from my posture or expression—that

I was not there for celebration.

Douglas followed me, pulled the library doors shut behind him, then turned to face me. He raised both brows in a questioning look, as handsome as ever and as perfectly dressed. Everything on the outside looked exactly right.

"You look lovely. Is this a new gown?" When I didn't answer, he stepped closer. "My guess is that you bring me bad news. Have you decided to refuse my offer?" I laid my cloak over a chair and reached into my purse.

"As a matter of fact I bring you good news. You've lost something that I think you must miss. No doubt it's worth a great deal of money to you." He stood an arm's length away, surprised by my words and mystified by my tone and actions.

"I don't think I've lost anything." Vaguely suspicious and—unusual for Douglas—uneasy.

"Nonsense. Incredible as it seems to me, you must have forgotten." I dropped the pin onto the nearest table where it lay, the sparkling *G* face up and clear to both of us. His gaze dropped to the table and he became completely still, looking down as if he had never seen either the table or the pin before, staring down and searching desperately for a way to explain what he realized I must know.

He raised his head to ask coolly, "How did you get this?"

"Mary Fay brought it." At his blank look, I asked with offhand disgust, "Didn't you even know her name? I'll help you remember then: fair, young, a little plump, good-natured, dressed in bright pink, cuts quite a figure on the stage, I'm told. Does that help?"

He dropped his eyes to the table once more, then made the leap and assumed I knew everything.

"Did you really think I was living the celibate life while you decided in your fastidious way if you could condescend to have me?" I didn't expect that mocking, cool tone, as if I were the one guilty of some exceptionally childish and embarrassing blunder.

"You know," I replied, "in my fastidious way, I didn't think about that at all." I picked up the small wrapped package I had set down and handed it to him. "Here. It's the piece of silk you gave me for my birthday. You can have it back. I don't think it's very pretty anymore. You must have touched it, and I can't seem to get the stains out." That angered him. I could read it in his face.

"I touched you, too."

"Yes, you did." He saw the little shudder of repugnance I gave and knew it was a spontaneous shiver accompanying my words, without conscious volition on my part. "I can't seem to wash that away either. I've tried but I suppose it will take time." I reached for my wrap, unable to find the right words that would express my revulsion for him and my disgust with myself.

Then, incredibly, he said, "This doesn't need to affect us, Katherine. I'm a man and I act in the unbecoming way that men sometimes do. If you were my wife, I wouldn't need other women."

"Wouldn't need Petra either, do you mean? Or wouldn't need other women in general?"

"What has she told you?"

"Everything."

"That she threw herself at me, told me she was looking for someone to help her career, and proposed we make a trade? Is that what she told you?"

I gasped in outrage. "How dare you blame Petra for your bad conduct?! Do you think I would believe that? You prey on the weak and powerless and when you're called to account for your actions, you blame your victims. Not only degenerate but a coward as well! You should know that I've shared your objectionable conduct with Miss Addams, so don't even think about pressing your attentions on Petra again. Miss Addams knows more people than you and she can make your life very uncomfortable." I turned, desperate to leave, but he caught my wrist in his right hand.

"Why does any of this have to matter, Katherine? It won't happen again, I swear. Do you think either of them meant anything to me? What can I do to make it right? I made an error in judgment. Can't you forgive me?" He was completely serious.

Held fast in his grip, I said, "An error in judgment? Is that what you call it? If you think it's consorting with a prostitute that disgusts me, then you truly never knew me at all. You beat a woman nearly senseless, you try to seduce a child, and you call it an error in judgment? My God, Douglas, I'm so shamed by you—and by me. What a repellent pair we are! I deserve to say yes to your proposal. It would be an appropriate penance for my vanity, but the proximity to you would be unbearable."

He took hold of my other wrist with his left hand and jerked me forward so that I stood against him. The man was furious, everything about him taut and tense and ferocious. That close, I could feel the quick, shallow rise and fall of his chest and the warmth of his breath on my cheek. When I looked at his face, I saw what Mary Fay must have seen. Felt the same panic, too, but instead of pulling away, I pushed myself closer.

"Will you strike me, too?" I spit at him. I lifted my chin and purposefully turned my head in profile. "Go ahead. I deserve it for being such a vain and stupid child. God forgive me."

I don't know if he would have struck me or kissed me because just then from the doorway Drew said his brother's name. We both turned to look at him as he gently closed the doors and came into the room.

"Douglas, let Katherine go. You'll hurt her."

"Perhaps that's my intention."

"No, it's not. You've never intended to hurt anyone in your life."

Douglas pushed me away so abruptly and so hard that I stumbled against a chair and nearly fell. I reached for my cloak, which had fallen in the altercation, put it on, and walked past the two men to the door, all without a word.

"You'll have to find your own way home," Douglas said meanly. "I've invested nearly a year in you without a return. I'm done with sending good money after bad." Keeping his gaze on his brother, Drew pressed his hand against the door as I went to open it.

"Don't be foolish, Douglas," he said. "How will it look to your influential friends out there? Several people saw Katherine arrive. What will the talk be if you send the woman you've publicly squired around town for months out into the winter night and let her find her way home alone? It's hardly the kind of publicity that will strengthen your business relationships. These are very proper people, in case you've forgotten. Pillars of the city. Have Fritz take Katherine home, and you can say she was suddenly taken ill. It's still a risk, but I can give support and between the two of us, we can make the story believable." Douglas chewed on his lower lip and stared at Drew as he thought through the proposition.

"All right. Just get her out of my sight," as if in some reciprocal way my presence now revolted him. Drew took me by the elbow, opened the door, and together we went down the hallway, past the room filled with light, laughter, and music, out the front door, and down the walk where Fritz waited.

When Drew got in next to me, I said, "Thank you, Drew, but you don't need to come along. I'm fine, and I don't want to spoil your evening." In the streetlight I could see that he gave a little smile but he stayed seated beside me.

"Does anything unsettle you, Doctor?" He reached to tap Fritz on the shoulder. "Dr. Davis is ill, Fritz. She longs to be home." None of us spoke a word the whole distance.

Before I got out I leaned forward to say, "Good-bye Fritz. Thank you for the driving lessons. I'll name my first automobile after you." He didn't misunderstand me.

"Good-bye, Doctor." It was the first time he'd ever called me by that title. "You've made a wise decision, and I'll sleep better because of it."

Drew accompanied me up the walk to Hull-House and stepped inside with me, where a welcoming blaze still crackled in the front room's fireplace.

"Can you tell me what happened?"

I related the story of Mary Fay without emotion, kept her nameless, and didn't mention Petra at all. Drew sat down, still in coat and hat, and watched me through the telling.

"I don't know why I couldn't see it," I concluded, "but your brother is damaged, Drew. He's terribly, terribly damaged."

"No, Katherine, not damaged," Drew responded gently. "Douglas is broken. And he can't be fixed." He sounded so sad and so tired that for the first time that evening I wanted to cry. "My brother has always had a terrible temper, but I honestly believe he never intends to lose it. When he does, though, he's uncontrollable. He can do—has done—serious damage, and it seems to be getting worse as he gets older. I've cleaned up several nasty messes behind him."

"You shouldn't allow him to be alone with women and

children, then. It's an unconscionable risk," I said without pity, my earlier sympathy for Drew completely gone.

"You're right. I should keep better track of him, but —" His voice trailed off and I thought he was done, but he finally finished, "My brother and I are both flawed in similar ways, Katherine, so protecting society against the Gallagher brothers can be quite an undertaking."

"Don't tell me you beat women, Drew. I won't believe it."

"Oh, no. No. I don't do that, thank God. I use them for my own delightful but totally carnal purposes and when they get clingy or boring—as they always do—I discard them with a pretty trinket and a kiss on the cheek." At my expression, he said, "I told you I was flawed, Doctor. Neither of the Gallagher brothers is worth your time or your energy. The difference between us is that I accept the truth about myself while Douglas continues to long for a normal, respectable relationship with a normal, respectable woman. A woman like you. Unfortunately, he has no idea what a normal, respectable relationship is or how to maintain one. He doesn't understand that there's an emotional investment involved, an investment that he is totally incapable of making. I don't believe either of us knows how to love, although Douglas came as close to it with you as I've ever seen him. There were times you made him very happy."

"How flattering," I said in a tone that belied the words.

"More than you know. My brother could never get enough of you, wanted to know where you were and what you were doing all the time, talked about you in a tone I'd never heard from him before. Did you know he hired a man to investigate and then follow you?"

I remembered wondering uneasily how Douglas knew things: the violets that matched my hat, my birthday, my parentage.

"I should have guessed it, I suppose, but it never occurred to me that a man would do such a thing."

"He couldn't help it," Drew said gently. "He's been holding on to you like a drowning man clings to a raft, afraid to lose you because somehow he knows that you're his last chance for a real life, a normal, real life."

"Am I supposed to feel sorry for him and approve his actions, Drew? Should I pat him understandingly on the shoulder and say, 'You had an unhappy childhood, poor fellow, so go ahead and beat up more women if it makes you feel better?'"

"You have a sharp tongue, Katherine, and it doesn't always become you. Yes, in a way you should feel sorry for him—and for me, too—you with your clear eyes and steadfast heart, so sure of what's right and wrong. There's nothing crippled about you, is there? So you should feel sorry for those of us who wander through life lame and blind."

"I'll save my pity for those who really are lame and blind, not for men who have everything and choose to act either brutally or stupidly when they know better and could make different and worthwhile choices."

He stood. "Is that what it's about, then? Choices?"

"You're all grown up, Drew. Don't you get tired of blaming your past life for your present actions? To answer your question, yes, it's all about choices, about thinking them through carefully and doing the right thing and living with the consequences when we don't. If you can't understand that, perhaps you really are as damaged as your brother."

My words caused Drew's face to tighten with a brief, almost imperceptible flinch, but he remained silent until he paused at the front door.

"You know, Katherine, a different place and under different circumstances, we might have made a match of it, you and I."

"I don't think so."

He replied very seriously, "Well, maybe not. Maybe I'm too shallow and frivolous a man for you, but you'll have a good life, I think. Lucky the man you finally love, Cowgirl Kate," and carefully closed the door behind him when he left.

I considered Drew's departing words as I lay in bed that night. I doubted that there would be a man I would 'finally love.' How could I trust myself to recognize that genuine emotion after all this? How could I ever be certain I'd found the right man?

Science and medicine were safe. Read the symptoms. Make a diagnosis. Get better or worse. Live or die. But my emotions could not be trusted in the same way. All this time I had believed it was Douglas who went along behind Drew to rescue and protect a younger brother gone bad, but the reality had been exactly opposite. If I could misjudge their relationship so profoundly, how could I ever trust myself to choose a lifelong partner?

Still, if I lived out my life alone, that was all right, too. I could be a force for good in the same way Jane Addams was, as Alice Hamilton and Mary Smith were. Husband or not, I could find fulfillment through service and vocation. My family needed a spinster aunt—every family worth its salt should have one—and I would be home in two weeks, ready and willing to fill the role.

PART TWO

1911

CHAPTER 14

From central Minnesota west I saw nothing but snow through the train windows, a curtain of snow day and night that blew and piled along the tracks so that on more than one occasion I thought we would come to a complete standstill. We slowed but kept on going, not even a ferocious January storm able to stop our progress.

All my good-byes were said: a little party in the nursery, a special dinner with Miss Addams, Dr. Hamilton, and Mary Smith, kind remembrances from Miss Flaherty and Mrs. Tabachnik, and tears from Petra. That sorrowful heart-shaped face and those overflowing violet eyes had been the worst, still so much a child and her world nothing but change and loss for so many years.

"You'll be so busy, you won't even miss me," I told her firmly. "You have your studies and your music lessons, and Mr. Sweeney says you're to perform in the Hull-House spring production. You know how you love that." But Petra would not be comforted, just looked at me with those big eyes until I was as weepy as she. Then the moment struck us both slightly silly and we were giggling together. "You're a sensible girl and you'll make good decisions. Just let Mr. Sweeney guide you. He'll always be your friend, Petra."

"I know. I trust him most next to you."

"And I know you'll be a help to Dr. Goldmeier."

My successor was a short, stocky, black-haired, and bearded young doctor from the University of Michigan, not particularly amiable but very bright and passionate about his vocation. He had good clinical skills and an encyclopedic understanding of the most recent medical discoveries. Dr. Pasca was clearly proud of him.

"He won't be the same as you, though."

"I'm several inches taller and a woman, so no, he won't be the same, but it will be good for you to see that it doesn't matter what a doctor looks like. It's what's in the head and the heart that counts."

The last thing I saw as the automobile pulled away from the curb to take me to the train station was Petra wrapped in a heavy shawl, standing on the porch and waving a frantic good-bye as the wind swirled her hair around her face. I waved, too, until I couldn't see her anymore. Petra Stravinsky would be famous one day, and happy, and I would have had a hand in that. The knowledge held some consolation to my remorse.

The train pulled into Laramie in the middle of the same snowstorm that had flanked it for days. Grabbing my large valise and my doctor's bag I stepped out into the wind and thought I could take refuge at the Johnson Hotel if the weather was going to keep me from making the trek a few blocks north to my sister's house. But Ben Wagner, Becca's husband, waited in the little station for me. He gave me a hug and took the larger bag from my grip.

"I'm glad to see you, Katherine. Becca's been going from window to window for the last two days worried you wouldn't get here at all. If you're dressed for the walk, I think we can make it home. Do I need to tie a rope from your waist to mine so you don't get lost?"

The thought of the two of us tugging each other down the main street of town made me laugh, but the idea wasn't all that farfetched because as we walked, the wind gusted with enough force that I had to hold on to Ben's arm to keep my balance.

My brother-in-law was one of the three local parsons in Laramie. He arrived fresh from Philadelphia seven years earlier, completely unprepared for what he found: Laramie, Wyoming, still raw and wild and a far cry from the amenities of the more civilized East. But he met my sister and loved her, learned to love Wyoming, too, I think, and became a part of the Davis family just as my brother's wife had—as if born into it. A fine man, fervently honest with not an unkind bone in his body, a man of surprising depth, unselfish generosity, and great tolerance. Becca once told me that she fell in love with his passion for good. I remember being impressed with the phrase and thinking it summed up Ben Wagner exactly right.

Lily Kate met me at the door, hopping on both feet, chanting, "Aunt Kat's here, Aunt Kat's here," so cute that my family duty as maiden aunt demanded I sweep her up in my arms and cover her little face with kisses.

Becca came from a back room holding the new baby and passed her to Ben so she could welcome me literally with open arms. She rushed from one sentence to the next.

"I was so worried you'd get stuck somewhere. Ben will tell you I've been acting like a child waiting for Santa Claus. You look wonderful, Katherine. Take your coat off. I have hot breakfast and fresh coffee in the kitchen. Yes, this is Blessing. Isn't she perfect?" Blessing *was* perfect, red curls and soft brown eyes and her little fists waving in the air as if in welcome.

I took my newest niece into my arms, cradled her, smiled at her in the way adults do with babies, and cooed in a foolish and fatuous voice, my lack of professional objectivity completely forgivable. Becca was so obviously happy with her little family with a look about her that reminded me very much of Mother, something warm and welcoming in Becca's face that I had also seen in my mother's face when she had first caught sight of me at Hull-House. I had been away too long, should have been here when Blessing was born, should not have missed Lily Kate's changing from toddler to little girl, should have been closer to Becca in her grief at her infant son's death. My existence had been only about me for too long.

After Ben drifted back to his study, Becca and I used the time to talk. Lily Kate sat on my lap with her head against my shoulder while Becca nursed the baby and brought me up to date.

"Everyone's doing pretty well, but we think Uncle Billy doesn't feel quite himself. You know Hope's due next month. She's more subdued than usual, Katherine, worried about the baby and as anxious as I to have you home. Maybe now that you're here she'll be more herself again. Are you home to stay?"

"I think so, although I'm not quite sure what to do with myself, whether I should check with the hospital or open a practice of my own. I haven't really thought through my next step."

"That doesn't sound like you, Katherine. You're usually just like Hope, always a plan, always sure where you're going."

After a moment I responded, "My self-confidence had a

little set back," but I didn't volunteer more and she didn't ask.

Outside the wind had quieted and I could see a touch of sunshine through the windows, so the snow must have tapered off, too. I felt very comfortable in my sister's warm kitchen, Lily Kate cuddled on my lap happily preoccupied with the buttons on her dress as she hummed a tuneless little song. Becca, with Blessing cradled in one arm, looked at me over her coffee cup with concern and affection in her clear blue eyes. I felt better already, the mantle of shame and regret I wore a little lighter on my shoulders. At the same time, I knew I could never be Becca, never feel completely content as wife and mother. The roles suited her perfectly and wholly in a way they would never satisfy me. I would always need more.

By noon the snow stopped and the sun shone and people were once again out and about. Becca, Lily Kate, and I went outside to build a snowman and somehow ended up throwing snowballs at one another, all of us eventually so lost in whoops and giggles, we could hardly stand upright.

Looking past me, Lily Kate waved a mittened hand and called, "Hello, Sam," and I turned to see Sam Kincaid still mounted and watching us with a big grin. He led a saddled horse behind his own. At first I was surprised to see him and then felt such a welcoming warmth that it must have showed all over my face. He slid off his horse to pick up Lily Kate with both hands and give her a bounce.

Still holding her, he came forward to say, "So you did make it, Katherine. Your mother was fit to be tied, sure you were stuck in a snow bank somewhere."

"I *was* stuck in a snow bank, but it was right here, just a minute ago, and all Lily Kate's fault, the little stinker." The child giggled, pleased at the attention.

I examined Sam's weathered face carefully, then smiled

and said with sincerity, “Hello, Sam. It’s good to see you.”

I knew I looked a mess, hair scrunched under a woolen cap, nose and cheeks bright pink, and my coat covered in snow. That didn’t seem to matter to Sam. He smiled in return, a nice smile that showed white under a dark mustache.

“It’s always good to have you home, Katherine. Hasn’t been often enough is all.”

“Come in for coffee and pie, Sam,” invited Becca, and we all trooped inside to the warmth of the kitchen where Ben joined us. Until then I hadn’t realized how much I had missed the casual company of family.

“We can’t get a wagon on the road until some of this snow melts,” Sam said to me, “but if you’re game, I brought Sol for you and we can get home on horseback.”

I turned to Ben. “Taking a page from my mother’s book, Ben, I’d like to borrow a pair of your trousers. I can’t let anyone think I’m not game enough to make the trip home.”

Later, warm and bundled against the weather, my doctor’s bag fixed to the saddle horn, I sat atop Sol, my favorite mount, and gave a final wave to Lily Kate. She pressed her face against the window, squashing her nose flat and turning herself into an unrecognizable—but still adorable—creature. Becca had repacked some essential clothes for me in a smaller bag that Sam rolled in a blanket and tied behind his saddle.

“Are you ready?” he asked.

I didn’t answer, just smiled at him and pulled on the reins to turn Sol for home, more than ready, past ready, to get there.

The horses’ breath showed in the frigid air as we traveled, our pace slow but not unpleasant. With the sun out full force and no wind to speak of, the countryside looked beautiful, a study in white and black and gold. The distant mountains showed in conspicuous contrast to the clear blue sky.

Next to me, Sam, dressed in heavy coat and gloves and a well-worn Stetson, asked, "Are you doing all right, Katherine?" I couldn't tell if he was asking about my life in general or this ride specifically.

"I'm fine. I forgot how beautiful snow can be."

"Not this pretty in Chicago, then?"

"It only snows dirty snow there, I think. At least that's the only kind I ever saw."

After a little silence he asked, "How long are you home for this time, Katherine?"

"I don't know. I may be home for good and that would be all right with me."

"That would be all right with me, too," and at my sideways glance he added, "All right with all of us."

I didn't recall that Sam's eyes were such a deep brown, almost as dark as Douglas's, but a world of difference in their color, nevertheless. Nothing glittered or lurked in the depths of Sam Kincaid's expression, no tingle of excitement and no promise of pleasures yet to be discovered. I needed to banish Douglas more completely from my mind, I thought, because despite my best intentions, he came to mind at odd and disconcerting times. Sam's plain brown eyes and likable smile were a good foil to the memory.

"Thank you for your letters, Sam. They really meant a lot to me. More than you know. I'm sorry I wasn't a more faithful correspondent in return."

"You were busy these last years and I know you didn't have much extra time. I was happy whenever you spared me a minute."

I could have spared him more minutes, I thought, and wondered if I would ever be able to tell him what his last letter had meant to me, how I had clung to it for normalcy and comfort. Probably not, but it seemed right that he should know someday.

Aloud I said, "I wish I had done some things differently, Sam, but I can't go back and change the past."

I could tell from his expression that my serious tone surprised him, but he answered easily, "Everybody wishes that, Katherine. My mother always said that only the future matters. The older I get, the more I think she was right."

"You've never spoken of your mother before."

"No? Well, not to you maybe." Which made me think he had to others, who'd been willing to take the time to listen to him.

We plodded down the road and turned off on the drive that led to our house. Someone had been there ahead of us. The drive was cleared of snow and a big paper sign with streamers hung over the entry arch where the letters JL, our ranch and our brand, were usually prominently displayed. The sign read *WELCOME HOME KATHERINE* in bold black letters. Without warning, the sight of the sign brought tears pricking at the back of my eyes.

"Fiddle tears?" asked Sam, too observant for a woman's peace of mind.

"I guess so. I didn't expect such a special welcome." That comment made him shake his head.

"You have been away too long if you thought your homecoming wasn't special. Your mother's been shining like one of those electric lights since she got your letter, and before the snow hit, Hope was over here every day to make sure you hadn't changed your plans."

"Are they doing all right, John Thomas and Hope and the boys?"

"Fine as far as I know. Seems to me they're both a little worried about the baby due next month, but they haven't said anything to me about it. I'm just reading the signs."

"Is Gus home?"

"For a few days yet. When school's in session, he stays in town with Ben and Becca, so with the prospect of having both you and Gus home, your mother's been walking on clouds."

Coming up on our house, I had to stop to absorb the view. When I was a little girl, the house had looked considerably different. Then it was a simple square building of four rooms where all winter we lived around the stove in the kitchen. Over the years, though, the house had changed, added on to more than once until it sprawled across the property, the walls of whitewashed logs interrupted by a massive chimney and fireplace, their stones whitewashed, too. An impressive sight, as full of light in its own way as Douglas's beautiful house, but I clamped down hard on the thought. Douglas Gallagher did not belong in the world of warmth and memory that lay before me.

In the summer Mother planted her brilliant yellow sunflowers by the corner of the porch, and with all the outbuildings in shades of red and brown, on some days the place was as pretty and colorful as a painting. That January day everything looked white, though, yard and house and snow-covered roofs, everything except for the spot of blue on the porch: Mother waiting for me, watching for me, the prodigal daughter come to her senses and finally home.

We had a celebration that evening, despite the snow that kept John Thomas and his family away. Mother made all my favorite foods and Uncle Billy, who could neither read nor write but had one remarkable musical gift, played a joyful and lilting tune on his fiddle in my honor.

Becca had been right to be worried about him, I thought critically. He was much too thin. A stocky man in his forties, Uncle Billy had never been sick a day in his life that I could recall. Something didn't seem right.

My younger brother, Gus, was in his second year at the university in Laramie and looked completely grown up. When had a gawky adolescent transformed into a young man with auburn hair and hazel eyes just like mine?

Mother, stopping long enough to plant a kiss on Gus's cheek, as happy as Sam had described and illumined by her joy, asked rhetorically, "Who ever would have thought we'd have both a doctor and a lawyer in the family? Your Grandfather Caldecott would be so proud and delighted!"

Age allowed her to speak about her family more easily and more often than I remembered from years ago. They were all gone and I think for a while, through at least some of my childhood years, their memories had brought her only pain. But like Gus, that had changed in recent years without my really noticing so that Mother mentioned those early times more frequently and casually, brought up her parents and her older sister Lily, who had all died before my parents married. My father's last relation, his brother Thomas, died well before he met my mother, too, so when Louisa Caldecott and John Davis started their married life together thirty years earlier, it had been just the two of them, no other family around for encouragement or support. No wonder they were as close as they were at this stage of their lives, that they finished each other's sentences and had been known to read the other's mind. Douglas Gallagher and I could never have reached that kind of closeness, no matter how many lifetimes we would have been given.

Sitting with the noise of family around me, I closed my eyes, relaxed, and tried to picture Douglas among us. I despised him and yet felt something for him, something I named pity that hovered at the edge of my mind. If what I felt was more than pity, I would not name or admit it. A stunted man, I thought, who had never been given the opportunity to experience the kind of gathering that surrounded me. The words almost came: *Poor Douglas*, but I remembered Mary Fay and Petra and the phrase died before it was born.

"Katherine." Sam said my name and sat down, straddling a chair beside me. "Tired?"

"No. Deep in thought is all." I smiled over at him and put a hand on his arm. "It was good of you to come and get me, Sam. I wouldn't have wanted Father to get out in the snow, but I'm glad I didn't have to wait to get home."

"You should know by now I'd do anything for you." He paused the briefest moment before he added, "And your parents. No one's ever been as good to me as they have."

"I believe they both think of you as a third son."

"I'd be honored if that was the case. But are you sure you need another brother?"

"You can never have too many. Besides, with John Thomas all domesticated and Gus off to school, you're the only one I have around to tease."

"If another brother's what you need, that's what I'll be."

His comment made me think of the question he had asked me years before: *What do you need then*? At the time I'd answered *friend.* Now it was brother.

His thoughts must have run to the same memory because Sam said, "And I'm still a better rider than you are." It surprised me that he remembered our exchange from years ago, made me laugh and pleased me, but I couldn't have said why. I hoped it wasn't vanity again.

That night, sleeping in the bed I had shared with my sister until her wedding day, the house settled around me, the whistle of the wind and the snow that once more pelted against the glass as effective as a lullaby. Just before I drifted asleep I recalled what Sam had said: *Only the future matters.* I hoped he was right.

In the morning, life as I remembered it at home resumed. All the men were already up and gone by the time I finally made it to breakfast, and Mother had something in the oven and was busy heating water for laundry that she would eventually hang on the inside back porch. She interrupted her work to join me.

"They'll be dropping hay all morning. I sent lunches along with them so I don't think we'll see them until supper." As she poured herself a cup of coffee from the stove, she asked casually, "Did you and Douglas have a nice Christmas? I wish you could have been with us. We had everyone here on Christmas Day. John put up a big tree in the parlor and I made Gus climb and drape greenery from the rafters. It was beautiful. John Thomas brought Hope and the boys, and Ben and Becca and the girls came after church. Everyone stayed the night. We loved having little ones in the house again." She had allowed enough space between her first question and her last sentence so it wouldn't seem like prying. My mother was very good at that sort of thing.

I started to say something purposefully vague, caught her loving and knowing eye on me—that *mother* look she had perfected through the years—and ended up telling her everything. A good listener, she didn't interrupt, just sat coffee cup in hand and watched my face as I talked.

"You always told us how important it was to make thoughtful and sound choices, but I guess I forgot. Or I let my vanity get in the way. Becca and Hope chose the right man from the start, knew the one they wanted and never lost sight of him, and I thought it would be the same for me. I don't have very good judgment, I'm afraid. Not exactly an admirable trait in a doctor."

Mother got up to pour both of us fresh coffee and rested one hand on my shoulder as she did so.

"You're not Becca and you're not Hope. You've always carved out your own way and followed your own dreams, Katherine. Don't be too hard on yourself. You finally made the right choice, and you did the right thing when it mattered and that's what counts." She began to clear dishes from the table but paused to ask, "What were you thinking, Katherine? Were you out to reform him? Did you think you could change Douglas into the kind of man you wanted him to be?" She asked the question with gentle and sincere curiosity that didn't offend or—as had happened on other occasions I could recall—cause me to bristle defensively.

"I don't know. I don't think so. Isn't that what you had to do with Father, though?"

She stopped what she was doing and came to sit in the chair next to me, reached a firm hand to my arm, and held my look with the intensity of her own gray gaze.

"Oh, no, Katherine. Where did you ever get that idea? Your father is the truest man I've ever known, and he was that way long before he met me. He never needed to be reformed, only loved, and that came easy to me from the start. If that's what you've thought about your father all these years, you've been wrong. I loved John Davis from the first moment I saw him, loved the clear, unbending honor in those blue eyes of his. I've never held much confidence in trying to reform a man from the outside. From what I've seen, it either doesn't work or it doesn't last." We sat there quietly awhile, and then she put the back of her hand against my cheek. "I'm happy to say it doesn't sound like your heart's broken. Is it?"

"No." I saw Mary Fay's misshapen face, heard Petra's words: *I thought I was the bad one.* It wasn't just men who could break a woman's heart. "I don't think so, but that makes it even worse, doesn't it? I spent a year in his company, took his gifts, ate at his table, enjoyed his compliments, allowed him to lavish me with attention, but didn't love him. I don't know if I feel more ashamed of my conduct or more relieved at my escape." She laughed.

"You aren't the only one who's relieved. Your father has been fretting about Douglas Gallagher since we boarded the train in Chicago to come home. He really took a strong dislike to Douglas. I can't recall John having that same deep aversion for a man since before we were married. Your father will dance a jig when he hears we won't have to welcome Mr. Gallagher into the family."

"I'd like to see that." I laughed at the mental picture but sobered to ask, "And you?"

"Oh, I knew it would never come to that. You were swayed for a while, I could tell. Your Aunt Lily struggled with similar provocations and I sensed that same conflict in you. But I understand you, Katherine, better than I ever understood Lily. Your inner voice is as strong as mine, and when the time came, I knew you'd make the right choice." I was warmed by her confidence but not nearly as certain as she. Had Mary Fay not shown up at the dispensary door, I may not have come home to stay. Then Mother tossed me a cloth to dry dishes and the time for confidences was over.

That afternoon I rode to my brother's place, a few miles southeast of us. To be accurate, I should say Hope's place because the house in its original, more primitive form had belonged to her, but John Thomas had transformed it into a comfortable, spacious, yet snug home.

Jack, almost four, answered my knock, examined me a minute, then with his father's and his grandfather's slow, sweet smile said, "Hello, Aunt Kat," and naturally held up both arms toward me. I lifted him into my arms, planted a kiss, then stepped inside and closed the door behind me.

"Hello," I called as I walked toward the back room. I

had heard the snap of the loom when I entered and knew Hope was busy at her work. My sister-in-law, heavy with child, came to stand in the doorway on the far side of the kitchen.

"Katherine!" she cried, flattering me with the look of pleasure that crossed her face. "I don't think I can get close enough to hug you, but I'll try."

My brother had had the good fortune to marry an exceptional woman, strikingly beautiful, strong despite her small size, steady in temperament, driven by a pronounced sense of purpose, loving, and smart. Besides that, she was by far the best cook in the family, which from the beginning my mother readily and cheerfully admitted. Even with a husband and two children and all the day-to-day activities of ranch life, Hope still found time to weave, with the resulting fabric a work of art. Like all of my family, I am a hard worker, but none of us can match Hope in energy and resolve. She was the reason John Thomas successfully ran sheep along with the cattle on their range. I knew that my brother, at first attracted by Hope's sparkling emerald eyes and her mass of unruly hair the color of sunlight, had ultimately fallen in love with her heart and spirit. Everyone who knew her understood exactly why he fell as hard as he did, and years later the attraction showed no sign of abating.

Eighteen-month old Tommy woke up as his mother and I talked and when she brought him in, acted shy, snuggling against her and pretending not to notice me. I'd seen his photograph as a newborn, but in the intervening months he'd turned into a long-legged little man with his mother's curly blond hair. After several minutes of furtive examination, he decided that I was acceptable, slid off his mother's lap, and came over to me to squeeze in next to Jack.

"I don't have enough room," I protested, laughing, but

hauled him up next to his brother. This spinster aunt role would work out just fine, but I'd have to figure out how to make more lap space.

When I asked Hope how she felt, she gave a little shrug.

"Like a ship out of water, but otherwise I feel fine. It's nothing physical, Katherine, but I know this baby is different from the other two. It's as if she's speaking to me, like she wants to be born but she's warning me about something."

"She?"

"Oh, yes, it's a girl. I know that."

Hope was serene in her confidence, a quiet woman with a rich inner life, at times almost mystical compared to the prosaic and practical Davis clan into which she married. Two hundred years ago she might have been suspected of witchcraft. Sometimes I found it extraordinary that my brother, whose heart hung openly on his sleeve and whose face reflected every emotion he was feeling at the time, should be loved by this poised and private woman. Lucky man, I thought, but Hope would have said she was the lucky one.

"Well, let me take a look." I scooted the boys into the back room to play while we went into the bedroom. Listening with my fetoscope pressed to Hope's abdomen, I told her, "This niece of mine has a good strong heartbeat and her head is down right where it should be. When did you say she's due?"

"The end of February, Dr. Jeske said. Why?"

"I would have said sooner than the end of February, but I don't know how you carried your other two so I could be wrong. Everything sounds and looks all right, Hope."

She sat up. "Dr. Jeske's probably right, and I just have baby jitters."

"Is that what it feels like to you, a case of the jitters?"

"No, but if I told him what it really felt like, he'd have me locked up."

"You can tell me."

She smiled her gratitude. "I know. That's one of the reasons I'm so happy to have you home." She lowered her voice. "Honestly, Katherine, I'm not crazy, but it's like a little voice speaking to me. I hear it in my dreams: a little girl's voice that sings and calls my name, calls 'Mama.' She tells me she loves me, and she can't wait to see me, but then in my dream she falters a little, like she's waiting for me to assure her that everything will be all right. John Thomas says I talk to her in my sleep."

Hope looked embarrassed by the confession but relieved, too. I knew she wouldn't have told John Thomas all this detail, wouldn't have wanted to worry him, and I imagined that holding it all inside had become something of a burden for her.

"He's caught me talking to her around the house, too. He never says anything, but I know my conduct worries him. It worries me, too, but I can't help it. I don't like what I hear in her voice so I tell her out loud, 'Little Beatrice, everything will be all right.'"

"Beatrice? Is that her name?"

"It was my mother's name."

"I didn't know that, Hope. It's a lovely name. I can't wait to meet my niece." Hope grabbed hold of me as anchor so she could swing both legs over the side of the bed and pull herself upright.

"It's funny, but I think she feels the same way about you. I told her that her Aunt Kat was a doctor and would be here to make sure she came into the world safe and well. I may be losing my mind entirely, but I swear she's been calmer and happier since I told her about you. Do you think

I'm crazy? John Thomas is the only other person I've told any of this to. I haven't even said anything to Lou. I'm afraid she'd think I'm not a fit mother."

"That is the only crazy thing you've said today. Mother thinks you're wonderful. Sometimes it's made me jealous because it seemed she approved of you much more than she ever approved of me."

"Oh, no. Lou is so proud of you! Always 'Katherine this' and 'Katherine that.' 'My daughter the doctor,' she says, and her eyes light up."

"I still have a lot to learn," was all I replied and let Hope make of that what she chose.

Going home, I considered what Hope had told me and supposed, like Dr. Jeske, that I should chalk it up to whatever changes were going on inside her body. But I had a lot of regard for Hope Birdwell Davis as a woman not given to exaggeration or hysteria, so perhaps Baby Bea really was speaking to her mother, whatever the message might be.

My brother met me as I left, not suppertime yet but he was clearly in a hurry to get home.

"We're sorry we missed your homecoming," he told me, "but I didn't think it would be wise to get everyone out in that weather." John Thomas looked older than his years, a vertical crease of worry between his brows and a touch of gray at his temples, neither of which had been there when I'd last seen him. No longer the boy I remembered, so another person who had changed while I was away. Our horses stood stirrup to stirrup, close enough so I could reach out a hand to him.

"I would have been disappointed in you if you had gotten out. The boys have really grown, John Thomas."

He gave his old grin. "They're something, aren't they?" Then the grin faded. "Did you talk to Hope?"

"Yes, and I gave her a quick exam. She looks fine. I

didn't see anything to be alarmed about."

"That's what Jeske says, too, but she's been so funny about this one. Nothing like she was with the boys. They were born before any doctor could have made it, easy births for her and a relief for me, but this one—"

Both of us were thinking about Becca's baby, a difficult labor and a weak little boy from the start, lethargic and sickly and gone in a month, leaving a gaping grief in his parents' lives.

"I know. I'll come every day, twice a day as it gets closer. I wish we had a telephone out here. I don't know how you could get word to me if you needed me in a hurry."

"Maybe you could plan on moving in with us for a while," he suggested. "When it gets closer to the time, I mean."

"I could do that," I agreed and in fact planned on it, but it wasn't necessary. The very next week on a frigid, mid-January morning, I made the trip over to check on Hope. Snow had fallen again and the men were once more dropping hay, a lengthy job necessary to make sure the cattle didn't starve. They would be away all day, and John Thomas had come by earlier than necessary to make sure I knew he would be gone. He seemed restless and worried.

"Why don't you stay home?" I said, "No one would think the worse of you."

"I wanted to do just that, but Hope wouldn't have it, said it was too early to be worried and she'd be fine. Sometimes you can't tell her anything, and you just have to do what she says." That from my brother, who had bossed me around unmercifully for the first eighteen years of my life, who as the oldest always felt he knew best and was never too timid to tell you exactly what that was!

"I'll go over and spend the day. She won't mind me and

I can help with the boys, maybe give her a chance to rest."

"Good luck with that. She never slows down." That he was deeply concerned was written all over his face. "I can remember what life was like without her, Katherine, and I couldn't go back to that. I just couldn't." He had never spoken so seriously or seemed so vulnerable before, and I was touched.

"Stop thinking the worst. There's not one reason this delivery should be any more difficult than the others." But I well knew that each birth was different, and there were no guarantees for the safety of either mother or child. He knew it, too. We were far away from town besides, and from the security of the hospital and its medical staff. His concern was only natural. I wanted to say just the right words of confidence and reassurance, but I couldn't find them, so instead I reached over awkwardly to put both arms around him in a quick, hard, quiet hug.

"I'm glad you're here," was all he said in response, but I thought he held onto me a little desperately. I found I was more comfortable with the old interfering and bossy John Thomas and hoped he'd reappear after the baby was born. It was like some other man was inhabiting my brother's body.

CHAPTER 15

That day when I got there and knocked, Jack met me at the door again.

"Mama's sick," he said with unnatural gravity. I heard Hope cry out behind him, picked him up briefly just to move him to the side, and threw off my coat and scarf as I hurried into the house.

Hope stood next to the stove, doubled over, gasping, pale, and sweating. Tommy sat on the floor next to the table, looking like he wanted to cry, and I scooped him up quickly before putting an arm around Hope.

"You'd better get into bed," I told her. I grabbed Jack by the hand and took both boys into the back room. "Jack, you and Tommy must play in here. You're a big boy and you need to watch your brother. No fighting, no crying. Do you understand?" He looked at me soberly, four going on fourteen, and nodded.

"Mama's sick," he said again.

"Only a little sick and she'll be fine. You play in here

and don't be scared. Aunt Kat will make everything all right." An easy enough boast to a little boy, but I had my own misgivings.

Hope made another, more subdued sound from the bedroom. Trying not to frighten the children, I thought, and hurried back to join her.

"How long has this been going on?" I asked as she clutched my hand.

"As soon as John Thomas disappeared from view. To tell the truth, probably even before that. I should have said something but when Tommy was born I made the mistake of thinking it was time. John Thomas went to get Dr. Jeske and rousted him out of bed in the middle of the night. Then when the doctor got here, he said it wasn't time yet and he turned around and went home. I think he was disgusted with me. I didn't want to make the same mistake twice, so I didn't say anything to John Thomas this morning. By the time my water broke, he was gone, and it was too late." She gave a deep groan, crushed my hand for almost a minute, then lay back down, panting a little. "I guess I just can't get the timing right."

As I examined her I commented, "That's not true. You got the timing right for this one. Baby Bea is well on her way. I'm going to go heat some water and get plenty of clean rags so we're ready for her. We'll need them soon enough. I'll check on the boys, too, and be right back." I leaned down and pushed her hair back from her face. "Everything will be all right, Hope. Trust me. Everything will be all right." She didn't want to let go of my hand and I had to physically lift her fingers with my free hand so I could leave.

For the next hour I wore a path between Hope and the boys. When I wasn't checking on the imminence of the baby, I played with Jack and Tommy or fixed them a treat, anything to keep them occupied. They were good boys but active, and I thought that when this baby finally arrived, Hope would need all the reserves of energy she could find. Three children under five would keep her more than busy.

I heard her cry out and had reached the bedroom doorway when the outside door opened. John Thomas stood there, heard Hope's cry, and gave me a quick, inquiring look.

"You were right," he admitted, "I should have stayed home today. I don't know what I was thinking of. Is it time?"

"Yes. It could be any time now. Make yourself useful and keep the boys occupied. I'll call you if I need you." Although he had been through this experience twice before—the first time during a blizzard so fierce that my brother had had to be both father and doctor—I thought he would never really get used to it, loving Hope as he did and worrying about her safety. I knew John Thomas very well, a hardworking man like our father, who felt most comfortable with action. He needed to be busy and liked to feel he was in control. Times like this made him realize how false his notion of control was. He loved Hope, and the idea that she was in pain and danger and he couldn't do a thing about it both frustrated and humbled him.

When I got to Hope, she had already begun to push and was panting hard, unaware of anything except the baby so that I had to say her name loudly twice before she heard me.

"Listen to me, Hope," I said, pushing down the sudden panic and fear I felt. "I don't want you to push. You must not push." I had seen something that chilled me. At least eight inches of the umbilical cord showed, a shiny, twisted, faded-purple, almost-gray rope that should never appear before the baby. If Hope continued to push and baby Bea came into the world as things were, the baby's head pressed against the cord would cut off her essential supply of oxygen. If Bea somehow managed to survive the birthing, it was unlikely she would be whole and healthy. I had little time to consider options. Very simply, very basically, I knew I had to relieve the pressure on the cord.

"I have to." Hope wailed her response to my instruction, not sounding like herself at all, but I had seen childbirth turn women into strangers before.

"Listen to me," I repeated, as stern as I could be. "You need to trust me. Do not push." Hope's pain slowly subsided, and I thought I might have two minutes at the most before the next wave began. Snatching extra pillows from the head of the bed, I pushed them under Hope to raise her hips, anything to offset the inexorable pull of gravity. Then I listened quickly for the baby's heartbeat, decreased now, a sign of distress. I knew I couldn't afford to waste a second.

"You'll be fine, little Beatrice," I murmured softly. "Your Aunt Kat's come all the way from Chicago to meet you."

I called my brother's name and he came to the door, would have come inside to his wife except I told him urgently, "John Thomas, I need you to do something right away. I've torn a sheet into strips and left them by the stove where the water should be boiling by now. Drop the cloths into the water, then bring everything, pot and all, to me. I'll need a wooden fork besides. Be quick about it, and be sure your hands are clean." He started to say something but I frowned and turned back to Hope. "I don't have time to explain. Trust me and do what I say." When I looked back, my brother was gone.

"I can't I can't I can't," Hope was saying over and over, all in one breath and without pause. "I can't help it. Is it all right now?" Another contraction started and sweat drenched her face.

"No, but it will be, Hope, I promise. Think of baby Bea, picture her in your mind, and think about her. Focus on her. This is what she's been trying to tell you. It's not time for her to join us right now. It will be in a very little while but not right now. Keep her with you. Don't push just yet." Hope lay panting, crying out some unintelligible syllable that was almost a howl, powerfully agitated.

"I have to, I have to, I can't stop." But I could tell she was trying to hold back, drawing from that strength of will and purpose that must have characterized her all her life, even from childhood. Slowly the pain eased and she relaxed as much as she could, already tensing for the next assault.

John Thomas carried the pot into the room carefully, the water so hot that steam still rose from it, and sat it on the floor at the foot of the bed where I crouched. I talked as I busied myself, carefully using the fork to fish out a ragged strip of cloth. After holding the cloth up just long enough to cool, I used it to grasp the exposed and slippery cord.

As I worked I made casual conversation. "There's something different happening right now."

John Thomas, still present, turned abruptly away from Hope to look at me with a sharp expression that narrowed his eyes. He didn't speak, just watched me, his sun-browned face as pale as Hope's. I knew my brother well, knew he wanted to *do* something, knew this forced helplessness was chafing at him, but I didn't have time to allay his fears. I needed to concentrate on Hope and the baby.

Hope shook her head as if doing so would help her hear and understand my words. "What? What's wrong? Tell me!"

"I didn't say wrong, just different, but you must not

push until I say so. The cord is coming ahead of the baby and that's not good. It's not good for the baby." Because I knew my time to act was limited by the contractions, I continued to work quickly as I talked, all the time trying to sound as if my actions were common and no cause for alarm, as if I had experience with such a situation when I had really only heard about it from an instructing doctor years before. In one clean and uncluttered part of my mind, I tried desperately to remember what I had read as follow-up in the medical textbook.

Hope was frantic to do what I told her but was unable to control the urge to push. Struggling to hold back caused her such pain and confused frenzy that when John Thomas went to her to try to take her hand and comfort her, she shook him off, beyond hearing by then. Hope's whole body told her to do one thing and only my calm, repetitive voice—"Don't push. Don't push."—opposed the fierce and natural urge that pulsed through her. I despaired that I had waited too long, was too fumbling in my approach, too slow in remembering what I had heard and read years before, but I allowed none of my despair to show. Instead, I spoke in a cool, matter-of-fact voice.

"I'm going to reach up and push our baby back a little, Hope, push the cord back in, too. I'll be careful not to hurt her, I promise." My fingers felt the top of the baby's head and I pushed gently, knowing how soft her little head was and careful not to do any damage. Time was going too fast but I couldn't rush this, not if I wanted to protect both the child and the mother. During that relaxed phase between contractions, I used the cloths to grasp the slippery cord and tucked it back inside, back past the baby's head, as far back as I could get it. I was done just as the next contraction came.

"It's all right now," I told Hope, although I wasn't at all sure I spoke the truth. "It's time to let our Beatrice come into the world." I tried to listen for the baby's heartbeat and caught it: a good, strong, defiant thump that declared, *Get ready, I'm coming*. I saw the top of the baby's head appear once more, no cord showing this time. Hope grunted and pushed, all the while repeating the same two words over and over; I couldn't make out what they were.

In a voice as composed and pleasant as if I were discussing the weather, I continued a mild monologue of my own: "Bear down a little, keep pushing, let it happen, everything's good, it won't be long now, you're doing fine, just trust me, everything's going to be all right."

I had directed John Thomas to find a soft towel or blanket to clean and cradle the baby, and then I lost track of him. There was no place for him in the room then, anyway. Hardly a place for me, either. It was Hope's and Bea's time, the two of them, mother and daughter, working in concert, one focus, one desire, one need.

Although Hope had been repeating a refrain for some time, it took me a while before I could make out her message. *Come home,* Hope was saying over and over in a cadence that rose and fell but never stopped. *Come home come home come home come home.*

And then the baby was home. In graceful slow motion, small and slippery, whole and healthy and as beautiful an infant as you can imagine, with Hope trying to push herself up on her elbows to see, Beatrice Davis slid into my waiting hands and into the world.

I turned the baby onto her side, used my finger to clear her mouth, throat, and nose, and rubbed her back for just a moment until she gave a squeak followed by a healthy cry. I placed the child on her mother's stomach.

"Here's your Beatrice," I said and watched Hope cradle her daughter's head with her palm. Hope's hair was plastered against her face with sweat and she was pale and drawn, but she had such a radiant glow about her that at that moment she looked beautiful.

"Is she all right? Are you sure she's all right?"

"She's perfect, a little thing but all her parts seem to be in good working order. She may be a bit early, but my niece is obviously a force to be reckoned with and couldn't wait to get here. A woman with a mind of her own already and not even an hour old."

John Thomas came to crouch next to the bed and take his wife's hand in his.

"Thank you, my love. It's just what I prayed for," he said to Hope in a low voice. "A girl just like her mother, strong and determined and beautiful." He leaned closer to Hope and whispered something in her ear that made her smile, then rose to rest his hand on the baby. John Thomas and I looked at each other for a brief and wordless moment across the bed and I scooted him out quickly before he had time to say something that would make us both cry.

Later, the cord cut, Beatrice wiped, washed, and wrapped, and Hope's hard work finally done for the time being, I put fresh sheets on the bed, cleaned up everything that needed to be taken care of, and sat down at the kitchen table for a much appreciated break. John Thomas came out of the back room with a boy by each hand.

"Papa," Jack announced, "Mama was sick, but Aunt Kat made her better."

"Yes," said my brother, "Your Aunt Kat is something, isn't she?" He handed Tommy into my arms, sat Jack on a chair, laid one hand briefly on my shoulder as he passed me, and went back into the bedroom, closing the door behind him. He stayed in there a long time, long enough for me to put Tommy, who had fallen asleep on my lap, into bed and to clear the table and wash the dishes. When John Thomas finally came out, he sat down at the table.

"Well," he said, and nothing more.

Jack crawled into his lap to ask, "Where's Mama?"

"She's sleeping now, son. She has a surprise for you, though. Come on, I'll show you, but we need to be quiet."

I followed them into the bedroom and watched from the doorway.

"This is your new baby sister, Beatrice," John Thomas told Jack. My brother's voice was so absurdly sentimental when he said the baby's name, it was clear that my niece had already wrapped her father around her little fingers. Clever girl to have figured out that trick so soon.

Jack gave the baby a critical look and remarked, "She's awful little."

"She's brand new."

"Well, I don't see what good she's going to be that small. You shoulda got a bigger size." Then he turned and walked past me out of the room, shaking his head at his parents' lack of foresight.

"She *is* small," said John Thomas, apparently desperate for something to worry about.

"She's fine. She'll grow," I told him and took his arm to bring him back into the kitchen. "Come and sit down and have something to eat. Let Hope sleep a while. She'll need all the rest she can store up to handle these three." I set food on the table for him, but he just sat there watching me.

"What if you hadn't been here?"

"I believe we would have lost the baby, but why think about that? I was here and we didn't."

"We're naming her Beatrice."

"I know."

"Beatrice Katherine."

"Oh." I repeated the name aloud. "It's a big name for such a little girl," but I was pleased at having a namesake of my own.

After a moment my brother, who has a heart like cornmeal mush, said, “Thank you, Katherine.” He tried to say more but something seemed to be caught in his throat. He gave a little cough, as if to hide the emotion, but I wasn’t fooled. Rising, I went behind him to put both my arms around his neck in a hug.

“You’re welcome, big brother.” Then I reached for my coat. “I set what you need to burn outside. You should take care of it before the coyotes get wind of the blood. I’m going home with the good news, but I’ll be back in the morning, and I’ll tell Father not to expect you tomorrow. Someone will come by later tonight to see if you need anything.”

I left him sitting with Jack on his lap. The boy, almost asleep, leaned his head back against his father’s chest and John Thomas carefully, tenderly brushed crumbs from Jack’s cheek. My brother always favored our father in appearance and just then I had a quick glimpse back in time to what Father must have looked like thirty years ago.

I knew some people assumed that our parents’ property, livestock, and bank account would one day make up the Davis children’s inheritance, but those people were fundamentally and extravagantly wrong. Long before our parents’ passing, my siblings and I had already inherited what would prove more precious than any material goods, something intangible and of far greater value, something I saw that afternoon on my brother’s face as he cradled his son.

In the morning Mother and I both went over for a visit. I examined Hope while John Thomas got the boys ready to go to my sister’s for a few days, an arrangement sure to make everyone happy. Hope was herself again, calm and steady, quietly delighted with her daughter. She raised a smiling face to me as she nursed Beatrice.

“Both the boys were bald when they were born, but

she's so pretty with all this dark hair. Lou said John Thomas looked like this when he was a baby."

"Poor child then," I replied. "I don't think you want your daughter to grow up looking as long and lanky as her father. We'll hope she's as pretty as you instead. How do you feel?"

"I'm fine." Then with a warm look, she added, "Thank you, Katherine. Bea and I are both glad you came home."

After I left I wondered about whether I really was home, whether I would stay or was just passing through to some other place, location as yet unknown and home still undetermined. I knew I should go visit Dr. Jeske and the city hospital to see if there was a place there for me, but I was strangely reluctant to do so. In my whole life I had never felt so aimless or been so directionless, a situation that made me jumpy and unsettled.

That evening my father pulled me aside to ask me to talk to Uncle Billy the next day. He didn't like how he looked, Father said, and thought there might be something seriously wrong. In the morning I tramped over to the cookhouse and caught Uncle Billy as he was on his way out with Sam after breakfast.

"How are you feeling, Uncle Billy?" I asked. I noticed again that he was thinner than he should be. Sam stopped to hear the answer.

"Not so good," he answered honestly.

My Uncle Billy wasn't a blood uncle, but he'd been a part of our family since I could remember. As a boy of thirteen, he'd accompanied my parents when they settled in Wyoming as newlyweds more than thirty years before. Always a simple man, Uncle Billy was by nature uncomplicated and kind, the only thing extraordinary about him that special gift of music for which there was no explanation.

I had him sit down and then sat across from him, almost

knee to knee.

"What doesn't feel good?" I asked.

He looked a little sheepish but trustingly opened his mouth to point to several sores on his gums and wiggle a loose tooth.

"Can't eat so good. Hurts."

Behind me Sam said, "Billy, you never said anything about that."

"Waitin' for Katherine."

"Well, I'm here now, Uncle Billy, so let me have a closer look." After a while I asked, "How long have you had these problems?"

He shrugged, either not remembering or not knowing how to tell me, and Sam volunteered, "Lou took him to see Dr. Jeske about six months ago. It wasn't long after that before he started losing weight."

"No wonder since it must be too painful for him to chew. Can you ask Fergy to cook soft foods for him for a while?"

As foreman, Sam gave out most of the general directions, even to the cook. I turned my attention back to the man sitting across from me.

"Uncle Billy, what did Dr. Jeske tell you?" He looked at me dumbly, then reached into the inside pocket of his vest to bring out a small white envelope.

"Got to take these pills. He said I got to take one every day."

"Let me see." I took them from him, read what was written on the outside of the envelope and asked, "Do you have a bottle of these pills somewhere?" When he nodded, I said, "I don't want you to take them anymore. I'm going to keep these and you go bring me that bottle right now."

He balked for just a minute. "Doctor said I'm to take one every day, Katherine."

"Uncle Billy, Dr. Jeske doesn't love you. I do. So please do what I say and bring me that bottle."

"Okay, Katherine." He gave me a sudden big smile, its message clear as could be. I love you, too, that smile said.

After he left, Sam asked, "What's the matter?" My anger must have shown on my face as I held the small envelope of pills out on my palm.

"This is calomel."

"I don't understand."

"Doctors stopped prescribing calomel twenty years ago, Sam. Even first-year medical students know that. It was the most prescribed drug for stomach problems for years until doctors figured out it did more harm than good, caused all the symptoms Uncle Billy has, loose teeth and open sores in the mouth. Calomel has even been known to eat away the jawbone. No reputable physician would prescribe it today." I would have said more, but Uncle Billy came back with the brown bottle of pills and handed it to me.

"Didn't mean no harm. Just doing what the doctor said."

"I know. You didn't do anything wrong, Uncle Billy, but from now on the only doctor you listen to is me. Do you understand?"

"I'm only listening to Katherine now," he told Sam happily. "Wasn't the same without Katherine being home, was it, Sam?"

"No," said Sam, "it wasn't. Let's get going Billy. We've got work to do." Sam stopped in the doorway to look back at me and say, "You're in a temper."

"You bet I am. I intended to pay the good doctor a call anyway, so it might as well be today."

"Don't you think you should calm down a little first, Katherine?"

I responded with a wordless, scornful look, and he

added with a half-smile, "I guess not."

"Calm down!? Any doctor who would hand out calomel to a patient today, with its dangers well documented for over ten years, is incompetent. That he's a practicing physician and an active member of the new hospital's planning board makes it even worse. This on top of what I knew about him from Hope is enough for me to suggest he take his practice elsewhere."

"A lot of people like Dr. Jeske, Katherine."

"A lot of people like to drink rubbing alcohol, too, but that doesn't make it good for you." I stood up and went out past him. "It's a good day for a ride into town."

"No violence," Sam said.

I frowned at him only to catch another small smile and then had to smile in return, despite my intention otherwise.

"I'll try to control myself but send someone into town with bail money if I'm not back by supper."

My visit with Dr. Jeske started off poorly and degenerated from there. By the time I got to his office, I had calmed down considerably and had planned out what I would say, something respectful but firm. That all changed, however, when I was confronted by his patronizing and condescending attitude.

"It's little Katherine," he said as he came out from his examining room, that despite the fact that I stood four inches taller than he. "Back from your adventure. I imagine you enjoyed the sights and sounds of the big city." The doctor was a rotund man in his fifties, with a small, neat beard and heavy sideburns, always impeccably dressed in the finest suits and with a showy gold watch draped into his vest pocket. "I hear you were there for Hope's new arrival. I told her there was nothing to worry about, but she wouldn't listen." His tone and expression were so offensive to me that I had to take a deep breath before I spoke to keep myself from saying all the wrong things.

"It could have been very serious if I hadn't been there," I said evenly, "if not for Hope, certainly for the baby." He waved his hand in the air, brushing me off.

"Nonsense. Women are inclined to exaggerate when they're expecting, and they fall prey to all sorts of imaginary fears. I knew everything would be just fine."

"You weren't there. I was."

"Someday, when you have my length of experience, you'll understand; however, I don't think a pretty girl like you will spend much time as a doctor. Some young man will catch your eye and that's all you'll be thinking about."

Surely, I thought, the man must be provoking me on purpose, but one look at his smug and smiling face told me he meant to charm. I took out the bottle of calomel and dropped it onto a table in the waiting room. He glanced briefly at the bottle, raised his eyebrows to me, and waited.

"You prescribed this for my Uncle Billy."

"Yes. He was complaining about cramps in his abdomen and I prescribed the calomel to clear out his stomach and intestines."

"Calomel," I pronounced with undisguised scorn, "causes mouth ulcers and jaw degeneration. It offers the patient nothing but unnecessary pain and it will eventually cripple him."

Dr. Jeske's eyes narrowed at me, but he kept his same unexcited tone. "You have been out of medical college—if you can call Kansas Medical School a valid medical college—for what? Two years, if that. I am a graduate of the University of Michigan and have been a practicing physician for over twenty-five years. Are you presuming to question my medical counsel?"

"I have read articles from at least ten years ago written by very reputable physicians, some of them University of

Michigan graduates in fact, that called calomel a poison and described exactly the symptoms my Uncle Billy has experienced. First, it's medically irresponsible of you to prescribe this. And second, you have not followed up once with your patient in over six months to see the results of your prescription. I may be a new doctor, but I recognize a deplorable lack of medical ethics when I see it."

"I will not be criticized by a woman pretending to be a doctor."

"I am not the pretender here."

"You are a spoiled young woman, over-indulged by her family, and should be home doing what God intended women to do, not criticizing her elders and her betters."

"Elder, yes. Better remains open for debate."

He went to the door and held it open. "You may leave, young lady, and if, as I heard, you expect to practice in conjunction with any hospital within city limits, you may think again. I will make sure that never happens." I felt frustrated and angry with him—and with myself, too, because I had lost my temper and said exactly what I'd vowed not to say.

At the door I turned and spoke in a temperate voice with no disrespect intended.

"Dr. Jeske, a physician doesn't have the luxury of resting on his laurels. Medicine is changing practically daily. For the good of your patients, you must keep abreast of the latest medical and scientific news. If you're not doing that, you put people's lives at risk."

"Do not presume to lecture me."

The man was implacable as he continued to hold open the door, a stern and righteous father forced to banish his intractable child from his sight. I could only shake my head at his stubbornness and leave.

That night Sam came up to the house after supper.

"How'd it go with the doctor?"

"Not good. I should have been more diplomatic, but the man was so annoying, so contemptuous and superior, as if Hope's and Billy's feelings were unimportant—only patients after all!—and I was some upstart female, who dared to question his omniscience. He infuriated me. Now I don't know what to do because he as much as told me I would never have the chance to practice out of any Laramie hospital as long as he's here.

"Maybe you could smooth the waters."

I reacted with outrage to the suggestion. "Me?! He's the one who needs to change, not me." Then I added, reluctantly laughing at myself, "I guess I could stand to change, too, and be a little more tactful and have a little less temper. But to risk people's lives is unethical and inexcusable, and it just infuriates me!"

"I can see that, Katherine."

The man was a master of understatement, I thought, and had to laugh at myself again.

"What stops you from opening up your own practice?" Sam continued. "It doesn't seem to me you'd need Jeske's approval to do that, would you? No matter what he says, I don't see how he could keep ordinary citizens from choosing you as their doctor."

"No," I responded thoughtfully, "I suppose he couldn't."

I considered that conversation for several days, considered opening my own independent practice with my name on the sign outside the door. I would need to find an office in town, then figure out a way to outfit it, but why not? I had no other plans and felt more and more restless as the days passed. In fact, I had noticed a small vacant storefront on Second Street, right next to Mr. Downey's law office, that would do fine: a front waiting area, two rooms in the rear that could be used for both examination and consultation, and a small apartment on the second floor.

I approached my father for a loan, serious about it and about drawing up proper papers if he said yes. He agreed, of course, but not until we had talked the matter through and he understood exactly how I would use the money. The loan was a big step for me because I didn't want to be obligated to my parents any more than I already was for my education.

With the money finally in hand, I began to feel an anticipatory excitement. If I put my mind to it, I would be ready to announce the opening of Dr. Katherine Davis's medical practice by spring.

At the end of January, I received two letters, one from Petra that caught me up on her life and on the day-to-day activities of Hull-House, and the other in the dark, bold script I recognized from cards attached to flowers and gifts. Douglas. His letter was completely unexpected so that for a moment all I could do was stare at it, dumbfounded. Then, because I simply did not want to remember him, I threw the envelope unopened into the fire. Nothing he could have said would have interested me, and I was perplexed that he would try to contact me after our last meeting. 'Get her out of my sight,' he had snarled as if he couldn't bear being in the same room with me. Why follow those unambiguous words with a letter? That December evening in Douglas Gallagher's library seemed like a different world entirely, and that Katherine Davis a different woman.

In February, Klaus Haberdink, a neighboring farmer to our north, came thundering up to our house in his wagon. Mother and I were home and hurried out to the porch to meet him.

"Can you come? Elsa fell outside on the ice, broke her arm, and it looks like a bad break. I can see the bone. I can't get her into town. Can you come and set it?"

Klaus was talking to Mother but I answered, "I'll come. We'll hitch Sol up to the back of the wagon and you won't have to bring me home." I went inside to change into warmer clothes and grab my bag, while Mother asked one of the hands to ready Sol.

"You watch the clouds, Katherine," my mother warned. "I think we could see snow again." I knew how treacherous the weather could be this time of year, how quickly a norther could blow in, bringing with it pelting snow and ice that obscured familiar surroundings and blocked the roads.

"Don't worry. I'll be careful."

Elsa Haberdink was Klaus's sister, a large woman of ample proportions. She had tried to catch herself when she fell, a move that shattered her forearm as her full weight fell on it. Her arm was a mess, and she was in such pain that I administered opium before I began the grim and lengthy process of realigning and setting the bones. Elsa still slept when I finally got ready to leave.

After I finished my instructions to Klaus, he commented worriedly, "Maybe you should stay. Your mother's right. There could be snow before long."

I eyed the sky and assured him I could make it home before flurries flew, but I was wrong. Midway home, I saw a few flakes in the air, and then suddenly and furiously it began to snow hard accompanied by an icy wind that both Sol and I felt clear to the core. As the snow thickened, I couldn't see very far in front of me, got off course, nearly ran into a wire fence and began to think seriously, although not desperately, about shelter. There were enough line cabins along the fences that I knew if I just followed the fence long enough I'd find some place for refuge. The line cabins, used by the ranch hands as they rode the range mending fence and seeking out lost steers, weren't fancy, but they generally had a stove for warmth and enough firewood stored for just this kind of situation. I was nearly frozen solid when I finally did run into a cabin. Literally. I couldn't see the building through the snow and poor Sol bumped into a corner of one wall. By the time I maneuvered Sol into the adjoining shed, freed him from the saddle, gave him a quick rub down, and tossed him some hay to munch, I was as cold as I'd ever been, teeth chattering and my feet and fingers numb.

Once inside the little cabin, I started a fire in the cook stove and looked around for creature comforts. I found canned goods, a lamp and oil, a small bed, a table, and two chairs. Nothing fancy but enough to wait out the storm safely. I felt fortunate that I had made it that far and hoped no one was worrying about my safety, although I supposed they were.

The little stove warmed the room nicely and after a while, as the wind rattled the roof and rustled the paper that lined the walls for insulation, I curled up on the narrow bed, pulled the single blanket up to my chin, and went to sleep.

I was dreaming about pounding on the door and awoke to the realization that noises in the real world had invaded my sleep. Someone really was banging on the door and shouting. Before I could even swing my feet onto the floor, the door flew open and a figure, bringing a swirl of snow along with him, stepped inside. I could hardly believe the sight.

"Sam?" I asked, incredulous and still bleary from sleep. No mistake. The figure was Sam, with a look on his face hard to interpret, first severe and then soft with relief. "What in the world are you doing here?"

He came farther inside, carefully shut the door, beat the snow off his hat, stomped his boots, moved over to the stove, and took off his jacket, all without saying a word. Snow sizzled as it hit the heat.

Finally he spoke. "I was looking for you, Katherine. The more it looked like snow, the more worried your mother got, so I said I'd head over to Haberdinks just to make sure you stayed put. But you were already gone by the time I got there, so then I thought I'd follow you home. The last tracks I could make out were Sol's veering from the main road, so I figured you'd follow the fence and hole up in the first line cabin you came to."

I sat on the edge of the bed, everything about me a mess, hair tousled and clothes wrinkled, and listened to Sam talk. I thought how he filled the room and brought energy and his own kind of warmth into it and surprised myself by realizing there wasn't anyone I'd rather have seen step through that doorway than Sam Kincaid. When had that happened?

"Don't be too smart about reading my mind," I retorted, standing and trying to straighten both hair and clothes, "because just when you think you know what I'll do next, I'll surprise you."

He grinned as he hung his coat over the back of a chair.

"I think I know you pretty well."

"Do you? That's presumptuous, especially since I've been gone the better part of the last six years."

"Doesn't matter. What you were at twelve you still are today."

"I don't think that's exactly true. I've grown up."

"You have done that." He gave me a long, unblinking look, and I was suddenly self-conscious, warmed by more than the stove. We shared a curious little quiet moment and then he turned to ask, "Is there coffee here?" and busied himself with looking on the makeshift shelves.

"I saw some. If you go fill the coffeepot with snow, I'll

make it. Coffee sounds pretty good right now." We acted like a comfortable old married couple as we put coffee on the stove, opened a can of soup, and found some stale crackers.

When we sat down at the table, I asked, "What were you thinking of to get out in this weather? You could have frozen to death as easily as I."

"I was going to rescue you," Sam answered humbly, sipping his soup from a cup and looking at me over the rim, "but as usual you didn't need rescuing. I figured that was probably the case, but I needed to be sure."

"Sure?"

"That you were safe. That's always been important to me. I remember the first time I really noticed you, Katherine. I'd only been at JL for a day or two. It was calving time and you were determined to come along with the men. I can still see you. You must have been about twelve and you had on a hat that was way too big for you, a red flannel shirt, and a pair of your brother's Levi pants. You had a pencil stuck behind your ear and a notepad with you. You were the strangest girl I ever saw."

"Well, thank you," I responded with a touch of indignation. "I planned to take notes about pulling calves. I don't know why you'd think that was so strange." He gazed at me without a word until I finally admitted, "All right, I suppose it was a little odd, but my family was so used to my curiosity by then, I guess we didn't think about how it would look to someone from the outside. It didn't scare you away, did it?"

"No. I already figured out that I was going to stay as long as your folks would let me. Nothing would have scared me away."

"I remember you coming up to the house with your saddle over your shoulder. You were so skinny that I didn't see how you could carry it on your own. I remember Father went out on the porch to talk to you for a while and then—"

"Then your mother came out," Sam finished for me, "just as if she'd known me all her life and said I should come in for supper—she'd set an extra place at the table. That was it for me. I'd been on the move for years and I thought if your parents would let me stay and work, I'd never leave."

"I know you came from Texas, but that's about all I know. Do you have family there?"

I was embarrassed that through all the years I'd known him, I had never bothered to find out more about Sam's past. Like a spoiled child, I had taken him for granted. He'd been around for so many years that I complacently thought of him as family, as if he hadn't had a life before the Davises.

"Not anymore. I was born in Oklahoma but when my father died, my mother moved back to her folks in Texas. They raised me after she died, and when they were gone, there wasn't anything to keep me in Texas any longer so I took to the road."

"How old were you?"

"Fourteen and big for my age. I didn't have any trouble getting work but I was a pretty dumb fourteen, and every time I got some money in my pocket, I lost it at cards and dice to men who were a lot smarter than me. You couldn't have told me that at the time, though. One day I woke up and realized I'd been working for four years and had nothing to show for it. The last game of cards I ever played I lost everything except my saddle and the clothes on my back. I told myself then that if I could find a place with regular work, I'd settle in and I wouldn't go near a card game again. So when I walked onto your front porch and your father offered me work and your mother offered me supper, I knew that was home and where I was meant to settle."

I put an elbow on the table and rested my chin on my open palm so I could watch his face as he talked. Sam Kincaid wasn't a handsome man in any traditional sense of the word and there wasn't anything smooth about his face, but he had warm brown eyes, an engaging grin under a heavy brown mustache, and thick, unruly dark-brown hair. My father trusted him completely and my brother considered him his best friend. I thought suddenly that I was fonder of Sam than I'd realized, and I didn't think I wanted to consider him as a brother anymore. What I felt wasn't that kind of fondness.

"You're looking like you've never seen me before, Katherine, like I'm some sort of specimen you want to make notes about." I had been staring with enough intensity to make him redden a little at my look.

"I was just thinking that you had a lonely life for a few years, and I wish you would have come onto our front porch sooner. We would have had room for you. And I was also thinking I should have known all that about you before today." My words took him by surprise.

"There's no reason you should have involved yourself in my life. I never met a woman who had her future all mapped out like you did and it sure didn't include me. Why should it? Why should a woman like you take notice of me at all?"

"'A woman like me'? What does that mean?"

"You know."

"No. I don't know. Unless you mean a self-absorbed, spoiled child who only thinks about herself. Then I know."

"That's not what I meant at all."

"But I think that's what I've been." He reached across the table and took my free hand in his.

"You are talking plain foolishness. That's not what you've been at all. You're the smartest, kindest, prettiest girl I ever saw. That's what I meant. I never knew a person, man or woman, to set her sights on something and work toward it and not let anything get in her way like you, Katherine. There's nothing spoiled or selfish about that."

His voice was low and clear and passionate, and for a moment I saw something in his eyes, some deep and fierce feeling that took my breath away. Then the look was gone. But he still held my hand and I was not about to suggest he let go.

"I think you see me through the eyes of friendship, Sam, and that's good of you. I don't deserve it, but it's good of you and I appreciate the kindness."

He let go of my hand then, back to his usual smiling and easy-tempered self.

"When you get humble, Katherine, you scare me. Is there more coffee?"

When I stood up to get the pot, I felt the mood pass, but I knew I would think about this conversation later, about what I had seen in his eyes and the way my heart had turned over at the expression.

"I'm going to check on the horses and bring in my bed-roll. You can have the bed. I'll stretch out by the stove and probably get the better deal because it will be warmer." He said that so I wouldn't protest his taking the floor while I kept the bed, always a step ahead of me as if he really did know me better than I knew myself, knew what I felt and how I thought. When he came back in, bringing somc of the weather with him, he grimaced.

"The snow hasn't let up. Your folks'll be worried, but I don't know what else to do except wait it out. I hope they know I wouldn't let anything happen to you."

"If you recall, I was safe and sound, sleeping in fact, all

without your help." Then at his rueful expression, I lay down and pulled the blanket up to my chin again, smiling to take the sting from my words. "But I was still awfully glad to see you step through that door, Sam." He stood and stared at me for a moment, trying to figure out what exactly I meant by that last remark, but because I couldn't have explained it even to myself, I closed my eyes and without thinking it possible, fell immediately and soundly asleep.

As soon as I awoke in the morning, I knew the snow had stopped. The wind no longer made the little shack creak and no icy grit spattered against the door. There was no Sam, either. His blanket was rolled up, tied, and sat against the wall by the door. Coffee perked on the stove. I had slept soundly through his moving around to do all that, which said something about my trust in him.

When he finally came in, he said good morning and added, "I've saddled us both up. There's no reason we can't get home. The snow stopped during the night and I felt a Chinook wind coming off the mountains that will melt most of what fell yesterday. Your parents will be fit to be tied. I don't think we should wait."

He was right, of course, but without saying so aloud, I was reluctant to leave. I could have stayed there, wintered in with Sam Kincaid, for much longer and been perfectly happy. From yesterday to today, something had changed for me that caused all sorts of butterflies in the pit of my stomach when I thought about it. But there he stood, looking at me expectantly, and all I could do was agree. He might think he knew me pretty well, knew how and what I thought, but I don't think he had a clue about what was going on inside my head and heart just then. Fortunately.

What I felt was nothing like what I had experienced when I was with Douglas Gallagher. Nothing at all. This new emotion was quiet and true and deep, a trusting, warm contentment with no hard edge of excitement and no warning voice telling me to watch myself. I knew instinctively and without a doubt that with Sam Kincaid I had nothing to fear. I hardly understood the feeling myself and couldn't have talked about it to anyone just then.

Halfway home we met my father and John Thomas.

"I told Hope there was no way a winter storm would get the better of you," my brother said with a grin, relieved and doing his best not to show it.

Father gave Sam and me a quick, speculative look, although he would never have said what he was thinking aloud. Sam met his look straight on, and then my father gave the briefest of nods to him and turned to me.

"Are you all right, Katherine?"

"Hungry, but otherwise I'm fine. I thought I could beat the snow. It still looked distant when I left Haberdinks but I should have known better. I followed the fence until I reached the line cabin that's just north of the Wildflower. The one along your northern border, John Thomas. Sam found me there. We were warm enough although we used up most of the coffee and you'll need to restock."

Once home, my mother said, "John told me you'd be fine, Katherine, and Sam would be, too. I shouldn't have worried." But it was clear she had. Her face remained drawn and the fine lines around her eyes and mouth were pronounced.

With a little pang I realized Lou Caldecott wasn't a young woman any more, that she was aging. She'd grown thinner with the passage of time and the silver streak in her hair had become more than just a streak. I never thought of my mother as anything but vibrant and invincible and to see age on her face sobered me. Somehow I had forgotten that I wasn't the only one growing older.

I put an arm around Mother's shoulders and we went

into the house.

"I was never in danger, but I am starved. I think Sam is, too. Is there any breakfast left?"

Behind me Sam called, "I'll get breakfast over at the cookhouse," and was gone without another word. I wanted to summon him back, tell him to sit down across the table from me so I could still look at him all through breakfast, tell him to talk to me as he had last night, as if we were a couple that had been together for years, easy and comfortable. I wanted him to give me that look again, the one that had caused the quick, responsive flutter in my stomach. But he was gone, back to life as usual. I felt suddenly bereft and abandoned and did not blame the February snow for my sudden chill.

CHAPTER 16

The sign went up over my office door the last week of February despite Dr. Jeske's public and frequent predictions of failure. He might be right, I grimly conceded, but I wasn't going to admit it aloud. Laramie's growing population would certainly support a new physician's practice, even if that physician were a woman. At first I had only female patients, young mothers-to-be with whom I'd grown up, family friends, women who knew my mother or my sister and thought they were doing them a favor by coming. I wasn't proud and I didn't care why patients came to me; I was just glad to have them cross my office threshold. It was slow progress, and sometimes I grew impatient or frustrated, but not often. From the start I loved being on my own and never viewed the sign over the door—*Katherine Davis, M.D.*—without smiling. As usual, Sam had been right to suggest the idea.

I knew Dr. Jeske was not complimentary about me and that people liked and trusted him from a natural loyalty for all the years he'd been in Laramie. He was a man besides, a comforting example of the natural order of things to many people who had doubts about a woman in the medical profession.

As in my academic years, however, I didn't let skepticism or disapproval bother me. My little office was just right and the rooms on the second floor, small but comfortable. My mother told me they reminded her of the rooms she lived in over the family business in Blessing, Kansas, before she met my father and left it all behind to move with him to Wyoming. I knew she didn't have any regrets about that choice, but she still sounded wistful when she commented about my little apartment and seemed nostalgic and reflective. I sensed that she'd been happy living on her own in Blessing, had appreciated the independence and not been bothered by solitude.

When I asked her about it, she admitted, "I *was* happy in Blessing, very happy. I can remember telling my sister that I'd never leave. I planned to live in Blessing all my life, I said, and at the time I meant it. But I was happy the day I left, too, a brand new bride sitting next to your father on the wagon seat, Billy and all our worldly goods piled in the back. Everything's a choice, Katherine, and I have never doubted I made the right one. It doesn't do to look back."

I knew Mother missed my company at home, that the big house was empty with both my younger brother and me living in town, but she understood my need to be on my own and never discouraged me.

I received a second letter from Douglas, his persistence annoying. I supposed finding my address wasn't difficult. After all, he'd met my parents and apparently done some research on them, but I still found his tracking me down distasteful. How could he have spent nearly a year's time in my company and not realized I was deadly serious in my desire to have nothing to do with him? Did he think time would soften my memory of poor Mary Fay's battered face or Petra's distress? I burned that unopened letter, too.

Sam came to visit me my first Friday evening in town. As I sat at my desk in the back, I heard the bell on the door jingle. Hoping it was a patient, I went out to the waiting area.

"I'm not who you expected," he said, reading my expression.

"Not unless you've come to see me as a patient."

"No, just as a friend."

"That's even better then. Forgive me if I looked disappointed, Sam. It was a slow week, but I understand that it will take time to get established so I'll try to be more patient."

"Not your strong suit."

I grinned an acknowledgement. "No, that's for sure."

Then we just stood there wordlessly looking at each other until he offered, "I thought you might be hungry. We should celebrate your first week. My treat."

We walked over to Lepper's Restaurant, I talking a mile a minute and he just listening. It wasn't until we sat down that I paused for breath.

"I'm sorry. I should let you get a word in once in a while, out of courtesy if for no other reason. I guess I'm excited."

"That's all right. I've never known you to do anything halfway. I've always admired that about you."

"Really?" Supper had come and I had a fork midway to my mouth but paused, arrested. "I think that's one of my flaws. I get so intent on things that I forget what's going on around me, forget people's feelings sometimes, too."

"You're the only one who considers that a fault,

Katherine. No one I know holds it against you. There's something to be said for a strong-minded woman."

I thought that was a kind thing to say and told him so.

"Kindness doesn't have anything to do with the way I think about you," he replied and then proceeded to finish his supper, leaving me to consider exactly what he meant. by the words

That Friday was the beginning of a courtship, although at the time I didn't realize that's what it was. As long as the weather allowed, Sam came in every Friday, so frequently that I began to look forward to seeing him, grew accustomed to having him there, and missed him more than I would admit the few times he wasn't able to make it. He treated me as a brother would have, acted friendly and interested, teased sometimes, filled me in on the week's activities at home, was always circumspect and well-mannered. I couldn't decide whether I was relieved or disappointed at his conduct.

One Friday at the end of April, I heard the bell ring and, expecting it to be Sam, called out, "In here," but it wasn't Sam who stepped into the doorway. Douglas Gallagher stood there instead, so unexpected and extraordinary an occurrence that I couldn't quite take it in. I stopped abruptly as soon as I saw him and felt all the color drain out of my face and my knees almost give way. I was absolutely speechless. Douglas looked exactly as I remembered him: very handsome, very elegant, dressed in a stylish dark topcoat that made his eyes look as black as his coat. No diamond stickpin to be found anywhere, though, I thought, feeling a rush of some unnamed emotion course through me.

He stepped toward me eagerly. "Katherine, you look wonderful!"

Still speechless, I retreated from his outstretched hand

as if I thought his touch would burn. Perhaps it would have. Perhaps it did.

"I wrote you that I was coming, that I'd be en route from Chicago to San Francisco and would stop in. You must have expected me. Didn't you get my letters?" He saw my recoil and stopped his approach.

"I never read your letters. I wasn't interested. You should go, Douglas. I really don't want to speak to you. I wish you'd go."

He was quick in his reply, the words prepared and practiced. "I know I acted like a brute and that I said hurtful things. There's not a day goes by I don't regret it. I know you think you can't forgive me, but I've changed. I was a blundering, arrogant, and stupid fool and I did some terrible things, but I've changed. I'm sorry, Katherine. You've got to believe me and forgive me. Can't you find it in your heart to forgive me?"

"I don't know what my forgiveness has to do with anything, Douglas. You didn't do anything to *me* that calls for forgiveness. I simply want you to go away. I have no interest in seeing you or hearing from you again. Just go away."

As if I hadn't spoken, as if my words were just so much noise to him, he came closer, urgent and somehow pitiful. For the first time, I saw the desperate man Drew had been trying to describe the night he brought me back to Hull-House after my confrontation with Douglas, saw a frantic man stripped of dignity and superficial elegance.

"*He's been holding on to you like a drowning man clings to a raft,*" Drew had told me, "*afraid to lose you because somehow he knows that you're his last chance for a real life, a normal, real life.*

I recalled the words and watched Douglas drowning in front of me.

"It hasn't been the same with you gone, Katherine," he

continued. “I think about you. I dream about you. I need you in my life. My darling, give me another chance.”

He came close enough to try to place his hand on my arm and I jerked away, finally able to identify the emotion I’d first experienced, the emotion that was trying to immobilize me. Fear. Plain, old-fashioned fear. I found the sight and sound of Douglas Gallagher terrifying. Had that emotion always been there but I had refused to recognize and acknowledge its presence? I took a deep breath to try to hold onto my nerves when the bell on the door rang and Sam called my name from the front doorway.

“Back here,” I said.

Sam stopped abruptly in the doorway of the room where Douglas and I stood, his eyes deliberately resting on my face and reading something there that caused his expression to go blank and lose the warmth I was used to seeing there.

“What do you need, Katherine?” he asked quietly. He had asked me that before more than once, always willing to do and be what I needed. I thought Sam Kincaid was the best and most faithful friend I would ever know.

“Would you show Mr. Gallagher the way out, Sam? He seems to be lost.”

Douglas gave Sam a cursory glance, took in his muddy boots, faded denim jacket, and worn hat, and instantly dismissed him. I could tell Douglas was angry and annoyed at the interruption, but he had changed he told me, so he couldn’t afford to let his anger show.

“Of course I’m not lost,” he told Sam without bothering to look at him. “I was renewing an acquaintance with a dear”—his emphasis on the word made me wince—“friend.”

“I don’t see anyone in this room who fits that description,” Sam replied mildly, “so let me show you the way out." He put a hand around Douglas's arm, but Douglas shook it off.

"I can find the door." Then he turned back to me. "My train connection isn't until tomorrow evening, Katherine. Perhaps we could have supper together tonight. It would give us a chance to catch up and give me a chance to reclaim affection."

"I already have plans for supper, but even if I didn't, I wouldn't spend any time with you. There's no affection to reclaim and I want you to go away."

Douglas, frustrated at my unbending resistance, would have said more but Sam came closer to him and said in a quiet voice that was not nearly as easygoing as before, "I think that's real clear. You need to leave." He would have taken hold of Douglas again except Douglas stormed out past him. He brushed against Sam with his shoulder, purposefully, it seemed to me, and slammed the outside door with such force that the bell reverberated.

I was surprised to see my hands shaking and put them in the pockets of my smock to hide the tremors but not quickly enough. Sam saw and his eyes narrowed.

"Are you all right?" He didn't move any closer.

I lifted my gaze to his face and tried to smile.

"Yes. Thank you." When he remained silent, I added, "I suppose you'd like to know what that was all about."

"Only if you want to tell me."

I felt an inordinate gratitude to him, for his loyal trust and his warm regard, and I started to say, "I do want to tell you," but only made it through the third word before I had to stop, tears at the unexpected, unpleasant confrontation and the remembered shame of my poor judgment tightening my throat and filling my eyes.

"I'm sorry," I whispered. I didn't know if I was apologizing for my tears or for exposing Sam to that nasty little scene or for once willingly accepting Douglas Gallagher's attentions or for something else entirely. All I knew for sure at that moment was that I didn't want Sam Kincaid to think poorly of me.

Sam said my name and took a step toward me, put both hands on my shoulders and pulled me into his arms and kissed me passionately as if he'd devour me. I stood for just a moment with my hands at my side, the sensation of being that close to him overwhelming, and then somehow, without conscious volition, my arms went around him and I was kissing him back, feeling more at home in his arms than anyplace I had ever been.

"You are not to cry," he said softly. "I cannot bear the sight so you're not allowed to do it." I pushed away from him, engulfed by the flare of emotion and wondering if he felt the same.

"I don't do it very often," I told him, searching for normalcy. "That's why you're not used to it." He let go of me quickly.

"Katherine, forgive me. I lost my head."

"Me, too. The emotion of the moment, I guess." We stood there with everything important still unsaid until I took a deep, somewhat shaky breath and repeated, "I do want to tell you about Douglas Gallagher. May I?"

"If that's what you want." He sat down immediately, took off his coat and tossed it over a chair as if he planned to stay a while. "But you don't have to."

"I know. That's why I want to."

He sat forward in his chair all the time I spoke, hands clasped, and never dropped his eyes from my face. I suppose I should have found his uninterrupted gaze uncomfortable but it was just the opposite. Like my mother, Sam Kincaid was a good listener; maybe he had learned from her. At first I paused now and then and tried to read his expression, but I finally gave that up. All that ever showed was his intent interest, no other emotion, not surprise or disappointment or curiosity and never a flicker of judgment.

When I finished, exhausted from the telling, Sam sat quietly. Still digesting the information, I thought.

Then he asked, "Did you love him, Katherine? Before you found out the kind of man he was? I don't think I'm mistaken that you don't love him now, but did you care for him at first?"

That was a good question, a question I had asked myself more than once, trying to understand what all those early emotions had been about.

"I don't think so." I looked at Sam and thought, it's not like what I feel for you and that might well be love. But I didn't say those words out loud. "I hope not. I'd know, wouldn't I, if I really cared for him? I think I'd feel something other than shame and guilt." Sam smiled at that, then reached to pick up his coat from the chair.

"You're right. You'd feel a lot different and you would know for sure. You're always so hard on yourself, Katherine. You don't let yourself make mistakes like other people."

"A doctor can't afford mistakes, not when people's lives depend on her good judgment."

He took my chin between his thumb and forefinger and turned my face so he could look at me straight on, which he did with the same objective and unflinching scrutiny I might give a patient.

"So that's what it is," he said at last, a certain satisfaction in his tone. "Your self-confidence got shaken up and now you're worried about your ability to make good decisions. That's what's been different about you. I never saw that in you before and I couldn't quite place it."

Sam was exactly right and I was relieved but not surprised that he understood.

"Listen, Katherine. One bad man does not change what and who you are. Nothing could ever change that."

"Not a good man either?"

"A good man wouldn't want to." He dropped his hand and stood up to put on his coat. "Are you hungry?" I stood up, too, resisting the impulse to drift right back into his arms and stay there considerably longer.

"Yes."

At the door he turned long enough to say, "Katherine, about that kiss—"

I smiled and looked up from buttoning my coat long enough to say, "It's all right. You don't have to apologize again."

He put on his hat, grinning. "I wasn't going to apologize. I was just going to say thank you."

He held the door and I went out past him, certain I was blushing. I wanted to say more but decided that pursuing the topic would only make his grin broader and my face redder.

Late Saturday morning Douglas returned to my office, his manner guarded and careful. He stood just inside the door and made no attempt to come closer. The fear that had so paralyzed me the day before was gone completely—purged by my long talk with Sam, I thought—and all I felt at the man's presence was something like fatigue. I so wanted to be done with Douglas Gallagher.

"I came to say good-bye," his words terse. I couldn't tell what he felt.

"We did that already, but Good-bye."

"Listen, Katherine, if you change your mind—"

"I won't."

"But if you do," he persisted, "wire me. I'm traveling to

Europe this fall and it could as easily be a honeymoon trip for us. Wouldn't you like to see the great capitals of the world? Doesn't Rome or Paris ever beckon you out of this backwater? We could have gone earlier this year if you'd only read my letters. I made tentative reservations for two on the *Olympic*, hoping you would see things differently over time. When I cancelled the trip, I heard that the White Star Line was readying a sister ship for a maiden voyage from England to New York next spring. We could leave on a honeymoon trip to Europe this fall, spend our winter in Rome, and return home next April in the lap of luxury. That new ocean liner sounded like a floating palace. You deserve a palace, Katherine, and I could give that to you."

I knew that what he pleaded for was not me, not Katherine Davis. What Douglas wanted was a life he would never have. He wanted it so very much! That's what he thought about and that's what he dreamed about and that's what he realized—in some private, despairing place—would never be his. At that moment, Douglas Gallagher was as terrified as I had been the day before.

But all I could do was look at him helplessly, completely at a loss as to how to make him understand, really understand, that the life he yearned for with such desperate urgency would not be lived with me. Power meant so much to Douglas that he wielded it like a scepter. Stronger and smarter than his business associates. Brutal in his dealings with women. Scornful of the commonplace. And now, incredibly, I was the one with power. Power over him. We both knew it to be true, but the knowledge didn't gratify. It only made me sad.

Something of what I felt must have shown on my face for he added, humble and desperate as I remember him to this day, "I'll make fall reservations for two just in case you change your mind, in case you could forgive me and learn to love me again. I don't remember the name of the new ship, but it's supposed to be the grandest vessel ever to take to the waters. They say it's unsinkable. We could have the trip of a lifetime, you and I."

Almost exactly a year later I found Douglas Gallagher's name on a black-bordered list published in the newspaper, so I knew he had followed through on his travel plans without me. He died in good company, I thought sadly, feeling a compassion for Douglas in death that I could not find in his life. Perhaps it was some comfort to him at the last that he had perished with men as wealthy as he: John Jacob Astor and Benjamin Guggenheim and Isidore Straus. Not to mention over 1,500 other poor souls. The name of the ship Douglas could not recall, the floating palace, the proudly unsinkable vessel, was *Titanic.*

CHAPTER 17

All that spring and into summer, slowly and painstakingly, patient by patient, my medical practice grew. Word filtered out into the community that a woman doctor was not so unnatural after all. Nothing fazed me, neither blood nor bones nor babies. I battled illness and disease with the passion of Dr. Alice Hamilton, as if those scourges were my personal enemies and must not be allowed to triumph. With a portion of my small profits, I purchased a larger sign for the door, a clear and defiant message to Dr. Jeske, to anyone who doubted, that I intended to stay. At first people may have come to my office as a family favor or to satisfy their curiosity, but they returned because I was a very good doctor.

My family stayed well, nieces and nephews had birthdays and milestones: first tooth—first word—first step, and without the corrosive effect of calomel, Uncle Billy slowly grew stronger; the gentle Uncle Billy I knew and loved returned. I heard from Petra frequently, too, and was pleased with her progress. My days fell into a pattern that were as comfortable and predictable as the medical profession allowed.

Sam stayed in my life with brotherly attention, no repeat of any conduct that he thought he had to apologize for—to my secret disappointment. Summer kept us both busy so our time together was infrequent. I missed him more than I could tell anyone, certainly more than I could tell him, although I wished I could find the right words. It seemed I could talk to him about anything except how I felt about him. Those words wouldn't come, and I didn't know why or what held them back. With hindsight, I believe I feared spoiling what we had, a warm friendship being better than nothing at all. What if that kiss really had been just an emotional and momentary lapse? What if I was wrong about the feeling I thought I saw in his eyes now and then, a deeper emotion that was a far cry from brotherly affection? What if I said something to spoil it all and he became uncomfortable with me? What if I was wrong about myself and my own emotions, a doctor able to diagnose patients but unable to read and interpret her own heart with any accuracy? I had been very mistaken once and had missed every crucial sign. What if history repeated itself? What if what if what if? And all the while time slipped by. Irreclaimable moments. Lost opportunities.

I kept quiet about the feeling I suspected might be love, a seed that had been planted a long time ago and had begun to blossom slowly, fed and nurtured by Sam Kincaid's solid decency, strength, and kindness. There was a natural penance in my struggle to understand my feelings, I told myself irrationally, as if my uncertainty could somehow make up for putting Petra in harm's way or betraying the values I had been taught.

My birthday came and went with a family party, cake

and presents, Uncle Billy's music, my older brother teasing me about being an old maid, and my younger brother surprising me with a poem. Gus was the wordsmith of the family, intelligent and literate with an easy and sincere charm, the baby and cherished as such by both my parents. None of the rest of us children resented their attention; it was impossible to begrudge Gus anything. Like Mother, he was kind and transparently honest. I remembered last year's birthday and was glad to be home with the people who were dearest to me.

One Saturday in late June, Sam came knocking at my door early. I was just dressed and still braiding my hair when I answered the door.

I said my first thought. "Is something wrong?"

"No, I'm just appreciating the day. Look at it."

I obediently stepped onto the landing next to him, gave a cursory look, then brought my unreceptive gaze back to him.

"Yes?"

"Katherine, look at it. It's a perfect day. I'll go get Sol from the stable while you put something on that's more comfortable for riding. Your mother packed us lunch."

"I can't just—"

He interrupted, unnaturally impatient with me. "Why not? Do you have appointments today?"

"No, but I—" He waited as I searched for a practical reason, didn't find one, and concluded unconvincingly, "I can't just close the office, Sam."

"And I repeat, Why not? You're not the only doctor in town, Katherine, and it's not like you'll be in California."

The morning *was* beautiful, lots of blue sky and sunshine that promised a perfect temperature, no breeze to speak of and everything summer quiet.

"Oh, all right." My ungracious assent sounded as if he

had asked me to do something tortured and arduous, but he only grinned, unruffled.

It didn't take long for me to acknowledge that Sam had been right to treasure the day and I shrewish to protest. It couldn't have been more perfect, the kind of day that years afterwards could still make me smile with pleasure at its memory.

"I'm surprised you could get the time away," I said. I spoke with my mouth full and a piece of my mother's fried chicken held in both hands. Sam and I sat along Wildflower Creek, enjoying the rare circumstance of doing absolutely nothing.

"I told John I had some personal business and he never flinched, said to take all the time I needed and that was that. I mentioned to your mother that I planned to see you, and she's the one who suggested I take along a picnic. Before I knew it, she had it put together and was handing it over to me."

"What was your mother like?"

"She was a schoolteacher in Texas before she met and married my father. He was a cowboy, a pretty rough man and used to a wild life. Her folks were dead set against the match. They told me that often enough later. My mother was small and feather-light and she had a little voice. You would have thought one good wind would blow her away, but she was strong-willed like you. She did what she thought was best and never apologized for it. Married my dad and left for Oklahoma and never looked back as long as he was alive. Sometimes when your mother talks about her early life here, I think that's how it must have been for my mother, too."

"How old were you when your father died?"

"Not quite five. I don't remember much about him or about that time, just my mother crying in the night and me going over to comfort her and tell her not to be afraid, I'd protect her. It was hard for her alone and she decided we'd go back to Texas. Then she got sick and was gone before I was ten and both my grandparents were dead by the time I was fourteen."

"You lost a lot in ten years, didn't you?"

He had stretched himself out on his side, his head propped up on one hand as he watched me eat. Sam Kincaid had length and breadth, long muscled legs slightly bowed from the saddle, a lean waist, broad, firm shoulders without an ounce of fat, all the result of years of hard, physical work, a strong man in more ways than one.

At my comment, he looked at me and answered thoughtfully, "I guess I did, but I gained back some of what I lost. Got more than I ever expected when I walked up onto your front porch."

"Almost twelve years ago now."

"You had just turned twelve and that day you were wearing boys' pants and one of your father's shirts tucked into the waistband."

"You don't forget much, Sam."

"Not when it comes to you, I don't." He was suddenly so serious and his tone so forceful that I was startled. He pushed himself to a sitting position, one knee pulled up and an arm resting across it. "I've been careful around you, Katherine, and I've been patient. I'm a patient man by nature. But life's awful short and lately I've felt time getting away from me, so I thought I'd just ask you something." He paused but I was wordless; there was no way I'd interrupt him. "I wondered if you thought you could ever learn to love me or am I just a nuisance to you? Am I just wasting your time?"

"I never consider any time I spend with you to be wasted, Sam, and you've never been a nuisance to me. You never could be. We've been friends too long."

"More than friends, Katherine, at least for me. You have to know by now that what I feel for you is a lot more than friendship. You're a bright woman."

"Not always."

I stood up, wanting to say more, wanting to tell him that lately I thought about him more often than not, wanting to answer his question from my heart, but fear held me back. Not what I'd felt that afternoon in front of Douglas, not that kind of fear. This felt as different from that as love and loathing. Take the step, a part of me said, open your mouth and tell this man he makes you happy. Trust yourself. Trust him. You won't lose yourself in him. Two people can be bound together in love and still retain their own separate sovereignty. I saw the proof in my parents' lives, but still I held back.

Such indecision was uncharacteristic of the Katherine I used to be. That Katherine had been a locomotive barreling along the tracks, headed in one direction, one destination in mind for years. The Katherine I'd become was a different woman, someone not yet completely defined. I knew the direction of my life had changed—whether I liked to admit it or not, I had Douglas Gallagher to thank for that—but did a changed direction mean my final destination had changed, too? I couldn't quite make out where I was headed, and Katherine Davis always knew where she was headed. Always. Not knowing was like walking in the dark.

I picked up the blanket we had used as a tablecloth and started to fold it, a distraction for me, a chance to take a breath and figure out what to say. Sam came up behind me and put a hand on each arm to hold me still. Douglas had once done the same, but the panicked sense of entrapment I'd felt then was completely absent with Sam. I could have leaned back against him and never known a moment of anything but contentment.

"I loved you from the first moment I saw you, Katherine. I know we were both kids then, but I knew from the start there would never be anyone for me but you. I understood that you had it in your mind to be something special, and that was all you could see and think about. It never mattered because you were the only woman there would ever be for me and like I said, I'm a patient man. But I'm closer to thirty than twenty, and time doesn't slow down. I got to thinking that maybe I expect you to read my mind and that's not fair just because I can read yours. So I thought I should tell you how I feel. I should say the words to be sure you know." He said everything from behind me so I couldn't see his face, his hands on me strong but gentle and his lips against my hair. I stood still as a statue and listened. Then I turned, very close to him, practically into his arms, and his hands moved up to my shoulders.

"I don't know what to say, Sam. I believe I do care for you, more than a brother and more than a friend, but how can I know for sure? How can *you* be so certain?" This time he was speechless.

"I just am," he answered finally. "A man just knows. Seems like I've always known and nothing's ever been able to change the feeling. Or ever will."

"But how can *I* be as sure as that?" I was dead serious. I wanted him to give an answer that would remove my doubts and spread a future out in front of me that was as certain as he was. Sam laid his hand against my shirt over my heart.

"You know here, Katherine. Your inner voice, your mother calls it. You just need to listen." He met my eyes and at the expression there said, "Don't look like that. I wouldn't have said anything if I'd known it would put that look in your eyes. I didn't mean to trouble you. Can you forget it? I can be awful clumsy sometimes." I put a hand up to his mouth.

"Don't say that because it's not true. Sometimes I think there's no one in the world dearer to me than you, but then there are other times I'm so happy doing what I'm doing that I don't want to give it up. If I couldn't be a doctor, I believe I'd wither and die. It seems to me that this past year I've changed and so have all the people around me and I just can't seem to get my bearings."

He took my hand in his and dropped a kiss in the palm before he released me and stepped back.

"Well, I'm not going anywhere so you do whatever you need to, but I'll say this: you haven't changed, not to me. You're the woman you always were, with a heart as big as Wyoming, doing the right thing at any cost. Your mother's daughter." He couldn't have given me a more generous or touching compliment.

"I wish that were true," I said quietly, "but I'm nothing like her, not in looks or temperament. Becca inherited all that."

"Oh, Katherine," was all he said, shaking his head as if he couldn't believe what I had just said. Then he leaned down to kiss me lightly, barely brushing my lips with his. "We should start back. The day'll be almost gone by the time we get home." As he moved away, I captured his arm.

"We're still friends, Sam." A question, not a statement.

"Always, Katherine. Like I said, I'm a patient man. When you're ready to be more than friends, you let me know."

He smiled when he said that, the old smile again, and I was humbled. What had I ever done to deserve such devotion?

"You'll be the first to know. I promise."

He nodded, then helped me pack up everything for the

ride home. Friends again and the burden on me if that was ever to change.

***

There are moments that redirect the course of our lives, moments so significant and meaningful that ever after we use them as dividing lines to separate what came before and what followed. As innocuous as it began, Independence Day, 1911, was such a moment in my life.

I stopped by Becca's house that July morning to scoop up Lily Kate, all dressed in patriotic red, white, and blue, and wait for Becca and the baby to join us. We were off to the annual July Fourth parade, probably the highlight of the year for Laramie. After the noon parade, made up of a procession of floats, the university band, and several costumed riders, we would go out to the ranch where my parents always put on a big spread with barbecue roasting in pits and tables that groaned with food, festive streamers festooning the porch, and a wild game of baseball toward the end of the day. Independence Day had been a particular family celebration as far back as I could remember.

My mother once volunteered that my father kissed her for the first time on the Fourth of July and it was a date she would never forget.

"Although," she added with slow thought, "I suppose it was already July fifth by then, but I'm not going to get lost in the details. Don't tease your father about it, Katherine, or you'll embarrass him."

I thought that with several years passed since that early confidence and with my father giving Mother diamond rings and pretty speeches, the teasing probably wouldn't embarrass him at all. Age had somehow softened John Davis, and I believe he relished the change more than any of us.

"Ben will join us later," Becca said when she stepped outside. "He's in the middle of a conversation with some-one and not to be disturbed."

My sister was sparkling and happy that day. She looked so much like my mother that I was still surprised by the re-semblance, same thick chestnut hair, same broad mouth and glowing complexion, same warmth about her that reflected her happiness in a similar tangible way, as kind and wel-coming as my mother had always been.

I took Lily Kate's hand while Becca pushed Blessing in the baby carriage along the rough walk toward Front Street. Lily Kate skipped along next to me all excited about the day, about the prospect of the parade and the promised fun at Nana's, as she always called my mother.

We stopped midway down the street and waited for the parade to start. As Lily Kate hopped up and down, a bundle of energy, her curls bounced up and down, too.

"Is it coming? Is it coming?" she cried.

From behind us, Sam picked her up so she could get a better view and said, "Not yet, Toot," his pet name for her. Becca and Lily Kate were glad to see him. I was, too, but was a little more reticent about showing it. I hadn't seen much of him following our Saturday together and felt un-accountably shy. Sam stayed the same, though, straightfor-ward and friendly, always careful to be sure I was at ease.

"Did you bring anyone with you, Sam?" Becca asked.

"John Thomas was going to bring the boys but when I stopped by, he said the baby was fussy and they'd just come over to the ranch in the afternoon."

Sam looked fine that Fourth of July, hatless, the sun picking up a few red glints in his brown hair, his face weathered to an attractive tan, tall and broad-shouldered, nothing pretentious or false about him. I had never found him so physically appealing before and felt the stir of a strong emotion somewhere between my stomach and my heart.

I pulled my gaze from Sam when Lily Kate squealed, "I see it!" She wiggled out of his hold and her mother, busy parking Blessing and the buggy against the front wall of the building where we stood, took her by the hand.

"It's coming, Lily Kate. Be patient." But my niece wasn't patient. She kept up a running monologue of questions and answers as the first float got closer, jumping up and down on one foot and then the other, a bundle of irrepressible energy.

"I never realized she took after her aunt so much," Sam whispered in my ear.

I laughed. "Was I like that do you think?"

"Was? Still are. Always wanting to run out and meet life, never patient enough to wait for it to come to you." I thought he was exactly right but wouldn't give him the satisfaction of agreeing with him.

All the churches had built floats along with the Farm Bureau, the Elks, the Library Association, the Civil War veterans (my father, never one to make a public display of himself, did not participate), the Cattleman's Association, and all the other fraternal organizations that made up Laramie. From a distance I could hear the unmistakable rattle of an automobile, a few backfires now and then and its distinctive rumble of sound.

"Elmer Lovejoy," announced my sister, laughing. "I heard he ordered a Model-T Ford. It must have arrived." As it got closer, everyone stared and chattered. We had a few automobiles about town but more wagons and buggies and certainly more horses. Remembering Chicago, I thought that would change soon enough so that an automobile coming down Laramie's main street would not be so remarkable. That day, though, the Ford was a rare and spectacular sight, black and shiny with the sun gleaming off its white wheels and an ear-splitting horn that Elmer blew for all he was worth, proud of the effect and the attention. He'd always had a mechanical aptitude and had been the first to experiment with steam-powered automobiles. Gasoline-powered engines made him euphoric.

The auto was preceded by a contingent of riders bearing an assortment of flags. The beautiful horses usually walked at a stately and dignified pace, their tails and manes braided the way a woman might primp for a special occasion. Putting a chugging and honking automobile right behind a contingent of horses and riders was a mistake in planning, however. I could tell from the way the animals pranced and snorted that the mechanical pops, sputters, and honks made them jittery.

When the group of riders was right in front of us, Lily Kate slipped out of her mother's grip—to get a closer look, perhaps, or because she loved horses or just to stare at that contraption of an automobile, the likes of which she had never seen before. For whatever reason, the child hopped away from her mother, past me, down off the boardwalk, and onto the street. I heard "Look, Mama! What's that?" in Lily Kate's childish voice, a little girl five years old and excited about all the sights and sounds of the parade, not a care in the world and life one big adventure.

It took my sister's scream of "Lily Kate!" before I realized anything was wrong. At the anguished cry, I turned to see Becca push past the people in front of her to get to her daughter. But that took time, time she didn't have, because by then Lily Kate was standing in the street and peering down at the automobile, oblivious to the horses that pranced nervously next to her.

Two things happened simultaneously. Elmer Lovejoy's auto gave a loud backfire, louder than a gunshot, and the big palomino horse next to Lily Kate reared up, its pawing hooves as deadly and heavy as anvil irons. All in an instant it was clear to me that neither Becca nor I could get to Lily Kate in time to keep those hooves away from her, that the animal was out of the rider's control and would most certainly crash down on top of the little girl. Nothing could stop the inescapable tragedy.

I shoved the person in front of me to one side with all my strength and leaped down to the street, crying Lily Kate's name in unison with Becca but knowing all the while that we would both be too late.

When the horse came down, its shod feet made a sickening thud as they collided with human flesh. From a distance it seemed I could hear Becca screaming her daughter's name over and over, repetition and volume the only means she possessed to hold off the inevitable.

Everything came to a standstill. People suddenly hushed. The horses pulled away. Elmer shut off his automobile. I pushed through the crowd that had gathered, afraid of what I would see on the ground and amazed when I saw Lily Kate in Becca's arms. The child, completely ignorant of the heart-stopping terror we had experienced on her behalf, safe and sound and my sister weeping, still repeating the little girl's name but not screaming any longer, murmuring the words instead like a prayer. Becca held her daughter so tightly I thought the child might be in danger of being suffocated. I knew an immediate and enormous relief and then as quick a fear. I'd heard those deadly hooves hit flesh, and if not Lily Kate, then who?

The unconscious figure on the ground lay sprawled on his face. Blood from a terrible gash along the side of his head just over the left temple drained into the packed ground. Sam lay there. For the briefest of moments I was absolutely frozen, unable to believe what I saw. How had it happened? When I heard Becca call out and turned to her, he must have already seen the danger to Lily Kate and taken action.

The queer, still moment passed and I pushed through to him, the doctor in me taking over. I felt for his pulse, which was still there—faint but still there, thank God—and asked for someone's shirt to use for pressure against the wound. I spoke from the ground where I crouched, holding the makeshift pad against the gash as Sam Kincaid's blood stained my skirts and the cuffs of my shirtwaist.

"I need someone to help carry him to my office right away."

Three men came forward and lifted him carefully. I rose, too, and walked next to him, still holding the shirt, now almost sodden with blood, to his head. Behind us people began to talk and I could hear Elmer's automobile being cranked to start again. The parade would resume and the day's activities continue. But not for me. If I lost Sam, nothing would ever continue for me. I might go on living, might breathe and eat and sleep as if I were alive, but I would be frozen in time, stunted and withered like a plant that had lost its supply of air and light.

He needed more than twenty stitches over his temple, the gash just missing his eye and angling up along his eyebrow instead. A terrible wound in a terrible place. The results of such a forceful head wound could be anything. There were no guarantees, but for now he lived and that was all I could think of. It was a matter of extending consecutive moments of life, one right after the other, hour after hour, day after day, until he was whole again. When I finished, everything stitched and washed and Sam lying in the bed in the back room, his chest barely moving with faint shallow breaths, I sat down next to him, took his hand in mine and just sat there, speechless with need.

My brother-in-law, Ben, said my name from the doorway—I didn't know how long he'd stood there— and came into the room. He rested a firm hand on my shoulder.

"How is he, Katherine?" I couldn't answer, couldn't take my eyes from Sam's face. Ben pulled up a chair next to me and sat down, stating the obvious. "He's alive."

I roused myself to say, "Yes, thank God, thank God, he's alive. But head wounds like this are still a mystery. All sorts of things could be going on inside his skull that we can't see. His brain could be bleeding and swelling and we'll only know that in time. He could be unconscious for a long while, so long that he never wakes up. He might wake up but with damage, not able to speak or think the way he used to. No one can say for sure about head wounds."

"It's all in God's hands."

"And mine," I said, my voice cracking a little, "God's hands and mine. Between the two of us, we ought to be able to make him better."

We sat there quietly for a while, then Ben offered, "Do you want to move him to our house? He might be more comfortable there."

"I'm afraid to move him. He'll be all right here."

"I'll go home so Becca can come for a while. I sent word to your folks and John Thomas. They were busy getting ready for the party and didn't make the parade."

"Thank you."

"Katherine." I turned toward Ben and he took my hand in his, emotion plain on his face. "I don't know how to thank Sam for what he did, for giving us Lily Kate's life back. If he comes to, will you tell him?"

I tried to smile but found that I was unable to, could only say, "Yes, I will," in a small voice, then added with more strength, "But it's not *if* he comes to, Ben, it's *when* he comes to. I'll tell him then."

When Becca arrived, she was once more her cool, practical self, a parson's wife and used to the unexpected, her early panic and fear for Lily Kate, if not forgotten, at least controlled.

"I'll stay with him for a while, Katherine."

"No, I need to be here when he wakes up."

"Katherine," my sister insisted, "you need to get out of those clothes. They're a mess and you should get something to eat while you can. I promise I won't leave him."

I knew Becca was right but that was one of the hardest things I've ever had to do before or since: stand up, turn my back on Sam, and walk out of that room, not knowing if I'd see him alive again. I did it. But I didn't like it.

By the time I got back, Mother was there, her face a study in concern and love for Sam and for me, too. But she was as cool and calm in an emergency as my father, a quality she had to learn from all those years spent alone with a young and growing family, no one around for miles, doctor and teacher and preacher to us and never allowed the luxury of panic or hysteria.

"Tell me, Katherine." I didn't pretend to misunderstand.

"I don't know," I replied helplessly. "It was a terrible blow, but I don't think his skull is fractured and the bleeding has stopped. The brain takes time to heal, sometimes a long time. It's as if it shuts down and shuts the person down, too, so it can devote all its energy to getting better. There's no way to tell what will happen and nothing anyone can do now but wait."

"What can we do to help?"

"Pray. After that there's not much anyone can do." I sat down next to the bed and rested my hand on Sam's as it lay atop the blanket. "I'm not going anywhere, and I'll just wait for him to come back from wherever he is. I'll just be here waiting for as long as it takes."

That night after Mother left, I stretched out in a chair next to Sam's bed and thought about what I had said, how I had volunteered to wait. Sam Kincaid had been waiting for me for a long time, for years. Uncomplaining. Careful not to get in the way of my dreams. 'A patient man by nature,' he said, content to wait for me to come home. I don't think he ever doubted that I would eventually find my way there, and he was right—I had, but not in the way I expected. Not home to Wyoming, to a place or a house or even to my family. In an unexpected but absolutely right way, I had come home to him, to Sam Kincaid, long-time friend and honorary brother and so much more. Love and life and necessity.

I sat with him through the night, all the next day and into the next night and could do nothing but watch him as he slept, if sleep is what it was. He had no fever and the swelling around the wound slowly subsided, but still he lay unmoving, no sound in the room but his light breathing.

People came and went, Becca and Mother and Hope all coming to sit for a while so I could get up and walk around, stretch, and try to think of other things, try to eat and sleep. But I couldn't stay away very long. As still and quiet as Sam was, he called to me all the time I was not with him.

My father came and sat with me, too, a formal man not easily given to words but who spoke from his heart just by being there. He took my hand between his work-roughened palms.

"Sam will recover, Katherine." I turned to him and my eyes filled with tears, the only time I cried since the accident had happened.

"I couldn't bear it if he died, Papa," I said. My lips trembled and the tears overflowed down my cheeks. "It would be worse than dying myself. I just couldn't bear it." He pulled his chair closer, put both arms around me, and quietly let me cry against him, wise enough not to offer false comfort.

"Sometimes terrible things have to be endured, but I know," he said. "I know."

Yes, he knew. He had loved my mother passionately and faithfully for over thirty years and that's how he felt about her, that he couldn't have borne it if anything happened to her. John Rock Davis was a deep and quiet man, and I had inherited those same qualities from him. The faithfulness and passion, too, I hoped.

Forty-eight hours after the accident and still no change, so I settled in for another night, watching Sam as he slept, occasionally brushing back his hair or laying a hand against his cheek, more for my comfort than his. Sometime after midnight, half-dozing in the chair, I thought I heard something and sat up. Someone called my name, I thought, and looked quickly, hopefully at Sam. But whatever I'd heard, it didn't come from Sam, who lay quietly, eyes closed and his face in repose. He was a ruggedly attractive man, his face too craggy for conventional good looks and his nose crooked—broken more than once, he told me—but in sleep some of the lines smoothed away and he looked younger and more vulnerable. I pictured him as a little boy creeping over to his mother as she wept and trying to console her, distressed for her, wanting to offer comfort but just a little boy himself, who needed someone to reassure him, too. The thought made my heart ache, and I slipped off the chair to kneel next to him, pick up a limp hand in both of mine, and hold it to my cheek.

"Listen to me, Sam Kincaid," I said aloud. "You need to come home. I miss you. Nothing's the same without you. It's dull and dark. You told me to let you know when I was ready to be more than friends and I want to tell you that now, but how can I when you won't wake up? I don't know why I waited. You probably do, though. You've always known me so much better than I know myself. I love you, Sam, and I want you to come home. I want you to open your eyes and ask me what I need like you've done so often before. It took me a while but I've finally figured it out. Open your eyes, Sam, because I know the right answer to that question now."

But he slept on, his chest rising and falling imperceptibly, in some other place that I couldn't get to. After a time, still seated on the floor, I fell asleep with my cheek against his arm. A few hours later I awoke stiff and cramped from the unnatural position, crawled into the little cot I had set up in the corner of the room, and slept again.

Becca stopped by early the next morning, saw there was no change, and literally pushed me out the door.

"Go upstairs and get some sleep, Katherine, some real sleep. I promise I'll come and get you if there's the slightest change."

I lay down to placate my sister but didn't sleep, then changed clothes, tried to eat, and wandered back down too soon.

Becca wanted to scold but said instead, "I'll stay a while with you. Blessing will sleep for at least an hour yet, so I don't need to hurry back."

Looking at my sister, so much my mother's face and so much her character as well, I asked, "When we were children, do you remember how John Thomas used to tease me about not really belonging to the family and how they found me in a box by the side of the road?"

She nodded, no idea where I was going with the conversation but willing to humor me.

"Sometimes I think that might be true," I went on. "You look so much like Mother and Gus favors her, too. And John Thomas looks exactly like Father must have looked thirty-five years ago, but I don't resemble either of them. Maybe I really did fall off a passing wagon." She smiled at that.

"You aren't able to see yourself clearly, Katherine. Being part of the family is more than hair color and height. I think family resemblance is more inside than out. It's what you believe, how you live and act and talk and carry yourself. That's why Ben and Hope and Sam fit in so well from the start."

And why Douglas Gallagher wouldn't have, I thought.

Becca continued, "You're so clearly a Davis you might as well have the name printed on your forehead." I must have looked at her doubtfully because she added, "Trust me, Sister. You have the look of Lou and John Davis all over you, just like the rest of us. We couldn't escape the connection if we wanted to."

After she left, I busied myself in my office, checked on Sam periodically, read some medical study findings so halfheartedly that I ended up reading the same paragraph three and four times. I was pretending normalcy when life could never be normal again as long as that figure lay so still in the back room. Three days now and no change, but for me the time didn't matter. There were specialists I could consult and hospitals we could visit, but if none of that worked and Sam lay in half-sleep for years to come, I would sit here and keep him company for as long as it took, for a lifetime if necessary. Patience wasn't my strong suit, but I could learn to wait. Hadn't he waited for me all those years, satisfied with sporadic and haphazard letters, forcing himself to be content with whatever time we spent together on my infrequent visits home? Hadn't he trusted that I would see past the adventure and the sparkle and someday discover what home really was, *who* it was? He had known all along and I, with my knowledge and education, had been the one slow to understand. So I could wait as long as I had to, into eternity if that's what it took.

Fortunately, blessedly, it didn't take a lifetime or an eternity. Late that same Friday afternoon, I sat in the chair next to Sam's bed, reading and not paying much attention to him. Mother had come around lunchtime to take my place so I could see a few patients and try to act as if it were business as usual. Grown suddenly tired, I read and dozed a little, so exhausted and drained from the last three days that at first I thought I had imagined the slight stir in the bed next to me. I returned my attention to the book in my lap when I again heard a sound, nothing intelligible, but a real sound.

Sam was gently moving his head from side to side, his breaths deeper, his hands fluttering like butterflies that couldn't quite get into the air. Immediately I was on my knees, pushing back his hair and saying his name.

He opened his eyes—I will never again take those brown eyes for granted, I promised myself—and looked around the room in confusion. He seemed to be searching for something. Then he turned his head just enough to see and recognize me, tried to smile with dry lips, and tried to speak with a drier throat. No sound came out. I scrambled up to get him water and put an arm under his head to lift him up so he could drink from the glass I held to his lips. His eyes never left my face. I couldn't stop watching him either, but mine was the impersonal gaze of a doctor as I tried to gauge the effects of the blow, tried to see whether he were himself with all his senses and faculties intact. When I lay him back down, his hand came up to grasp my wrist as I set the glass on the side table.

He tried to speak again and I said, "It's all right. Everything's fine. You don't need to say anything right now. Just get your strength back." Then I added, my voice shakier than I expected, "I've been so worried, Sam."

He said my name, his voice cracking, then repeated it, stronger the second time, and gently pulled me down closer to him.

"What is it?" I asked. He seemed agitated and compelled to speak, and I thought he might be worried about Lily Kate. "Lily Kate is safe, Sam, thanks to you. Ben and Becca, all of us, we don't know how to thank you." He shook his head slightly, as if to say that wasn't the issue.

"Katherine." His voice a croak but the fact that he recognized me and could enunciate my name made me want to sing for joy.

Possessing none of Petra's talent, however, I contented myself with a quiet, "I'm here, Sam."

He looked at me, smiled enough to wrinkle the corners of his eyes, licked his lips, and in a raspy voice from an unused throat asked, "What do you need, Katherine?" He spoke softly, but I heard the question as clearly as if he had risen up in bed and shouted it at the top of his lungs.

I didn't hesitate, didn't stop to wonder how he knew to ask and didn't need to think about the answer.

"You," I said, somewhere between laughing and crying. I leaned over him to put both my hands against his face, feeling his rough and stubbly cheeks against my palms. Then I looked squarely into his eyes so there could be no misunderstanding and repeated my answer with a slight embellishment I thought he might appreciate. "I need you, my darling."

"Good," he responded and closed his eyes to sleep again. A natural, healing sleep that held all the promise of the future, the promise of love and family, the promise of home.

EPILOGUE

1936

Both my parents have been gone almost five years, in body if not in spirit. Sometimes in the big house I think I hear a laugh or a contented murmur from a room that shows empty, and I wonder if they're there, my father's arm around Mother's shoulders and her face glowing the way it did when she was very happy. The sound of Sam's and my children gave her joy when she was alive, so I can't imagine she would let a little thing like death stop her delight.

I married Sam Kincaid on Christmas Day, 1911. We planned it earlier, but snow shut everything down for weeks, so the first day we had a thaw and were able to get out he said, "I know I said I'm a patient man, but this is ridiculous. Do you care that it's Christmas?"

Of course, I didn't care. My brother-in-law married us,

Lily Kate threw dried rose petals, and Uncle Billy played something lyrical and beautiful in honor of the day. Sam and I honeymooned in the Johnson Hotel longer than we had planned because another snowstorm blew in and we couldn't get out. Neither of us minded.

We didn't live in any one place or even think about a house until our second child was born. Before that I kept my practice in town and we lived over the office, Sam up and out early to his work at the ranch every day. Sometimes we spent weekends with my parents. We were vagabonds in those early days of our marriage, but it didn't matter as long as we were together.

After Louisa was born not much changed except I took her to work with me, walked down a flight of stairs to my office and that was that. She was my constant companion, her father's darling and a beautiful child, the image of her grandmother Davis from the start, affectionate and generous with her smiles.

But when Sam Junior was born, I realized something had to change. Two children complicated things. That was when my mother invited us to move into the big house with her and Father. When I hesitated, she assured me that it was large enough to support two families with relative privacy for both. She chuckled at the unintended play on words and continued to explain that the arrangement would allow me to practice medicine while she watched Louisa and little Sam during the day. Sam and I both thought her proposal made sense, but when we tried to thank her for her generous offer, she just laughed.

"Don't delude yourselves. There's nothing generous about it." She cradled Sam Junior as she explained. "With your schedules, I'll never get to see you otherwise, and I'd like to spend more time with my grandchildren."

She got more than she bargained for because Jane was

born three years after Sam, and Will three years after that, a houseful of children. I may be wrong, but I believe Mother enjoyed every minute of it. She and Father had one side of the house to themselves so sometimes we saw them only at meals, and even then I sometimes missed them. I juggled my role as Katherine the doctor with that of Katherine the wife and mother, so the Kincaid family's schedule was always a little chaotic.

Sam and I have celebrated twenty-four years together and they may not have been perfect, but I can honestly say they've come close to it a time or two. Sam knew all along, long before I ever considered it, that we were meant to be together, that we suited each other, body, mind, and spirit. What he gets from me I still don't quite understand although I'm grateful I continue to hold appeal. What I get from him is timeless and as necessary as air. Sam Kincaid anchors me to life, accepts without resentment that a part of me belongs to my profession, loves me when I'm not acting very lovable, calms me, makes me laugh, looks at me sometimes in a way that still holds such warm desire that I read his mind and blush, despite four children and all the years that have passed.

Our days are too fast-paced for much introspection, but sometimes at night I lie with an arm across my husband, feeling his chest rise and fall in sleep, and consider this thing called family and this place called home. I think about how we got to where we are, how all of us are a living legacy of one man and one woman who chose a life together and never looked back, and how we still stand on the foundation they built.

John Thomas and Hope are grandparents themselves, their two oldest boys married with their own families. My niece Beatrice, who spoke to her mother so clearly before she was born, is in a graduate medical program in Michigan, a single woman as focused as I ever was. She is determined to be a surgeon and if any woman can accomplish that, it's Bea. Her younger brother Charlie just graduated from the university here in Laramie and will teach. Hope, who never had any formal schooling and whose early years were solitary and isolated, finds all that remarkable.

When my mother died, Hope was inconsolable. A concerned John Thomas asked me to talk to her and I did, but my counsel didn't help.

"I can't explain it," said Hope. The poised and quiet woman sat in front of me with tears streaming down her face, and I don't think she even realized she was crying. "I know I'm too old to act like this, Katherine, but I can't help it. I can't accept that Lou's gone. It's like going out and seeing the same star in the same place in the same night sky, year after year, its glow always there to show the path and always able to see yourself clearly in its light. Then one day you go out and it's not there and you can't find the path and you can't find your own reflection." Hope looked at me helplessly. "I don't want Lou to be gone."

"I know," was all I said. I grieved my mother's passing, too, but Hope had come to Wyoming thirty years before, motherless and without home and family, and from the beginning she had found all three in the welcoming person of Lou Davis. Hope had lost a mother twice, and that seemed to make Mother's death more poignant and painful for her. Later, when John Thomas asked how our meeting went, I could only shrug and tell him that all of us grieve in our own ways and the only cure I knew of was time.

Time helped but not as much as my father. Hope rode her bicycle over one late May afternoon. I had just come home and stood on the porch watching her progress up the drive.

"What's the matter?" I called, surprised by a suppertime visit. "Is something wrong?"

She parked the bicycle against the steps.

"No. John Thomas told me his father needed me. Is something wrong here?" Hope was slightly winded from the trip and her face shadowed by worry and perplexity.

"No." Suddenly worried myself, I looked around to locate the familiar figure and with relief motioned toward the distant pines where the family cemetery had been established nearly forty years ago with the grave of my infant sister, whose death had been an early grief to my parents.

"He's up at Mother's grave. I can see him from here. He spends a lot of time there, and I worry about him walking on his own after what happened to Mother. But he's clear about preferring his own company." She followed my gesture and we both saw Father rise, stand, and look in the direction of the house. Waiting for Hope. She and I both knew it as surely as if he'd called her name. Still puzzled, Hope turned and without a word took the path to the cemetery.

I watched shamelessly and although they were too far away for me to make out much detail, I saw my father standing, cane in hand, until Hope stopped in front of him. She was a petite woman and my father a tall man even with age, so he still had to bend down to talk to her. He put both hands on Hope's shoulders and spoke for a full minute, maybe two. Hope stood as motionless as a statue, transfixed and listening. Then, in a remarkable tableau, my father held out his arms and she went into them. The two reserved people, who had learned years ago to hold their emotions deep and private, finally sat down together on the bench side by side and very close. They spent so long there that I eventually went inside and began to get supper ready. Hope left before it got dark but I didn't see her go.

I never knew exactly what they talked about. It wasn't my business and neither of them volunteered much, but from that afternoon on, Hope was her peaceful self again. The grief wasn't gone but it settled into her in a way that was natural and healthy. When I asked Father how he'd been able to help Hope, he gave a little smile.

"I can't take credit for it, Katherine. I learned from your mother. I was never very good at saying the right thing and she always has to give me instructions."

Until the day he died, my father spoke of Mother in the present tense, as if she were still alive to him, still at his side and giving him that quick, knowing look she reserved just for him.

Louisa Caldecott Davis died in March of 1931. She had been restless and suddenly determined to take a fresh cake over to the cookhouse for the hands. An early February snowstorm had been followed by a thaw that made the ground wet, slippery, and treacherous. I should have stopped her or taken it myself, but we had all been cooped up too long and she could never be persuaded otherwise when she set her mind to something. Closer to eighty than seventy, Mother stayed slim to the point of frailty. As age can, it made her seem small, bent, and fragile, no longer the tall woman with strong brown hands who had risen from her chair in the front room of Hull-House and opened her arms to me. The silver streak in her hair disappeared as she turned completely silver-white. But her smoke-gray eyes never dimmed and she was always quick to smile and laugh. She kept that special, welcoming way about her that drew people into her orbit, a perpetual warmth, a genuine interest in others that made her seem youthful. Only at rare times did I ever think of her as old.

She and Father danced a waltz on their fiftieth anniversary and it seemed they both shed forty years as they did so. My father whispered something to my mother as they danced that caused her to color with pleasure, and I was reminded of the night at the Palmer House Restaurant when she had looked exactly the same, her face touched with pleasure and surprise that John Rock Davis loved her so devotedly, that she continued to stir such passion in him.

When Mother held her first great-grandchild, Lily Kate's baby, she showed the same soft tenderness about her. She had looked sixteen.

I couldn't dissuade her that February day, so I helped her on with her coat and told her to watch her footing. I should have gone along but didn't, and even now I feel a sharp regret.

She was hardly gone any time at all when my father lifted his head abruptly from his newspaper and said sharply, "Katherine, go check on your mother." He didn't have to say it twice. By his tone I knew something had happened.

Halfway to the cookhouse, Mother had slipped on a patch of icy snow and fallen with her leg twisted under her. Her hip snapped the moment she hit the ground. It must have been terribly painful, but she didn't complain. After that, settled in bed for the bone to mend, she caught pneumonia and was gone in a month.

Toward the end, when I had done all I could and knew it wasn't enough, when it was clear she would soon leave us, Sam sent word and everyone came home.

Gus and his family came from Cheyenne, where he practiced law and served in the state legislature. Uncle Billy sat rocking in the kitchen corner, unsettled and unhappy, a man past sixty with the intense, simple devotion of the boy he had been fifty years earlier when Mother first adopted him. All of Sam's and my children were there. Bea came from Michigan. Becca and Ben with their youngest, Davis, and a grown-up Blessing came. Lily Kate and her husband and baby. Hope and John Thomas and their boys with their families. All of us crowded into that large, rambling house, took up all the bedrooms and floor space, and forced some of the men into the bunkhouse. No one complained. We made haphazard conversation and readied ourselves for the news.

My father sat quietly next to Mother's bed, held one of her hands in both of his, and willed her to stay. She had lain immobile and barely breathing for some time, and I could see her shutting down organ by organ, a gradual decline that would lead to one inexorable conclusion. I stayed in the room with them, helpless in the face of her death, and turned my back to look out the window out of respect for their privacy. I didn't think Mother strong or conscious enough to speak, but I was wrong.

"I have to go, John," she said. Her voice was whisper-soft but carrying. "Please let me go."

She heard it then, I thought, my father's unspoken plea that she stay. I wasn't surprised. They were very close.

With an obvious effort, she focused her gray eyes on his face. Worried for him, as always, but ready to leave, too. They'd been together for so many years that I never thought I would see so clearly in her face the desire to be released from his devotion. My father saw it, too, lifted one of her hands, and brought it to his cheek.

"I'm sorry, Lou. I don't mean to hold you here. You go on and don't fret. There's a home waiting for you there, too, and I won't be that far behind." Then he leaned forward and added softly, as tender a lover as he must have been fifty years before, "Thank you, my darling girl. Thank you for it all."

She tried to smile at him but couldn't for weariness. I stepped up to the bed and lifted her other hand to feel for a pulse at her wrist. Very, very faint by then. Almost gone.

"Remember John," she said and her heartbeat stopped

with the words. I didn't know if she was talking to Father or me, wanted to share a memory with him or was asking me to take care of my father. I'll never know.

"She's gone, Papa," I said. My voice caught and I couldn't say anything more. Father laid Mother's hand on top of the blanket as if handling delicate crystal, then sat there, his palms resting on his thighs, and stared at nothing. For a moment I didn't recognize the stricken, aged man that sat in front of me. Then the moment passed.

"Thank you, Katherine," he said quietly and formally, himself again. "It comforted your mother to have you with her."

He stood up and went out to where the family was gathered, walked through them as if he didn't see them, took his hat and coat from the peg on the wall, took his cane, and stepped out the door onto the porch. None of us said a word. We watched him as he descended the porch steps, a man well into his eighties who walked slowly with a pronounced limp, but who still carried himself with dignity, his bearing invariably upright, a formal man not given to public emotion. The years had robbed him of any extra flesh so that his profile was sharp enough to cut, and just that morning I had seen his hands, rough and strong for so many years, shake with tiny tremors he could not control, forcing him to hold his coffee cup with both hands just to keep it steady and raise it to his lips. But even then, with all the frailties and indignities of age, none of us wanted to disappoint him or risk his disapproval.

"Grandpa John's here but where's Nana?" asked Caldecott, my brother Gus's son and the youngest of the grandchildren.

"Home, Cal," said my brother-in-law, Ben.

He looked at me for affirmation and I could only nod, my throat too tight for words. My husband came up to me and put both his arms around me so I could cry into his chest. Sam's eyes were wet, too. He had loved Lou Davis as a mother for over thirty years, since the day he had walked up on our porch and she had set another place for supper.

Then Ben said it again, not just to Cal this time but to remind all of us in the room. "Nana's gone home."

That happened in March. My father grieved in his own private way, moved out of the room he had shared with his Lou for fifty years, and spent many nights in the rocking chair by the window, looking outside but seeing nothing. Finally he told Sam and me that we should take the bigger bedroom and he would move into ours. The trade might help him sleep.

"When I married Lou, she told me there was just one rule for our marriage and that was we were never to sleep apart. Not once, not ever, she told me, with that look on her face that said it wasn't a subject open for discussion. Not that I wanted to argue about it. I thought at the time it was a miracle she'd have me under any terms, and I wasn't about to do anything that might make her change her mind. So I'll take a different room and sleep in a different bed. The old one's too big now without her."

Father walked the path to her grave every morning and sat with her there, then walked back down and around the ranch, keeping busy, marking time. I believe sleeping apart from Mother those last months was the hardest thing he ever did in all his life.

One night in August of that same year, on the eve of what would have been my parents' fifty-first wedding anniversary, Father and I sat on the porch and looked out at the moon-shadowed sunflowers growing in their usual place by the side of the house. In late spring my children and I had sown each seed carefully, each a little memorial to Mother. For fifty years Lou Davis had planted and harvested and delighted in the flowers of her girlhood. Hope had planted a few to shade Mother's grave.

"Lou got awful homesick for Kansas those first few years," Father told me.

His reminiscence came out of nowhere and, surprised at the unexpected sharing, I sat attentive and quiet.

"Being your mother, she didn't say anything because she thought it would trouble me, and I pretended not to notice because that's what she wanted. Every year, though, she planted her sunflowers and took pleasure in their growth. Hope keeps them in her garden, and you'll keep up the tradition, too, won't you, Katherine? It would please your mother."

"Yes," I told him, picturing Mother as she used to walk through the flowers, many as tall as she, all the while smiling and fingering their bright petals, lost to us for a time. She never said much about it and because we came to take the ritual for granted, we never asked.

Father pushed himself up from his chair. His legs were unsteady and he needed both hands to grasp the head of his cane for balance. I knew he would refuse any assistance I might offer so I stayed seated and quiet as his soft voice of memory continued.

"When we first pulled up in front of this house, the place was a mess, the walls lopsided and the door off its hinges. I thought, what had I been thinking to bring a woman like Lou Caldecott to a place like this? I was ashamed. But your mother hopped off the wagon, gave me that quick smile of hers, and said to Billy, 'Come on, we're home now,' just like it was the place of her dreams. From the beginning, she was the one who made it a home. She left everything behind to come to Wyoming, but when I tried to tell her what that meant to me, she wouldn't listen, wouldn't let me get the words out."

"Mother told me once that she never looked back or regretted anything, Papa. She came with you willingly and said she'd do it all again in a heartbeat, no questions asked. 'Where your father is, that's home for me,' she said."

He blinked at that, tears maybe, but it could just as well have been the silver glisten of moonlight that I saw in his eyes.

"Lou always believed me to be a better man than I really was, Katherine, and I never had the heart to set her straight. After a while I guess I started to believe it myself. Your mother had a way about her that was hard to resist sometimes."

Father hesitated as if he wanted to say more, but he remained a reserved man and heartfelt words still did not come easily to him.

All he finally said was, "Good night, Katherine."

"Good night, Papa," I told him in return, and he went inside to bed.

That night my father fell asleep and didn't wake up—or more accurately, he woke up somewhere else. If you can will death, I believe that's what he did. He had marked every wedding anniversary that I could remember with something special, and I like to think that that year the gift he chose for Mother was himself. It was a peaceful departure for a man with a distant past of violence, but those of us who knew and loved him still find that hard to believe. All our lives we received only protection and patience from him. The man with the shadowy past my mother first described in her journal as John Rock Davis, the man she loved and eventually married, bore only a superficial resemblance to the man I called Father. In a way, that early man was like clay, and time and my mother molded him into the man he became: a faithful husband, a devoted father. We chose that epitaph for his grave marker.

My Uncle Billy put his fiddle away the year they died, put it in a box under his bed and stopped playing for a long time. For years.

"Can't hear the music no more," he explained simply and without noticeable emotion. Now he says he may get it out again to play at my Louisa's wedding.

Jane Addams died last year, Dr. Hamilton at her side. Amid deserved honor and great pomp, people filed by her bier and mourned the loss of so grand and compassionate a woman. Petra, who doesn't sing under her maiden name of Stravinsky or her married name of Sweeney but under a different stage name altogether, honored Miss Addams by singing at her funeral. The papers said the performance moved even the most indifferent hearers to tears. Petra wrote later that she could hardly get the words out, that she remembered those early years at Hull-House with such affection and gratitude that the memories threatened to drown the music. But she's a consummate performer and in the end she thrilled her audience with her tribute to Miss Addams.

My mother exerted her own influence on a much smaller scale, and I couldn't judge which woman had more impact on the world around her. Both of them were great women in their own way and left great legacies behind.

I'll be fifty years old next year, Sam even older, and the world is changing so fast I don't think I can keep up. I drive my own modern motorcar—affectionately dubbed *Fritz III*—to visit patients. Times are hard right now but for all the country's problems, we still have a telephone system and electricity, central heating, and inside running water that doesn't freeze up in winter. I've seen an airplane flying overhead and I can sit in front of the radio in my parlor and hear Petra performing in New York City. We lived through The Great War and now I fear the world may be teetering on the edge of another, even more horrendous, conflict. I'm frightened for my youngest son, Will, and for Gus's two sons as well. All three boys will come of age soon, and I can't bear the idea that all their energy and promise might be consumed by the mindless destruction of war. But in the end, children must grow up and make their own way and find their own home, just as I did, as my parents did, as we all did.

If I were a philosopher or a poet, I might be able to find exactly the right words to describe the cycle of family and home, what it means and where it is and how it forms us, but I don't have the talent for that. Or the patience. Sam's the patient one, patient lover, husband, father, friend. A good man and a hard worker, as passionate and faithful to me as my father was to my mother, and like my mother I am humbled, pleased, and slightly surprised that it's so.

When I came in last night, I found Sam in the study, reading. The light shadowed his face so that the scar above his eye was barely visible. Even now, I never see it without a slight catch in my heart, remembering how he was gone for all those days, how he heard me in the faraway place to which he had traveled, and how he came back to me.

He looked up as I came into the room and asked, "Do the Blakes have a new baby?"

As usual, I detected relief in his tone and on his face when he saw me. I knew he worried whenever I went out on a late call, but from the beginning he never voiced his fears. That's one of the many reasons I love Sam Kincaid: for the freedom he gives me, for the way he trusts my judgment and accepts my calling without complaint, for understanding that while marriage makes us one, we are still two independent beings.

"Yes, finally," I answered. "A boy. Number three. I thought it was going to be a longer labor than it was, but when the baby decided he was ready to join us, he didn't waste any time." I came and sank down on the sofa next to Sam and rested my head against his shoulder. "It's such a mystery, isn't it?"

"What? Babies?"

"No, not babies. I believe I've got them figured out. Life, I mean. What it's all about. The endless cycle of living and dying, how the past links to the present at the same time it forms the future—" I sighed, tired but happy to sit with my husband's arm around my shoulders, and continued to reflect, "—what makes home and family, how we become who we are, and how unimportant bloodlines are compared to what's in a person's heart. Sometimes I think it's all a mystery we weren't meant to understand."

"There's no mystery about it, Katherine, not the home and family part anyway. That part's easy."

I pulled back to gauge his expression and see if he were teasing me in my philosophical state of mind, but he was watching me tenderly, so much love in that look that I would need several lifetimes to take it all in.

"You think so, do you?"

"I can show you home and family in a minute, take all the mystery right out of it so it won't keep you awake at night."

"Really? Aren't you the smart man? Show me, then."

Sam grinned, then gently put his hand under my chin and turned my face so I looked directly at the dark glass of the window beside us. The backdrop of the black, moonless, winter night sky made the window as clear as any mirror. The two of us showed in the reflection.

Sam sat dark-eyed with a faint smile, the gray hair at his temples showing white in the glass and his scar invisible in shadow. I leaned back against him and looked squarely and soberly at the window, a challenge in my expression that had not faded and never would. I saw a woman with a thin face beginning to show age and honey-colored hair that still looked too heavy for her neck.

"There," Sam said, no longer smiling. He met my look in the reflection and held my gaze with the force of his own. "There's home. It's that simple."

Meet Johanna Swan, Titanic survivor, social worker, and suffragist, an independent young woman of strong will and sizable fortune. Johanna has survived two deadly catastrophes and is determined to spend her life doing exactly what she chooses for the sensible purposes she selects. When she meets Drew Gallagher, Johanna decides to use him to accomplish her worthwhile goals. To her, Drew is a man of little moral or intellectual worth, but their combined fortunes could make a difference in the lives of poor urban women and that is what sets her on his trail. It doesn't take Johanna long, however, to discover that there is more to Drew Gallagher than she first supposed. When Drew draws a circle around Johanna's heart and makes it his target, a war of wills between two strong, smart people begins. Read Circled Heart, *the next book in the Laramie Series, to see how the battle ends. An excerpt follows.*

***

Hilda Cartwright waited for me at the doorway of the meeting room where Mrs. Trout was to speak and together the two of us made our way to the front row of chairs where two seats had been reserved for us. The room filled up quickly—mostly with men, I noticed—and I wondered if Hilda had been right to believe this would be an unsympathetic and hostile crowd. If that were so, the knowledge did not appear to make a difference to the speaker.

Grace Wilbur Trout was an imposing woman, a stately and elegant brunette nearing fifty but with the animation and energy of a woman half her age. She took the podium comfortably after a brief introduction and began to speak with intelligence and passion about the necessity for women to have the vote for the good of the family, the nation, and society in general.

"That youths can vote on issues that affect their mothers while their mothers cannot vote at all is preposterous. How can we say *that* is good for society? Would such an arrangement not create a natural scorn and disrespect in the hearts of young men for their mothers if a nation implies that their mothers are not informed or intelligent enough to make decisions at the ballot box? Doesn't the inability of mothers and sisters to have their voices heard in elections create disunity in the family, the very effect that suffrage opponents fear?"

"Wasn't any complaints heard before women like you stirred things up," one man grumbled audibly from the back of the room.

Mrs. Trout continued until another negative comment was made: "Seems to me the family was doing just fine before women stepped out into the streets. They've got plenty to do at home without interfering in men's business."

And still Mrs. Trout continued with her speech undeterred, calm and competent, intelligent and unflappable. I admired her perseverance and was outraged on her behalf at the rude comments still filtering through the crowd, nothing boisterous or overt so that I could tell the person to sit down and be quiet but spoken in a murmured voice just loud enough to produce subdued laughter from those in the critic's general vicinity. I considered it a carefully planned conspiracy to discredit Mrs. Trout and her message and longed for something more confrontational that would allow me to respond in kind. As it was, all Hilda and I could do was sit quietly and considerately, give the speaker our full attention, and ignore the derisive remarks that rippled as an undercurrent through the room.

Mrs. Trout was a vigorous but disciplined speaker who ended with a flourish. "The struggle for social change has often been met with ridicule and scorn by small minds who live in the past and cannot think beyond the present. My challenge for all of you in this room is to step out of your constricted and complacent lives and look frankly into the future. Honestly ask yourselves if our present situation, where women are second class citizens at best, is what you want for your daughters and granddaughters. We cannot stay bound to old ways from an old century. Now is the time to free the intelligence and the energy of your daughters so they may blossom into mature, responsible women, capable of making sound decisions for the family and just as capable of making responsible judgments to influence the progress of our state and federal governments."

Her last ringing words fell into a deep silence. No one spoke or laughed or even coughed. She might as well have been speaking in a foreign language for all the response her stirring conclusion generated.

Stubborn and arrogant men, I fumed, with your minds already made up before you even got here this evening. As I raised both hands to applaud, a male voice spoke from somewhere to my left.

"Well done, Mrs. Trout."

I turned to see a man several seats down in my same row rise and face the podium. With his right hand he gave Grace Trout a small, charming salute and then methodically and purposefully he began to applaud, a smile playing around his mouth as he did so. He's enjoying the attention, I thought, so why shouldn't I do the same? I took one more quick look at his handsome profile, stood quickly, and began to applaud, also. From the corner of my eye I saw the man turn to give me a brief, curious glance. For what seemed like an interminably long time it was just the two of us standing and showing our public approval. Then Hilda stood and joined us, and a few other women in the room joined in, and finally several men stood, too. At least half the room remained seated and silent, but those of us who had risen made up for their bad humor with our enthusiasm.

Mrs. Trout smiled very specifically at the attractive, fair-haired man who had begun the ovation, gave Hilda a nod and a smile, and made an elegant but silent bow to the room before she exited down a side aisle.

When the applause faded, I asked Hilda, "Has Mrs. Trout met with such an ill-mannered reception before? I admit I was surprised by the open resentment that greeted her ideas. She made good, practical sense and didn't play to the emotions, as other women in her position are so often accused of."

"I had heard in advance that this evening's group might be more antagonistic than usual, but I certainly didn't expect the level of hostility they displayed," Hilda answered, then turned to look past me at the tall, blonde man in the perfectly cut dark suit who had so nonchalantly—and gracefully—voiced his approval before the crowd and led the applause.

Apparently oblivious to the disapproving glances around him, he slowly made his way from the room, one hand on the arm of a woman whom he maneuvered protectively through the crowd. When they reached the door, he leaned forward to say something close to her ear. The woman turned to look back at him and despite the extravagant, broad-brimmed hat she wore, I caught a glimpse of rich brown hair and an impossibly red mouth. For some reason, that quick look gave me the impression that she was not particularly pleased about something. Perhaps the press of the crowd made her uncomfortable.

"And who would have imagined that?" continued Hilda, her gaze still following the man.

"Imagined what?"

"That *he* would be the one to lead the defensive. There's no doubt he made a public stand tonight, but I never imagined he had the slightest interest in universal suffrage. In fact, with his disreputable reputation for enjoying the company of women, I thought he would surely prefer the status quo. Well, life is full of surprises, and I give him complete credit for the unpopular stand he took tonight. Perhaps all those stories about him are just so much rumor and innuendo."

"I don't recognize him, Hilda. Should I? Who is he?"

"There's no reason you would know him, Johanna. I'm sure you don't move in the same circles, and he's always lived in the shadow of his successful older brother," adding thoughtfully, "Until recently, of course, poor man. Considering your recent distressing experience, you can appreciate his situation more than the rest of us." With unsuspecting impact, Hilda concluded, "The man's name is Drew Gallagher."

If you enjoyed Where Home Is and haven't read the first two books of the series, you can find Lily's Sister and Waiting for Hope at www.barnesandnoble.com, www.amazon.com, and many other online booksellers. The fourth book of the series, Circled Heart, will be available soon. Find out more about the author and her books at www.karenhasley.com.